DREAMREAPER

BLOOD OF KAOS SERIES

BOOK 2

NESA MILLER

ACKNOWLEDGMENTS

A SPECIAL THANK YOU TO

Daniel, my incredible husband

Amy Briggs – Editor Extraordinaire

@rebecacovers on Fiverr

Daniel Palfrey – the talented artist who designed the beautiful roses strewn throughout the series.

My Beta readers and friends who have advised and provided their invaluable assistance along the way.

Many years ago, a small group came together in the spirit of community.
They called themselves superheroes.
Super they were and super they remain.
Thank you for your super ways, support, and continued friendships.

Long live all you Superdudes!

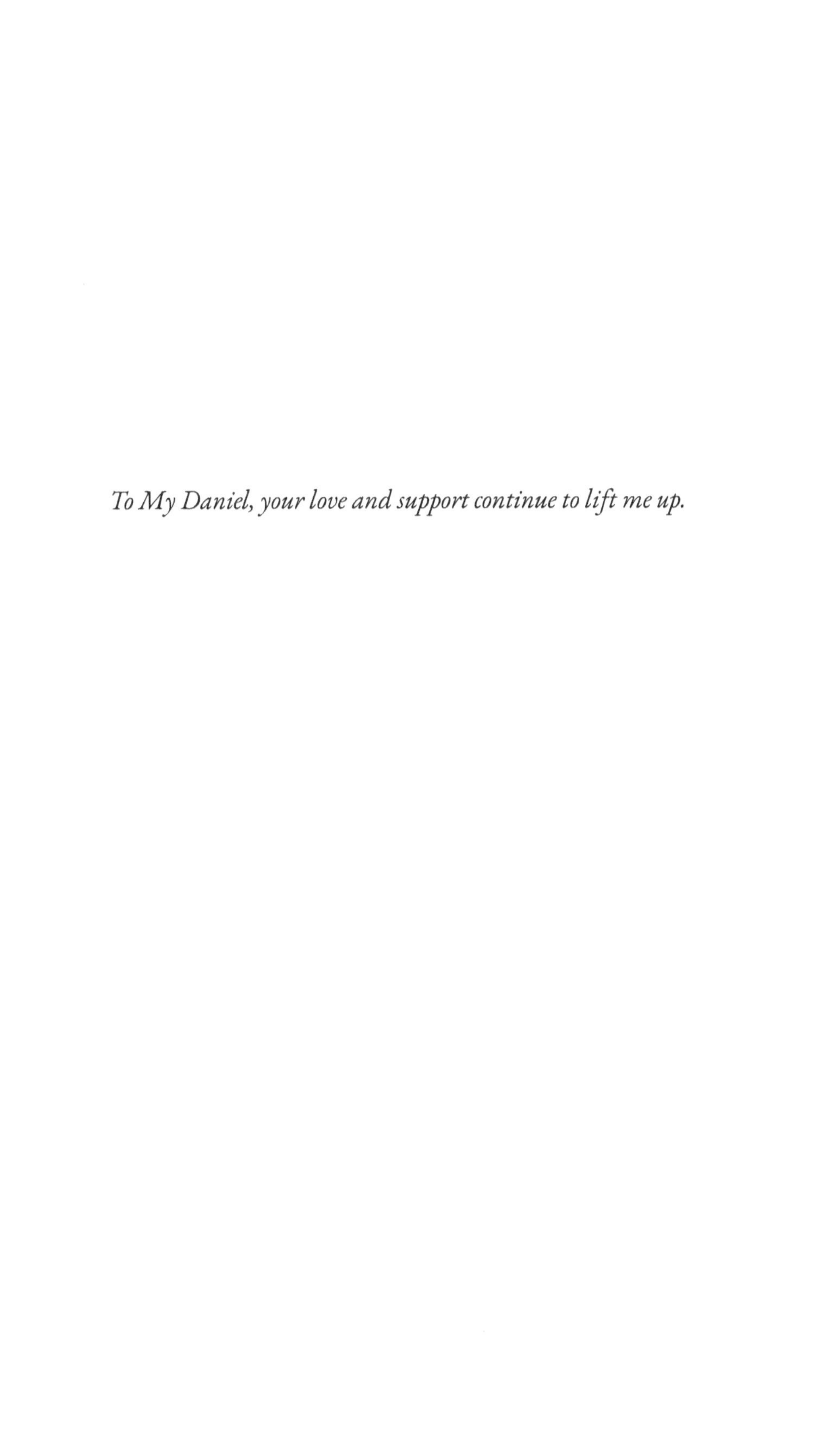

To My Daniel, your love and support continue to lift me up.

LAUGHARNE

*H*ome. Etain stood at the new bay windows in the lounge and hugged herself, thankful for her good fortune. It was good to see the room restored after Midir's impromptu visit, which had been the cause of the damage. The encounter almost ended with her and her sister, Faux, dead. Fortunately, Dar proved the better warrior, despite his brother's under-handed attempts. Midir was no longer a concern.

From her viewpoint, the autumnal colors of the countryside seemed richer. Perhaps by her becoming the High Lady of Kaos, more had changed than just her appearance. Or maybe she saw things differently because Dar was alive, Faux was on the mend, and according to Dar, Spirit survived her run-in with his brother. It seemed things were finally—

A cough and the clearing of a throat broke into her thoughts. She turned to an amused Inferno.

"Etain, lass." He grabbed her in a tight hug. "It's good to have ya back."

Felix and Ruby, his Irish Wolfhounds, one black and the other red, joined in the reverie, barking and tails wagging.

Caught up in his bear-like hug, Etain uttered a muffled, "Sorry for the delay." The smoky smell of his skin was a welcomed scent, and the bristles of his unshaven cheeks scratched her face. "Inferno, let go."

With a good-hearted laugh, he set her free. "Ya look like hell."

She breathed in, enchanted by the gold flecks sparkling in his hazel eyes. "Aye, well, rough day at the office." She noticed his dark hair was longer than usual as she patted each dog on the head. "You aren't much better."

Inferno scrubbed his knuckles along his jawline. "Aye, well, no time for shaving, what with yer running off and the hellions showing up."

Etain smirked at his casual reference to her abduction as she glanced over his shoulder. She cringed inside and frowned. Seated on matching brown leather sofas were five of Dar's most trusted clan members. His High Council. "What's going on here?"

Inferno faced the group and crossed his arms over his chest. "Accordin' to this lot, their chieftain's been neglectin' his bloody clan."

Her eyes fell on the woman in dark green leathers, Dar's second-in-command. "I find that hard to believe. Dar lives and breathes LOKI."

Savage tossed her blonde hair back with a glare in her eyes and came to her feet. "Who are you to be calling him by his given name?"

Etain felt the hairs on the back of her neck rise, a common occurrence when dealing with this woman. She and Savage never saw eye-to-eye, although they came nose-to-nose on many occasions. She learned the hard way that from Savage's point of view, cooperation meant doing what she said when she said it, no questions asked. No matter how many times Dar demanded their cooperation, their differences had clearly escalated to the realm of never going to happen.

"What's the problem, Savage? Jealous of a lowly Warrior Caste member who's on a first name basis with his lordship?"

Inferno raised his eyebrows and grinned.

Pyro, *Nae'Blis* (Commander) of the BloodCore Caste, distinguished by his black armor and blood-red cloak, stood next to Savage. "Our clan business has nothing to do with you, realm shifter."

Felix and Ruby growled at the man.

"Hypocrite. I was acting under Dar's orders," Etain said, stunned by his words. If not always supportive, she thought the man sympathetic to her situation.

He sneered at her. "What orders? Nothing came through the Council."

"Not every decision requires *your* approval. He *is* the chieftain."

On the other side of Pyro was Swee, a slim young woman with brown hair streaked by golden highlights and dressed in the green armor of a healer. "She has a point, Pyro."

Etain's piercing gaze made the woman move closer to the *Nae'Blis*. "Swee. You're a part of this, as well?"

Gentle blue eyes smiled back at her. "The voice of reason, Etain."

"Reason dressed for battle?" she replied, angry that the "voice of reason" chose to wear armor instead of her usual riding leathers. "Excuse me if I don't believe you." She unconsciously placed a hand on the hilt of her sword, her gaze shifting between Pyro and Savage. "It was a surprise for *both* of us to find out I'd been expelled from the clan. I don't suppose you'd care to elaborate?"

The frown lines on Savage's face deepened and her hand lingered over the handle of the whip at her side. "You lost your LOKI status when you went on a destruction blitz with the demon girl. That alone forced the clan into weeks of damage control. Even now, we must prove to the Ambassadors and our fellow Alamir you acted without clan approval. Your dirty bit of business can't be finished until our *chieftain* deigns to meet with the Ambassadors. And here you are again, sticking your nose into our business."

"We were not—" Etain sucked in a breath and ran a hand through her hair. It was Freeblood's debacle and his merry acceptance of his Alamir powers. Her only concern was to keep Faux from joining in the revelry and condemning herself to permanent exile. "I don't have to explain my business to you."

The other blonde in in the group, Shera, Councilor of the Judicial Caste, stood. "Perhaps we should all calm down."

"Shut up, Shera," Savage said with a condescending air. Shera's mouth opened and snapped closed without a sound. Savage smirked as she faced Etain. "No, you *don't* owe us an explanation, but you won't get off so easily with the Ambassadors. They still have a team in the human realm trying to smooth over your stunt with the truckers."

Inferno came to her defense. "None of it would've happened if yer bleedin' chieftain hadn't poisoned her with his demon blood. Yer damned welcome to take him off to hell with ya."

"*Oi.*" Etain narrowed her eyes at the man.

Warden, a tall young woman with dark hair and eyes, the *Machin Chin* (First Instructor) of the Warrior Caste, joined the conversation. "Sharing of his blood is forbidden. A rule set by the man himself."

Shera found her voice again. "It is high treason against the clan."

"LOKI wouldn't exist if it weren't for Dar," Etain argued, her narrowed gaze moving to each of the Council members. "If anyone's committing treason, it's you, marching in here with your ridiculous accusations."

"Come on, guys." Swee tried again. "Etain isn't the one we've come for. I'm sure Dar will put things right once he arrives."

"Hmph," Pyro grunted. "We have no proof Dar approved anything, or that he's even aware of *her*. If presented the right way, shifting between Alamir and the human realm is as treasonous an act as breaking a clan code. To turn her in would raise LOKI's standing with the Ambassadors and further support our charges against our renegade chieftain."

Etain gripped the hilt of her *Nim*. "And lower *yours* by a head."

"Tell me that wasn't a threat against me girl here," Inferno blustered, snapping his fingers. Felix's ears pricked as he bared his teeth. Ruby did the same and stepped closer to the Council.

"Etain?"

All eyes turned to the doorway.

"Spirit."

The face of the mage reflected the confused feelings of both women. "You *are* alive."

Etain's gaze was for Spirit alone as she walked toward the young woman, afraid she may well be a ghost. But with a touch of her arm, she found it warm, soft, and pliable. Definitely not dead.

I survived Midir. Why not Spirit too?

"Aye. I thought *you* were dead." Etain didn't know whether to laugh or cry and realized she was doing both as she lifted her friend in a tight embrace. Her hair smelled of freshly cut apples and cinnamon.

"Dar said you were alive, but I daren't believe him until I saw you with my own eyes."

"Me, too."

"You're pale, lass. Are you sure you're all right?"

Etain swiped at her eyes. "A lot has happened."

"We need to talk." Spirit grabbed her by the arm, and despite the ruckus raised by the others, led her down the hall to the kitchen.

Fresh herbs lay by the Belfast sink and a stewpot simmered on a buttery yellow range. The aromatic mix of herbs, garlic, and meat stock made Etain's mouth water. She giggled as Spirit pulled her toward the pantry, her free hand drifting over the cool granite of the island in the center of the room.

Etain closed her eyes and breathed in the conglomeration of smells. Savory scents of fresh onions and rosemary blended with the earthiness of potatoes. With a turn of her head, she caught a whiff of sweet cinnamon and spicy nutmeg. She opened her eyes to Spirit's brazen once over.

"What happened there?" She nodded toward Etain's ripped sleeve.

"Oh, well. Midir." Etain shivered at the memory of his failed seduction and placed a hand over the pale scar where he'd driven his blade in his final attempt to take her away from Dar. She thought it best to tell the truth, despite Spirit's prejudice against the sharing of blood. "But Dar fixed it. Uh, me."

Spirit crossed her arms. "You must be as Krymerian as he is, what with the man's generous nature with his blood."

Etain spied a jar of chocolate buttons just beyond Spirit's head. "Ooh, chocolate." She reached for the jar, twisted off the lid, and popped a few into her mouth, then tipped the jar to Spirit.

She waved off the temptation. "I saw the man stab you in the heart."

"It hurt like hell too." She rolled her shoulder. "But he missed, and now he's dead." She nodded at Spirit's wide eyes. "Aye. It's over and done. Dar put an end to his miserable life."

"How's Dar?"

Etain returned the jar to the shelf. "He's good, considering what he's had to do. When did LOKI show up?"

"The pot's been simmering since Dar left to find you, lass."

"Oh, Lord." Etain rolled her eyes. "How's Faux?"

"She stirs now and then but hasn't opened her eyes."

"Damn Midir. Will she recover?"

"Aye. Me potions are stronger than his poisons. She'll come around."

Inferno's voice boomed from the living room. "Sit yer nazzy knickers down and stop worryin' me damn floors. The bleedin' bastard'll be back. Felix, Ruby, sit, ya wee hounds."

Etain raised a brow. "I'd best get back in there. Dar shouldn't be far behind me."

Spirit reached for her, "There's something else," but she was already out the door.

Etain passed through the double-sized archway into the living room. She noted a body in the worn leather chair just inside the room and the hounds reclined on the floor but didn't pay much attention.

The rubber soles of her boots whispered over the stone floor of the light and airy room, yet she felt the weight of anticipation in the air. A distinct tang of nervous perspiration grew stronger as she skirted around the matching sofas.

She joined Inferno in front of the fireplace and turned to the cold faces of the High Council, while an enthusiastic blaze warmed her backside. "So…"

Felix eased up next to her and leaned into her. She smiled at the loyal hound and gave him a scratch behind the ear.

The movement of an unexpected figure in the hallway caught both their eyes. Inferno whispered into her ear, "Another Council tosser?"

To smile would have been so inappropriate. Instead, she bit her bottom lip and turned. "You could say that."

"Hmph."

"Don't turn your back on me," Savage snapped. "We're not going anywhere until we have our chieftain in hand."

A growl rumbled from deep in Felix's chest as he took a protective stance in front of Etain. At his move, Ruby inched closer to the strangers.

Etain flashed Savage a fierce grin. "That should be entertaining."

The sun, having peeked out from behind a cloud, filled the living room with its brilliant light as Dar walked in. "I agree, Lady Etain." Dressed in a fresh shirt and his hair loose over his shoulders, he was every inch the powerful chieftain. The sight of his newfound love in a face-off with his High Council pricked his anger, but at the same time, she made him proud. His authoritative gaze swept over the Council. "What part of 'stay put' did you not understand?"

Except for the deep-throated growls from the dogs, the noise abated for a brief moment. Savage glanced at her fellow Council members, who shared the same addled expressions.

Inferno waved his arms. "Sit yer arses down before I set me hounds loose on yer bloody carcasses."

Felix barked in unison with his master's commands and was soon accompanied by an equally vociferous Ruby. Etain rolled her eyes.

"Call off your dogs, Inferno," Savage yelled.

Felix lunged at the woman, forcing her to step back. She lost her balance and landed on the sofa, the hound on top of her. Confronted by a lethal set of white fangs, she lifted her arms over her face. Pyro took a step toward the hound.

"Don't touch me dog." Inferno snapped his fingers. Felix growled one more time, leaped off the sofa and joined his master.

Etain cocked a brow as Dar walked toward her. "So many talents in one so young, milord. You've not only wreaked havoc by entering the room, it appears you've brought the sun with you as well."

He grinned at her sarcastic tone knowing she would have preferred a moment alone to prepare him. The flash in her eyes and added color in her cheeks made him wish they were alone. "The Lord of Kaos, at your service, milady."

"It's gonna take time to get used to the new look. I like the blond," she ran her fingers through the long length of his heavy mane, "but I think I preferred your eyes blue."

He shrugged. "We have the rest of our lives, *a chuisle*."

"Who the hell are you?" Savage asked, pushing up from the sofa.

Etain smirked at Dar as she answered the question. "You don't recognize your own chieftain?"

Everyone stared followed by a few gasps and a definitive "Fuck me" from Inferno. The last time any of these people saw him, his hair was brown and his eyes a deep blue. He now had blond hair and golden eyes, all because he was the victor in the battle against his evil brother.

"Dar, my darling. Your Council, hand-picked by you..." She turned her gaze on the Council, "is under the impression you're no longer fit to lead."

The LOKI chieftain crossed his arms, his eyes on his second-in-command. "Is this how you lead? Abandoning your responsibilities to the clan to traipse across the countryside, chasing after some whimsy you've fabricated in your head?" His stern gaze swept over the rest of the Council. "And you let *her* lead you by the nose."

Savage's jaws flapped. "I... We... Th-this *is* clan business." She lifted her chin and straightened her shoulders. "Unlike you, we aren't in pursuit of debased pleasures."

"However..." A young man popped up from his chair and joined them at the fireplace. "I was here first. Someone," his gaze landed on Etain, "owes me an explanation. I've come a long way for answers."

"God," Etain groaned, rolling her eyes. "Where did you come from?"

"Please, let's keep it informal. Call me Freeblood."

"Now isn't the time." She remembered the boy, broken and bleeding as a result of a tap dance with two semis. She rushed him to a hospital and given a lifesaving blood donation. Within a few hours, a completely healed, fresh new Alamir dashed out of the room.

"Too bad. I had plans before you screwed with my head. I wanna know what happened in Mexico."

All eyes went to Etain.

"Technically, it wasn't Mexico. It was the Mexican *sector*."

"*Technically*, I don't give a damn what you call it." His eyes on Dar, he stepped closer to Etain. "Why was I banned from an entire region of the planet?"

She sighed, considering how to answer his question. The glower on his face, coupled with the fact he didn't belong there, fueled a childish devilry within her. "It wasn't an entire region, just the UK sector."

Despite the tension in the room, she heard a few snickers. So did Freeblood.

"Wait a minute. Wait a damn minute! I've gotten the cold shoulder ever since I got here. That's okay. I don't know these people and they don't know me. But with you, the cold shoulder ends here." He stabbed a finger toward the floor.

Her nerves were on edge, and he made things worse. The palm of her hand itched, wanting to release an electrical charge. Then she noticed his choice in footwear. "You *do* know your glow-in-the-dark sneakers make you the perfect target, right?"

His eyes narrowed. "Don't change the subject."

"Well, it appears our dance card is full," Dar remarked with a sardonic tone.

"You shouldn't be so cavalier, High Lord," Pyro snapped. "You're charged with dereliction of duties and treasonous acts against the clan." The fire cast a reddish tint to the stubble along his clenched jaw, but it was the one burning within that fueled the dangerous glint in his grey eyes.

"Stand down, *Nae'Blis*. You go against Alamir protocol by showing your faces here unannounced and uninvited spewing your false accusations." Dar's height lengthened a few inches. Pyro and Savage stepped back. Even Inferno backed away. "I have heard every word spewed from your mouths today. The Ambassadors were informed and lifted the restrictions on the clan weeks ago. On the same day, I sent a messenger to advise my Council of the decision." He eyed Savage. "What is this really about?"

"You're different," Swee said from her seat on the sofa.

Dar's steely gaze turned to the healer. "Pursue this matter and it will become all too evident."

Savage refused to back down. "You will do as the Council orders, or you will be stripped of your title."

"Careful, Savage. You can be stripped of more than a title."

Etain stepped between Dar and the Council. "I'd be happy to show you the way out."

Spirit gasped from across the room. "Not me new windows."

"The witch has cast a spell on you," Warden said, nonplussed by the changes in Dar. "She will answer for that."

"Why wait?" Etain's hand smoldered with an electrical charge. "We can—"

Dar placed a hand on her shoulder. "No, this is not the place." He eyed the others as he leaned down to her ear. "It is best we take the boy away from here to conduct our business. Let things cool down before they get out of hand. Take Faux to *Sólskin*. I will come to you there."

Etain studied his face from over her shoulder, turned, and kissed him on the lips. "Don't be long."

"She will be dealt with next," Pyro muttered, watching her walk through the doorway.

"You will not touch her," Dar said. "She no longer answers to your rules."

"She is Alamir and subject to Alamir law," he countered.

"This has nothing to do with Alamir law. I am the chieftain of this clan. You will do as I command."

"Calm down, Dar." Swee shifted on the sofa, chastising Pyro with her eyes, but a low growl from Ruby gave her reason to keep her seat. "You're the one we've come for, not Etain." She turned an accusing glare on Savage. "I, personally, have not been advised of any messengers sent by the Ambassadors or yourself." She returned to Dar. "But there are *other* problems only you can resolve."

"We *will* talk, but my lady and I have unfinished business with this one." Dar nodded at the lurking young man.

"*No!*" Savage yelled. "We will not be ignored. This has gone beyond your incessant need for chitchat. You will return with us immediately."

Felix lunged. Only Inferno's iron grip held him at bay. Ruby growled in reaction to the outburst.

"You will wait until I return." Dar turned to Inferno, who was crouched beside Felix. "I apologize for the rude behavior of my Council. They will repay your good graces, milord."

After murmuring soft words to settle the hound, he answered. "Take care of business with this wee brat. Don't worry about the others. We'll keep 'em busy."

Dar grabbed the scruff of Freeblood's shirt and disappeared amid a flurry of angry protests.

Enlightenment

A small rise in an otherwise desolate landscape held the only item of interest—a red castle with four large turrets, one facing each direction, their rooftops lined by row upon row of skulls darkened by the elements. The walls gleamed as though covered in fresh blood.

At the entrance stood two immense gates of solid metal marked by substantial studs tapered into lethal points. In this dimension, the sky above was as grey as the dirt below.

Commander Thamuz stalked down the corridor toward a set of heavy wooden doors, his muttered condemnations echoing off the walls. *I will be straightforward, as always.*

A rather fantastical idea flitted through the mind of the steadfast military man. *Dathmet will understand.* His broad shoulders slumped with the burden of his news.

Stopped short of his destination, he slid a hand over his close-cropped grey hair and adjusted his dark uniform. *Hell may well be an amusement park.* He curled his fingers into fists, splayed them out and fisted again. Composed, he reached for the bronze handle.

Thamuz found his blood-skinned master behind an elaborate Louis XV-style desk in front of the only window in the room, its size equal to half the wall. Impeccably dressed in a black suit and crisp white shirt tailored to accommodate the ridge along his spine, the master's focus was on the courtyard below. Thamuz noted the black boots with their excruciatingly pointed toes and clenched his jaw. He knew from personal experience the pain they could inflict. Despite his master's taste in sadistic footwear and that he was only twenty-six in human years, the commander appreciated the image he projected. The young man's confidence was indomitable.

The commander's voice revealed nothing of his apprehension. "Milord, we have news."

"Thamuz." Dathmet stared out the window. "I take it my father was successful?"

"The target was acquired."

"Was," he echoed, stated as a fact rather than a question. Tendrils of fire that passed for hair flickered around his strong features. "But..."

Thamuz cleared his throat, the room closing in on him. "The brother—"

"Yes. The fucking brother." Dathmet's voice carried a lethal edge. "How did he interfere *this* time?"

Impaled by his master's black gaze, Thamuz shifted his shoulders in response to the trickle of sweat making its way down his back. "Midir underestimated the bond between them."

Dathmet's head of flames surged and licked out. "Do not judge, Thamuz. You have no idea the estimations or sacrifices of my father."

"It is fact, milord. Your father placed me in this position because I say what must be said, not what you wish to hear."

After a long moment, his gaze returned to the window. "Where are they, now?"

"Midir is dead, and his brother has disappeared. My assumption is he has taken his body to Krymeria for burial."

Light gleamed along the tapered edge of Dathmet's ridged back as he came around from behind the desk. "Why take him home? They hated each other."

Another line of sweat slithered along Thamuz's spine. He lifted his shoulders and lengthened his neck in an attempt to match the young master's six-foot-five frame. "It is where all Krymerians are buried, milord. It would be sacrilegious to bury him elsewhere."

Dathmet slammed his hand on the desk. Flames billowed about his head, his eyes burning coals. "The fact my father is dead and his arrogant brother lives is sacrilege! It is *my* right to bury him, not that excuse of a Krymerian."

Thamuz blinked, unsure of how to respond. The young demon spun on his heel, jamming both hands through his fiery locks. The commander stepped back to avoid the ridge of his master's back.

Dathmet returned to the window. "Where is *she*?"

The bulldogged light in his eyes revealed an inner turmoil. Thamuz had seen it throughout the boy's life.

"She's gone back to the Alamir realm. To Laugharne."

Dathmet's gaze turned thoughtful as he twisted a diamond cufflink. "He won't be far behind. What of our other plans?"

The conversation now focused on military matters, Thamuz's heart returned to its normal rhythm. "Several moles have slipped through the Alamir net into the human realm and are proving their worth."

Dathmet shifted his shoulders as he straightened his suit jacket. "We cannot afford to repeat the mistakes of the past. There will be no assassinations. Human martyrs tend to unify, which does not serve our purpose. Understood?"

Thamuz bowed his head, proud of the astuteness of his protégé. "A certain number of deaths will be required, milord. However, none will be high profile. Religious fanatics abound in the human realm. Suicide bombers vie for a one-way ride to hell, believing they serve a greater good. The spread of disease has also proven effective in the past, albeit somewhat more difficult to control. Whatever methods we implement, the death of insignificant minions will work to assassinate reputations and credibility.

With the human realm in flux, our plans to neutralize their leaders will be realized. The chaos will keep the Alamir so distracted they won't notice our movements. By the time they do, it will be too late."

"Total chaos. I like it."

"Pardon my asking, milord."

The master raised a brow but motioned him to continue.

"How do you propose to rebuild the Krymerian race?"

A sinister grin came to Dathmet's lips. "No one has ever confirmed what happened to the Krymerians. I believe there are others out there, somewhere."

Thamuz furrowed his brows. "Milord, our antiquarians have found nothing to support this. As far as we can tell, the race disappeared completely, aside from yourself and the other two."

He returned to the oversized chair behind the desk. "I believe when the precious High Lord left his people and went wandering after the death of his family, the others followed his lead and integrated with other races."

"Where is the sense in Krymerians—"

"Krymerians are survivors. If they found a way to cooperate with disgusting Draconians, they would find other races easy to manipulate, especially humans and these Alamir. No doubt some would have retreated to the Elven and Faerie realms as well."

"Milord, had they intermingled with the human race, I doubt the Alamir would exist today."

Dathmet leaned back into the chair. "Feel free enlighten me, Commander."

"You should know the Alamir are human, albeit on a higher level." At the raised brows, Thamuz explained further. "It was a part of your education Midir and I argued over many times. He saw no reason to familiarize you with a race he believed to be far beneath the Krymerians and certainly had no intentions of you having any involvement with them."

"Yet he conducted business with the father of this woman. Was he Alamir? Was he why she became one?"

"He was not." Thamuz approached the desk as he spoke. "An Alamir is born human and raised as a normal child, oblivious to their destiny until it presents itself. The manner of induction varies from person to person. Few hear the call, and none refuse. They consider it an honor to serve as protectors of their human counterparts."

The young man considered his elder for a moment. "Are you sure he wasn't Alamir?"

"We have no reason to believe he was."

"I find it hard to believe my father dealt *directly* with these creatures."

"Only her father, who served as liaison for any business Midir had in the human realm. His fascination with the man and his family always puzzled me."

"Maybe he saw beyond the human aspect in him. He certainly saw something in the daughter."

"Perhaps."

"What honor is there to die for so primitive a race?"

Thamuz tilted his head. "Every species fights to survive, milord."

Dathmet pushed out of his chair and returned to the window. "We'll see how far their honor gets them. Harborym has been briefed on the infiltration?"

"He has, milord." Thamuz joined him but kept a respectful distance. "Once the Alamir are engaged with the happenings in the human realm, his team will move in and acquire the stones."

"Good." He seemed momentarily preoccupied with other thoughts. "Midir never explained their importance. All he talked about was her."

"Control the stones and you control the Alamir."

"Their power comes from a handful of rocks?"

Thamuz shifted on his feet and placed his hands behind his back. "In the beginning, it was a single stone, but after years of fighting amongst the Alamir, it was split into pieces and entrusted to the five strongest clans."

"How did *she* become the key?"

"Midir believed it is due to her mixed blood. If we strengthen the darkness within her and turn her to our cause in conjunction with the stones, we will be able to turn the Alamir. Control them and the human race will follow."

Dathmet stroked his chin. "How do we know if she carries the darkness?"

"Every soul is made of light and dark. Neither exists without the other. Our aim is to trigger an imbalance in her loyalties."

"Interesting." He turned to Thamuz. "Does the woman know her history, or from where her mother came?"

"I don't understand what significance it would have."

Dathmet dismissed the question with a shake of his head. "How much does she know of me?"

"She is not aware of your existence and should remain so. If she knows too much too soon, the Krymerian is sure to learn of it. Our plans, *your* plans, would be disrupted."

"Assemble your officers, Commander. It's time to move forward."

"Shall I assign Togor to the woman?"

"No. I will take on the task myself."

Thamuz cleared his throat.

"Don't be concerned. She'll never know it's me." He placed his hand on his chest, giving the commander a fanged grin. "Until I'm ready for her to know."

"Tread carefully, milord. She's not a helpless little girl anymore." Thamuz saluted and left his master to his thoughts.

Dathmet stared into the courtyard. "Indeed. She is not." The beauty of the pebbled walkways and multi-colored flowerbeds belied the torturous monument at its center—two black stones nine feet tall and spaced the width of a man spread-eagled.

He considered it unnecessary to admit his presence at his father's death. His reasoning wouldn't have set well with the commander. But the desire to see this brother, and more importantly, her, was too great to resist.

He vowed to keep the sight of Midir's body reduced to ashes and his essence consumed by the other alive in his head in order to repay them both in kind for his demise.

"I will finish what we started, Father. Their dreams will turn into nightmares and nightmares into reality. Their days are numbered."

Freeblood paced the dark cavern of a room. The unexpected transport left him disoriented and being left alone hadn't helped either.

He'd always thought of the Alamir stories as fairy tales, anecdotes created by parents to pacify the wild imaginings of their children. He'd never considered the Alamir to be real, much less his destiny. From the moment he opened his eyes in the hospital bed, everything was different.

A light suddenly appeared from above spotlighting a silver-haired Amazon who sat on the lap of nothing less than a god crowned by a mass of golden locks. Perched on a massive black-and-blue-flamed throne, skulls formed the arms of the great seat that tapered down into griffin feet, its back carved into a winged serpent. He peered over his shoulder. *When did they come in?* The sight of the duo made him hesitate, but the clearing of a throat prompted him to speak.

"Okay, okay." Freeblood blew out a breath. *Take it slow, Joe.* He directed his first question at the Amazon. "Why did you leave without explaining what happened to me?"

Her eyes darted to the side. "At first, I wasn't sure anything *had* happened." But once said, her steady ice-blue gaze met his. "Not until I saw you dash down the hallway."

His next question was for the man. "How is it you know me, yet I've never heard of you?"

The big man sat back. "I became aware of you through my Etain." The couple shared an intimate smile. "There were difficulties with her sister which required my assistance. Had it not been for her, you and I would have never met."

Freeblood thought back over the days since he'd met the silver-haired woman and tried to envision a sister. "Short black hair, horns, and a kinky tail?"

"Aye." Dar combed his fingers through the ends of Etain's hair.

"Whose name is?"

She answered this time. "Faux."

"Hmm." Freeblood narrowed his eyes. The study of her face sparked a memory. "You were chasing me."

She frowned and straightened her back. "*Faux* was chasing you. *I* was trying to stop her."

"Really? Why would she be chasing me?"

"Who knows why Faux does anything?"

"Then why try to stop her?"

"Well…" Etain rolled her shoulders and glanced at Dar, who rejoined the conversation.

"We are not here to discuss family matters."

Freeblood eyed the big man. "What's so damn special about you?"

Dar grinned as he trailed a hand down Etain's back. "I will leave that to my lady. Tell us, *a chuisle.* What is so *damn special* about me?"

The gaze exchanged between the two was intimate, intense, and charged the air with sexual energy. Freeblood slid his eyes to the right, and to the left, anywhere to avoid being the sordid voyeur.

Etain broke their connection and turned to him. "Have you declared a clan?"

"Answer my question first."

She inhaled slowly. "Have you been invited to join a clan?"

Maybe it's going somewhere. "Well, yeah. I thought about it in Australia. I'm sorry, the Australian *sector,* but the fog in my head lifted and here I am. Why—"

"What made you want to be a part of the clan?"

He shrugged, watching her descend the steps toward him. "I don't know."

"Was it the clan? Their politics?" She walked in a circle around him. "Their beliefs? Or was it a person?" She placed her hands on her hips and faced him. "A person you liked or admired?"

He stared at her.

"Clans are serious business within the Alamir. Being part of one is an important decision and affects your future and your clan. I joined LOKI because of Dar." She glanced over her shoulder at the man. "I knew him to be a good leader and strong, but more importantly, honorable." Her countenance turned sour when she turned back to Freeblood. "I learned the hard way that he was the only one in the clan I could trust. We may have become superhuman, but we're still human. Not everyone has integrity."

"Yeah, I get it. Choose carefully. Am I Alamir because of you?"

Her warm smile lightened the mood. "After your tap dance with the eighteen-wheelers, you needed a lot of blood. The doctor took as much from me as he thought I could handle." She chuckled. "You should've seen his face when I walked out of the room."

He smiled at the memory of the stoic doctor and glanced at his arms. *Good ol' Dr. Green.* One was covered in gashes and scrapes, the other broken.

She continued speaking as she ascended the stairs to Dar and sat on his lap. "I had no idea my blood would do anything more than save your life.

But I figure the change wouldn't have happened if you weren't meant for the Alamir."

Etain was on the same road and took him to the hospital. His injuries, severe and life-threatening, had healed within hours of her donation.

He shifted his weight from one foot to the other and crossed his arms. "You're saying this would've happened anyway, whether we met or not?"

"Probably. Yes." She pushed a hand through her hair. "Most likely."

This was too provocative. He uncrossed his arms. "Are you fucking with me?"

Dar answered with the voice of a flustered father dealing with a thick-headed son. "Before you met my Etain, could you move faster than the speed of light? Did you see things the way you see them now? You would certainly not be standing here before me were you a mere human."

"What does it mean to be Alamir?"

Etain leaned forward and rested her elbows on her knees. "It means you are a protector of the human realm but are no longer a part of it. We live in a parallel dimension. It's our duty to ensure their world continues without interference from evils that don't belong there."

His laugh was more of a grunt. "What evils would those be?"

Dar answered but his focus was on Etain's backside. "Demons, recruiters."

Freeblood raised a brow. "You?"

A steely, golden gaze met his. "*Bok.*"

An uncomfortable darkness teased at the fringe of Freeblood's consciousness. He sucked in a breath and turned from the unspoken warning. Imagine what his family would say if they knew. He dismissed the thought with a shake of his head and returned to the cozy couple lost in their private world. *Like it or not, this is my future.*

"Were all those people back there Alamir?" His question brought their attention back to him.

"Spirit and Inferno are Etain's Alamir family." Dar smoothed a stray lock of hair from her face. "The others are the High Council of the LOKI clan, my most trusted friends."

"If Spirit and Inferno are your Alamir family, do you have a human one? Do you ever see them?"

Etain's head jerked around. A palpable sadness hit him in the heart, followed by a pain permeating from the center of his brain. Tears glistened in her eyes as bloody images ripped through his mind. A girl pursued by a red-eyed monster.

She closed her eyes and escaped into Dar's arms.

Freeblood's hands went to his head as he fell to his knees. "Make it stop! I'm sorry! I didn't know."

"Shall we not go down that road?" He heard the man say.

The cool of the stone floor against his forehead eased the pain. Freeblood drew in a shaky breath. "Agreed. I just wanted to know if we can go back."

"It can be done," Dar said. "But I suggest you not make it a habit. The Alamir frown on it if for personal reasons."

They can frown all they want. "You seem different from the other Alamir. I'm not sure how to explain it."

Dar raised a brow. "I am Krymerian."

"Krymerian?" The word felt strange on his tongue. Freeblood sat up and crossed his legs. "What is a Krymerian?"

Dar's jaw clenched and unclenched. "Krymerians are a race as old as time. Due to wars against opposing clans, the *Bok*, and even the Alamir, few remain." He and Etain glanced at one another. "Come to think of it, I am the only one left."

He contemplated the significance of the statement, piecing the information together. *Etain was already Alamir when she gave me her blood. You gotta be kidding me.* "Are you why she's Alamir? Did you use your blood to turn the others?"

"My blood has nothing to do with the Alamir."

"Etain, when I found you two in Mexico, you said the connection was your sister and not you. How is that? What happened to *our* connection?"

"Well," she chewed the inside of her lip, "a few things got in the way."

"Like what?"

She rolled her eyes and sighed. Dar wrapped his arms around her waist and leaned his head against hers. "You do not have to say, *a chuisle*. We can save it for another time."

"No, it's okay. I should tell him."

"Tell me what?" Despite the warmth in her eyes, Freeblood shivered.

"During our conversation at the hospital, I sensed something. By the time I realized what I felt was real, you shot out of the room." She glanced away as she ran a hand through her hair. "I've never seen anyone move that fast. Faux felt it too. I went to stop her from going after you."

"Why?"

"Because..." Etain paused and glanced at Dar. "She can be difficult."

The young man hid a grin behind his hand. "Really?"

She pressed her lips together. "Her intentions are not in your best interests."

"*My* interests," he repeated, doubtful *his interests* had anything to do with it. "I'm guessing it didn't go well."

Dar hugged her close, his golden gaze for her only. "Faux tried to remove her from the equation, which forced me to take action."

Visions of the arrow-tipped tail lashed through Freeblood's mind. "She tried to kill you because of *me*?" His mind whirled as he came to his feet. Pacing back and forth, he eyeballed Dar. "*Your* blood saved Etain."

"Aye."

So that's the difference. Freeblood shoved his hands into his pockets. "If there's a link between me and Faux, did you share blood with her too?"

Etain stood, growing taller with every step toward him. White wings tipped with crimson fanned out and settled on her back.

"Faux is none of your concern." She grabbed the front of his shirt and lifted him a good foot off the floor. "Do you understand *that*?"

Eyes wide, his thoughts tumbled as he struggled to break free.

Dar chuckled and joined them at the base of the throne. "You have been warned. Faux is one with whom you should not toy. My love, turn him loose. She will handle him in her own way."

"That's what I'm afraid of." She set Freeblood down and retracted her wings.

"I will allow one more question," said Dar.

They act like it's nothing to sprout wings. Freeblood straightened his shirt and tried to appear unaffected by her transformation. "How does Midir fit into all this?"

Five talons instantly appeared from Dar's hand. "What do you know of Midir?"

Freeblood realized his mistake in time to deflect the attack with his blue-gemmed sword. "Nothing, hence the question. Inferno said you'd gone to visit your brother and his name came up in the conversation." His eyes narrowed. "You know, the one with your *most trusted* friends."

One side of Dar's mouth twitched as he eyed the unusual sword in Freeblood's hand. "Midir was misguided and desired something never meant for him." He retracted his talons and took Etain's hand in his. "We have personal business. Make yourself at home. The kitchen is in the next hall if you are hungry." They walked toward the door. "Then pick a room and rest."

Freeblood cracked his neck and grinned at his prowess in tempting fate at least three times in the past half hour. There was an added bounce in his step as he followed his nose toward the kitchen. In the doorway, he searched for a light switch, but found only a cool, smooth surface. When he stepped into the room, a soft light illuminated the warm color of the walls. *Nice.*

He circled the dark stone island and searched through the mahogany cabinets. Across from the island sat a massive range that dominated most of the wall. Not far away stood a large refrigerator.

"Already feels like home."

He noticed a set of frosted glass doors on the opposite side of the room. Opening them with a great flourish, he grinned at the wonderland of treats within.

"Heh, Krymerians aren't so different when it comes to food. Dar's gonna regret this." Within a few seconds, he assembled a king-sized sandwich and sat at the island, savoring his creation as he reflected on the day. Despite a few tense moments during the interview, he was happy with how it went.

A Krymerian. He shook his head and smirked. *Ancient.* He ran a hand through his curly mop of hair. *And I'm Alamir. Damn.* Would it make any difference to his apathetic father to know his son was now a defender of the earthly realm instead of the family wealth?

Then his mind went to the fourth piece in the jumbled puzzle. *Faux.* He had no words to describe that sexified demon of a woman.

A sudden yawn reminded him of the late-night party he was enjoying when memories of Mexico returned as well as Etain's attempt to erase those memories. He immediately left, following the burn in his blood.

"There's something they aren't telling me, I'm sure of it. But..." He stretched and pushed away from the island. "I need sleep."

The dishes placed in the sink, he ventured upstairs and paused on the landing. *North, west, east, or...* He turned. "South it is." Not far down the hallway, he came to a set of three doors and pondered the purpose of their close proximity to each other. He pressed an ear to the center door and heard nothing. After a shuffle to the door on the left, he smiled. "Mom and Dad."

The door to the far right was no different than the others, yet it held an indescribable allure. Freeblood pressed his ear against the smooth wooden surface. Tingles in his belly niggled farther down to the beast below. He bit his bottom lip and balled his hands into fists.

"Sleep first."

He forced himself to move far enough down the hall to afford him a peaceful night. Within moments of slipping between the sheets, the newest family member of the *Sólskin* estate was fast asleep.

TIME ALONE

In their private domain, Dar reached for his fiery vixen, his sole intent being a slow seduction. She surprised him by capturing his hands in hers.

"Not just yet, milord," she whispered as she backed him into the room. "When I think of what almost happened. I could've killed you."

"It is over. He is gone." His mouth claimed hers in a long, savoring kiss. "We are here, together." His forehead to hers, he caressed her lips. "I need you, *a chuisle*. I need to lose myself in you."

"And I you, my love."

The bed pressed against the back of his legs, what he saw in her eyes told him he would be a fool to resist and willingly sat at her slight insistence. His hands itched to rip the leathers from her luscious body. "You have me at a disadvantage, milady."

She stood between his legs, a shadow of a smile on her lips. "When I'm with you, my sweet savage, I feel like I can do anything."

Her earthy fragrance, a fusion of warm vanilla laced with sex, smelled of life, love, and home. His hands drifted up her thighs to her rounded backside. "Sweet savage. Is that how you see me?"

She traced the faint scar across his left cheek and eye. A gift from the assassin he killed for her. "Sweet?" Her fingers trailed down to his broad shoulders. "Sometimes." She continued along each muscular arm to his hands on her bottom. The move stretched the fabric of her top and accentuated her breasts. "Savage?" Mesmerized, his gaze went to her mouth, watching her tongue run over her red lips, and ending with the lower one tucked seductively between her teeth. "Always."

She plucked his hands away, a mischievous glint in her eye, and returned them to his own leather-clad thighs.

"A woman in control." He gripped said thighs to keep himself in check. "I like it."

Etain glided across the plush rug. After a suggestive wink over her shoulder, she leaned her head back shaking her silvery mane, and tossed it forward as she bent over, pushing her backside in the air.

He licked his lips and reached for her as she pulled the laces of one boot. She almost smiled but caught herself and gave him a pouty shake of her head. Although she felt downright scandalized, having never done anything like this before, his reaction told her she was doing something right. The captivated expression on his face unleashed a wild abandonment within her.

She undulated to her right and raised a graceful arm, her fingertips dancing over her curves down her hip to the top of the other boot. Its laces loosened with the slightest pull. With a turn, she straightened and approached her prey with what she hoped was a sensuous look, hooded eyes, and pouty lips. In getting Faux situated and squeezing in a quick freshen up, she hadn't the time to practice. From the desire burning in his eyes, it didn't matter.

As she unbuttoned his shirt and pushed it off his shoulders, her lips hovered close to his, raising goosebumps over his skin. The kiss a mere taste of breath, she twisted around and held onto his muscular thighs to lower herself onto his lap.

His breath was hot and heavy against her neck, making her nipples ache and her clit pulse. She leaned into him and snaked her arms around his neck with the thought of taking him there and then. But as he made his move, she bent over to remove her boots, pushing her backside against his restrained invitation, and slipped between his legs. Facing him, her fingers slid along the collar of her top, right versus left in a tug of war, exposing her flesh, one popped button at a time. His hungry gaze shifted from her chest to her eyes, his tongue darting over his lips.

She groped her breasts, and slid her hands down her stomach to the waistband of her trousers. Her thumbs separated the deep blue leather from her pale skin, the two sliding toward the button below her navel. Emboldened by Dar's undivided attention, she slipped the button, flipped the zipper tab, and pulled the leather from either side.

A simple shrug slid her top down her arms. Before it dropped to the floor, she snapped it up around his neck and pulled him in, her mouth beneath his.

"Etain."

"Not yet."

She cast her top aside and grazed her nails down his chest, over his abdomen, and along his thighs. Silver strands swept forward as she removed his boots and massaged each foot, her knuckles working into the arch. Dar sighed and relaxed back onto his elbows.

"*A chuisle,*" he emitted more as a guttural grunt. "Come to me."

Her nimble fingers worked their way over his leathers. "You first, my love."

Dark eyes fluttered open. The red-stained glass of the Tiffany lamp cast a soft light throughout the room. "Halle-fucking-lujah. Back where I belong." Faux sighed at the red-and-black furnishings, then frowned. *Midir. Asshole.* After a quick check of her torso, she sighed, reassured by the mark on her stomach but noted the small alteration caused by Midir's blade. The crown of swords was no longer the eternal circle of protection.

He's gonna pay for that.

Happy to be pain free, she nonetheless took her time to adjust being upright, swung her feet over the edge of the bed, and used the bed post for support to stand. At the same time, her tail snapped out to keep her on her feet. The coolness of the black lacquered post helped slow the spin in her head.

"Damn, how long has it been?"

She eased down onto the bed and held her head in her hands. Her stomach growled. "I need to eat." It took several stabs of her shaky limbs to slip on the robe left at the foot of the bed, but eventually, she stood on her own and shuffled to the door.

At the kitchen, residual vibrations of danger made her skin tingle. She licked her lips and poised her tail for attack. One step into the room, and another. When the lights came on, she jumped, and laughed at herself. "Don't be such a lame ass."

Once her heart settled, she checked the refrigerator for something to make a quick meal. It surprised her how the simple act of making a sandwich helped her relax.

She closed her eyes and sank her teeth into the soft bread, her first solid food since Midir's attack. "Oh my god," she mumbled. She even scooped up the stray crumbs with her fingertips, happily licking them clean. When she left her dishes in the sink, it struck her as odd to find a plate and glass already there but didn't make much of it.

Faux roamed about the manor, poking into various rooms, imagining how they would be with a woman's touch. As much as she wanted to continue exploring though, the aches in her body forced her to admit she wasn't ready. She stopped several times to catch her breath in her slow procession up the stairs.

At the landing, another presence in the house came to her. *Something is different.* She pressed her ear against Dar's bedroom door. "I'm sure one of them brought me here."

She moved to Etain's door and smirked, the mystery solved. The muffled voices were familiar, but she wasn't in the mood to face either of them tonight. The delicious tingles in her blood tempted her to a room at the end of the hall. *I haven't felt this alive since…*

Her bare feet whispered over the large rug in the room. "So, you're back." A not so manicured nail trailed along his cheek. "Oh." She did a quick inspection of the disasters at the end of each finger. "Someone could've at least used a nail file."

Freeblood shifted in his sleep.

"Move over, lover boy. I'm too tired to walk all the way down that long, lonely hallway back to my cold, empty room." She went to the other side of the bed, slipped off her robe, and slid in between the sheets. "You don't mind, do you?"

Curling close to the young man, she drifted to sleep.

Arms and legs intertwined, the couple murmured soft words of love against skin slick from the flush of passion. Their lips met in a salty embrace, tongues caressing in tender exploration.

Dar released a contented sigh. "I could stay here with you forever, *a chuisle.*"

She swept her finger along the line of his jaw. "I'd gladly forget the world, my sweet savage."

"Aye." He caught her hand and brought her fingertips to his lips. "Your performance has me perplexed." At her raised brow, he added, "I am not complaining."

The invitation in his gaze intensified the pulse between her legs. To avoid melting into his golden pools, her gaze followed her fingers as she traced the outline of the shared mark on his chest. "It's funny the things you see when sitting in a corner, minding your own business."

Dar chuckled. "I did not take you for a voyeur."

"Hmph. It's not my fault people don't check the room before getting down to business."

"And far be it from you to gracefully retire."

"Grace is not one of my strong points. You know, with all the talk about the blood today, I've been wondering."

He twirled a lock of her hair around his finger. "About what, my beautiful lady?"

"You've told me not to share it, no matter what. You even outlawed it within the clan but never said why."

"Might we talk about this another time? Our private time is so precious I hate to waste it discussing such things." He leaned in for another kiss.

Etain turned her head. "Not today."

"I have good reason. Can we leave it at that?"

She pushed away and sat up. "With your Council at Laugharne and Freeblood here, who knows when I'll get another chance. I need to know, Dar. Your blood has saved my life more times than I care to remember. Because of you, mine saved Freeblood. Holy hell, our sharing of blood created Faux, a totally different person. And now your clan wants your head because of it. Why would you outlaw such a vital part of you?"

He sighed as he shifted and leaned against the headboard. "The Council wanting my head because I shared my blood is an excuse to remove me as chieftain. Savage has become power hungry."

"Can they?"

"They can try. But in the end, it is *my* clan."

"I have every confidence you will prevail." She laced her fingers with his. "Now tell me why."

"When I joined the Alamir long ago, there were bloody clashes between the clans in their struggle to come to terms with their new lives and the overwhelming responsibilities it entailed."

"Worse than the one where your found me?"

"Oh, aye. Much worse." He gave her hand a loving squeeze. "I witnessed the death of many who should not have died, many who could have taken the Alamir in a direction of peace and harmony instead of the senseless brutality we endured.

"There was one man—noble, well-spoken, courageous to a fault. He was a born leader, and his clan followed him without question. We both recognized a kindred spirit and developed a deep respect for one another. He taught me as much as I taught him.

"There were those who despised the clan and thought their loyalty to the man inane. Those who hated him laid a trap and waited until I was away." He breathed in and released it slowly. "The plan succeeded with deadly precision. Most of his clan could not be saved."

"Oh, Dar. You must've been devastated."

"Fellow Alamir donated blood but still his life threatened to slip away. When I received the news, I rushed to his side and offered my own blood. I was certain the superior qualities of mine would prove a turning point."

"You saved him?"

He turned his head, lost to another time. "Aye, I saved him, if you can call it that." She placed her other hand over his. After a few moments, he came back to her, hesitant to meet her gaze. "He was never the same afterward."

"Well, neither was I."

An unusual expression something akin to pride tempered with sadness passed over his handsome features. "Your reaction was different, *a chuisle*." He squeezed her hand again. "Your system absorbed the light in my blood rather than the dark."

"Oh." They sat quietly as Etain pondered on what he'd said thus far. "It doesn't make sense. You told me the priests removed the darkness when you were a child. It was your separation that made Midir."

His smile held no humor. "They could not remove it all. How can light exist without the dark?" He shook his head. "No, a portion of the darkness remained. I have thought on it often, trying to understand how you were not affected by it."

"Maybe it's like playing roulette."

He raised a brow.

"You know…" She let go of his hand and turned to face him. "Spin the wheel and hope the ball lands on your number." His furrowed brow told her he had no idea what she was talking about. "A crap shoot?" He pursed his lips. She twirled a strand of her hair, trying to find a phrase he would understand. "A toss of the dice?"

"Aye, perhaps."

"This friend who you saved. Is he still alive?"

"As far as I know. He murdered his caregivers and disappeared into the night, taking with him those few of his clan who still lived."

She bit her bottom lip, unsure whether to ask the question.

Dar saved her the effort. "He turned to the *Bok*." He closed his eyes and leaned his head back. "He has risen within their ranks as an intelligent and ruthless commander."

"I'm so sorry, Dar. When was the last time you saw him?"

"It does not matter, my love." He pulled her into his arms. "Tonight, there is only me and you."

"One more question, please," she said, intent on an answer. "Could the man you saved have been one of Midir's men?"

He stroked her body, sparking the fire in her blood. "I doubt it."

"Why?"

"If Thamuz was working for my brother," he mumbled, his teeth raking her bottom lip, "we would not be here now. He would have seen to it."

DIRTY DEEDS

Sunlight shining on his face dragged Freeblood to consciousness. He raised an arm to block the light and was surprised to see Etain, her arms crossed and fire in her eyes.

"What're you doing?" he mumbled, his eyes squinted against the brightness.

"What the hell are *you* doing?"

He blinked. "Uh, well, I was sleeping until someone opened the curtains. How about doing me a favor by closing them?"

"You wanna rethink that, bub?"

He followed her gaze to the lump beside him and sat up. "Whoa! Where'd you come from?"

Faux stretched, a dreamy glint in her dark eyes. "Good morning, handsome. Best night I've had in ages."

Her sexy smile gave him a thrill. "Handsome, huh?"

The clearing of a throat brought him back to earth.

His eyes darted to the Amazon and was certain the Four Horsemen rode in the ice-blue apocalypse. "Nothing happened here." He glanced at the impish Faux. "Not that I would've minded, but..." He turned to the face of his reckoning. "*Nothing* happened."

"You were warned, Freeblood."

"Shut up, Etain," Faux barked, pushing up on her elbows. "You're such a drag."

"It's a miracle you're even alive. You're jeopardizing more than *your* life by cavorting with this heathen."

"There was no cavorting," Freeblood threw out, in case anyone was listening. "And—"

"Shut up, Freeblood," the sisters snapped in unison.

He slid under the covers when a spiked tail whipped over his head and peeked out from behind the sheet just as a naked Faux stood on the bed.

"I have rested for what feels like *for-ev-er* with only your mindless mage for company. I've heard all about raising four fucking kids and am convinced I don't even like kids. And then you take Dar for yourself. Well, you're not taking this one. He's mine!"

Freeblood grinned from behind the duvet as his gaze shifted to the other sister. *Not a happy face.*

"You ungrateful shit. We have all risked our lives to ensure your recovery." Her wings fanned out. "All you care about are your own selfish pleasures."

He heard a gasp and turned to the succubus as she plopped down on the bed, speechless.

"Fun time is over, Romeo." The threat in Etain's voice was loud and clear.

An amused Dar, who languished at the door, came into the room, and stood next to Etain. "What have we here?"

Freeblood displayed his best innocent face in the hopes it would help. "I swear, nothing happened."

Etain hissed through gritted teeth.

Dar frowned. "Faux." When she didn't respond, he yelled, "Faux!" Her head snapped toward him. "Go to your room and get dressed. Now." She stared at the man as she shuffled to the edge of the bed. "Freeblood, gather your wits and your trousers." He turned to Etain. "We will get this straightened out, *a chuisle*. However, we must deal with the Council first."

"Are you serious?"

Dar lowered his voice. "The boy is telling the truth, Etain."

"He ignored what I said."

"We can address it upon our return. We will not be long."

"You go ahead." Her piercing glare at Freeblood forced him back under the duvet. "I'll make sure it gets sorted now." She snapped her wings to her body.

"Etain." Dar gripped both her arms. "Look at me."

"What?"

"We will deal with these two later."

"You take care of your business," she pulled from his grasp, "and I'll take care of mine."

"I would prefer you come with me should anything go awry with the Council."

"I'll come along once I'm done."

"Remember her condition, Etain."

Feathers ruffled along her wings. "How could I forget? I wonder if you'd be so blasé if Midir were alive."

His hands fell to his sides. "*Breakfast* will give everyone an opportunity to cool down."

After a final glare at the couple, she stalked toward the door. "I'll be in the shower."

Dar watched her stride from the room and turned in time to catch the smirk on Freeblood's face. "Get dressed. Breakfast in thirty."

Freeblood rolled out of the covers, grabbed his jeans from the floor, and yanked them on. "You seem surprised." He walked around to offer Faux a hand.

"*I'm* the demon, not her," she muttered. "And what the hell happened to Dar?"

"We all have a little demon in us," he said as a joke, but her lack of response changed his tone. "People change, which reminds me…" He raised a brow. "*Nothing* happened last night."

"So what?" She smirked, back to her old self. "Tell me her reaction wasn't worth it."

He pulled on his shirt and waited at the door. "No more than yours."

"Hmph." Faux rolled her eyes. "I tripped over *your* lame ass." She grabbed her robe and walked toward him.

He followed her out the door. "That's me. The lame ass heathen."

In consideration of the explosive start to the morning, Dar thought it the perfect time to indulge his culinary talents and give everyone in the house time to settle down, especially Etain. With a generous portion of bacon under the grill, he stood poised at the counter, onion in position and knife in hand.

Visions of the past leaped forward in his mind. A horde of *Bok'Na'Ra* riders crested a hill overlooking a castle he knew all too well, walls of white stone shining in the morning's light.

With a shake of his head, the image dissipated.

Soon, onions, peppers, tomatoes, and ham, mixed in a creamy concoction of whipped eggs, stood ready for their transformation into omelets. Pancakes with the sweet, spicy warmth of nutmeg brought back memories of his days as a boy in Krymeria. He laughed quietly, remembering his early morning forays into the castle kitchen in an attempt to beat the old chef at his own game. No matter how early the boy rose, the old Krymerian was there, surrounded by the smell of fresh bread, bowl in hand, whipping up a delicious family breakfast.

You taught me many things, Ramsey.

After dotting the griddle with batter, he turned to the strawberries. A few made it to the dish, but the fragrance of their magical sweetness proved too irresistible. His lips red with their juice, Dar poured the omelet mixture into four separate pans. A pot of grits bubbled, while bread covered with egg batter sizzled on another griddle. He pivoted on his heel and was back to the pancakes. Within minutes, his breakfast concerto was ready for its audience.

Dar stepped into the dining room and set the large tray on the table. Although Etain did not acknowledge him, he took it as a good sign that she was at the table, angry or not.

Faux acted nonchalant.

Freeblood rubbed his hands together and licked his lips. "That's what I'm talkin' about."

Dar took his seat at the head of the table.

"I can't possibly eat all this," Etain grumbled.

"You don't have to." Freeblood shoveled food onto his plate. "I'll take care of it."

Faux puzzled over one particular dish. "I didn't realize grits were popular where you come from."

Dar enjoyed a few bites, swallowed, and dabbed his lips with a napkin. "I have learned to appreciate a thing or two in my travels. They are one of my favorites. Does it trouble you?"

She stabbed her fork into the food. "Weird."

Dar winked at Etain, who responded with a glib expression. "You appear to be a most generous employer."

"I do not follow," he said, reaching for his cup of coffee.

"Another holiday for the minions?" She snapped her napkin out and placed it across her lap. "And so soon after the last one."

His eyes crinkled with amusement as he gently blew the steam from his hot coffee, the memory bright of the last meal he prepared for these incredible women after an artful transport to his abode. A summons, to be exact. In his haste, he forgot to mention his expected guests to the housekeeper, making it impossible to get a cook on such short notice, so he cooked the dinner himself.

"The locals like my laid-back style." The coffee now at a tolerable temperature, he enjoyed a sip.

"Hmph."

Dar set down his cup and leaned toward her, placing a hand on her knee. "I thought it best to give us time to get used to each other and our new home without the hindrance of watchful eyes. The townsfolk are good people, but rather curious and talkative."

"Oh, well..." She acted as though it was of little consequence. "Good thinking, I suppose."

He sensed the mellowing of her anger and turned to the other two. "I trust you both slept well."

Freeblood indulged in a sip of juice. "It was a good night." The cool words did not sit well with Dar or the lady sitting at his side.

"Don't count on having another one," Etain said, casting a stern eye at her sister.

Faux brushed off the scowling faces. "I appreciate your saving my life, but I feel great and ready to get on with it."

"We will have a proper discussion when Etain and I return from Laugharne."

Faux turned her black gaze to the Krymerian. "No. We will talk before you go."

"I have a Council to sort out. We will talk *after* our return."

She slapped her napkin on the table. "I don't care about your stupid Council. My life has been on hold long enough. Whatever you have to say can be said right now."

Dar sat back, coffee in hand. "You will do as you are told."

Faux pushed up from her chair, snapping her tail like a whip. "You will *not* treat me like a child. I took a sword through the gut for you and kept my mouth shut during the constant drivel from that mouse of a woman. Not to mention your conquest of my sister."

He gently set the cup on the table. "I distinctly remember your accusing Etain of the same thing earlier."

Her eyes smoldered. "You look different, Dar. She *is* different. Did big bad Midir piss in your cornflakes?"

"Faux." Etain set her fork and knife on the table.

"Shut your mouth." Dar felt his casual demeanor deteriorating with every word. "I have heard his name more in death than I ever heard in life."

"Or what?" Faux puffed up in defiance.

Dar abruptly stood. She stepped back but lost her balance. He had the opportunity to catch her but did not move. Freeblood shot out of his seat, wrapping his arms around her, and took the brunt of the impact when they both hit the floor.

"My *gift* is what keeps me from sending you back to your island." Dar turned his back on the commotion and went to Etain. "*A chuisle*," he whispered into her ear, "Were the Council not at Inferno's, we would handle this now. But I cannot further impede on his good graces."

"I think you've put the fear in them." She pushed out of her chair and walked with him.

He stopped at the door. "I cannot agree. Explore his mind and dip into hers, then you will understand. I doubt his earlier words will ring true for much longer."

She touched his cheek. "It appears we've switched places. What's made you so angry?"

But his attention remained on the couple sitting side by side on the floor. He pulled away and strode into the room.

Freeblood jumped to his feet. "Back off, Dar."

"She carries *my* child." He slammed his fist on the table, making the dishes rattle and jump.

"You have a shitty way of showing concern for the mother of your child."

"She is not in danger. However, the same cannot be said for you. I suggest you not act on those thoughts in your head. You will not like how it ends."

"Your threats don't scare me." Freeblood came from around the table, his hands balled into fists. "She's free to do as she pleas—"

He hit the floor, a boot on his throat.

"Stop it!" Faux screamed.

"It is a promise, you insolent pup." Dar ground his boot into his neck. "Do not test me." He released the boy and stormed past Etain.

Hearing the front doors slam, she cast a glare on the couple. "Listen to me and listen well. Promises are serious business for him. He doesn't make them lightly."

Faux gently rubbed her stomach. "Since when did his Council become his pet project? I thought Midir—"

"Midir is dead." Etain flexed her hands at her sides. "I have half a mind to bind each of you in an electrified bubble." With an angry flip of her hair, she stalked out of the room. "Keep your legs together for once, Faux."

Freeblood winced as he touched his neck. "What's your story? I'm having a little trouble putting it together."

"Midir showed up at Laugharne one day with a murder hard-on for Dar." She bumped his shoulder with hers. "He didn't count on someone like me. I had plans to rip his head off. I could've too," she gave him a sideways glance, "if he hadn't stabbed me with his stupid sword. That's why I'm stuck here."

"So if he's with her, how is it you're having his baby?"

"He couldn't resist my charms."

Freeblood chuckled. "I think that train left the station."

"Hmph." She rolled her eyes. "I could get him back easy if I wanted him. Is what she said true? About Midir?"

"I think so. All I know is Dar left Laugharne in a hurry and returned a changed person." Faux sighed in resignation. "Well, as long as he's dead."

"I guess I'm the new punching bag."

"Honey, they aren't gonna hurt you or me."

"You sure?" he asked, adjusting his jaw.

"Like he said, he gave *me* his baby." Her hand circled over her stomach. "He wouldn't do anything that would hurt his child."

"From what I just saw, I wouldn't count on it. Something tells me he has a helluva temper."

Etain caught up with Dar in the courtyard. "What's going on with you?"

"As if the High Council is not enough." He stopped and faced her. "The boy flaunts his insolence and will betray our trust."

"Hmm." She crossed her arms over her chest. "Or maybe you're angry because he fancies your mistress?"

"What?"

"You heard me." Afraid she had miscalculated his loyalties, she raised her chin in a charade of strength, despite the fear thundering in her heart. *Maybe Midir was right after all. Maybe Faux means more to him because of the child she carries.* "You're making an awful lot of noise over a few dirty thoughts."

"Etain..."

"Don't! Don't you dare say another thing about her *condition*. I'm trying to be strong, Dar. I am." Her hands ran through her hair. "I bloody fucking am. Aye, they're a handful, and I was ready to kick him out, but after a long think in the shower, I realized if Faux wants to be with him, she'll be with him or anyone else she chooses. Well, except you. *You* are off limits, which I think she understands. But I don't know *you* do." She paced back and forth, angry tears in her eyes. "It seems to me you want to have your cake and eat it too. I'm telling you right now. I deserve better."

She stopped in front of him, legs shoulder width apart and hands on her hips, shaking from the angst churning in her stomach. "I thought I could take it. I thought I was strong enough to watch another woman bear your child. But if you're gonna play the jealous lover, I cannot. I *will* not. You decide right now." The words spoken out loud gave her a surreal sense of calm.

"Etain. You are my heart. I would travel to hell and back for you." He moved toward her, but she avoided his touch.

"I feel like I'm already there," she murmured.

"Can you not understand what this child means to me?"

"If you want Faux and the child she carries, let me go. I won't be your fool."

He stared at her. "Not so long ago, you stripped me to the core over Midir. Yet you are completely blind in this?" His hands traveled down to capture hers. "We have a case of a wild child crossed with a wild card. There is nothing I can do about the child she carries, except remind you it is a part of me. I know I ask a lot, but we must be of a like mind to get through all this.

"I know you feel what I feel." He pressed her hand to his chest over the mark they shared. "See me, Etain. Trust in what your heart tells you."

His touch, his body so close made it difficult for her to remain distant. The heat of the mark warmed her palm, his golden gaze an invitation to forget everything and everyone outside of this moment. *I want to believe you, but should I?* She held his gaze for a long moment before entering his mind left bare for her intimate scrutiny. Her heart pounded as she searched, finding his emotions as raw and exposed as her own. "I see."

"Please, do not doubt who you are to me." His voice was as soft as the caress to her cheek, but the depth of his conviction was indisputable.

"I'm sorry, Dar. I don't know what I'm supposed to do."

"I know you are where I belong. Forgive me for not realizing how different it is for you."

She almost smiled. "It's crazy sometimes."

He lifted her hands to his lips. "It is about to get worse. Will you stand with me, my precious lady?"

"I *am* with you." She pulled free from his grasp. "But where Faux is concerned, you have to be patient."

"Like a saint, *a chuisle*."

"Shall we go before we're detained by something else?"

"Give me five minutes." His smile chased away any lingering doubts in her heart. "I have a special gift for Inferno to thank him for hosting my Council. It could not have been an easy time."

She laughed. "Not for them, I'm sure. What is it?"

"He may not care much for me, but I believe he will appreciate the work of an old Krymerian swordsmith."

After a long kiss in the Laugharne courtyard, Dar admired the view of Etain's backside as she strolled through the front doors to find Spirit. Voices from the direction of the back garden reminded him of why they had returned. He closed his eyes and breathed in the crisp afternoon air. The simple act helped bolster his resolve to settle things with the Council, but rather than walk around the side to the back garden, he made his way toward the front doors. Another simple act to delay the inescapable confrontation.

His foot on the first step, a blinding vision pushed in.

Well-honed steel sliced through soft flesh, mirthless laughter overshadowing a woman's screams.

He stumbled up the steps and raised his hand in time to protect his face from the door. The phantoms faded with a ragged intake of breath. "*Tartarus.*"

Lost in his thoughts, he walked through to the kitchen where Etain, Spirit, and Inferno were engrossed in conversation and absentmindedly acknowledged them on his way to the back door.

"About bloody time," Inferno muttered.

Dar paused at the door. *Keep your cool and stay in control.* The moment he stepped into the garden an assault of questions hit him.

"Where have you been?"

"Why have we been kept waiting?"

"What right do you have to leave us here with no explanation?"

"I am here now," he said, closing the door. "Shall we get this done? I have other matters to attend to."

"*We* are your only business, Lord Darknight," Savage hissed.

Pyro sidestepped to flank Dar. "Who is this Midir we've heard about?"

Warden threw in another question. "Why did you share blood with another? You know it's forbidden."

"One question at a time." Dar raised his hands and cast an eye on Pyro. "Midir was my brother." He turned to Warden. "It is *my* blood to share as I please, but as you have asked so eloquently, it was done to save someone dear to me."

Without warning, another vision tore him from the present.

A small boy strapped to a table, crying for his father, the familiar knife slicing long lines into the child's flesh.

Dar's body quaked in the realization that the child was his long-dead son, Henrí.

"What business is so important you neglect your duties to the clan?" Pyro asked. "Where have you been all this time?"

Dar stared at a man with his head on fire and blood on his hands. Henrí's blood.

The dagger grazed along the top layer of flesh, peeling it from the small body.

The rush of pleasure he felt turned his stomach.

"You will return to the LOKI castle to face the charges of dereliction of duty and treason laid against you," Shera stated as the others moved toward their chieftain. "It will go easier if you come peacefully."

"Treason?" he echoed in a trancelike state. The brutal visions and reality blurred into one. Dar rammed into the fire-headed monster, slamming him into the stones of the castle. He caught the arm wielding the bloody knife and twisted until he heard the bone snap.

The monster screamed.

Dar heard footsteps come from behind and lashed back with his elbow. At impact, he whirled his fist into a face.

Warden bent over and collapsed, blood gushing from a broken nose.

In an instant, Dar released an energy blast. "I am the High Lord of Kaos. You will listen to me."

Knocked to the ground by his blast, Savage was the first to her feet. "How dare you attack the High Council!"

Screams of the child dropped him to his knees. "Stop!" he cried out, his hands going to his head.

"Not until we get what we came for." Savage cracked him in the back of the head with the handle of her whip. Dar went down, face-first into the dirt.

The moment Dar stepped out the back door, Etain cringed at the bombardment of questions. "I wish I could help him fight his battle."

"Well, ya can't. He's a man. It's bleedin' time he acted like one."

"Inferno."

"Steady on," Spirit said. "We've more important things to discuss."

"You're right." Etain agreed. "What is it you wanted to tell me?"

Spirit turned to her husband first. "Love, you need to listen and let me finish what I'm about to say."

"What could ya possibly have to say that I wouldn't listen?" He sat back in his chair. "Unless it has to do with the sucker-punching wanker and his yapping dogs." Her no-nonsense gaze told him it did. He wiped a hand over his face. "For fuck's sake."

With him subdued, she addressed the immediate problem at hand. "Etain, love, you know when you told me Faux is pregnant?"

"Aye."

Recovered from his moment of quiet, Inferno blurted, "She's preggers?"

"Love, please," Spirit said.

"It's his, isn't it?" Inferno violently pushed away from the table, his chair crashing to the floor.

"About that—" Spirit started.

He turned a raised brow glare on Etain.

She stared in return and realized what he must be thinking. "I am *not*."

"Small blessings. I was right about the soddin' bastard. To hell with his Council of tossers, I'll kill him meself. They can drag his corpse back for trial."

Etain stood. "You won't touch him! He has enough to deal with and doesn't need your threats piled on top."

"How can ya defend the cunny-dipping prick? Have ya no pride?"

"I won't have her child grow up without its father."

"Yer a daft one. He's fried yer bloody brains."

He made a move toward the back door, but Etain blocked his way. "*You're* the daft one if you think I'm letting you go out there."

"Both of you sit!" Spirit surprised them both. "I'll not have the two of you fighting."

Etain's shoulders sagged as she pushed a hand through her hair. Inferno had the sense to step away and right his chair.

Spirit sighed. "I think a cuppa would do us all good."

"No!" Etain suddenly screamed.

The intensity of the fight outside vibrated through her. She dashed out the door just as Savage hit him in the back of the head with the handle of her whip, knocking him out. "Have you gone crazy? He's your *chieftain. Nim'Na'Sharr!*" Her crystal sword materialized in her hand.

The four Council members gawked at one another in stunned silence.

"Get the hell out of here! All of you! Leave!" Her sword took on the same white light in her eyes. "Do as I say, or I'll wage my own war here and now."

"There's a dirty deed," Inferno said as he stepped through the back door. "Ya best do what the lass says if yer to bugger off in one piece."

In response to the ruckus, members of the UWS clan appeared from various directions, Felix and Ruby included, tugging against their restraints.

Savage and Shera helped a wheezing Warden to her feet. Shera offered the *Machin Chin* a handkerchief for her broken nose as they joined Pyro, who held a broken arm to his chest. Watchful of the threat around them, the Council gathered close and conferred in quiet whispers.

Savage sneered as she straightened her shoulders. "This isn't over. Once we've dealt with him..." Her gaze went to Etain, "I will deal with you."

"Ooo, I'm scared now," Etain sniped, lowering *Nim*. "The only way he'll be taken is over my dead body."

"Works for me," Savage said.

Pyro leaned toward Savage, his gaze traveling around the yard. "It's not going to happen today. We should go. We know where to find him. Wherever he is, his bitch won't be far behind."

Etain stood over Dar, happy to see their backsides as they marched toward the stables.

Inferno came up next to her. "It could be the whole clan next time. Is he worth it?"

"What would you have me do? Dar would never see justice from that mob."

"This comes of his own doing. Ya should've let 'em have him." He nudged the comatose man with the toe of his boot. "When they come back and a war starts, who do ya think he'll side with?"

"I'll kill them all before he knows they've arrived." Etain sheathed her sword and crouched next to Dar. Her eyes closed, she delved into his mind to ensure he was okay, and fell onto her knees, her head in her hands.

"Lass!" Inferno was quick in getting to her. "What's wrong?"

"His family," she cried.

"Whose family?" Spirit asked.

"The blood." Her eyes reflected the horror seen in her mind. "His memories are so vivid."

Inferno wrapped an arm around her. "What memories?"

"Midir murdered everyone."

Inferno looked at Spirit, who shrugged. "Come on, lass. Let's get him upstairs."

SILENT WARRIOR

---

*S*creams in his head drove him near to madness. Before his eyes, blood-covered hands performed their gruesome deed with great precision, the sharpened edge of a knife separating skin from glistening tissue.

He shook his head. "Not by my hands. I could never do such depraved things."

"Are you sure, brother?"

His gaze moved to the boy's eyes squeezed shut, his innocent face twisted in agony. The body Dar inhabited shivered with delight. A scream to his right made him turn. There was a woman chained to the wall, tears flowing down her cheeks, her arms bloody in her struggle to break free. He saw through her torn clothes the bruises of varying colors on her body. But it was her beautiful face that spoke the loudest of the abomination she was forced to watch as she begged for the life of her son.

"Alexia."

Next to his wife was a small, chained heap. Although he could not see her face, he knew it was his daughter, Victoria. Her pain would be the most intense. After watching her brother and mother die horrible deaths, it would be her turn. Tears blurred his vision, but the hands would not cease in their morbid task.

Dar forced himself to turn away. A glint from across the room caught his eye. Propped against the wall, a large mirror reflected the light, the room, and the disgusting images.

"You disgrace my family in this manner and admire yourself as you do so?"

The knife clattered when it hit the floor. He stormed toward the reflection and came face-to-face with Midir. Dar's bloody hands pierced the silver façade, grabbing the muscular neck so much like his own. A sense of gratification sent a warm flush through his body. His scalp tingled. The flesh yielded to his command, the muscles just below the skin slackening bit by bit as he squeezed the life from his dark brother.

"Dar!"

Sparks lit inside his head, his jaw on fire. He opened his eyes to a familiar face topped by a distinctive strip of thick, blond hair, his fists drawn back for another cuff. Dar's first instinct was to punch the Elf, but realized his hands were otherwise engaged. He remembered Midir's neck locked in his grip and the satisfaction of his brother accepting the inevitable.

But why would Linq try to stop me? No. Midir is dead.

He followed Linq's blue-eyed glare down to the hands that in his mind gripped the neck of his murderous brother. "*Tartarus*!" His release was immediate.

"Give her to me." The authority in Linq's voice compelled him to obey.

Dar sat up a bit too fast, "Oh," and rubbed the back of head as he leaned against the headboard.

"Bad head?"

"Something like that." Dar reached out to touch her, but the Elf pushed him away.

"You have done enough." Linq pressed his fingers against the side of her neck, and leaned into her face, listening for a breath. "What the hell were you thinking?"

"I had to stop Midir." Dar's thoughts were jumbled. "He was killing my family."

"Hmph. Inferno tells me Midir is dead, by your blade, no less."

Dar heard the doubt in his voice. "Inferno? How does he fit into this?"

The Elf pursed his lips. "Do you know where you are, High Lord?"

"I..." At first, the room was strange, unfamiliar. His gaze went to Etain, and the Elf. "Laugharne. My Council—"

"Has left." Linq crossed his arms and leaned against a bedpost. "Apparently, Pyro's arm was broken, and Warden's nose shattered."

Dar gently touched Etain's hair. "They should not have come here. There was no need of it."

"What is going on with you?"

Dar gave his friend a long, hard look. In light of how the day had gone, he decided to share something he considered no one's business but his own. "Visions of the death of my family have been haunting me since Midir's death."

"Was he involved?"

Without Dar saying a word, Linq seemed to understand the glint in his eyes.

"So, you have taken on his *cuimhní cinn*, his memories?"

"I expected it would happen, but not to this degree."

"I remember you telling me he was the darkest part of you when you were a child. If the darkness was so powerful it required an intervention, how could Midir not be as strong as the one from whom he was created?" Linq sat on the edge of the bed. "Alatariel could help you conquer those demons. Your ladylove may not be so lucky next time."

"You have always spoken straight with me. Your honesty is greatly appreciated."

He acknowledged the sentiment with a tilt of his head. "I expect no less from you in return."

Dar sighed. "You deserve the truth, but not today."

"Not today then." Linq checked on Etain. "She appears to be breathing easier now. Except for the marks, I think she will be fine."

"Thank you." Dar laid a hand on her shoulder. "Tell me what brings you back to Laugharne."

The Elf grinned. "Anytime the High Council deigns to leave the LOKI castle is big news. Add that their destination was a small clan in the Welsh district made it all the more monumental. Why else would they come this way except for you?" He shrugged. "I thought you might need my assistance. After a short chat with Inferno, I came upstairs to check on you and overheard what I thought was a scuffle.

"I was afraid they had come back. What a surprise to find you strangling your lady." He eyed the bruised knuckles on his hand. "You have a jaw of pure iron, my friend."

Dar rubbed his jaw. "No less than your left hook. Have Spirit put ice on it." He rolled to the other side of the bed and onto his feet. "I am better now, thanks to you."

At the door, Linq grasped his shoulder. "Let Alatariel help before it gets worse."

"I will consider it. And, please, nothing of this to Inferno." Dar opened the door.

"The bruises on her neck will tell him all he needs to know."

Dar nodded, unconcerned. "We will be down soon." He mused over his friend's words as he quietly closed the door. *Surely it is from the stress of the day.*

Hearing her stir, he rushed to the bed and wrapped his arms around her. "Dar..."

"Shhh, my love. No need to talk. Just rest here with me."

She touched her neck. "My throat hurts."

"A sip of water will help." He scooted out from behind her and soon returned with a full glass. He hesitated, uncomfortable under her narrowed gaze. "What is it?"

Etain took the offered glass, sipped slowly, and placed it on the bedside table. "You were choking me."

"You remember."

"I should think so."

He reached for her, but she leaned back. "It was not you, Etain."

"Bullshit." Her voice caught. She grabbed the glass for another sip. "I'm sure I have the bruises to prove otherwise."

Dar sat on the edge of the bed. "It was you, here with me, but in my mind..." He touched his forehead, "it was Midir. I saw him murdering my—" He shook his head. The words were too horrible to utter. "I had to make him stop. I am sorry, *a chuisle*. Please, forgive me."

She stared at him for a long moment. "I saw them, Dar."

He went with what he thought was a change in the conversation. "The Council will not be back anytime soon."

She inhaled and softened the features of her face. "I'm not talking about the Council. I saw what Midir did to your family."

An emotional whirlwind made him lightheaded. He thought his heart would implode. This one time he wished the connection they shared was not so strong. "It is something no one should have to see."

She placed her hand over his. "Or to bear alone."

The contrast of his large hand covered by her delicate one proved the truth in her words. He was no longer alone. "It was a long time ago. You are my family now." The heaviness in his heart lifted.

Her fingers intertwined with his. "Aye. I am yours as much as you're mine."

She lost her family, too, but at a young age, thrown into an alien world without warning or preparation. His eyes came up to meet hers. "Aye." He frowned at the sudden tears in her eyes, afraid the chaos of his life might have driven her to the edge, despite what she said. "Etain…"

"Our family is more than just you and me." She gave his hand a loving squeeze. "We have Inferno and Spirit." When he shrugged and rolled his eyes, she smiled through her tears. "We have Faux and Freeblood, wild child and wildcard, and the baby." Etain touched his cheek. "We have both suffered great loss, but we have so much to be thankful for. Let's make a fresh start."

Ghabháil ar na déithe (Thank the gods). She would stay.

"However…"

Dar raised a hand in surrender. "I promise you, milady." He reached for the dirk in his boot and held it up. "My heart, my blade, and my body are yours—"

She placed her hands over his on the blade. "My love. I know. What I need from you is a promise to be open with me. Tell me when something bothers you or if your dreams are troubled. We *did* agree to be honest with one another."

"Aye, milady. I will do my best."

Linq inspected his hand as he made his way down the stairs and into the kitchen. Spirit and Inferno were sitting close together, their voices low. Felix, sprawled at Inferno's feet, raised his head with a low growl, but Ruby trotted over to the Elf. He offered his knuckles for inspection. "*Bore da*, Ruby."

Inferno gave Felix a good scratch behind his ear. "Good boy."

"Linq. Have a sit." Spirit waved him over. "Ruby, come. That's a good girl."

After a licked acceptance, Ruby wagged her russet tail and returned to her mistress.

"I need ice." Linq raised his bruised knuckles.

"How'd this happen, love?" Spirit stood and gently took his hand in hers.

"A point proven between old friends."

Inferno snorted. "The bugger deserves a lot worse."

"No broken bones. Sit whilst I put together an ice pack."

Linq sensed the turmoil between his friends. Judging by Inferno's reaction, Dar had not made the best impression. "How much do you know of Dar before he met Etain?"

Inferno turned away, crossing his arms. "I know he's an arrogant prick."

"Things are not always as they appear, my friend. Maybe if you knew his story, you would better understand his ways."

"Here you go, love. Keep it on top there." Spirit reclaimed her seat. "We should listen to Linq. He's known the man longer than any of us."

A glower on his face, Inferno leaned back. "I doubt the Elf has anything to say I'd wanna hear."

"Maybe not, but I do." She turned to Linq. "Tell us about Dar."

"I will but you must tell me about Etain. I have not known him to be smitten by a woman. A new blade, perhaps." He smirked. "But never a woman."

Spirit glanced at her husband. "It sounds a fair trade."

Linq adjusted the ice pack as he gathered his thoughts. "His father was a king." Inferno's raised brows gave him a degree of satisfaction. "Dar should be in Krymeria ruling over his warrior people rather than suffering the disrespect of this realm. What *you* see as arrogance is his sense of responsibility for a more primitive race."

"Hmph. Are ya inferring we're stupid?"

"*That* I would never do. But you must admit the Alamir are somewhat backward in their ways."

"Then explain why we're still here and they're not. Never heard of another Krymerian until his nasty brother came along."

"Nunnehi is full of stories about the Krymerians. Every child knows them by the time they can walk. The stories became all too real the day he and I met on the road." He ran a hand along his thigh to take away the chill of the ice. "I remember when I first saw the man." His eyes widened. "By the stars! None of us in my troop had seen anyone like him and were not sure if he was friend or foe, so we followed him. If he were *Bok*, he could prove dangerous.

"He staggered for days, lost in another world. The only time he slept was when he fell to the ground from sheer exhaustion. Even then, he twitched and muttered. When he woke, he would resume his aimless staggering."

Linq gently flexed his hand. "One afternoon, he collapsed, as expected. It had been a few days since his last sleep. But something was different this time. There were no twitches or mutterings. We thought he found his nirvana and passed into whatever afterlife his kind believed." He paused for a moment.

"We drew sticks." He shrugged. "Someone had to confirm. Lucky me drew the shortest one." A smile came to his lips. "Damn near lost my head. I thank my Elven fathers his reflexes were off, or I would not be sitting here today."

"I hear that," Inferno said. "The bleedin' bastard's got a mean arm."

Linq turned thoughtful. "It is not our custom to ignore a cry for help, whether voluntary or involuntary. It took every one of us to carry him to camp where our healer took over his care. He caused quite a stir with his outbursts. Such strange words came from his mouth."

He chuckled at Inferno's raised brow. "Although his return to health was slow, the healer eventually began to see progress. I visited him every night after my rounds and talked to him. He did not speak. But I knew from the sparkle in his eyes he was listening." Linq stretched his legs in front of him and grinned. "I felt very foolish when I realized he understood every word I said."

Inferno shifted in his seat and crossed one leg over the other. "Wanker."

"Dar is a noble warrior who has proven his worth many times, in battle and out. I would ride with him anywhere."

Inferno tapped a finger on the table as he leaned forward. "Aye, the man's a fighter, but it doesn't make him noble."

Dar, you have a tough row to plow with this one.

"Would you like a brew, love?" Spirit asked, rising from her chair. "You must be parched with all this talk."

"Thank you, milady, but the telling of this tale requires something stronger. Do you have a pint you do not mind parting with?"

"Cheers." She patted his shoulder and went to the cupboard. "Etain mentioned a family - a wife and children."

Despite his hesitation to talk about Dar's private life, Linq hoped by telling a few things about his family and his loss Inferno's paternal instincts would help bridge the gap between the two men.

"Alexia was his wife. Victoria and Henrí, his children."

Inferno jumped up, knocking over his chair. "So it's true?" Felix's nails clattered against the stone floor as he scrambled to get out of the way. Ruby barked, surprised by the noise. "The lass mentioned a family earlier, but I paid no mind. She was fair upset with what happened. This proves what I've been saying all along. He's a lying, two-timing bastard."

"I am getting to that part," Linq said calmly. "Sit down and listen."

"I've heard all I want to hear," he bellowed.

Spirit returned with three full pints and set them on the table. "Pick your chair up and sit your arse down. Let him finish the story. Our lass wouldn't be involved with him if he were such a man."

Inferno scowled at his wife. "Her judgment of the man's character isn't the most reliable. She's lost her fecking mind." He righted the fallen chair and sat with no small amount of muttered curses. After a long draw on his pint, his eyes darted from one to the other. "Well, what're ya waiting for? Make with the telling."

Felix snorted and lumbered around the table to stretch out next to Spirit. Linq drained half his glass and licked his lips. "Ah, thank you, Spirit," he said, grateful for more than just the opportunity to quench his thirst. "Before I continue, tell me how these two met."

Spirit gave Inferno a sideways glance. "You should ask Dar, love."

He raised a brow and grinned. "Complicated?"

"Aye." Inferno lifted his glass for a drink. "We're still trying to figger it out."

Spirit sighed, shaking her head. "She joined LOKI about a year ago."

"I see." Linq's eyes brightened. "That would explain the angry Council."

"They weren't here because of her." She chuckled. "But I think they've added her to the list."

"Our girl's been caught up in his web of lies." Inferno huffed. "Maybe they are too."

Linq knew Dar did not deal in lies. But rather than argue with the man, he leaned back and gazed at the chieftain. "Earlier, you mentioned a new name. Faux. Tell me how she fits in."

Spirit spoke before her husband could launch into another tirade. "Etain showed up not long ago with the girl behind her. A couple of weeks later, she received a summons from Dar that included Faux. They weren't gone for long but when the girls returned, they were different. And they brought the man with them."

Linq raised a brow this time. "They *brought* him?"

Spirit chuckled. "Oh, aye. He was laid out on the gravel when I opened the door."

He tried not to smile. "That must have been a sight. What happened to him?"

"Etain said he killed the assassin who murdered her family. From the looks of him, he took some hard hits."

Inferno scooted his chair closer to the table. "Then his bastard of a brother shows up, tries to kidnap our lass, stabs Faux through her gut, and damn near did the same to Dar. I give it to the man; he gave as good as he got. Too bad he didn't kill him then. It would'a saved us all a lot of grief."

A grandfather clock chimed down the hall. "Pardon me, gentlemen, whilst I start tea. You're welcome to stay, Linq. We have plenty." Spirit turned to her husband. "Love, would you light the barbecue?"

"But the Elf hasn't finished with his side of the story."

She rested her hands on her hips. "Can you wrap it up in twenty-five words or less?"

He laughed but turned serious as he spoke. "His family died long before we met. Dar did not say *how* they died, only said they were gone."

"It was Midir." Spirit blushed, realizing she had voiced her thoughts out loud. "He murdered Dar's wife and children. And there's the wee babe."

Linq tilted his head, intrigued by her insight. "What did he tell you, Spirit?"

"It was something the lass said after his bleeding Council attacked him. She went into his mind to make sure he was all right, and said Midir murdered everyone."

"His brother was a subject we were not allowed to discuss. You say there was a baby? I was not aware Alexia was pregnant."

"No, not his wife," Spirit said. "Faux."

"She is with child?"

"Only after they returned from Dar's."

Linq couldn't hide his shock. "So it is his?"

"Aye."

Inferno practically preened. "Yer holier than thou lord ain't as high as ya make him out to be."

"Love, please!" She took a breath. "The poor thing didn't survive Midir's attack."

Linq lowered his head at the devasting news. His heart ached for his friend. How much more could the man endure? As if sensing his inner turmoil, Ruby sat up and rested her head on his lap. He stroked the dog's wiry fur as his mind drifted to memories of the Krymerian, his quiet brutality and fierce loyalties, and on to what he had seen upstairs. He feared for the man's sanity and for the life of his new lady. "Did Etain know she carried his child?"

"She did but I've not had the chance to tell her Faux lost the baby." Spirit sighed. "The whole affair is beyond me."

"You are a bonny lass, Ruby."

"Well, let's move on to happier things. It'll get sorted," Spirit said as she turned away.

Inferno rose from his chair and walked to the door. "Tap us another glass, mate, and join me and me hounds. Come, Ruby, Felix. Let's stretch our legs before supper."

Linq grabbed both glasses. "I will tell you the story of how Dar became known as *Rólegur Kappi*, the Silent Warrior."

DERAILED

E tain walked into the kitchen expecting to see Spirit busy with supper but found the room empty. Hearing voices in the garden, she stopped at the kettle on the countertop and checked her reflection in its mirrored surface. Not a bruise in sight. She popped her head out the back door.

"Anyone need a refill?" Everyone raised their glasses to show they had plenty. She ducked back in and tapped a brew for herself.

"Then it's all set," Inferno said from behind the grill as she stepped into the garden.

"What's all set?" She chose an empty chair between Linq and Spirit. "Hi, Linq. When did you get here?"

Inferno cut him off before he could answer. "Weren't ya just upstairs with the man?"

Etain frowned. "What?"

"I left ya with Dar."

"So you did." She turned to Linq and smiled. A slight shake of his head and stern gaze made the hairs on the back of her neck prickle.

"Don't tell me ya left yer poor wee man on his own after what that pack of mad dogs did to him?"

She closed her eyes briefly and peeked at the man from the corner of her eye. "What's with the sudden concern for Dar?"

He stepped from behind the grill, the barbeque tongs in hand. "Makes me wonder what's been going on whilst ya been up there."

As she stood, Linq reached for her. "Etain."

She flicked away his hand. "If you must know, I fell asleep and only woke a few minutes ago. Dar wanted to freshen up before he came down."

Inferno placed his hands on his hips, his head bobbing like a bobblehead toy on a dashboard. "Was that before or after he and the Elf had their scuffle?"

The prickles moved over her scalp as she glanced at said Elf. "Scuffle?"

"I—" Linq started.

"Oh, aye! He's got the bruises on his knuckles to prove it. Was it sleep or was it something Linq felt ya needed saving from? He's told us plenty about yer Krymerian."

"Inferno." Spirit stood. "Not now. She's only just—"

"It *will* be now." He waved the barbeque tongs in her face, his eyes ablaze. "I'll not have any more shenanigans under me roof."

Etain rested her hands on her hips. "What *shenanigans*?"

He narrowed his eyes, the tongs now aimed at her. "I've seen the change in ya, I have. And there's the bloody mark on yer chest and his. I know what it means." He slapped his chest with his other hand. "Me and me wife share a mark too."

She raised her hands in a shrug. "Then you know we belong together. What's the problem?"

His eyes bulged. "Not in me bloody house! No! I'll not have it. I don't give a tinker's damn what's happened in his past. He'll not be using ya like a bleedin' tart."

"I thought this was *my* home, too."

It was as though he hadn't heard a word she'd said. "And, *bach feinir* (little lass) ..." The tongs came dangerously close to her chest, "ya'll be properly wed to that demon by the end of the week or ya'll be banished from me home."

She squeezed her hands so tightly her nails cut into her palms. "I will *not* be dictated to."

"Ha! Ya have a way with yer words, *merch* (girl)." Flames licked out from his fingertips. "Ya been nothing *but* dick-tated to since ya met the wanker."

"You will *not* force me to marry."

"Oh-ho!" Inferno rocked on his feet in a Victorian show of piety. "So, he's good enough to bed, but not to wed?"

She circled to his side, turning him away from the house. "It has nothing to do with my feelings for Dar."

Dar walked through the kitchen on his way to the back garden. As he neared the door, Spirit rushed through, tripped over the step and lost her balance. He caught her before she hit the floor. "Oh, Dar. *Ta*. You're up."

"Aye, for a while now. Are you all right?"

"I was coming to get you."

He glanced out the window. "What's going on out there? Sounds like my Council's come back for another round."

"Not even your Council would want a taste of that. Linq's keeping watch."

Inferno's voice boomed through the door. "Ya been daft since ya went to his blasted castle with yer so-called sister."

"Not daft enough to be coerced into marrying against my will."

"And what *will* would that be? Ya been too busy acting the lapdog to use any will of yer own."

Dar peeked out the window again and caught the violet flash in Etain's eyes. "Holy mother of..." He dashed out the door as her wings arced over her head.

"Let me show you the will of a lapdog."

In response to the raised voices, the wolfhound brigade dashed from around the corner. Dar burst into the garden just as Etain's feet left the ground. "Etain!" His cry was lost in the whoosh of air from her wings and the barking dogs. She soared high beyond detection, but Dar knew her thoughts.

Felix and Ruby chased after her, whining and watching the skies while Dar sprinted toward Inferno and dived, knocking him off his feet at the moment she swooped past. Upon impact with the ground, Inferno inadvertently released a fireball. Etain curved and flew toward the horizon.

"*Oi,*" Inferno murmured, the breath knocked out of him. "That was close." The hounds snorted their concern as they sniffed their master.

Blood oozing from his side, Dar pushed away from the man and rolled onto his back. "Closer than you think."

Inferno gasped at the shreds of his own shirt. "Hells bells."

Spirit reached the men as Linq offered a hand up to Dar, who winced as he came to his feet. "Another shirt gone."

She bypassed her husband to inspect his wound. "Let me bandage it for you, Dar."

"Thank you, but it will not take long to heal." He held out a hand to Inferno. "You have to stop making her angry, or it will be the death of us all. She is not the girl you first met."

In a daze, Inferno stared at him, and accepted his hand. "*Ta.* I'll keep it in mind."

Dar turned to Linq, who tilted his head toward the south. He gripped the Elf's shoulder in thanks and spread his wings. "Watch those steaks. I want mine rare."

"There's a shocker," Inferno grumbled, inspecting the rags of his shirt. "Bring her home safe."

At the front door of a ranch-style house in the human realm, a sense of déjà vu crept over him. It brought back memories of when he was here last. He thought her dead, her life taken by Midir.

Why would she come here?

Consider what has befallen this lady you call yours. Remember her free spirit. Where would you go if you were backed into a corner by someone you trusted?

Then it dawned on him. This was her haven from everything Alamir including him. He turned the knob and found her on her knees in the middle of the room.

Her back to him and wings tucked close to her body, she lifted her head. "Are you in on this?"

He murmured a silent prayer of thanks. "I have no idea to what you are referring, but I am confident when I say no."

Her head turned slightly. "We're to wed this week or Inferno will disown me."

Dar heard the man's declaration before Spirit dashed through the kitchen door. "I take it is not to your liking." He walked around to face her. Now he understood why she had not tucked away her wings. The scorched feathers on her upper right wing were hard to miss. It was painful as a veteran, unbearable as a novice. "You are hurt. Let me tend to you."

She flinched and crossed her arms over her chest, resting her head against her shoulder. "No, please, don't touch me. It's too painful."

"Are you referring to your wings or our wedding?" He crouched in front of her. "Etain, where did you think we were headed? We talked about our future and of having a family. I admit it is not quite how I intended for it to happen, but here we are."

Her eyes remained downcast. "I know."

He felt her pain, the physical and the emotional, but had to ask. "Is the thought of being my wife so horrible?"

"*That* is not the issue," she snapped, dropping her hands to her lap. "You are forever my heart. My life's breath." Still, she would not meet his gaze.

"Then what?" He hoped his patience would bring her to him. "We owe it to ourselves and our children. None of us has a legacy if we do not wed."

Her eyes met his. "Legacy be damned if you're not there to share it with me."

Dar recognized her fear yet did not understand from where it came. "I have no plans to go anywhere without you."

"Marriage is a death sentence, Dar." She blew out an exasperated breath, rolling her eyes. "The look on your face... You think I'm crazy."

"No, but I do wonder why—"

"My parents loved each other to distraction. They let down their guard, became comfortable, and now they're dead. Your own Alexia is dead. Your parents are dead. Marriage makes you vulnerable, weak. It's a lethal distraction. A warrior must always be alert and ready for battle."

"Aye. I agree a warrior must be alert." He sat on the floor cross-legged, suppressing the urge to wipe away her tears. They deserved to be shed. "Do you consider Inferno and Spirit weak?"

The color drained from her face. She sniffled, wiped her eyes, and rubbed her nose. "I-I never thought of them that way."

"*A chuisle*, marriage did not kill our parents or Alexia. *Evil* did. Marriage united them, made them strong enough to face anything at all costs."

Eyes full of innocent anguish bore through him. "But marriage is so...so...final."

His heart lifted. Her reluctance had nothing to do with him. It was more a matter of having no idea what marriage entailed. He took her hands in his. "*Our* marriage will be a new life for us both, a new beginning, a blessing."

A fresh set of tears trickled down her face. "I miss my mom. How do I do this without her or dad?"

"They are with you. Always." He lifted her hands to his lips. "You and I will start a new dynasty. Be my wife, Lady Etain. Be my queen."

She squeezed his hands. "I love you so much, Dar, but I'm not ready. I hope you understand."

He pressed his lips together and lowered their hands. Her admission was not a complete surprise. He sensed her hesitation the moment Inferno made his declaration, but the words stung all the same. "There are no rules, no boundaries. It is ours and ours alone. When you are ready, we will marry."

"Thank you." She shrugged. "So where do we go from here?"

"To *Sólskin*, our home."

"It'll take time to get used to having a new home."

Her words calmed his heart. "We will work together to make it ours. Go on to *Sólskin,* get settled. I will return to Laugharne for our things and to explain."

She narrowed her eyes.

He released her hands and leaned back. "What?"

"I think I would rather face Inferno than deal with Faux and Freeblood."

He laughed and came up onto his knees to mend the burned wing.

"You're hurt!" She reached for his torn and bloody shirt.

"It suffered a far worse fate than I." He lifted the tattered edges. "See? No harm done."

"Is that Inferno's blood?"

"The only thing he suffers from is a bruised ego." Dar noted the realization in her eyes of what happened.

"Because of you," she whispered. "Thank you. I'm sorry—"

"Shall we go? The sooner we deal with our demons, the sooner we can get on with our lives."

With her wing healed and tucked away, they stood together. "I'll get there as soon as I can."

"You do not have to face him alone. I can go with you."

"No. He needs to know he can't bend me to his will. This is *my* life, *our* life. We make our own rules on how our relationship will be, not him." She pulled him close. "Besides, I'm sure the wild ones could use a strong hand right about now."

"Call to me if he gets out of hand."

"Don't worry. I'll be fine."

Stretched out on a large, brown leather sofa, Freeblood cast a quizzical eye at Faux, who reclined at the opposite end. "Two questions."

She smirked and raised a brow.

"Do you think they even know what a heathen is?" He waited for her laughter to subside. "Now for the serious question. Are you *really* carrying his kid?"

"I am." Faux moved toward him and pressed her body to his, twining a lock of his hair around her finger. "But it doesn't mean *we* can't have fun."

"I don't know. I mean, I like the unusual, sometimes on the verge of what could be considered the macabre, but..."

Her bottom lip pushed out in a seductive pout. "Don't you like me?" Innocence flashed in her eyes while her hand traveled in a southerly direction. The pout melted into a knowing smile. "You *do* like me."

He swatted her hand away. "I didn't say otherwise. It's just, well, Dar." A movement outside the window caught his eye. "Oh, hello. We have company. Not the good kind, either." It would seem innocent enough if not for the greenish mist rolling off his tattered rags and the rusty axes. With the house situated on a cliff's edge, it was too out of the way for a traveler to stumble across. He disentangled himself and jumped to his feet. "I'll take care of it."

Faux peeked between the curtains. "Friend of yours?"

"More like an annoyance who doesn't understand the meaning of the word 'no'." He scrambled to the door. "You stay here." And stepped outside. "Canker, you old fart recruiter. What're you doing so far from your hole?"

His black-toothed grin was as menacing as his axes. "Guess you fergot my little recruitin' motto. Join or die."

"Simple and to the point. Just your style."

Canker's chuckle rumbled in his throat. "As I see it, you got one invite. There ain't no more. So it's time to die. I got a rep to protect." His beady brown eyes roamed over the manor, and zeroed in on the face peering out from the window. "You've come to such a perty place with a perty little toy. I like the horns on her head. It's been a long time since I had anything that tasty to play with." Two more arms equipped with axes emerged from the rags. "Her tail around my neck'll make a right nice trophy."

"She's out of your league, scumbag." The gem embedded in Freeblood's hand glowed with blue light.

A ragged laugh came from the recruiter. "Always been an ambitious son of a bitch."

"But not very smart. You know I'm not a *Bok* kinda guy."

"That's *your* problem, Ala-meer. Me and my clean-up crew are here to..." He laughed. "Clean up."

Freeblood turned in time to see an undead minion shuffle into the courtyard. A pair of mud demons burrowed up from the earth, their eyes nothing more than empty sockets. From the clouds came another agent, one with clawed wings covered in a black oily substance.

"Meet Cadaver and Darkwing. You know the saying. Friends who play together live to fight another day." Canker snorted, amused by his witty comeback. "How about a little show and tell?" His axes clanged off one another. "Your head shows my axe a good time, and I tell your toy to suck my cock."

Freeblood grinned and spun a blue staff, his weapon of choice for the first round. "I'd rather see your cock shoved down your throat."

Canker smirked. "Let's go, boys."

Freeblood ducked and swerved, blocking the swings of multiple axes, and jabbed the tip of his staff through the belly of a mud demon. It splashed on the ground, bubbled, and turned back into solid form. Freeblood twirled the weapon over his head and altered its shape from a blunt-tipped staff into a blue-bladed Chinese polearm. The blade separated the pair of mud minions into pieces, but Darkwing intercepted his backswing, nearly knocking him off his feet. He caught himself and was able to sever Cadaver's head from his body instead of those belonging to the mud minions.

"Seems your friends have a hard time keeping it together, Canker."

"Yeah, but they git over it quick." Canker exposed his black teeth in a lethal sneer as he and Freeblood watched Cadaver's head roll back onto his stump of a neck. "Not bad, eh?"

"Just means this'll take a little longer than expected."

Faux watched through the window as Freeblood battled the misty green apparition and his band of miscreants. Fascinated by his movements, she was especially intrigued when the blue staff appeared in his hand. Excitement fluttered in her belly watching him slice the intruders to pieces. Her eyes flashed red when the grotesque figures kept reforming slash after slash.

"No, you don't. You're not gonna steal *my* fun." Her body lit in a blazing fire and her tail snapped like a whip as she ran to the door.

Freeblood twisted out of an attack prepared to deliver a mortal blow to one, but the deformed body crawled to its lost head. Faux cast a power blast at the head moments before it reattached to the body. The burning torso convulsed, filling the air with the stench of rotting flesh, and withered to dust.

She wrinkled her nose and winked at Freeblood. "The poor thing looked cold."

With a grin, he turned and swung his weapon. Canker stumbled, pushing against Darkwing, saving them both from a fatal blow. Darkwing attempted to distract Freeblood while Canker weaved back onto his feet. "She's a feisty one. Glad the boss said I could have whatever's left."

"You're never gonna touch her." Freeblood ran toward the winged creature but at the last minute turned toward the old recruiter.

Faux worked her way closer to Freeblood. "Let me get Etain here to help."

Between blows, he yelled, "I don't need her. This is *my* battle."

"Have at it." She shimmered out of the courtyard. Once in Freeblood's bedroom, she sat on the bed and leaned over, her arms wrapped around her stomach. "Not a smart move."

After a few steady breaths, the pain seemed to subside. She stood in the hopes of rejoining the fight, but the world spun, and went dark.

Upon landing at Laugharne, Etain heard Dar's voice in her head. *"He thinks of you as a daughter, a chuisle. Forgive and forget."*

Her back stiff, she huffed through terse lips. "I bloody well *won't* forget."

"Etain..."

"No promises on the forgiving, either"

From across the garden, she noticed Spirit and Inferno at the barbeque, her expression stern, his eyes narrowed. He stepped out from behind the grill and met her halfway.

"Inferno."

"Etain."

They stared at one another for a silent moment. She shifted on her feet and glanced at Spirit, who responded with a reassuring wink. Linq, comfortable in his chair, raised a mug in greeting.

She glanced at the barbeque tongs in Inferno's hand. "You plan on using that thing?"

He brought the tool up in speculation. "Ya think it would do any good?"

"Doubtful."

"I'm not happy with the shenanigans happening under me nose."

"I'm not happy being told what to do or being referred to as a *little lass.* I'm a grown woman."

"Hmph." He lowered the tongs. "Ya damn near gutted me."

"You roasted my wing."

"I thought it was me steaks burning."

She almost smiled. "Were you hurt?"

"Ah, well, I did lose me favorite shirt. Are ya all right?"

"Ah, well," she said, mimicking him, "it takes more than a fried wing to keep me down."

He chuckled. "Think a steak can keep yer arse on the ground for a spell?"

"I'm not here to eat."

The smile on his face faded as his eyes darted left and right. "Where the hell is Dar?"

"He's gone to *Sólskin*."

"I see. Sent the little woman to do his biddin', did he?"

She clenched her jaw. "We will *not* be forced into marriage. Not by you. Not by anyone. *We* will decide when and where."

"Ah. He's got the milk from the cow, why bother making it legal? Yer a fool, girl."

Her hand twitched with an electrical charge. "You are so fucking rude." It took a great force of will to quell the desire to zap him. "Dar is ready to marry. *I* am not. I will marry him on *my* terms, not yours."

"So yer turning yer back on yer family?"

"No!" The man knew how to get under her skin. She rolled her shoulders. "You're the one who's drawn the line in the sand." Her gaze went to Spirit. "I wanted to explain so you wouldn't worry."

"Bleedin' hell!" Inferno turned his back and stormed to the grill. "I'll burn the flesh from his cunny-dippin' bones."

Spirit threw the sizzling steaks onto a plate and made a mad dash toward Etain. A single fireball flashed from Inferno's hand, upending the grill. Another one blasted it into oblivion.

"Come with me, lass." Spirit grabbed her arm and pulled her toward the house. "You've certainly upset the apple cart today."

Etain went with her willingly. "He started it."

"Let's make sure he doesn't end it, too." Safe inside the kitchen, she set down the plate. "You could've been a wee bit gentler with your delivery."

"He's a Neanderthal! I thought he would respect the fact I came to explain."

"In time. Perhaps. What are your plans?"

"We'll be at *Sólskin* for a while. I hope *you* understand. I love Dar with all my heart but getting married right now is a step too far."

"Aye, lass. I'd say you've been thrown amongst the wolves." A loud bang from the garden made them both jump. "You best get going before he storms in here. You can get your things later." As Spirit turned toward the back door, she stopped. "*Ta* for being the woman I know you to be and telling us yourself. He'll appreciate it too once he's cooled down."

"*Ta*, Spirit." She gave her a warm hug. "I'll be in touch." In a blue shimmer, she disappeared.

The shit hit the fan from the moment Dar appeared in the courtyard at *Sólskin*. Freeblood suddenly rushed out the front doors moving so fast he collided into him, spouting his words so quickly he could not understand.

Dar grabbed hold of the whirlwind. "Slow down, boy. Where are you off to in such a hurry?"

He gave Dar a wide-eyed stare as though he did not recognize him. "Dar? Oh, god. Dar!" Freeblood held onto him, doing his best to pull him toward the doors. "You gotta come quick. I don't know what to do. That old recruiter and his thugs showed up."

"Old recruiter?" Dar dug his feet into the ground.

"Canker. I was holding my own until Faux jumped into it."

"Take a breath and tell me what happened."

"She was magnificent, throwing fire blasts, blowing their minions into next week." He sucked in a deep breath as he rubbed his forehead. "I should've listened when she wanted to call Etain. I thought I had it under control. I took care of the others, but Canker ran off before I could kill him."

"The girl," Dar quipped at his wits' end. "What happened to Faux?"

The boy's head snapped up. "After they left, I went inside to get a drink. She wasn't in the living room. I checked the whole house before going to my room and found her unconscious on the floor." Panic seeped into his voice. "I thought she just needed to rest, so I put her in bed and let her sleep. I keep checking on her, hoping she'll open her eyes. She won't wake up." His eyes glistened with tears. "She won't wake up, Dar."

"Take me to her."

They made their way upstairs where he found Faux unconscious on the bed. Dar performed a cursory examination. "She is bleeding inside." He glared at Freeblood. "She was not healed enough to be fighting. Why did you—"

"You try telling the woman no." He ran his hands through his curly mop. "I was too busy fighting off Canker and Darkwing to stop her. But if she hadn't helped, we'd both be dead."

"Why was he here?"

"Sore spot, I guess. I turned down his invitation to the *Bok* and he didn't take it too good."

"You would have been safe if you stayed in the house."

"How was I supposed to know? Can you help her?"

"I have never shared blood with a creature like her." Dar reached for the dagger in his boot. "My blood may be too strong."

"What about me, my blood?" Freeblood pulled up his sleeve and stuck his arm out. "Etain's blood put me back together. Maybe mine will do the same for Faux."

He glanced at the girl. "Are you sure you're up for it?"

"Yes."

Dar grabbed his arm and slid the blade across his forearm. He barely flinched, watching as Dar brought the welling blood to the girl's lips, chanting strange words.

"*Smaointe leighis a sheolaim uaim. Ní maith le dorchadas ar bith fanacht ionat. Cuirim cosc ar bhreoiteacht agus tugaim smacht, chun do chorp, d'intinn agus d'anam a leigheas* (Healing thoughts I send from me. No darkness dares to stay in thee. I banish illness and take control, to heal your body, mind, and soul)."

"What do we do now?"

"We wait. Will you sit with her?"

"Try and stop me." Freeblood pulled a chair as close as he could to the bed and took her hand in his.

"Good. If you see any change, no matter how slight, send me a message." Dar tapped the side of his head. "Etain should be here soon." He placed a hand on the boy's shoulder. "We will get her well, once and for all."

"Thanks, Dar."

⁂

As Dar walked down the hallway, he noticed the door to Etain's room ajar and poked his head in. "Etain?" Not receiving an answer, he stepped inside. It had to be her. Her *Nim* was on the bed. "Etain?"

"In here." Her voice came from the bathroom. "How are the demon and the brat?"

He met her at the door with a grin. "They are situated. Welcome home."

"Hi, handsome." She gave him a quick kiss. "I was claiming my own space in this cavern of a bathroom."

"Is this how you greet the man of the house?" He wrapped an arm around her waist and pulled her to him. Warm and vibrant, her body stirred a yearning within him, a need to be close, intimate. "I believe I deserve more than a peck."

A devious smirk on her lips, her arms slinked around his neck. "Because you're the man of the house?"

"Because..." He lifted her into his arms. "I am *your* man and have a great need for *my* woman."

She laughed as he carried her to the bed. "I haven't been gone that long."

"It has been an eternity."

Her luscious lips begged to be kissed. His lips touched hers gently, his heart pounding. The desire to rip off her clothes was overwhelming, yet he resisted and set her on her feet. His hands ran up her arms to her beautiful face. He much preferred to take his time, to hear her sighs and the other small sounds she emitted when they made love.

Her hands busy at unbuckling his belt, she whispered into his ear, "Save your slow seduction for next time. I need your naked body next to mine and your exquisite cock inside of me."

"As you wish, milady."

No Rest for the Wicked

Happy in each other's arms, Dar rested his head against Etain's. He hoped to broach the subject after they were married but perhaps it was best to get it out into the open. "Once we have things sorted here, I will go to the Council and relinquish my title."

When she didn't respond, he asked, "Did you hear what I said?"

She sighed. "Are you sure you want to?"

"Aye. It is time. Not to say I agree with their methods, but some of what the Council said was not far from the truth. My heart no longer belongs to LOKI. It is yours, *a chuisle*, forever and a day."

"Just don't do it on my account. I'm with you no matter what you decide."

"I do it for us." He hugged her close. "We must find a replacement to fill Swee's position before I go."

Etain yawned. "Do you intend to leave Savage in charge?"

He kissed the top of her head. "Her strength of will is matched only by her strong-minded ways but she reveres the clan and will ensure it remains strong."

"If I were you, I'd make sure Swee's replacement is as bullheaded and outspoken as Savage."

He contemplated what she'd said, twirling a lock of her hair. "One person *does* come to mind, but I do not believe I will pursue the matter."

"I understand your decision to step down." She pushed away to face him. "I also know what the clan and the people mean to you. If you know of someone who can keep her in check, you owe it to the Council and the clan."

"Perhaps," he mused, "but I seriously doubt she would be willing to accept the position."

"She?" Etain frowned. "You know another woman as ornery as Savage?"

"Oh, aye. Definitely every bit as much if not more."

"Then you must talk to her, Dar." She was adamant. "For the sake of the clan, you have to convince her to join LOKI. Surely, if she is a friend of yours she will accept."

"If I thought she would listen—"

"Why wouldn't she? Unless she's involved with another clan." Dar saw the wheels turning. "Even if she is, you have to try."

"Well..." He rubbed his chin. "That is not the real issue. As far as I know, she is not with a clan."

She crossed her arms over her luscious breasts. "Then what is it?"

"Her partner." He sensed a shift in temperament, knowing her opinion of a chauvinistic point of view.

"What does he have to do with it?"

Oh, how he loved the indignant flush of color in her cheeks, the fight in her eyes. He could almost feel the electric charge crackling beneath the surface.

"Do you not think he would have a say in the matter?" It was all he could do to keep a straight face.

"Why? As you said, marriage is not a prison. She has every right to join any clan she chooses, and he should respect her freedom to do so." The flush spread farther down, tinging her skin pink. "It's the perfect time to set him straight. Let him know her wishes and wants are just as important as his."

"And what if his wishes and wants..." He nuzzled into her neck, feathering her skin with kisses, "are like this?"

"Well... She, uh... Bloody hell. What were we talking about?"

"Nothing important," he whispered into her ear. "It has been a long day. Shall we get some sleep?"

She snuggled into him again. "I *am* exhausted," she murmured. "Lucky for you."

Dar relaxed into the quiet moment at peace with the world. "How so?"

She yawned again. "I'm too tired to pay you back for comparing me to Savage."

"You must be mistaken, *a chuisle*. You are far and away in a league of your own."

"Something you should always remember."

He chuckled to himself. To have found this incredible woman who so easily became a vital part of his life, his heart, and his soul. *How did that happen?* Whether it was by chance or by design was not important. His arms tightened around his sleeping lady. *When?*

Memories flooded in, vivid as the day they happened. The first time he met the raggedy girl, she was held fast to a brick wall by his own sword. His brother, Midir, evil incarnate, had thrown the beast of a blade. She was so young, so vulnerable, and still carried the taint of human frailty. *Tartarus.* Although two years as an Alamir, she was only a babe, finding her way.

How? He was lost the moment he pushed back the tarnished silver hair and touched her face. The jolt that ran through him when she fell into his waiting arms staggered him. The vibrations of her song swept him into its whirling vortex and pierced straight into his core. It was the moment he knew he would sacrifice everything to have her in his life, to keep her safe.

"*A chuisle*," he whispered into her hair, the heaviness of sleep tugging at his eyelids. Before he slipped under its spell, Linq's words came back to haunt him.

The next time, your ladylove may not be so lucky.

He jerked awake. "I cannot fall asleep." Without disturbing his love, he eased out of the bed, slipped on a pair of trousers, and walked downstairs to the garden. A few twinkling stars greeted him, but his mind was elsewhere. "My best course of action is to stay awake until I find a way to stop the dreams."

The weary warrior focused on the variations of plants in the garden, reciting the common name in his language and its Latin counterpart to keep his mind alert. Just as the skies lightened, he returned to her side.

"Wake up, sleepyhead."

An ice blue eye peeked out from beneath the duvet. "What're you doing up so early?"

"It is a new day and we have things to do."

"Like what?"

"We should check on Faux."

The cover over her head muffled her voice. "What has she done now?"

"She and Freeblood were involved in an altercation."

Etain pushed back the duvet. "What happened?"

"An old recruiter came for the boy, and she wanted to help get rid of him."

She scooted to the edge of the bed and grabbed her clothes from the floor. "Did they?"

"It appears so."

"Great." Etain shoved one leg and the other into her leathers, wiggling them up over her bottom. "What did she do?"

While she dressed, Dar explained it as Freeblood detailed it to him. Within a few minutes, the two were headed toward his bedroom.

They found the young man, his back hunched, and head on the edge of the mattress, Faux's hand in his. Etain gently touched his shoulder. "Freeblood."

He jerked awake. "Is she okay?"

Dar pressed two fingers against Faux's wrist and touched her forehead. "She survived the night. It is a good sign."

Freeblood lifted her hand to his lips. "I need her to open her eyes."

"Give her a little more time." Dar eyed the young man with a raised brow. "You should shower. We will sit with her until you return."

"Not until she wakes." He suddenly yawned and stretched his arms wide.

Etain wrinkled her nose. "For the sake of us all, take a shower. If she wakes, you'll knock her out again with your smell." He shot her a narrow-eyed glare from over his shoulder, but a whiff of an armpit told him she spoke the truth. "Go on. Once you're done, Dar will whip up breakfast and bring a tray."

He reluctantly let go of the sleeping girl's hand. "I won't be long."

In the bathroom, Freeblood dragged his hands through his wild mane, staring into the bloodshot eyes peering back at him. "Damn, man. Maybe she *did* wake up but passed out at the sight of you."

Once the stink was washed away, he turned the water on cold to ensure he was wide awake. A screech and a jump later, he was out of the shower, dried, dressed in fresh jeans and shirt, and was back at Faux's side. Her eyes fluttered open just as he slipped into the chair and took her hand.

"Faux. Can you hear me?"

She squinted from the brightness of the room, licking her lips. Dar rushed to the window and closed the drapes against the morning sun. "What's he doing here?"

Etain leaned over Freeblood's shoulder. "We're both here."

"Saving you from yourself." Freeblood squeezed her hand.

"Huh? What's going on?"

He shifted from the chair and sat on the side of the bed, facing her. "I should've listened to you."

"About what?"

"The blooding seems to have worked," Dar said. "We shall leave you two alone."

Etain gave her a stern eye. "You stay in bed this time and get well."

Faux waited until they left the room, and tried to sit up. "Ooo..."

"No, you don't." Freeblood held her down. "You overdid it this time."

"What the hell are you talking about?" A sour expression puckered her face. "I didn't do something stupid like save one of them, did I?"

He chuckled. "Well, not them. You saved *this* stupid Alamir."

She closed her eyes. "You're too cool to be Alamir."

He laughed, happy she was alive. "If it helps, Canker was the only one to get away."

"Fantastic." She tried again to sit up. "I could use some help here."

He leaned her against him as he reached around her to prop pillows against the headboard and eased her back. "Darkwing was clipped in the process."

"Great."

"While in the air."

She rolled her eyes. "You're bragging now. What are those two doing here?"

"Be glad they are. Dar helped me save your life."

Faux attempted a laugh, but a sharp pain cut it short. "Oh, damn." She drew in a slow breath. "Now *that* is funny."

"What's funny?"

"Them." She patted the spot next to her on the bed. "Sounds like he finally got his shit together."

Freeblood carefully slipped in behind her and leaned her against his chest. "What about the baby?"

"Etain can raise it. I have better things to do than be tied down by a screaming kid."

"Wow. I, uh... I thought you were excited about being a mother."

"I don't know what got into me. Settling down was not part of *my* plan." She shifted in his arms. "Do you think they'll last?"

He shrugged. "They share a hobby of trying to keep us apart. It might work."

After a superb morning meal, Dar smirked and raised a brow. Etain pushed her plate away. "Okay. I'm game. What?"

"You stay there." He rose from his seat and cleared the table with one sweep of his arm. Dishes and silver crashed onto the stone floor. While offering her one hand, he pulled out her chair with the other. Once on her feet, he sent the chair skidding across the floor with a single kick and lifted her onto the table's edge. She smiled as he unbuttoned her top and tossed it over his shoulder.

"What about breakfast for the two upstairs?"

He knows where the kitchen is."

"And what if he comes in here?"

"If he values his life, he will leave and keep his mouth shut."

"But I told him—"

Dar removed the dirk from his boot. "We are going to have a little fun."

"With a blade?" she asked, swinging her bare feet.

He surprised her by catching one leg and slicing up the length of the leather, and the other, leaving her naked.

"What am I supposed to wear now?"

"Who cares?" Between her legs, he leaned toward her and stabbed the blade into the tabletop. "This time we do it my way."

In a sweet assault, he laid her back and draped her legs over his shoulders, trailing kisses along each one. His deft tongue made her moan and her body quiver. A quick glance at her beautiful face, her bottom lip trapped between her teeth, told him she was lost in a heavenly torment. Her grip in his thick mane tightened as he brought her to the edge of orgasm and loosened when he backed off only to take her to the edge again.

Assured of her satisfaction, Dar straightened, undid his leathers, and came back with a sharp thrust. Her hips firmly encased in his hands, he continued until his moans joined hers. Just at his peak, he opened his eyes, eager to see the pleasure on her face.

Rather than Etain's ice-blue gaze, he met one of a different color. Amusement danced in the green depths as her red lips distorted into a sneer and her thighs clamped around his hips, imprisoning him within their powerful hold. Horrified, his cock slid free and hung limp between his legs.

"Come on, brother. Fuck her one more time."

Dar grabbed her legs, doing all he could to break free without hurting her. When she finally released him, he staggered back against the wall and reached for a sword that was not there.

"Does she taste as sweet as when I had her, brother?" At the edge of the table, she spread her legs and groped her naked breasts, testing the weight of each one, and rolled the pink nubs between her fingers. "What a sensation. To feel what she feels is exquisite." Midir's gaze came up to meet Dar's. "I've missed the feel of her flesh next to mine." The hands caressed their way to her thighs. With a wicked smirk, she dragged her fingers through the wetness between her legs and brought them to her mouth. A flick of her tongue licked away the stickiness. "Mmm. VonNeshta cream... The best in the land."

"Shut up, Midir," Dar croaked, his heart hammering and stomach churning. "Your lies have no power."

She reached back and pulled the dirk from the wooden surface. The green eyes glowed bright as she slid to her feet and moved toward him, waving the knife back and forth. "Lies? There is no need for lies now, dearest brother."

Etain glided the blade through her tangled mass of hair. The brothers watched as a tendril of silver drifted to the floor. Midir's gaze returned to Dar as the blade drew a red line across her stomach. She slinked up to him, blade first, an evil grin distorting her beautiful features as the knife kissed the skin of his throat. Blood welled to the surface. Her naked body pressed to his issued an immediate betrayal of his true feelings.

"Can't resist, can you?" Midir whispered into his ear, encasing Dar's erect cock with Etain's free hand. Dar grabbed her by the wrist. Midir laughed, letting the hand fall away, but the knife hovered over his heart.

"She is my wife." Dar raised an arm to push her away.

"Who is the liar now?" Midir cut deep into Dar's forearm.

"She will be." Blood flowed as Dar's free hand dove into the silver locks. Twisting her around, he ripped the knife from her hand and brought it to her throat. "Tables turned, brother. What will you do now?"

Certain he had the upper hand he yanked her head to the side. An icy blue glower sparked with flashes of violet killed his desire to laugh. A sharp pain shot through his foot making him drop the knife and an elbow to the belly doubled him over. In seconds, he was face down on the floor after a blow to the back of the head.

He flipped onto his back to a pissed Etain, her chest heaving and eyes flashing. "What the *hell* do you think you're doing?"

He could only think of one thing to say. "Midir."

"Midir?" Incredulous, her voice rose. "He's dead, Dar."

"He had a knife."

"What knife?" His eyes followed as she stormed to the table and extracted the blade from its surface. "You mean *this* one?" She marched back and crouched before him, waving the weapon in his face.

He flinched as though she had slapped him. "You... He sliced my throat." He touched the base of his neck but felt only smooth skin. There was no blood on his hand. "He... You cut me." Dar turned his arm to show her the injury.

"There are no marks, Dar." She swatted his hand away. "Why would I do such a thing? We were making love, and as I recall, enjoying it."

"He cut *you*." But her belly was pristine - no marks, no blood. "I *felt* it. I swear to you, Etain. There was blood."

She softened at the desperation in his eyes. "What is it?"

"Help me up." On his feet, he leaned against the counter and inspected his arm. "It *was* Midir."

"Dar..."

"No. He was here. He came through you. Your eyes were green like his. Your voice..." He faltered at the memory. "Your voice was his."

"He's dead."

"This is not the first time he has done this."

"Done what?"

"Spoken through you."

She stepped back. "Huh?"

"At *Sólskin*, the first night you and Faux stayed. He couldn't physically enter my home, so he used you. He spoke *through* you, claiming you were his emissary."

She placed her hands on her hips. "Please don't bullshit me."

He ran a hand over his face. "Like you said, we were enjoying each other. I would much rather be doing that than this."

"Why didn't you tell me about it back then?"

"You had enough on your plate at the time. If I told you..."

She placed the dagger on the counter. "Your plate was pretty full, too."

His eyes burned with sudden tears. "Am I losing my mind?"

She wrapped him in a protective embrace. "Oh, baby. Is it like what happened before?"

He held onto her, afraid to dwell too long on what it could mean. "This was worse."

"When was the last time you slept?"

"I cannot sleep, *a chuisle*." He kissed her forehead. "It is too dangerous. How can I sleep knowing the visions will come?"

"Darlin', the visions come whether you're awake or asleep." She framed his face in her hands. "I tell you what. You crawl into bed and sleep. I'll watch over you. Should anything weird start to happen, I'll wake you." She placed a finger over his lips when he tried to protest. "You can't keep going on like this. You must sleep. Get your rest, then we'll decide what to do next."

They walked upstairs to her bedroom. Dar climbed into the soft bed. "Don't let me sleep long. We must go see Alata..." He fell asleep before he finished the sentence.

Assured he was sound asleep, she tucked him in and kissed him on the cheek. "You'll wake when I see fit, and not a moment sooner. I'm gonna spend a little time on myself."

Refreshed after a long, hot shower, she glanced at the sleeping Dar as she walked to the wardrobe. Dressed in one of his white gauze shirts, she found a pair of leathers, although too big, were acceptable with the use of a belt, and pulled on her boots and went downstairs with the intention of cleaning the kitchen.

What a surprise to find everything in its place and the mess cleared. She noticed the pile of clothes on the table and walked over to pick them up. Dar's dagger was on top. "As long as he doesn't ask any questions, we'll be fine."

On her way back upstairs, she detoured into the study for a book and chose a thriller-adventure to keep her occupied a while longer.

Morning turned into afternoon and still he slept. Etain found it increasingly difficult to keep her eyes open. She rose to check on Dar and left a kiss on his forehead. She thought of going to see Faux but didn't want to leave him alone again, so returned to her book.

Time won in the end. Her eyes closed and the forgotten book slipped to the floor.

Freeblood glanced at the clock. "You up for breakfast?"

Faux laid her head on his shoulder. "Well, I would, but—"

"Dar was supposed to bring a tray."

She shrugged. "I guess he forgot."

"I'm gonna whip something up. You stay put." He pulled on a pair of jeans and padded downstairs. In the kitchen, he stood at the door and stared at the mess. "Thanks for thinking of us and leaving a disaster."

He ventured further into the room and noticed the breakfast nook. The chairs in disarray and broken dishes on the floor raised the hairs on his neck until he saw the clothes strewn about.

"Damn, Dar, I didn't know you had it in you." He grinned as he set the chairs right and picked up the clothing. His eyes widened at what was once a nice pair of leather trousers. "Etain, you naughty wench."

As Freeblood piled the clothing on top of the table an oddity on the kitchen floor caught his eye. In the center of the room lay a curl of silver hair. "Curious," he murmured and tucked into his pocket as he went in search of a broom.

With the kitchen returned to order, he got to work on breakfast for his lady. "I hope there's more dishes."

Not long after, he returned upstairs with a full tray. "I hope you like waffles."

"Everybody likes waffles."

He placed the tray on her lap and slipped in beside her.

"I was about to come looking for you. Did you get lost?"

"Not at all but I think Dar lost his shit."

She tilted her head. "What makes you say that?"

"The kitchen was a mess, broken dishes, and shredded leather, not to mention the dirty pots and pans. I don't know what went on down there, but I think we missed a party."

"It couldn't have been much if it involved those two."

"Oh, and there's this," Freeblood pulled the slip of hair from his pocket.

Faux raised both brows. "Was there any blood?"

"I didn't see any."

Seemingly unconcerned, she cut into a waffle. "Did you make these from scratch?"

"Is there any other way? A rub of the hands heated up the waffle iron." He performed a live reenactment, sans the waffle iron. "A quick whip of batter and *BAM*, homemade waffles, Freeblood-style."

She chuckled, reaching for the glass of milk. "I hope you didn't hurt your hands in the process."

"Oh, uh... No. Both are fully functional." All ten fingers wiggled in front of her face. "Shall I demonstrate?"

"I don't know, sir." She set down the glass and made a closer inspection of said fingers. "They appear to be somewhat lacking. I detect a short lag in the wiggle."

He frowned. "Really? They don't feel any different."

"The owner is usually the last to notice. There's definitely a lag."

Freeblood wiggled his fingers in front of his face while Faux placed the tray on the floor. "Trust me. I'm an expert."

"Expert at what?" he asked, impressed by her acute perception.

"To ensure they're fully functional." She lifted the comforter. His heart skipped a beat seeing her naked. "Step into my office."

"Physical therapy?" He grinned and jerked the comforter over their heads. "I've heard it works wonders. But are you sure—"

Her mouth on his proved the surety of her expertise.

Dar found himself outside, naked, shivering from the cold. He rubbed his arms as he walked toward a lighted window. Able to see into the room, he smiled when the familiar form of his ladylove came into focus.

In the next moment, she was gone as if someone had pulled her away. Concern for her safety put him in motion but his legs were heavy as stone. The harder he tried the slower he moved. Shadows gyrated across the ceiling and walls. Afraid she was at the mercy of an attacker he summoned his inner demon. His next step proved a disaster when something underfoot made him trip. His nose crashed into the stone surround of the window, exploding in a spray of blood. In a daze, he grabbed onto the sill and pulled himself up, peering into the room.

"Etain," he whispered, his heart in his throat and blood pouring down his chin.

Stretched across the bed, soft light shone off her sweat-slicked skin. A man loomed over her. Judging by the seductive smile on her lips, she was not afraid. Eager hands reached up and pulled the stranger down on top of her. Their tongues entangled in a sexual dance as his hands roamed over her naked body.

The breaking of his heart drowned out all other sounds. Dar gasped and unconsciously swiped the blood from his face. His mind refused to comprehend what his eyes told him. His hands curled into fists.

Despite the cold of the night, sweat covered his body. "Etain!" He slammed his fists against the glass, over and over, bashing at the window with every scream of her name. "Etain!" The glass never cracked, never broke. "Etain!" It never gave a goddamned inch.

NIGHTMARES

E tain startled awake and scanned the bedroom. Everything was as it should be. A paned window from across the room beckoned to her. As she walked toward it, she cast a casual glance at the empty bed. Outside of the window stood a dark form. A sudden movement to the left of the dark figure made her squint. *Dar?* His mouth slowly opened.

Screams ripped her from the dream. She shook her head to throw off the fog and realized the screams were real.

"Dar!" She lunged from the chair and grappled with his flailing hands as she crawled onto the bed and straddled his body. "Wake up!" She managed to pin his arms with her legs and in desperation slapped him across the face. His responding death stare made her heart hammer triple time. He could easily break her in half. In the next moment, his eyes rolled back, and the screams resumed.

"You have to wake up." Tears streamed down her face, struggling to gain control of herself. "I don't know what to do."

Void of conscience thought, her wings spread from her back as her body stretched to its demon height of seven feet. *Why didn't I think of this sooner?* Her increased strength made it easier to hold him down, but she wasn't sure how long she could keep at it. Frantic, she wrapped her wings around him and threw a mental message toward the first person who came to mind. Someone she knew would help no matter how estranged they'd become.

After a long day, Inferno eased back in his chair to enjoy a few rounds of ale in the garden with Wolfe and Elfin. Just as he raised the mug to his lips, his hand jerked and splashed the fresh brew down his shirt. In the next instant, he was sprawled on the ground, the mug shattering into pieces.

The light-complected Wolfe exchanged a raised brow grin with the dark-skinned Elfin and laughed.

"Argh! Stop yer infernal cackling and give me a hand."

The two jumped up to help, trying not to snicker in the process.

"Must be a bonnie mug of ale to knock you on your arse," Wolfe said.

Inferno rubbed his aching head. "Wasn't the ale, laddies. It was Etain."

Elfin grinned. "Whatever you say, boss."

"Arr, the two of ya," Inferno grumbled, shrugging them off. "She sent me a bloody message straight to me head. Something's wrong."

"Are you sure you want to get involved, boss?" Wolfe scratched his head. "From what I heard, you two didn't part on good terms."

"Doesn't matter. She's family."

"Do you know how to get to where they are?" Elfin asked.

Inferno attempted a smile. "'Tis the easy part. They're upstairs." In a flash of flames, he disappeared.

The screams came to him before he materialized in the hallway. Dashing into the bedroom, he found Etain crushed against the wall by a naked Dar, his hands around her throat. Her eyes wide and violet, she croaked, "Inferno."

"What the bloody hell?" He rushed at the man and brought the three of them crashing to the floor. Etain shoved her arms between Dar's and called on her transformation once again. With her added strength, she forced his hands apart and rolled away. On hands and knees, she gasped for air.

Dar took Inferno by surprise with a hit to the side of his head, but the determined Alamir strengthened his grip and hung on. "No ya don't, laddie boy."

Dar turned, raising a fist but Inferno dodged and grabbed him by the wrist. He twisted and sat square on the man's chest.

Etain regained enough breath to speak. "Since Midir's death..." She coughed and took another gulp of air, "he's been having terrible dreams, awake and asleep." She sat back and ran a hand through her hair, resting her elbows on her knees. "I've been able to see a few, but this one..." She shook her head. "He won't let me in. I'm totally locked out."

"How long's he been like this?"

"Just this evening." She inched closer to his side. "He hasn't been sleeping, so I told him to lie down while I watched over him. But I fell asleep. His screams are what woke me."

One of Dar's hands broke free and blindly reached for her neck. Etain fell back as Inferno caught his arm. "Not on my watch, boyo."

"Where's Spirit?"

"Away, but I doubt she could do anything fer him."

"She could knock him out with one of her potions. Where did she go?"

Inferno eyed the girl. "Oh, aye. Well, I can do something about that." He pulled back and delivered a perfect right hook, followed by a left.

"Inferno!"

"Payback, ya bloody demon." The convulsions ceased and Inferno slumped back, winded by the fight. "Don't worry about him. He's got a head like a rock." He rolled off Dar and laid on the floor. "Spirit's gone to get the kiddies."

"Are you all right?"

"Aye." He turned his head, giving her a smirk. "But neither of us will last another round. Maybe Elfin knows a spell, him being an Elf."

"Sure, but we have to get Dar dressed first." Etain stood and headed toward the wardrobe. "He should still have a few leathers here."

"Leathers? Are ya daft?" Inferno sat up. "How the hell do we get leathers on this oversized mass of demon? Can't we wrap him in a sheet?"

"He's the High Lord of Kaos, Inferno. The *chieftain* of LOKI." At the wardrobe, she shot him a defiant glare. "I don't care if we have to rip out the seams and sew 'em back on. He's not leaving until he's properly dressed."

"No need to yell, lass. We'll get him pretty as a picture."

Etain started the process by slipping the leathers over his feet, doing her best to snake the trousers up each leg in conjunction with his occasional twitch. The going got harder when it came to his thighs. Inferno stretched out over Dar, just in case he came awake, to help with the process of jigging the leathers over the hips. Suddenly face-to-face with the Krymerian's privates, he turned his head.

"For fuck's sake. Does the man not wear pants?"

Etain stopped. "I'm not going back now. Deal with it."

"I'll deal with it but ya best not be telling the man or anyone else of me introduction to his wee balls and cock."

She rolled her eyes, "I won't if you won't," and hunkered down, leather in both hands, inching ever closer to the product of Inferno's concern. "Besides, Dar wouldn't take kindly to his balls or cock being referred to as wee." Leathers in position, she wiggled them over his hips, careful to tuck his far from wee privates inside, sat back and pushed the hair from her face. "I'll get him buttoned up here and you can do the top half."

Inferno wrangled a shirt onto the man with only minor difficulties - a bruise here, a scratch there, nothing that wouldn't heal in a few days. With the man dressed, both noticed his bare feet.

"Have any boots for a big man?"

"Yer having a laugh."

Etain dragged a hand through her hair. "I'll pop back and get a pair if you'll sit here with him in case he wakes up."

"Works for me."

After her quick shimmer to *Sólskin*, the High Lord was properly dressed. A bit disheveled but in better shape than his attendants.

Inferno blew out a breath. "I'll find Elfin and be right back. The quicker we do this the better. A sucker punch gets the job done, but ya never know for how long."

"I'm scared, Inferno."

He draped his arm over her shoulders and gave her a fatherly squeeze. "Don't worry, lass. We'll get him straight."

Spirit and Linq appeared in the Laugharne courtyard at the same time as Inferno stepped out the front door. "Saints be praised. Yer back," he hollered wading through the gaggle of children.

All four grabbed hold of a leg, vying for his attention. "Da!"

"Hello me wee ones. Would ya give yer poor da a moment to speak to yer mum?" They quieted but didn't let go of his legs. "Love, ya need to come with me. Linq, would ya take the kiddies round back? Elfin and Wolfe should be lazing in the garden." He smiled at his children. "Ya don't mind playing with the likes of them for a wee bit, do ya?"

Seth, the oldest at nine years old, grinned at his siblings, who laughed and clapped their hands. "Don't worry, da. I'll take 'em."

Inferno beamed with pride and tousled his hair. "Aren't ya the big boy? *Ta*, Seth." As the children toddled off he turned to Linq. "Find Zorn and bring him to Etain's room."

"What're you on about?" Spirit tried to pull free from his iron grip.

"We're not done with the bleedin' brother." He practically dragged her through the house and upstairs. The answer was all too clear when they burst into the room.

"Your punch wore off," Etain growled through gritted teeth, struggling to stay seated on Dar's chest, her wings settled on her back.

Spirit glanced at her husband. "Since when do you make punch?"

Inferno opened his mouth to explain, but Etain spoke first. "Spirit! Can you make the potion you used on Faux? He's a real handful."

"What's wrong with him?" Spirit managed to get free of her husband.

"Midir. He needs something to give him peace."

"Aye, lass. Be right back." She passed Linq on his way in.

"I could not find Zorn."

"We'll worry about him later." Inferno waved him in. "We need ya here."

As the men converged on the bed, Elfin and Wolfe walked through the door. "We heard things are amiss."

"For fuck's sake." Inferno pursed his lips. "Who's watching the kiddies?"

Wolfe held his hands up. "Don't worry, boss. BadMan and Ciara are with 'em."

"One of ya stand with Linq and the other come to me." On opposite sides of the convulsing Krymerian, Linq and Inferno each took an arm while Wolfe and Elfin grappled with his legs.

"We should take him to Nunnehi," Linq said. "The war wizards will know what to do."

"War wizards?" She shook her head. "No. He's been through enough already."

Spirit returned in a flurry. "I grabbed the strongest draught I have." It took a joint effort by all four men to hold him steady while Etain assisted Spirit in prying open his mouth and pouring the contents of the vial down his throat. Dar went limp within moments.

"Thank you, Spirit. Thank all of you." Etain smoothed the hair from Dar's face. "Rest now, my love. We'll figure something out."

Linq clenched his jaw. "Etain, he needs help."

She kissed Dar's cheek, wiped her eyes, and slipped off the bed. "How in the hell are war wizards going to help?"

"He is fighting a war he cannot win – not alone. Only powerful magic can combat what haunts him. The wizards will know what to do."

"Linq. I know it's bad, but I've only met you a few weeks ago." She put her hands on her hips. "I don't know what a war wizard is, nor do I know what they're capable of. So, pardon me if I'm a little less than accepting of your suggestions. I will not take him to a strange place and leave him to a bunch of war wizards."

Linq glared at Inferno.

"Lass, he and Dar are old friends. If he says they can help, they can."

"Dar once told me it would take the strength of a demon to defeat his brother." Etain turned on the Elf and pointed at the bed. "Look at him! What good did it do? Midir may be dead in body, but his spirit lives in Dar. If a demon couldn't defeat him, how the hell are a bunch of wizards gonna do any better? He's beyond their magic."

Linq tried again with a softer tone. "How could we know Dar and not of his brother? Alatariel and the wizards can save him." He rested a hand on her shoulder. "Let us help our High Lord."

His words of support were too much. Tears slid down her cheeks as she jerked her hands through her hair. Resembling a lost child, she turned to Inferno.

Spirit went to her. "Come on, lass. Let's get you sorted before you go."

"No, I'm okay." Etain sniffled. "Really. You're right, Linq. I'm sorry." She bit her bottom lip as her eyes strayed to Dar, her hand lingering over his. "I can't give him what he needs. How do we get to Nunnehi?"

Linq lightly squeezed her shoulder. "There is a portal in the mountains at Torfaen Pass, no more than a few hours north of here."

"We'll help." Wolfe and Elfin volunteered.

"I can shimmer us there."

"No, Etain." Linq exchanged a glance with Elfin. "This afternoon has taken a toll on your energies." At her downcast expression, he relented. "You can take Dar and Wolfe. It would be faster and easier than carrying him. Elfin and I will meet you there."

After a quick farewell, the group departed - three in a blue shimmer, the other two in a mad dash to the mountains.

At Torfaen Pass, in the light of a full moon, Etain and Wolfe gently laid Dar on a small patch of grass as they waited for the Elves. Etain gave her arms a brisk rub against the cold wind blowing through the Pass. "I should've grabbed a cloak. I'd forgotten how chilly it gets up here." She walked in circles, hoping the constant motion would warm her body.

"Won't be long until winter. Any idea where the portal is?"

"I think Linq's the only one who knows."

He scratched his head. "Not even Elfin?"

"Hell, I don't know, Wolfe. Maybe he does, maybe he doesn't. Maybe we're the only two in this world who *don't* know."

"Don't worry, Lady E." He nodded toward the sleeping Dar. "He's strong. With a little help, he'll pull through."

She gave him a sideways glance. "I hope you're right."

Linq crested the ridge, Elfin behind him. "Are you ready, milady?"

"Aye. Are you? He's no lightweight."

It was a group effort. Sweat, muttered curses, and strained muscles finally got Dar to his feet and balanced between the four escorts. The group faced north as Linq uttered the words in his native tongue, opening the portal. The moon shimmered like a reflection on the water and the mountains appeared to recede. A line of white light emerged and formed into an oval door. On the other side of the portal the travelers spied a magnificent countryside, resplendent with large trees covered in deep green leaves, bathed in early morning sunlight. Grass as thick as carpet and dotted with multi-colored wildflowers, rolled toward a small, crooked river. In the distance, the tips of white spires peeked above the lush forest.

They were met by Elves dressed in shades of blue, green, and grey, seated on horses of white and dappled grey. Two more sat at the helm of a large cart drawn by Bavarian-style horses, their coats brushed to a high golden sheen, setting off their white silky manes. Five Elves dismounted and helped place the unconscious High Lord into the cart.

An older Elf, dressed in black, his brown hair pulled back in a silver clasp, spoke to Linq. "Her Majesty has ordered the High Lord be taken directly to his quarters." He turned to Etain. "My Lady of Kaos," he greeted her with a bowed head, "Queen Alatariel has requested your company while we see to the High Lord's comfort."

Etain grabbed Linq by the arm and pulled him close. "I thought Alatariel was a wizard."

He patted her hand. "You will meet her soon." Linq made a proper introduction. "Etain, this is Commander Crom, hand-picked by Dar as Commander of the Black Blades of Nunnehi."

She had no clue what he was talking about but smiled. "Nice to meet you, Commander Crom." He offered her a hand into the cart. "Thank you." Etain moved to the front where she placed Dar's head in her lap.

With a sudden lurch, the cart headed for the city. Linq, Wolfe, and Elfin were given mounts of their own and kept near the cart. The Elven troop rode in formation, two abreast, along a well-traveled, winding road into the city.

"What a place!" Wolfe turned one way in his saddle, and the other, his eyes wide. "Did you live here, Elfin?"

"No, but not far from here. It has been a long time."

An ancient stone bridge took the party over the river and into Nunnehi. The road branched out into cobblestone streets that lined the city of white. Each street corner bore testament to the inhabitants' celebration of nature. Lush greenery of aged trees draped over buildings while others boasted colorful red or green ivy. Jewel-toned flowers bloomed in meticulous beds set throughout the city.

Shimmering silver gates welcomed the entourage into the palace grounds where cherry blossoms swaying in the light breeze lined the drive to the main courtyard. Their delicate blooms twirled through the air adding a sense of serenity.

Wolfe appreciated the delicate architecture of the white stone buildings, some with thatch roofs and others adorned with regal spires that reached for the skies. He raised a hand to shield his eyes from the glare of the sun to follow the tallest of the spires to its tip and reined in his horse. "What the hell is that?"

Elfin pulled up. "What, mate?"

He leaned so far back he almost fell from his saddle. "That." Wolfe pointed past Elfin. "It's, well, massive. It is the most massive piece of massiveness I've ever seen." He stared at the structure.

Elfin chuckled. "It is the palace."

"It doesn't look like stone."

"She is wood."

Wolfe scratched his head. "I don't get it. There's no joints or seams. It's like one big piece."

He laughed. "Because she is a tree."

"A tree? But it's so…"

"Massive?" Elfin's face reflected his pride. "She is the center of the Elven world. Our protector, our shelter, our mother."

It was too incredulous for Wolfe to believe. "People live *inside* the tree?"

"Aye, my friend. Come. Let me introduce you to *Modertræ*, our mother tree."

Nunnehi

Once in the palace courtyard, intricately carved golden doors opened to ten warriors dressed in black armor. On the left breast of each was a crimson flame surrounded by a golden crown of swords and a sword strapped across their backs. Lost in her thoughts, Etain didn't notice the black-clad warriors reach in to relieve her of her precious package. Their movement of Dar brought her back.

"No! What are you doing?" She tried to hold onto him.

"Milady..." Commander Crom addressed her with the utmost respect. "He will be made comfortable in his chambers."

She blinked at the Elf. "He has chambers? Here?"

"Yes, milady."

"Oh, well, okay. But..." She lifted her chin. "But I will stay with him. I won't have him wake in a room full of strangers."

"Etain." Linq turned her attention to him. "These people are not strangers. Each man has fought by his side at one time or another. Alatariel has gone to great lengths to ensure he is surrounded by people he knows and trusts."

There's that name again.

The commander added his assurances. "We were informed he was administered a strong sleeping potion, milady. He should not wake anytime soon. You will be back at his side in no time."

"Speak with Alatariel," Linq said, an encouraging smile on his lips. "Get to know her. You will see you have nothing to fear."

A momentary panic churned in her stomach. "Aren't you coming with me?"

"I am going to see about quarters for the rest of us. You are among friends, Etain. You will be fine."

"Dar would want you close by." She touched Linq's arm and lowered her voice. "*I* want you close by."

He leaned in so only she could hear. "It would be good for our young friends to mingle with others like them. We will not be far." He gave her hand a reassuring squeeze. "You are the High Lady of Kaos. You do your part, and we will do ours."

"Whatever that is." She accepted his assistance out of the cart. "Will I see you later?"

"Of course."

With Dar safely placed on an elaborate litter, she kissed him on the brow in a silent goodbye. When the ten warriors lifted their High Lord, a line of similar clad warriors, two abreast, marched through the great doors of the Elven palace, lined the walkway on either side, and presented their blades in what Etain suspected was a show of respect. Their black blades reminded her of *Ba'alzamon*, the sword Dar once carried. Thirteen black-robed figures, who also displayed the crimson flame surrounded by a golden crown of swords joined the escort chanting as they made their way toward the corridors of white.

Commander Crom walked with Etain through the same doors and followed the procession for a short time. At an intersection of hallways, Dar's litter, the priests, and the warriors turned in another direction. Etain and the Commander continued down grand hallways adorned by great arches carved into the walls. Some were decorated with sculptures, a few with Elven artwork, and others offered marble benches as a place to rest.

Curious about these people who seemed to know Dar quite well, she asked, "Commander Crom, who were those men in the black armor?"

"They are our warrior elite known as the Black Blades second only to the Queen's Royal Guard. Both were the ingenious creations of our High Lord."

"Oh." Etain had to stretch her long legs to keep up with the Elf as he turned another corner. "How long have you known the High Lord?"

"Not long." He waved a hand in the air. "It has not even been a half-turn yet."

"Half-turn?"

Crom stopped before a set of magnificent golden doors. "Almost a half-turn but not quite." The blank expression on her face prompted him to explain further. "Forgive me, milady. In Alamir time, a half-turn would be two hundred and fifty years. To be clear, we met roughly one hundred years ago, give or take a few years."

"Not long at all," she murmured, fighting the urge to roll her eyes, and noticed the engravings on the golden doors. They depicted the scene of a great battle set in a dense forest with the ground littered by the fallen of both sides. A single warrior in black stood out from the others.

Crom noticed her interest. "Milady?"

"Who is the one in black?"

"The most formidable warrior of all. Death." He nodded to the guards, who stepped to either side of the grand doors. "This way, High Lady."

She held back. "We're going in there?"

"Yes, milady. The queen awaits."

"Behind Death's door?"

Crom sighed. "This is your first visit?" She nodded, captivated by the engraved scene. "It is merely a reminder of our mortality." He left her to her thoughts as he conversed with an attendant. The commander smirked, watching the young man rush off. "I do enjoy how the arrival of royalty sets everything in motion." Etain peered up and down the hall. "When the door opens, I shall announce your arrival, and you will enter."

"Uh, okay, but what about the royal—"

The great doors opened into a magnificent hall filled with Elves dressed in every color imaginable. Soft whispers and the rustle of fine fabrics made her heart race. She gazed up at the exquisitely carved ceiling miles above her head. Light poured in from the rows of curved windows atop panels of painted murals lining the walls on either side. The intricate carvings on the floor reminded her of fine lace. The attention to detail gave the room and the palace the impression of floating amongst the clouds.

A voice from within the great hall called out, "Our most gracious Highness, lords and ladies of Nunnehi, The High Lady of Kaos, Princess of the Realm, and Queen of Krymeria."

Etain glanced over her shoulder expecting to find a person of great import. *Wait a minute. Linq called me The High Lady of Kaos. Why? Queen of Krymeria?* It dawned on her. *Holy crap, they think we're married.*

Mesmerized by the grandeur of the space and the multitude of Elves staring at her, Etain swallowed the lump in her throat and lifted her lips in what she hoped would be seen as a smile.

Commander Crom entered the hall. "Our High Lady, Etain Rhys Von-Neshta."

She stared at the man as he stepped aside with a flourish, wondering how he knew her name and why everyone seemed to think she was Dar's wife. *When I meet this Alatariel, I'll get it straightened out. Let's get through this first.*

Silence. Etain stepped into the hall and made eye contact with as many Elves as possible until she came back to Crom, who motioned toward a violet-carpeted path between the sea of onlookers. She lifted her chin. *One foot in front of the other.* As she passed, each courtier either kneeled on one knee, bowed, or curtsied. *This can't possibly be for me.* As she approached the royal dais, a tall, slim red-headed vision clothed in a gossamer emerald gown stared at her from the throne. Next to her stood a small boy with the same hair color and dressed in a suit of emerald trimmed in gold.

Is this Alatariel? She doesn't seem too friendly. Great. She probably had her eye on Dar and now we're enemies.

Etain returned the lady's stare, unsure of what to do next.

The boy peered up at the woman, who continued to stare at Etain, and tugged on her sleeve. The motion was small but enough to break the spell. The red-headed woman winked at him, and faced her new guest.

"You are a true queen indeed, Lady Etain."

Etain bowed her head. Somewhere from deep inside came the proper words. "Greetings, Your Grace. May the light bless you and darkness flee before your presence."

"Greetings, High Lady. May the light bless you and darkness flee before the might of your blade." The lady stood. "Welcome to Nunnehi. I am Alatariel and this..." she smiled at the boy, "is my nephew, Raphael."

He executed a perfect courtly bow. "Welcome, Lady Etain." His formal greeting belied his young appearance, but his baby voice assured her he was in fact a child. "Please call me Raff." He lowered his tiny voice and leaned toward her. "Raphael is a sissy name."

Etain chuckled and bowed her head in return. "I'm happy to meet you, Raff."

She maintained a smile during the kissing of cheeks, handshakes, and warm embraces that welcomed her. Their acceptance put her at ease and made her feel like part of a large family. Once the introductions were completed, the queen dismissed the court.

"Etain, please join me in my private chambers."

"Thank you. Will you be joining us, Raff?"

His features screwed up into a sour expression. "No, milady. I do not like tea."

Etain grinned despite the churning in her stomach. She hoped to have at least one person in the room who liked her. "Will I see you again?"

He shrugged. "Maybe."

Alatariel linked arms with her while chastising the boy with a loving glare. "Raphael has studies to attend."

His face broke into a huge smile. "But I get cookies and juice first!"

The women laughed as he ran after the rest of the court. "I hope you do not mind if we do not join the others. I would like to get to know you, Etain."

The queen led her toward a suite of rooms off the main hall. At the door, she turned to Crom. "You may go, Commander."

"Pardon, Your Grace, but as the High Lord is in the capable hands of the war wizards and guarded by the Black Blades, it is my duty to watch over the High Lady."

With a slight bow of her head, she stepped back as Crom opened the door. Inside, the queen motioned Etain toward a deliciously overstuffed chair, one of four, covered in luxurious fabrics of spicy red, orange, and warm gold. Set in a sunken area draped in sheer voiles of red and orange cascading from a center point of the ceiling, the room was a bold contrast to the peaceful white and cream of the grand hall. The floor covered with a plush carpet of deep red tempted Etain to take off her boots and run her bare feet through its deep pile. Enchanted, she snuggled into a chair that offered her the full spectrum of the room, its perspective also giving her a glimpse of the innermost private garden sheathed in glass and framed by red sheers.

"You look exhausted, Etain." The queen turned to a young girl with long blonde hair dressed in soft pink who stood on the upper level. "Sasha." The girl curtsied and disappeared through an inner door.

Etain ran a hand through her hair. "It's been an eventful few days, Your Grace."

"Please, call me Rie." She sat in the chair across from Etain. "There is no need for formalities. We are equals."

A nervous laugh escaped her lips. *Maybe I misjudged her.* "Rie?"

"It is short for Alatariel." She leaned forward. "Dar has not prepared you. I suppose it is to be expected. It has been a long time for him."

"To be fair, all this has taken us both by surprise. Linq's the one who suggested we come here."

Sasha returned and set a tray on the low table in the center of the chairs. She smiled at Etain. "Tea, Your Grace?"

Etain stared at the girl, and realized she was speaking to her. "Oh, yes, please. Thank you." With the tea served, Sasha retreated from the room. Etain picked up her cup and blew lightly over the hot liquid. "A long time?"

Alatariel sat back, stirring her tea, her eyes on the High Lady. "Since Alexia."

"Of course." Etain dared a sip of the steaming liquid to collect her thoughts but found it too hot and set the cup down. "Being his wife, I'm sure she was well-trained in what was expected of a High Lady. However, Dar and I are not married."

Alatariel's eyes sparkled. "I am aware. To capture the heart of a warrior who has not loved in over one hundred years takes an exceptional woman. One our High Lord will not soon let go of, if ever."

"No disrespect to anyone, but I have a say in the matter too."

"Etain, you have proven your intentions by bringing him here." She delayed the moment with a sip of tea. "It is only a matter of time."

"Huh?" Etain lifted both brows.

Alatariel gave her an understanding smile. "We see your heart, milady. Eventually, you will see it as well."

Etain tried her tea again and found it easier to drink, thinking she'd become the butt of a bad joke. "It doesn't bother you?"

The queen furrowed her elegant brows. "I am not sure what you mean."

"That Dar has fallen in love with *me*?"

"Why would his love life be of my concern?" She raised her cup.

"Because you're a queen and he's a king."

The woman choked on her tea. Etain quickly set her cup aside and lunged out of her chair, catching Alatariel's cup and saucer before her beautiful dress was damaged. She set the items on the side table and patted her on the back. "Are you okay? I'm sorry if I upset you."

One hand on her chest, she waved the other at Etain. "I am all right." She coughed again. "I am not upset. Merely surprised." Alatariel picked up a napkin and dabbed at her lips.

"By what?"

"Did you think Dar and I were involved?"

Etain recognized the merry glint in her eyes and rolled her own as she returned to her seat. "I'm an idiot."

"I am sorry to laugh, Etain. I do not mean to embarrass you, but it is quite humorous. As we get to know one another better, you will come to understand why." She tilted her head. "I am curious as to what makes you think it would matter."

"And confirm what a fool I am?"

"You are not a fool." Alatariel chuckled. "Who better than family to tell your secrets to?"

Etain shrugged. "When I walked toward the dais earlier, your face was not very welcoming. Dar was my first thought. You've known each other for a long time."

The queen turned thoughtful. "It had nothing to do with Dar. I was not prepared for the person I saw walking toward me."

Etain huffed. "Am I so offensive?"

She pursed her lips. "Of course not. You remind me so much of a dear friend from long ago. If I did not know better, I would think you were the same." She chuckled again. "What am I saying? I thought you *were*, which is probably why you thought me a banshee ready to keen a death knell."

Etain laughed this time. "Well, not quite." Her sip of tea tasted much better than the last as the cloud lifted from around her heart. "She must be a great beauty." She winked at the queen.

"Lyoness was a strong Krymerian warrior, known for her courage and relentless energy in battle. She would fight until she dropped from exhaustion. On several occasions, her kinsmen carried her from the battlefield. If she was not *in* the fight, she was helping with the wounded or encouraging her fellow warriors." She leaned forward. "She was a fierce warrior with a fair complexion and silver hair. And eyes of ice blue, like yours."

Etain held her gaze for a moment, blinked, and lowered her eyes.

The queen sat back. "Sadly, she died before her time, betrayed by someone she trusted."

The story had a sobering effect. "I'm sorry you lost a good friend. Did Dar know her?"

"She was born a few turns before Dar." Alatariel raised a brow. "But he was intended for her. Lyoness was a princess in her own right."

Etain frowned. "Oh?"

The queen either ignored her change in expression or did not notice. "Krymerians do not age the same way as humans. There can often be what *you* consider several hundred years between the ages of spouses."

"Surely Dar was aware of his future."

"Not in this case. He never met Lyoness. She died when he was a child."

"Well, I may look like her, but I don't relish the fight, nor do I have what it takes to lead warriors into battle. Don't get me wrong, I *can* fight."

"She said the same when she was young. Her only desire was to be wed and raise a family, but fate had other plans."

Etain grunted in a most unladylike fashion. "Fate. What an interfering little bitch." Her cheeks burned at the realization of to whom she'd spoken. "Forgive me. A slip of the tongue."

"Not to worry. I admire a woman who speaks her mind. I hope our friendship is a long one."

"I'd like that." She raised her cup. "Lyoness must have been quite a woman, especially if she was deemed worthy of my Dar."

Alatariel flashed a knowing smile. "She was an indomitable spirit, milady. As are you."

Etain finished her tea and set the cup aside. "Linq said you knew Midir."

It was Alatariel's turn to frown. "Yes, I had the misfortune to meet him a time or two."

"Then you'll be glad to hear he's dead."

"Yet Dar lives. Tell me how that happened."

"You know the story between Dar and Midir?"

Her nod set Etain on a journey she was not necessarily ready to embark on. She started with Dar's severing the noose from his brother with the Jewel of Life. "Midir came close to killing him. Thankfully, he didn't." She told of their return to Laugharne, of the High Council's charge of treason, and how the confrontation ended with Dar unconscious. "I delved into his mind to make sure he was okay." A shiver ran through her. "His dreams have become nightmares."

Alatariel raised a brow. "You saw his dreams?"

"I did." Etain absentmindedly rubbed her neck while telling of recent events, uncomfortable in sharing intimate details with a woman she hardly knew, a queen, no less. "He said Midir came through me and cut him, but there were no marks or blood."

The queen leaned forward. "Did he hurt you?"

"No. I hurt him, though. A couple of punches snapped him out of his delusion." She curled her legs beneath her in the chair. "I don't know what to do, Your High... Ala..." She rolled her eyes, frustrated at her pitiful attempt not to sound desperate. "Rie. I can't get through to him."

"Dar is a man who believes he must handle things himself. He has always been stubborn in that way. You did right to bring him here."

A messenger rushed in and spoke with Commander Crom, who nodded and dismissed the man. "Your Graces..."

Etain didn't need to hear another word. She ran out of the room, Dar's thunderous shouts leading her to him.

TIME

————

After a playful session of sexcapades, Faux and Freeblood lounged on the bed. A ringing from his discarded jeans made her sit up.

"What're you doing with a phone?" She reached for the jeans.

He rolled off the bed and snatched them up, jabbing a hand into the front pocket. "To communicate. It's mainly for emergencies."

"Why, when we have this?" She pointed at her head, his and back.

"The only person I have this with," he copied her move, "is you." He held his phone up. "I need *this* to keep in touch with my family."

"Family?"

He nodded as he put the phone to his ear. A feminine voice on the other end began talking before he could say anything. "Joe. Thank goodness. I was afraid you weren't going to answer."

"Hey, Mom. What's wrong?"

"It's good to hear your voice. How are you, sweetheart?"

"I'm fine. What is it?"

There was a hesitation on the other end. "Son, I know you've been avoiding the family lately—"

"I haven't been avoiding anyone, Mom. I've had a lot going on, traveling and such. I've met someone." He winked at Faux. "Someone special."

"How nice for you, son." Her voice broke.

"What is it, Mom? What's wrong?" His heart skipped a beat, afraid of what she had to say.

"I'm sorry, Joe. This isn't the way to handle it, but no one knew where you were."

His stomach churned. "What?"

"Your brother..." She paused, sniffling. "Oh, Joe. He's gone. My baby is gone."

It was as though he'd been punched in the stomach. The air whooshed from his lungs, and he struggled to catch his breath. "G-gone? I-I don't understand, Mom."

"Not long after you disappeared, his doctor told us he had cystic fibrosis..." Her voice trailed off.

His legs turned to rubber, and he collapsed to the floor.

Faux peeked over the foot of the bed. "Who's gone?"

Freeblood shook his head, unable to say his brother's name. "Cystic fibrosis?"

"Yes." His mother's voice was tight. "Joe, he was so sick."

"My god, Mom." Nausea made his stomach roll. "I'm coming home. When's the funeral?" Silence. "Mom?"

"A month ago..."

The phone slipped to the floor.

"Joe? Joe, are you there?"

He wiped his eyes and picked it up. "A month? Why didn't you call me sooner?"

"Your father—"

He threw the phone across the room.

Faux watched him from the bed. "Who's gone?"

"My baby brother," he said, hopping from one foot to the other as he jammed legs and arms into his clothes. "He died a month ago." Freeblood dragged a comb through his hair for some ungodly reason, a habit inflicted on him by his mother.

"Is there anything I can do?"

He sensed her genuine concern and gave her a quick kiss. "I'm going to visit his grave. I won't be long."

After a sonic speed run along the southwestern coastline of the island, Freeblood jumped onto a land bridge connected to the mainland and breezed into the cemetery within a few hours of leaving *Sólskin*. He stopped just inside the gates and approached the family plot at a human pace.

This part of the cemetery was laid out like a family tree. His great-great-grandparents lay at the top, farthest from the gates, followed by their children, a spinster or two, a bachelor great-uncle, and so on. His brother's grave was the first of their immediate family, one small grave set apart from the rest. Freeblood recognized a familiar silhouette standing by the grave.

Damn.

He dragged his feet through the grass and stopped short of the fresh grave. "You should have let me come," he said to his father, who stood on the opposite side. "Why wasn't I told about Paul or the funeral?"

His father pulled out a pack of cigarettes and tapped one out. "You clearly have no interest in family." He reached into another pocket, brought out a lighter and touched the flame to the tip. After a long draw, he blew out the smoke and glared at his son. "Money, power, prestige... You threw it all away, walked out without a word."

"If you'd have paid attention, you would've known none of that means anything to me. However, my family means everything. I went out on my own, true. I had to. Don't you understand? I had to find my own way without your interference. It did *not* mean I didn't care." Freeblood couldn't believe what he was about to say but knew every word was true. "I've found a new family, people who accept me as I am, without money, power, or prestige. People who I respect even when we disagree."

"Lowlife trash, no doubt. You're an insult to this family." He dropped his cigarette on the ground. "Don't bother coming to the house. You're not welcome."

Freeblood chuckled. He knew it would come down to this, but a small part of him clung to the insane hope his father would experience a change of heart and accept him for who he was. "Glad I can finally make you happy, *Dad*."

Before his father finished crushing the cigarette butt with the toe of his shoe, Freeblood was gone.

Time was what he needed at this moment. Time to think, to sort out his feelings, to grieve. But not on the same ground his ass of a father walked on. Freeblood needed to be alone in a place that would help him come to terms with the passing of his brother. He needed to find a semblance of peace before he returned to Faux.

Aware of her nature, he also knew his own all too well and believed their budding relationship deserved his full attention—heart, mind, and body. It would take all his wits and energy to keep up with the likes of her, but he knew he was up to the challenge.

Life became a whirlwind after meeting Etain, and he doubted it would slow down. The small mishap with the eighteen-wheeler was a glitch, but one that paid off in the end, thanks to a blood transfusion given by the silver-haired stranger. Dashing out of the hospital, he'd felt stronger than ever and hadn't looked back, not even to think about the family he left behind in the human realm. Everyone was well. Life was good.

Freeblood lifted his head to a heart-stopping sunset in the Highlands, streaks of orange and gold blazing on the horizon cast a red glow on the clouds. Jagged silhouettes of trees and hills shadowed in black served as the perfect division between a sky on fire and its molten reflection in the loch below. He shivered from the cold evening air, but his mind was elsewhere. He knew where his future lay. As tough as his relationship was with Dar, he was more a father figure than his own father. He sat on a rock, pushing his hands through his mop of brown hair and let the tears flow.

THE BLEEDIN' BROTHER

E tain shoved through the throng of wizards and Black Blades to find her husband pacing around the bed, face blank, the neck of an unfortunate wizard in his grip.

"Dar." Etain moved toward him, but a forceful hand pulled her back.

"It is not safe, Etain." Rie turned to an intimidating Elf, who stood at her side. "Shalifi, open a small hole in the shield." She leaned toward Etain. "Shalifi is the most esteemed master of the war wizards. He will be responsible for the High Lord's recovery."

With the hole open, the queen chanted a spell. "*Róaðu huga þinn, slepptu þjáningum þínum, í friðsömum blundi sigrum við óvini þina* (Calm your mind, release your woes, in peaceful slumber we defeat your foes)."

"No!" Etain screamed when Dar collapsed.

"He is only asleep." Rie whispered to her, then spoke to the others in the room. "The shield is lowered. Place him on the bed and restrain him." Black Blades lifted the High Lord while the wizards carried the body of their colleague from the room.

At the queen's command, two chairs were brought in and set near the bed facing each other. She had Etain sit in the one with its back to Dar. "We will have to work together. I must join my mind with yours and perhaps we can see what ails him. Can you do that?"

"I'll do anything to help him." She cast a worried glance over her shoulder. "Is it necessary to tie him down?"

"Absolutely." Rie took the young woman's hands in hers. "Etain, focus. You have to be strong for his sake. Tell me what to do." She feigned ignorance as a way to help the young woman.

"Well, relax and clear your thoughts. I think it's best I come to you." She interlaced her fingers with the queen. "Close your eyes and breathe with me."

Once telepathically united, Rie sensed the intense love between these two beings and knew she was right about their future.

Together, she and Etain requested entrance into Dar's mental domain. A wall rose from the darkness so forcibly it pushed the women apart. Etain ran her hands through her hair, and reached for the queen, nearly pulling her from her seat. "Hang on, Rie. This could get ugly."

They inhaled as one again. This time, Etain mentally slammed into her head before she released the breath. Her trust in the warrior woman was so complete, she allowed her mind to be dragged to a precipice and tumbled over the edge into the black abyss.

As they descended deeper into Dar's consciousness, a warm breeze rose to meet them. Far below, a faint light shone. Etain instructed the queen to ease off slightly, thereby slowing their descent. As they fell farther, the light took on a greenish glow.

"It is important we stay connected," Rie said. "Do *not* let go of my hand."

A nefarious voice spoke from the dark. "Lady Etain. Your Grace. Two of my most favorite femme fatales."

"Lurking in the shadows, as usual," Etain quipped, unnerved by the man's refusal to die.

"It's fascinating to be dead, yet so alive." Midir stepped into the green glow, a smirk on his lips. "I have to say, I greatly enjoyed our time alone, sweet Etain. I hope you prove as ravenous after all this is over."

Rie squeezed her hand. "You will not deter us, Midir."

"Alatariel." Amusement shone in his eyes. "You are a special treat. Such delicate flesh begging to be taken. I've had many dreams of your body pressed to my slab, my knife loving you strip by strip."

"We've come to rid Dar of you, once and for all," said Etain.

"*Mon petit*, my brother and I are one. As the old saying goes, to harm one is to harm the other. *I* wouldn't feel the pain, but his screams would be delightful."

"As one goes so too does the other," Rie whispered. The women split, one hand in touch with the other.

"Is that not what I said?" Midir turned, keeping them in his sights.

"Goddess of us all, hear my plea. Do not be deaf to our cries," the queen chanted.

A growl rolled from Midir. "Stupid bitches. I will haunt you in your sleep and make your days a living hell."

Undeterred, the queen continued. "We call out to you for help, sweet Mother. Watch over our brother who was born in the light."

He turned his green gaze on Etain. "Your precious Dar cannot live without his dark half."

She remained silent, afraid if she spoke, the emotions held in by the fragile restraint would destroy the thin thread linking her to Dar.

"Make silent the darkness..."

Midir laughed, but his discomfort was easy to read. "I can fuck you as easily here as in the physical world. I will take you both."

A scene of Dar naked at a window appeared. Stunned by his sudden appearance, Etain released Rie's hand.

"No, Etain."

Midir laughed. "What will you do now, great queen?"

Etain's heart pounded as she approached the scene. "It's the same w-window I saw in my dream." Dar leaned heavily against the frame, his hand slamming weakly against the glass, his screams nothing more than ragged croaks. She went to stand next to him. "There was a dark figure. I-I thought it was Inferno, but the figure stayed in the distance." She looked at Rie. "Dar's screams woke me."

"Something inside the window has his full attention. Be careful not to touch him." Rie carefully ducked under Dar's arm.

Etain peered through the glass. "No!"

Angry tears stung as she watched Midir slither over an imitation of her body, biting her lips, caressing her nakedness, tasting every inch of her. The greater horror was the ecstasy on their faces. Their laughter was an abomination. She realized what Dar must think, what he'd been thinking all this time. Her fear urged her to revert to the scared little girl who ran for her life.

"Dar! It's not me." She came up between him and the glass.

Rie reached out. "Etain, no. It is too soon."

Midir's laughter mocked them both. "An inspired performance, don't you think? You do him more harm than I ever could, *mon petit*."

"Dar! I would not do this to you. To us." She grabbed his face in her hands. "Stop watching, please. Look at *me*, not her."

"Etain, please stop." Rie warned. "You could drive him over the edge."

"Don't you see? He thinks this really happened. I swear to you it's a lie." Her attention returned to her husband. "Dar. Please. It's me." She patted his cheeks. "*A chuisle*, listen to me."

"Yes, Dar. You *must* listen." Midir encouraged his brother. "Listen to your most precious love. Let her explain why she is with you but fucks your brother."

"Shut up!" she screamed.

Dar's gaze moved from the window to Etain. "Lying slut." He grabbed her about the waist and slung her like a rag doll across the phantom yard. Golden eyes flashed as he stalked toward her. "You played me for a fool. Is that why you lured me to his castle? To take his life so I would not learn of your betrayal? You should have killed me in the devil's courtyard. I would be better dead than to suffer this."

"Dar!" the queen yelled. "This will not stand."

Etain clawed at his hand as he lifted her by the neck.

"I loved you more than life itself." He shook her mercilessly. "Is this your revenge for Faux? I thought her the demon, but I now see the joke played at my expense. How long did you think you could keep this dirty secret?" Unprepared for his sudden release, she fell onto her hands and knees. When she tried to stand, he backhanded her. "Stay in the dirt where you belong."

Etain drew in several ragged breaths, trembling from the intensity of his hate. She stumbled to her feet and dared to challenge him with the only words she thought would cut through his delusion. "The very first time you saw me dangling on the wall." She recited the words he'd spoken not long ago. Words that made her stay. "The moment you held me in your arms." She stepped closer to him, her hands clenched into fists, and struck him on the chest over and over. "I knew. Just like you knew. Coming to my defense was your excuse to be close to me. I did *not* betray you."

He caught her by the wrists and twisted, making her scream. "You say excuse. I say curse."

"Have you no faith in me?" she cried, her pain almost too much to bear. He let go only to slap her across the face. A metallic taste in her mouth told her he'd split her lip. She winced as her tongue ran over the cut. "You are my sweet savage." Midir laughed when Dar raised his hand once more. This time, Etain hissed as she caught him by the wrist. "I love you forever and a day."

A moment of recognition lit in his eyes but quickly passed. "There is no forever with you."

She slapped his face as hard as she could, hoping he would wake from his nightmare. "You didn't trust Midir in life. Why would you believe him in death?"

Dar spoke through gritted teeth. "There are no lies in his memories."

Midir grinned, arrogant to the end. "Another old saying comes to mind. Blood is thicker than water. I've not understood it until now."

Etain peered over Dar's shoulder, pushed away, and stalked toward the insufferable demon of a man.

"No, Etain," Rie turned and went after her.

Midir howled with laughter. "Will you slap me, too, little Etain? Slap me deeper into my brother's psyche?"

Her hand came up with that thought in mind. Just as he caught her by the wrist, she dipped down for the dagger in her boot, its blade reflecting the eerie green light.

Midir clamped his other hand on her forearm and forced her arms behind her back. His lips hovered over hers. "You cannot kill me, *mon petit.*" She felt his breath warm and moist against her flesh. "I am a part of you as you are now a part of me."

"No." She shook her head. "Dar told me—"

"Dar told you what you needed to hear."

Rie hurled her body into his, digging her nails into Etain's flesh.

Pinned between the two women, Midir maintained an arrogant sneer as he wiggled, fighting to push Rie off. "Please, little queen. Your time will come."

She chanted quickly. "Goddess of us all, here my plea. Pay back the evildoer for his dark deeds."

Midir became more agitated. "Stop this."

"Reward him in kind. Strengthen our brother and bring him home."

He reached for the dagger in Etain's hand. "I will destroy him *and* her if you do not stop."

"Etain, I need your help." Rie dug her nails in deeper. "We have the power now. Hear the words and say them with me." She laid her head against Midir's back as he continued his attempts to push her away. "Save your son and bless him. You are all-powerful, Goddess. You are our strength and shield. Blessed be—"

"I will twist the goodness within your Dar until you no longer recognize him," he growled. "Then my brother and I will destroy you and turn your Alamir pets into rabid dogs. We'll see how well your Elven whoremongers fare without their precious High Lord."

Etain's protective nature burned bright. Unable to make use of her dagger, she leaned as far back as she could and banged her head into his. Stars danced before her eyes. She screamed when Midir sank his incisors into her shoulder.

"Etain!" Rie shouted. "Say the words with me. You are all powerful, Goddess."

She opened her eyes and concentrated on the queen's voice.

"You are all powerful, Goddess." Although weak, she continued to speak the words. "You are our strength and shield. Mother of protection, remove the spirits who do not belong here. Glory be to the light of the Goddess."

Amidst screams of vengeance, Midir ignited in a black fire and pushed the women apart. He turned on Rie and threw a stream of fire in her direction. Etain instantly reacted, engulfing the queen within a blue orb. On her knees within the light, the black fire ricocheted off its surface. Midir leaped aside to avoid the backlash. Green eyes aglow, his sights landed on Etain.

"Little bitch, you're like your mother and her mother before her." His black fire intensified. "I will not allow you to destroy what my son and I have started. We will come together and twist you to our will. Krymerians will rule the realms as they did in the beginning."

Blue electrical charges crackled around her. "What would you know of my mother?"

His laugh made her skin crawl. "You'll know soon enough." Midir raised his hands, transforming his black fire into a green blaze. Etain's blue charge encircled him and pinned his arms to his sides. His eyes burned into hers as the green fire seeped into the ground beneath his feet, his form fading.

"Stop him!" Rie screamed from her blue cage.

"But he's going away. Isn't this what we wanted?"

"He's going deeper into Dar's psyche. You must kill him now. If he bonds with Dar on that level, we'll never be rid of him."

"What do I do?" She tightened the electric lasso wrapped around the green beacon to no avail. "Bloody fucking hell!"

Midir's form transparent, his laughter drilled into her brain, transforming her anger into a white-hot fury. A bolt of perfect white light blazed across the void. Within seconds, she found herself flat on the ground and Rie standing over her.

"You did it, Etain."

"What?"

"I believe the old man is gone for good." Rie offered her a hand up.

"How do you know?"

"The look on his face when your light touched him."

Etain touched her jaw. "My head hurts."

"Sorry. I was afraid you would burn through all Dar's memories. He should remember some part of Midir."

"Burn?"

"We are not done." Rie pointed at Dar lost in his delusion.

"Maybe I should burn his memories of me."

"Stop it. The man loves you. Why else would he be in such a dither?"

"What good is love if he doesn't trust me?" She relented at the queen's raised brow. "Fine. I'll try one more time."

She walked toward him, her shoulders squared and head high. "We are blessed in the blood of Kaos. We are one. I am *your* High Lady." Tears threatened but she kept them at bay. "I trust you with my heart, my body, and my life." Dar continued bashing at the glass. Etain swallowed her humiliation. "If you can't return my trust, Dar VonNeshta, we have nothing."

The women awoke, their fingers still intertwined. Etain pushed away and fled the room.

The afternoon light sheened over the monolithic black stones in the center of the garden. Dathmet stood between them, his eyes closed, stroking their smooth surfaces as though they were favored lovers. "You will serve me well, my beauties."

Commander Thamuz, accompanied by his slim-waisted captain, Kromok, waited patiently for the master to acknowledge their presence. Kromok's brown-eyed glance to his commander conveyed his uncertainty as to whom the master spoke.

Eyes black as the stones popped open and scrutinized the two men. "Yes?"

Thamuz snapped to attention. "Harborym has gathered his team. They wait for your orders, milord."

"It won't be long now." Dathmet reached for the rings embedded in the stones and pulled himself up.

"The first will be the COL clan. Our man inside tells us the vault is deep below the fortress and is virtually forgotten. Our decoys will be sure to keep the other Alamir occupied while we move in to acquire the stone they hold."

Pebbles sprayed out when Dathmet's feet hit the ground. "Why not go for LOKI instead? They're in turmoil already. Literally falling apart."

"Agreed. However, the woman who plans to usurp the current chieftain keeps a vigilant watch over the castle. She would be more likely to keep her best warriors close at hand to protect her claim rather than send them to the human realm. Whichever way it goes, it would be to our advantage to wait until a firm decision has been made."

Dathmet's eyes gleamed. "You're right. We have plenty to keep us busy for now. In time, they will fall like the others and knowing it's *his* clan, whether he's the chieftain or not, will make it all the sweeter."

Thamuz watched his master walk toward him. "With our decoys in play, the *.com* clan will answer the call before the others and go to help COL. None of them will realize what's been taken until it's too late."

The master nodded. "I see. Good plan. You may go." Both men saluted. "Not you, Kromok. We have things to discuss." Commander Thamuz considered the captain with a shrewd eye.

"I am at your command, milord."

Dathmet's sinister grin spread across his fanged teeth. "Thamuz, you are dismissed."

The commander acknowledged the dismissal with a bow of his head and made a sharp turn. With his back to the master, he glared at the captain and marched off.

Kromok remained at attention.

"I have a private matter I would like you to handle. Do not discuss it with anyone, not even Thamuz. Do you understand?" Anticipation flamed in Dathmet's eyes, setting his hair to crackle and dance.

"Yes, milord."

"A plan is in motion that requires my return to the Alamir realm." Dathmet appreciated the interest in the man's eyes. "Discreetly assemble a small company of men and go to a village north of Laugharne Castle called Deudraeth. Locate the local apothecary shop and meet up with Cromorth. His troop is already in the area."

"Permission to speak freely, milord?"

"Yes. I value your opinion, Kromok."

The captain relaxed into a natural stance. "Does this have anything to do with the Krymerian?"

"He has been neutralized for now. He will not be involved."

Kromok raised his brows. "I thought he was the target."

"He is *a* target but not in this case." Dathmet returned to his black beauties, caressing each stone. "His time will come soon enough."

"Pardon, milord, but if we're not after the Krymerian, then who?"

"Someone with the power to bring the Krymerian and the Alamir to their knees." Dathmet's crowning glory flashed as though doused with lighter fluid. "Ensure Cloud is among the men who travel to Deudraeth."

"Cloud?" Kromok could not contain his distaste. "He is a human child."

"The boy's talent will serve you well, Kromok."

"A ragamuffin whose loyalties are questionable."

"You forget yourself, soldier." Dathmet lashed out with a rope of flame, burning through the sleeve of Kromok's uniform and into the flesh. The demon thrilled at the man's screams and the smell of burning flesh. His lips twitched into a seductive smile as he brought the insubordinate captain to his knees. "Collateral in the form of a younger brother removes all question of loyalty. You will take this boy with you and use him to our advantage. Remember, *you* serve *me*."

The man bowed his head, his face streaked with sweat and involuntary tears. "Apologies for questioning your wisdom, milord."

Dathmet hissed a calming breath. With a wave of his hand, the burning rope disappeared. "It will all become clear once you're in Deudraeth."

Kromok remained on his knees. "Are there any other accommodations required?"

The blood-skinned demon stroked his chin. "None come to mind. Find the apothecary, meet up with Cromorth, and wait for my signal."

Kromok struggled to his feet. "It shall be done, milord."

INTRIGUES

B eneath the long branches of a tree older in years than she could count, Etain sat at the river's edge and cried. She'd never seen Dar so cold, his eyes full of raw hatred. Not even in his fight with Midir did he show such rancor.

Holy hell. I tried to drown myself to get away from Midir at Laugharne. How can he believe such lies?

She screamed in frustration and threw herself back onto the ground.

A familiar face loomed over her. "A penny, milady."

She sniffled. "What do you want, Linq?"

"I saw you run out of the palace and thought you may need someone to talk to."

She flung her arm melodramatically. "What the hell. Have a sit."

"I take it things did not go well with Dar."

She placed her hand in the river, watching diamonds of sunlight swirl around her fingertips. "I don't know what to do. He won't listen to me. He stares with those golden eyes and accuses me of things I didn't do."

"The wizards will find a way."

Etain closed her eyes. "I should be the one to find a way, but I'm as lost as Dar. The man no longer trusts me because of a nasty trick his brother played. Even in death the bastard interferes."

"What do you plan to do?"

She turned her head to the water. "Maybe I should leave."

"I think you *should* go." The two jumped at Rie's intrusion. Etain sat up as Linq moved to stand. "No, no. Keep your seat." He held out his hand. "Thank you, kind sir."

"I can't leave Dar. No matter what was said, I won't go."

Rie folded her hands in her lap. "Dar is a confused man. He does not have the ability to discern between truth and lies at this point. I did not know before, but I now understand how much you mean to him and what he means to you. It is breathtaking, to say the least. But I believe your presence hinders his healing process."

Etain gave her an indignant glare and jumped to her feet pacing the river's edge. "He *knows* I would not betray him. He knows I would *never*—"

"Etain." The queen watched her pace. "He is not rational in his current state. I think by removing your influence he will be able to clear his mind."

Her heart skipped a beat. *Leave?* The world seemed to float before her eyes, black spots appearing.

Linq caught her just in time. "There now, milady. Take a deep breath." He held onto her until she was safely seated on the ground.

Rie scooped water from the stream and patted it on Etain's face. "It is only temporary. A few days. Give Dar the time he needs to sort through the delusions and come to terms with his brother's treachery."

"I don't know if I can. I think my leaving could make things worse."

"Nothing has to be decided right now." Alatariel adjusted her skirts and folded her hands in her lap again. "However, if I am to help Dar, you must be completely honest with me."

She returned the queen's steady gaze. "I guess it started with Freeblood." Etain told the story of the young man and the eighteen-wheelers, the blood transfusion, and subsequent antics between him and Faux. Mexico added Midir to the mix. She mentioned the summons to Dar's castle, his conquest of the assassin hired by Midir, and her trip to Texas. It continued through her time at Midir's castle and his ultimate death by Dar's hand.

"Y'all know about the Council. He had his first nightmare then. I don't know what he saw but if Linq hadn't been there, I'd probably not be here."

Linq raised his knuckles, still bruised from the encounter. "My persuasive skills were above par."

"Then it happened again at *Sôlskin*." Etain picked at the grass, throwing bits into the water. "He said Midir spoke through me and here we are."

Rie thought on her words. "Your time with Midir, did anything happen between you and him? Did he—"

Etain shook her head. "No! Hell, no! He tried, but I said no."

"Hmph." Linq was skeptical. "When did 'no' ever stop Midir?"

She shrugged. "All I know is he left me alone."

Rie patted her on the knee. "Midir was a self-gratifying man who did not wait for his pleasures. He took whatever he wanted whenever he pleased. Why would he delay in taking what he thought was owed to him?"

Linq offered a suggestion. "Perhaps it made him vulnerable because Midir was a part of Dar. They had a strong connection. It would not be too far-fetched to believe Midir felt as passionately about you as Dar."

"I think his passion was more about sticking it to Dar rather than caring about me." Etain picked at the grass again. "He was ready to sacrifice me on too many occasions to believe otherwise."

"It is true their conflict went deeper than mere sibling rivalry. Midir would have killed Dar a long time ago if the priests had not made it impossible."

"Oh, Linq." Rie sighed. "After Dar lost his family, I doubt he would have cared."

He stretched his legs out in front of him and leaned back on his elbows. "You know, Midir became the author of his own demise the day he threw Dar's sword, the one that nearly took your life, Etain. Because of you, Dar began to care again."

She perked up at the tidbit of information. "How do you know what happened? Dar didn't even know until recently."

Rie gave her a motherly smile. "The Elves preserve the history of those races no longer with us."

The hairs on the back of her neck prickled. "He was tortured for years. It would've saved him a lot of grief if he'd been told."

"Our interference could have proven fatal for Dar. He was not ready to face his brother. Midir's selfish nature brought you into Dar's life and changed his destiny." The queen touched Etain's hand. "You know of Midir's involvement in your parents' deaths?"

"He told me."

"By the time we discovered the time and place, your parents were dead, you were gone, and his hellion had absconded with your brother."

Etain stiffened. "What? No. My brother died with them."

"When our people arrived, there was not much of anything left. The assassin's jarvelin cleaned the site quite well. However, they were able to find *some* traces of blood," Rie countered. "All of which belonged to your mother and father."

Etain glared at the Elves, anger vibrating through her. She swallowed hard to tamp down the demon within and jumped to her feet. "My brother told me to run. *Something* chased me, but it wasn't him. No, if Robert were alive, he'd have come for me."

"Etain, our people *saw* them take your brother," she said patiently. "And with you becoming Alamir, how would he have known where to go?"

"Well, *I* would've looked for *him*. I wouldn't have spent the last five years scared and alone."

"At the time, we had no idea to where your brother was taken," the queen said.

Torn between anger at the secrecy of the Elves and the excitement her brother may be alive, Etain's voice deepened. "Midir's castle would've been a good start. I don't understand how a human could survive in his realm, but I have to find him."

Linq stood. "If he *is* alive, you will need help." He turned to the queen. "Is there something you can do?"

"It will be dark soon," Rie said. "We should return to the palace. I will make a few inquiries, but it could take a few days before we have an answer. Should our wizards find anything, I will send a messenger."

At the palace, Etain parted company with the two and went upstairs. Lost in thought, she walked past Dar's room and nodded at the sentry outside his door. Rie was thoughtful enough to give her the room next to his. As nice as it was to have him close, it occurred to her it was far more torturous to be so close and not be with him.

How am I going to walk out of here without you?

Etain relaxed in a hot bath mulling over the happenings since her arrival in the Elven city. Discovery of the Black Blades, the wizards, the castle, even the people themselves was surreal. Okay, she knew Elves existed. There was Elfin, whom she met through Inferno, and Linq, a more recent acquaintance, but she'd not considered from where they came or that there were more like them. Friends, families...

Holy hell. They must have families. Could Linq have a special lady?

She tried to imagine the savage Elf locked in a lover's embrace. Maybe she was what kept him busy while she'd been with Dar and the queen.

Charmed by the idea, she lifted the bathing sponge over her head. "Ow." Her left shoulder hurt. "What the hell?"

The sponge made a soft splash when it hit the water. Etain pulled her hair back, trying to see what it was out of the corner of her eye. She gently touched the area. It felt rough and hot. The memory of Rie's nails digging into her arms flashed in her mind. She checked the right and the left but there were no wounds, not even a scratch.

Water splashed onto the floor when she pushed to her feet and turned to the mirror on the wall. Her throat showed no signs of Dar's stranglehold. There were no bruises on her jaw. She carefully stepped out of the bath for a closer look at her shoulder. Then she saw them, red and hot. Two small puncture wounds right where Midir bit her.

"Holy hell. Hopefully, they'll be gone by morning."

She extinguished the lights, dropped the towel at the side of the bed, and slipped in between the soft sheets. Downy covers cushioned her from the rough reality in the next room as she sank deeper into sleep.

Outside her window stood a dark figure, vigilant in its scrutiny. She recognized the shape as Dar. No sooner had the thought passed than his gaze pierced through her like a golden fire. His hypnotic stare drew her to the glass. At the window, she closed her eyes to reclaim herself from the intensity of his glare. A scream from the other side of the glass made her open her eyes. She staggered back, startled to see Dar bashing his fists against the frame of the window, a forlorn expression on his face.

"Help me."

"Dar." She startled awake. Gathering the comforter around her, she shuffled to the bedroom door and peeked into the hallway. She slipped out into the empty corridor and padded to Dar's room. The sentry was gone. She tried the handle and experienced a mix of relief and concern by its easy turn. Her heart pounded. Where were the wizards and the guards?

The sleeping lord was clearly visible within the faint blue light of the containment spell, turning his blond hair silver. His hand fell off the edge of the mattress as though he beckoned her closer. The spell forgotten, she tiptoed across the stone floor and reached out for his hand. She bit her lip to stifle a scream and stuck her fingers into her mouth to suck away the pain.

Why are you alone?

The comforter fell away and a blue shimmer transported her from outside of the transparent wall to the inside. She lifted his hand and kissed the soft center of his palm, happy to be close to him again. Seated on the edge of the bed, she placed his hand against her cheek and closed her eyes. "I miss you." Gently setting his hand at his side, she climbed onto the bed and straddled his hips. The heat of him between her thighs made her wet and awakened an ache only he could satisfy.

"I'll be leaving soon my love." Her gaze etched every curve of his face into her memory. "I'm not sure when. Maybe tomorrow, maybe the next day, but Alatariel says I must. For your sake." She brushed her lips over his, her words mere wisps. His shirt grazed the sensitive tips of her breasts. "I love you, my sweet savage. You are the air I breathe. My heart." Her hair fell around his face, encasing them both in a silvery tent. "I won't be gone long. I promise." Tears formed in her eyes as she pressed her lips to his. "And you must promise to be my Dar again."

The naked nymph untied his bindings and dropped them to the floor. She unbuttoned his shirt admiring his lean, muscled torso and lovingly caressed his body. "You are so beautiful, so strong." She kissed him lightly across each shoulder and laid her head on his chest, pressing her body to his. The steady beat of his heart drummed against her ear. "I know you love me as I love you. You *will* come back to me."

Early the next morning, Linq made his way to Etain's room, thinking of how a tour of Nunnehi would be good for the High Lady and might take her mind off the ailing High Lord if only for a while. After several knocks, he tentatively opened the door. "Etain? Are you awake?" He stepped in and gave his eyes a few seconds to adjust to the darkness. The sheets were tousled but the bed was empty.

Troubled, he left the room but stopped at Dar's door and asked the sentry if anyone had passed. A flush tinged the young man's cheeks, but the soldier confirmed he had not seen anyone all night.

"I think it is best I check on the High Lord."

The sentry opened his mouth but opened the door without saying a word.

Once inside, Linq's gaze immediately went to the bed. White skin, glowing silver in the light, made him blink. He closed the door as he placed his hand on the hilt of his sword. Closer to the bed, he exhaled, relieved to see it was Etain rather than a *draugur* come to steal Dar's soul. He called her name as loudly as he dared. After several attempts, her eyes opened and her brows furrowed. She pushed up on her elbows.

"Linq?" she mumbled, her hair falling over her face. "What are you doing in our bedroom?"

"Etain, this is not your bedroom. We are in Nunnehi."

He turned his head as she sat up.

"What? Oh!" She covered herself as best she could. "Dar needed me. There wasn't a sentry at the door, so I came to him."

"There was no sentry?"

She shook her head.

"I shall mention it to Alatariel. We should be leaving. The wizards are rather rigid when it comes to crossing boundaries." He grabbed the comforter from the floor. "Here. Shimmer into this and let us get back to your room."

"Is there a guard now?"

"Yes. Hurry."

"But they consider me the High Lady of Kaos. Why do I need permission—"

"Shall we not press our luck? Give Nunnehi time to adjust to your presence."

She rolled her eyes and turned to Dar. "Get well, my love. I'll see you soon." She left him with a kiss, slid off the bed, and shimmered into the confines of the duvet. "Put your arms around me."

In her bedroom, Linq held the comforter until she had a proper hold of it. "Thank you." She gave him a nervous smile as he stepped back. "I didn't realize there were so many protocols where the High Lord is concerned."

"It is as much for your protection as it is for his and ours."

Etain picked up her clothes as she headed to the bathroom. "I'll only be a minute. What plans do you have for me today?"

"A tour of the palace, and perhaps a ride in the country."

Back in the bedroom, she donned her boots and strapped on *Nim'Na'Sharr*. "Can we grab a quick bite before we leave? I wasn't up for a meal last night, but I'm famished this morning."

As they passed Dar's room, Linq gave a nod to the sentry, who responded with a wide-eyed stare. Etain commented under her breath, "He looks as though he's seen a ghost."

Linq smiled and kept walking. He hoped a happy ending was in Dar and Etain's future.

AWAKENINGS

Later in the evening, Linq went round to Etain's room anxious to speak with her. When she opened the door wrapped in an oversized towel, he turned his head, surprised again by her state of undress.

"Apologies, milady. I was not aware you were bathing. I will come back."

"Linq. I wasn't expecting you. Has something happened with Dar?"

"No. Nothing has changed."

Etain glanced down at the towel, hitched it up a little higher, and reached for his arm. "Don't be ridiculous. Come in. I was just soaking my sore bum. It's been a while since I've sat in a saddle the better part of a day. Come on." She pulled him into the room. "I was turning into a prune anyway. Let's chat."

He moved no farther than the door. "Dar would not appreciate—"

"Dar doesn't appreciate anything at the moment." She linked her arm through his. "Please come in. I promise no one's honor will be compromised. You're as much my friend as you are his."

He displayed an uncomfortable smile, trying to forget the image of a naked Etain atop his best friend. "The wizards have found information on your brother."

"Already? How'd they find him so quickly?" She motioned him to the overstuffed chairs in front of the stone fireplace.

He sat across from her but kept his eyes on the orange-and-yellow flames of the fire. "He has been located in a village north of Laugharne."

"Seriously? How long has he been there?"

"Nothing is certain."

She popped up from her seat. "My brother," she murmured, pacing back and forth. "How far north?"

Unable to maintain propriety, Linq looked at her. "On horseback? A day, maybe two."

Her eyes glittered with excitement. "Forget the horses. Inferno's truck will have me there in a couple of hours." She let out a nervous laugh. "I wouldn't want to freak him out by showing up in a shimmer."

"It would not be in your best interests, Etain. With the High Lord out of commission, others may take liberties."

"What liberties? I'll be there and back before anyone even knows I've left."

"As you said Etain. You are thought of as the High Lady of Kaos."

"Linq." She sighed. "We're not even married. No one's gonna—"

He abruptly stood, making her step back. "Married or not, he has chosen you as his partner. It is a monumental event known across all the realms. Do not for a moment think a ceremony makes any difference to the *Bok* or Dar's enemies."

She blinked several times and turned her back to him. "*All* the realms?"

"Aye, milady. I am sorry if I speak out of turn, but it needed to be said."

She ran a hand through her hair as she turned to face him. "What if I left here without him and never returned?"

"You would not."

"It's my brother, Linq. I thought he was dead."

Confronted with the lady's stubborn streak, his voice took on a more commanding tone. "You would risk your life for a man you have not seen since you were a child?"

"I would do the same if it were Dar."

Suddenly, he understood Dar's desire to be with this vexation of a woman. Granted, her outward beauty caught one's attention, a misconceived perception of vulnerability drawing you in, but it was her determination and courage to face her fears that ensnared loyalty to the end. Although impressed by this sudden revelation, his words did not betray his thoughts.

"What happens when he turns out to be exactly like Midir? Dar will not be waiting in the shadows to step in and save you this time."

Sparks of silver glinted through her hair and her eyes sparkled with defiance. With a roll of her eyes, she threw herself into a chair and stared at the fire.

Linq returned to his seat, satisfied his point was made, albeit not well-received. "You will *not* leave this palace alone. Dar would have my head if he knew you left with no escort, nor could I forgive myself should something untoward happen. We have been friends for many years, and I do not intend to compromise our friendship by watching his lady traipse off after a boy raised by Midir."

She cut a sideways glare at the Elf.

"Have you forgotten the evil Midir perpetrated on Dar and his family? Or closer to home, *your* family? I do not see how living with that demon could have left a positive impression on a young boy."

She sat up straight, reclaiming a semblance of regal composure. "Fine. We leave before dawn. I suggest you get some rest. We have a lot of traveling to do." She walked him to the door.

Before stepping out, he had one more thing to say. "You are right about you and me, Etain. We may have met because of Dar, but we have become friends too. Something I would like to believe would have happened with or without the High Lord." He disappeared down the hallway before she could speak.

Early the next morning, long before most of Nunnehi awakened, Etain and Linq shared a light breakfast while the cook's assistants packed a bag with enough food and drink to last them several days.

As they finished their meal, Alatariel joined them at the table. "I am glad I caught you before you left. Linq, I know you will take good care of our Lady Etain."

"If for no other reason than to avoid the High Lord's wrath," Linq teased. He picked up the bag of supplies and headed for the door. "You coming, Etain?"

She didn't budge from her seat. "Meet me by the front gate in five minutes." As he walked out, her gaze moved to the queen. "I want to thank you again for your generosity. You didn't have to help us."

Rie gave her a serene smile. "Etain, you are a part of my family now. We take care of each other."

She ruminated over the queen's words and raised a quizzical brow. "You keep saying we're family. I assume it's meant in a figurative way?"

"All I will say is my and Dar's grandmothers were sisters. Both Elves. One fell in love with a tall, handsome Krymerian, while the other found love with one of her own."

Etain's eyes widened. "Shut up. He didn't tell me *that* part of his family history."

Rie chuckled. "I doubt he knows. His father swore us to secrecy."

"How do you keep such a secret? Didn't Dar know his grandmother?"

"He did, but she was a clever woman. Very few Krymerians knew of her heritage."

"Why hide it?"

The queen sighed. "A king of Krymeria must be of pure blood. A custom Dar's grandfather did not believe in. Or perhaps it was a show of rebellion. He and his father, Darieous, did not always see eye to eye."

"Well, I think you just broke your promise."

A mischievous grin on her lips, Rie winked. "I only promised not to tell Dar. The old man never counted on you coming along."

"I should go before Linq comes back." The women embraced. "You've made me feel so welcome. If I may, I'd like to think of you as a sister."

"I would like it very much. Be safe and return soon."

"Please tell Dar..." Etain hesitated, unsure of what to say. "Well, tell him I'll be back and explain why I left."

Rie gave her hand a comforting squeeze. "I will make sure he understands."

"Thank you." She turned to leave. "Oh, I forgot something in my room. See you soon, Rie."

A few steps down the hallway, she glanced over her shoulder and shimmered to a spot outside of the city beyond the front gates. Even though it was too early for most in the city to be up, she kept a vigilant eye to make sure no one followed her.

Please forgive me, my friend. Dar needs you more than I do.

However, once in the countryside she wasn't sure of her surroundings. None of the landmarks were familiar. Upon their arrival, she hadn't paid attention to the way they came to the palace. The only thing she *was* certain of, they had come from the mountains. It took longer than planned but she finally found the right path and meandered to the spot from where they originally entered. Happy as she was in finding it, she frowned.

"Damn."

"Not much of a strategist, are you?" Linq stepped out from behind a large boulder.

Hands on hips, she grinned. "Obviously not. How long have you been here?"

"I was about to head down when you came up the hill."

"Yeah, I didn't think I'd ever find the right place." She shuffled her feet. "You know, Linq—"

"Were I a younger Elf, I would have tried the same thing."

"Perhaps, but it wouldn't have taken you half the day."

"Definitely." He smiled. "Come on. We have a brother to find." He spoke the sacred words to open the portal back to the Alamir world. "Where to first, milady?"

"Inferno's, to beg the use of his horses."

He raised his eyebrows. "No Hummer?"

"No Hummer."

When they stepped through the portal into a wet and chilly Welsh evening, Etain clawed at her neck and fell to her knees.

Linq nearly went down with her but was able to maintain his footing. He crouched beside her. "What is it?"

"Can't breathe." She gasped and choked, desperately trying to pull air into her lungs. "Por-tal." She stabbed a finger at the opening.

Linq closed the rift with a wave of his hand. Her throat suddenly opened, and she gulped in mouthfuls of air.

He shoved his flask at her. "This will help."

She took a sip and handed him the flask. "Thank you. Dar's awake. And he's furious."

"You are doing the right thing, Etain. They will have him to rights in no time." He helped her up.

"I don't envy their task," she said, pushing the hair from her face. "It's gonna take the patience of a saint and whatever else a war wizard can come up with to deal with that tiger."

"Aye. Well, onward for us."

She shivered. "It was so nice in Nunnehi. I forgot how cold and bleak it is here. If we shimmer, we should get to Laugharne in time for an evening cuppa. Shall we scheme through the night by a warm, cozy fire?" Etain held out her hand.

"Sounds a plan, milady."

Hand in hand, the two disappeared in a blue shimmer.

Alatariel raced up the stairs at the howl echoing through the hallways. A violent tremor rocked the palace and knocked her to her knees. Trident, the Shalifi, met her at the top of the stairs. "My Queen. I fear he has awakened in a foul temper and destroyed the shield."

"Is anyone hurt?"

"Not yet. He overpowered a circle of thirteen, Your Grace. It is unheard of."

"Trust our High Lord to traverse new territory. It is obvious we no longer know the full extent of his powers." Nearer to the door, she heard the sounds of total chaos. "He has reunited with his darkness and is now a true High Lord of Kaos. He is like no other before him."

"Excuse me for saying this, Your Grace, but the laws of magic are specific. White magic is tied to the laws of light, while black magic is tied to the laws of darkness. If we can determine to which he is now aligned, we can neutralize—"

"Kaos is not bound by such limitations. It has no equal, Trident. *Dar* has no equal."

"What of the High Lady of Kaos? It is said he has shared his blood with her. Surely her strength is equal—"

"She has left this realm. I am sure it is the reason for his anger." She reached for the handle. "I underestimated the bond—"

The door burst open. The force from it tossed her back into the Shalifi and threw them into the opposite wall.

The commander came running from farther up the hallway. "Your Grace! Shalifi!" He helped a stunned Alatariel to her feet and assisted the battered Trident who suffered the brunt of the impact.

"Commander Crom, thank you," she said as she straightened her gown. "Trident, how are you?"

He leaned heavily against the wall. "I will be fine, Your Grace."

"Once we are done here, you get to Chelri." She turned to Crom. "We must get the High Lord settled before he brings down the entire tree."

The Shalifi stepped in front of her. "He has destroyed the room. We must ensure your safety, milady. I beg you, please allow the wizards to enter first."

Alert to the High Lord's movements, the wizards formed a living wall between Dar and their queen. Alatariel gasped at the enormity of the destruction. Pillows, sheets, and even the mattress were ripped apart. The bed and side table were pulverized. Books littered the floor, their torn pages still fluttering to the floor.

She pointed to ribbons of bluish sunlight filtering into the dark room. "Where did this come from?"

The Shalifi shook his head. "The containment spell held during his first attempt, but when he released a bolt of sheer force, it ripped through the shield, raining sparks over everyone."

"Where is she?" Dar's voice thundered.

The wizards answered with a singsong spell.

"*Móðir elds og íss, heyrðu beiðni okkar. Sendu honum svöl þægindi þín og frelsaðu hann frá draugunum sem ásækja sál hans og færa honum sorg. Kristallaðu hatur hans og ótta, gefðu honum léttir* (Mother of fire and ice, hear our plea. Send him your cool comforts and set him free from the ghosts that haunt his soul and bring him grief. Crystalize his hate and fears, give him relief)."

Minute crystals formed at Dar's feet and blossomed out, quickly creeping up each leg. Their journey sounded like ice cracking in the first thaws of spring.

In response, the veins in Dar's neck bulged as he shattered the spell with a simple hand gesture and sent three wizards flying backward into the wall.

"I will not be caged like an animal. Did you honestly think your puny powers could hold me?"

"Stop this madness, Dar," Alatariel commanded from behind the wizards. "This is not the conduct one would expect from a High Lord. You will abide by our rules while you are here."

Cold eyes bored into hers. "This is what happens when a High Lord has been betrayed. Have you any idea how it feels to be made a cuckold by one you trusted with your life?"

"Your *actions* have made you a cuckold, not Etain. You damn well know she would not betray you. Look past the lies left behind by your jealous brother."

Dar paced back and forth across the room. "What makes you think this has anything to do with Midir?"

Too late, she realized her mistake. She bravely stepped out from behind her wall of wizards. "I had a long conversation with your wife."

He raised a brow. "That must have been interesting since I have no wife. Etain has admitted her guilt by slinking away without as much as a goodbye."

"Yes, she has gone, but not for the reasons you think."

He moved quickly, grabbing a handful of her red hair, and pulled back hard, exposing her long neck to an extended talon. Her eyes rolled at the unexpected attack. "Do not cover for the whore. Did she run to her dead lover's realm?"

Crom was the first to reach for his blade. "Release her, High Lord," he commanded from outside the circle, "or your exit from this realm will not be the one you planned."

A concerted scrape of metal filled the room as seasoned warriors followed Crom's lead, encircling their queen and her assailant. The wizards filled the gaps between the Black Blades, ready to deliver a magical assault should the swords aimed at the High Lord not persuade him to release their cherished leader.

Dar's glare accosted each one as he spoke. "You are no match for me or the power I call upon. I do not wish to harm any of you, but if you stand in my way, I will lay waste to all."

"High Lord, your mind is not yet healed. Let us help you," Trident said.

Alatariel lifted a hand to stay their swords. A vision of the dead wizard flashed through her mind, but she pushed it away. She knew Dar better than anyone in the room and did not believe he would cause her irreparable harm. His anger was obvious, but she sensed something else far more dangerous. An irrational fear.

"Dar, these Blades are of your making, trained by your standards. A wizard has already died by your hand and now you threaten their queen. You know they will not allow you to pass, no matter what it takes." From the hallway came the sounds of an army on the march. In the next moment, the Queen's Royal Guard sealed the entrance to the room. "Are their lives worth that of a whore?"

He bared his teeth, pressing the talon against her skin. She flinched from the sharp edge cutting into her flesh.

"My Lady!" Crom shouted.

"If you believe she's betrayed you," Alatariel turned her head as far as the talon would allow, "let us remove the mark you share. Destroy it. Be done with her."

Dar considered the mark which bore testament of their union. It warmed his chest as it whispered to his heart. The protective shield he put up because of his evil brother, who continued to lie and scheme from beyond the grave, started to crack. Dar glimpsed the happiness and newfound trust of the last few days he and Etain shared since declaring their love. He clung to the cracks for dear life, willing them to tear apart and wanting more than ever to believe the good he desired, not the evil he had seen. He retracted the talon and pushed the queen away.

"I cannot."

"Why keep a stain given to you by a whore? What do you owe her that warrants the lie on your chest?"

He had no answers.

"Could it be your heart tells you differently?"

In another search of his mind, he realized something was missing. "What have you done, Alatariel?"

"I am merely trying to get into your thick head. Your lady is loyal to you."

Trident reached between the Blades and pulled the queen to safety, the warriors tightening the circle around the High Lord.

"I am not talking about Etain."

"Oh. Well..." She lowered her eyes, lifted her head and squared her shoulders. "We saved you from his lies."

"We?"

"Etain and myself. We rid you of his poison. Dark remnants of Midir were twisting your mind."

He drew in a slow breath, afraid of how many of his brother's memories had been destroyed. "It was not your place. Did you at any time consider the consequences?"

"Our main concern was to destroy his hold on you. He wanted to tear you apart, to ensure you were as unhappy as he. We did it to help you move on and live a happy life with Etain."

"You have erased memories I needed to come to terms with the blood he shed. A part of me committed those evil deeds. We are both to blame."

"Your way of coping would have been the death of your loving lady."

He shot a scathing glare at the straightforward woman.

"You cannot change the past, Dar. You had nothing to do with how he lived his life. The moment the priests separated you, he was his own person. Do you give him credit for the good you have done?" She pushed her way through the wall of Blades. "You have enough of your own guilt. Do not take on his as well."

He turned from her damning stare to the split in the wall. Through the opening, he caught the flight of morning songbirds, twittering among the branches of the old tree. A slight breeze entered the room, blowing the blond mane from his face. Inexplicably, his thoughts turned to the day he found Etain at Midir's, her sword in hand.

"You say you spoke with her. Did she tell you of the day she nearly took my life?"

"We spoke of many things, but I believe she mentioned it." She motioned to the others to leave them alone.

"He cannot be trusted, Your Grace," said Crom, a wary eye on the High Lord.

"She will not be harmed, Commander. You have my word."

Crom narrowed his eyes. "Your word means nothing today. You have *my* word you will not walk out of this realm should she come to any further harm, whether it be by your hand or another's."

Dar tilted his head in acknowledgment.

Alatariel stepped in between the men. "Commander Crom, despite this mess, he remains our High Lord. His word will be respected." Her features softened. "A few moments, please." Crom cast a warning glance at the man standing behind his queen. She turned to address her men-at-arms. "Not one word of this leaves this room."

Crom stepped back as the Royal Guard, the Black Blades, and the wizards retreated into the hallway. Before he joined the others, Trident offered her a cloth for the wound on her neck. She pressed it to her skin and waved him out.

Once they were alone, Dar submitted to his memories, reliving the day he appeared at Midir's castle and faced a warrior Etain. "In true Midir fashion, he tried to steal my life again. I have no idea what happened between them." He gazed through the cracks in the walls. "Her actions puzzled me, but then I realized she did not recognize me. When I noticed the green in her eyes, I knew she was under the influence of his magic." Arms over his chest, he shook his head. "My lady, left alone with that monster subjected to what I will never know."

"You could ask her."

"I could but she would not tell me."

"Do you not trust her?"

"It has nothing to do with trust. She would hold back the worst to keep from hurting me."

"A woman bent on betrayal would not do such a thing."

Dar's gaze returned to the openings in the wall. A long silence separated him from this place. In time, he sighed and crossed the bridge laden with memories. "Once *Nim'Na'Sharr* was in her hands, the valiant sword reclaimed her mistress." He suddenly turned. "Would you have a new room prepared? I promise to take better care."

"I have every faith." She walked to the doorway and instructed a Blade to have the room next door prepared for the High Lord. Before she dismissed her men-at-arms, she said, "Gossip is for old women and not a productive pastime for honorable men who wish to retain their post. Forget what you have seen here and enjoy your evening."

"Your Grace, with all due respect, do you think it wise?" Crom asked.

"He is on the road to recovery."

"High Lord or not, he must answer for his actions today," Trident said.

"So true, milady," Crom echoed.

"Gentlemen, please. We can discuss this later."

Trident exchanged a glance with Crom, bowed to his queen, and left.

Crom eyed the destroyed doorway. "It is against my better judgment, Your Grace. However, I trust your instincts." He turned to leave but stopped and glared at Dar. "I will be watching and will not hesitate should it come to it."

Dar met the queen at the doorway. "Thank you, Rie. I would do the same were I in their position." He took her hands in his. "My deepest apologies for today." The expression on his face mirrored the pain in his heart. "I know I cannot make amends for the life I have taken or for the troubles I have brought to this beautiful city, but I will find a way."

"Were it not for Midir, none of this would have happened. Do not worry about Shalen's family. They will be taken care of."

"I would request the opportunity to speak with them if I may."

She patted his hand. "Shall we leave it for now?"
"If it is not too much to ask, may I be left in peace to compose myself?"
"Take as long as you need, Dar."

Conveyance of Swords

The time spent in the Highlands gave Freeblood a sense of relief. Although saddened by the loss of his brother and abandonment by his human family thanks to his asshole father, his outlook on his future remained positive. He was ready to get back to Faux and even Dar and Etain.

He slowed his pace as he approached *Sólskin*, and stopped to listen, thinking it couldn't possibly be what he thought. *I wasn't gone long enough.* He took a few more steps. *Have Dar and Etain come home?* It was possible, but something told him this wasn't their brand of music. This was definitely Faux.

He walked through the gates into the courtyard, small white pebbles crunching beneath his neon Converse. The music grew louder with each step toward the front doors. Just as he reached the stoop, the doors flew open. A pair of blondes dressed in the skimpiest red plaid skirts he'd ever seen, their buxom chests covered with what he was sure were men's handkerchiefs in another life, and thigh-high boots stared at him. The two laughed and grabbed him by each arm.

"Oh, my gawd. Aren't you the cutest thing?" the one on the right said, her green eyes glittering.

"We've been waiting for you, sugar," said the one on the left. "We were on our way out, but now you're here..." He felt naked beneath her thorough scrutiny. "I think we'll stay a while." Each girl linked an arm through his and escorted him down the hallway.

The throne room was the place from where the ear-splitting music rumbled. People littered the room. Dancing, lounging, drinking, talking, laughing, and... He did a double take. *Should they be doing that in public?* Not a prude by any standards, he felt his face go red and turned away.

In the far corner was a live band. Death metal was the current choice, but the singer was an ear wrencher. Freeblood had heard a lot better from the garages back home.

Through it all, a familiar laugh caught his ear. He ignored whatever the blonde bimbos were chattering about and scanned the room. She was here somewhere. The laugh came again from above. Extricating himself from the twins, his gaze drifted up the steps of Dar's throne. There sat his horny little demon, deep in conversation with some lowlife who hovered over her like a vulture waiting to pounce. His jaw clenched. The twins tried to engage him once again, but his death glare changed their minds.

He attention returned to the woman lazing upon the throne. His stomach churned. She should've known he was back by the burn in her blood, but either she chose to ignore it or was too distracted. Something else made his breath catch in his throat.

Maybe she just doesn't care.

Faux turned her sparkling black eyes on him. He caught the slight change in her and felt the heat rise in his blood. Freeblood gave her a lazy grin. Wasn't it what attracted him in the first place? The audacious games she played, mesmerizing people with her hypnotic tail, taking them hostage with those bottomless black pools of pure sex until she grew bored and squashed them with a single comment. His stomach settled. Let her play her games. He was a fierce competitor and always won.

"I was beginning to think you weren't coming back." Faux leaned back in the oversized throne, watching him walk toward her. "How is the little family?"

"Hmph," was all he was willing to say, afraid anything more would end his hard-won peace.

"Are you here to stay?"

He gestured to the crowd. "Is this what I have to look forward to?"

A smirk lifted the corners of her delicious red mouth. "I was bored."

Freeblood grunted a laugh. It'd only been a few hours. "We should have a discussion about what that means so I'm clued in."

The forgotten vulture cleared his throat. A unified glare from the couple made him turn and graciously descend the grand steps acting as though it'd been his plan all along.

Freeblood walked around the throne. His fingers danced over her skin, sending vibrations through them both. A smirk lit his lips as he crouched next to the chair and trailed a finger along her perfect cheek.

"It's not often I find a kindred spirit." He took her hands in his and pulled her up with him, his eyes caressing her face, her lips, and traveling down the sumptuous body that drove him to insanity. "And what a spirit I have found." He held her tightly to him as he spun them around, making her laugh at the ending dip. "Mom and Dad should be home soon."

In complete control, his hand glided up her back, bringing her to him. A snap of his arms pressed her body against his. "Shall we make plans for a hellish homecoming? Surely the two of us have been left alone far too long."

"You don't suppose they've come to trust us, do you?" she asked, more than a little breathless.

He spun them again and laughed. "Dar and Etain trust us? You must be mad, woman."

The laughter of children and dogs barking drifted on the breeze as the two travelers came into the courtyard. Etain smiled, eyes bright. "I haven't seen the kids in so long! I hope they remember me."

Seth yelled at their approach and waved his arms, leading the charge. "Etain! Linq! Hallo!" Felix and Ruby raced past the children to meet the newcomers first.

"Hello, Felix. Hi, Ruby." Etain laughed giving each a pat on the head.

Three-year-old Tegan, the youngest, did her best to keep up with the older children, pumping her chubby little legs as fast as she could. "Tain! Ink!" she shrilled, laughing when she fell. She picked herself up, squealing with excitement, and waited for them to bridge the gap.

"Hey, kiddos!" She and Linq suffered an onslaught of boisterous greetings and hugs. Seth, Molly, and Dylan, ranging from ages nine to five, kept close on their heels as they walked toward the back garden. Etain scooped the smallest of the four into her arms. "Hi, Tegan. You've gotten so big."

"Tain," she giggled, taking Etain's face into her small hands. "Me miss you."

"I missed you, too," Molly yelled. "You didn't say 'bye."

"I'm sorry, Molly. It wasn't that I didn't want to see you." She stroked the little girl's soft brown hair. "You know, you have a new uncle. His name is Dar."

Molly's blue eyes lit up. "Mama says he's handsome."

"Ugh, girls," Seth grumbled, making a face. "Da says he's a great warrior and has two black swords. Can I see them, Auntie Tain? Can I?"

His little brother joined in the chant. "Me, too. Please? Can we? Can we?"

Inferno walked up. "Good to see you back. Spirit's in the kitchen." He took Tegan from Etain's arms and set her on the ground. "Get on, kiddies. Take the hounds with ya."

Seth frowned. "But, Da."

"It's getting dark. Time to get ready for bed."

"They just got here," Seth argued.

"Get to it, boy. There'll be plenty of time to talk over breakfast."

The children grumbled amongst themselves as they stomped toward the house.

Inferno waited until the small army of imps disappeared around the corner. "Where's Dar?"

"Can we get inside?" Etain rubbed her arms. "It's chilly out here."

In the kitchen, Spirit gave Etain and Linq a hug and offered each a whiskey to warm their insides, then led the way to the living room.

Inferno followed, a mug of ale in his hand. "Why'd ya not send news of yer coming? I'd of met ya in me Hummer and saved ya the walk."

Linq answered before Etain could. "One of us has a new task and is hell-bent on seeing it through as soon as possible."

Etain's eye roll ended with a glare as she sat on the sofa. Linq's grin confirmed his strategic move, both knowing it would set Inferno on the warpath.

"Task?"

May as well get it over with. "To find my brother."

Inferno sputtered ale from his mouth. "Yer brother?" Using the back of his hand, he swiped at the golden beads in his beard. "Fucking hell."

Etain wrapped both hands around her glass. "They say he lives not far from here."

"They?" he echoed, swatting at the dribble down his shirt.

"The Queen of the Elves and her wizards." Etain kept an eye on him, hoping things wouldn't go downhill.

"Damn Elves. They couldn't tell ya this five years ago?" He raised a brow at the only Elf in the room.

"We thought Etain knew he was alive but chose not to search him out because of the circumstances."

Inferno emitted a disgruntled snort. "Could ya not ask? Do ya have any idea how this girl's suffered thinking her whole family was dead?"

Etain tried not to smile. Things were working to her advantage rather than the Elf's. "There's more to it."

"Not much goes on with the Elves he isn't in the middle of," he said, jerking his mug at Linq, sloshing what little ale remained. "There's no excuse for keepin' ya in the dark all this time."

Etain ran a hand through her hair. "You should sit down."

"For fuck's sake. What else?"

"Love," Spirit said, "let the girl talk. It's best to know what we're up against rather than going off half-cocked."

"Ain't nothing half about me cock." He set the mug down and crossed his arms over his chest. "And I'm damn happy to stand."

"Then stand." Etain downed the rest of her whiskey, stood, and walked around to the back of the sofa, strategically placing it and its twin between her and Inferno. "The night my parents were murdered, Robert told me to run, so I ran. At first, he was behind me."

Visions raced through her head, her parents cut down before her eyes and her brother's attempts to drag her out of the car. She remembered the evil threatening to blast her head apart and how she ended up running for her life. The whiskey warm in her belly gave her the courage to continue. "Since he didn't come for me, I thought the assassin killed him too."

"Hmph."

"Where's he been all this time?" Spirit asked.

Etain gazed into the eyes burning into her. *He knows it's not good.* "He took him instead." She bit her lip, unable to say more.

Linq sighed. "The boy was taken to Midir."

Inferno's glare gravitated to the Elf. "Are ya bloody daft, man?" He stormed around the sofas toward Etain, who moved a safe distance away. "After all we've been through. After all *you've* been through. I'm tellin' ya, lass. Leave him be. It won't be the reunion yer hoping for."

"He's my brother. I don't give a damn where he's been. He's the only family I have left."

"I suppose yer wanting to bring this soddin' brother into me home?" Her silence angered him further. "Goddamn it, Etain! For once, think of someone besides yerself! Children live here and not just ours. What about me clan and their families?"

The children rushed in, cheeks rosy, dressed for bed and full of stories.

"We saw a rabbit, Da!"

"Tegan saw it first."

Molly giggled. "Seth and Dylan tried to catch it."

Tegan laughed and danced around, singing, "Me first! Me first! My wabbit!"

The scowl on Inferno's face melted into smiles for his children.

Seth frowned. "The rabbit got away."

Spirit laughed. "Then we'll have to make do with pot roast for tea tomorrow."

Molly sidled up to Etain and grasped her hand. "Mum, can we stay up for a little while? Please?"

The other three echoed her plea.

"Ya wee devils," Inferno said. "Not tonight. We have grown up things to discuss. They'll be here in the morning. Ya can talk then."

With the children tucked in their beds, Inferno revisited the previous conversation about Etain's brother. "What does Dar have to say about this?"

She sat on the edge of the sofa and shot a sideways glance at the Elf before she met Inferno's gaze. "Dar's busy with other things."

"He doesn't know, does he?" Inferno barked, the color rising in his face "Why am I not surprised?"

From the opposite sofa, Spirit leaned forward and placed a hand on Etain's knee. "How is he?"

She did her best to ignore the looming threat at Spirit's side. "Not well. Midir haunts him with his twisted lies. I hope the Elves can help."

Worry lines creased Spirit's forehead. "Was leaving him the right thing to do?"

"I don't know." Etain stared at the flames ablaze in the fireplace. "Alatariel thought it best. My being there seemed to make him worse."

"I hope she's right, lass." Spirit tilted her head to catch her eye. "No matter what they may think, you're a comfort to him. If she's wrong, things could go bad for everyone."

Etain met her gaze. "I have to believe we're doing what's best for him. In the meantime, I intend to find my brother."

Inferno looked ready to burst out of his skin. "What is it ya need me to do?"

Relieved by his resignation, Etain told him of her plans to take Dar's scimitars with her and the need of a scabbard to carry both blades. "The one he has fits him but it's too large for me. Can you make something I can strap across my back and be serviceable for Dar afterwards?"

Inferno rubbed his chin. "Won't the fancy sword he made for ya be enough or are ya expecting trouble?"

"No one even knows we're going except the people in this room and the queen. There shouldn't be any problems."

"Mmm, hmm." He moved toward the fireplace. "I wonder at the need to take his blades at all. They'll be safe enough here."

Etain watched him walk around the room. Should she tell him the truth or give him an excuse about how persnickety Dar was with his swords? The concern in his eyes made her decision. "I'm not taking them as protection. They'll make me feel closer to Dar."

She expected laughter and a snarky comeback, but her admission seemed to have the opposite effect on the man.

"I'll do some sketches before bed. It'll take a few days to construct it." He returned to his wife and motioned her to move over. "Ya said yer brother's not far. Where is he?"

"Deudraeth," said Linq, who leaned against the door jamb. "I think going the back way would work to our advantage."

"Aye," Inferno agreed. "I'll lend ya a couple of me best horses." He leaned back, crossing his arms. "Where does that leave Dar?"

"It leaves him to get well. I don't need him to find my brother."

"No, just his blades," he mumbled. "Ya'd be better off going back to yer boyfriend and let this brother of yers be." He turned on the Elf. "And you encouraging her."

Linq shrugged. "Who am I to tell her no? Dar would have my head if I let her go alone."

"If *I* don't do it first, damn Elf."

Unable to sit any longer, Etain stood and walked around to the back of the sofa. "Inferno, Alatariel said it would be best if I left, so I did. I can't sit around doing nothing."

The man exploded off his seat. "Ya could go home, girl, and forget this madness."

"To Faux and Freeblood?" She threw her hands in the air. "No, thank you! I'd end up killing them both."

Inferno's face turned red. "I meant *your* home in Texas. Get away from the Alamir for a while."

"My brother is *here* in the Alamir realm. Dar will come *here* when he leaves Nunnehi. This is my life, Inferno. I won't run from it."

Inferno huffed and cleared his throat. "Stay with us. Help with the clan and the kids until he shows up."

"I have to find my brother."

They stared at one another for an interminable moment. Inferno scrubbed his face with his hands and blew out a long breath. "Aye. I hear what ya say, lass," he conceded. "It's a bloody bad idea. But if yer determined to walk into a snake pit, it's down to me to see yer ready."

After an early breakfast, Etain grabbed one of Spirit's cloaks and wandered into the back garden turned frosty faerieland overnight. The cup of hot tea in her hands helped keep her warm as she walked down to the forge where she found Inferno and Linq leaning over a messy stack of papers. Upon her approach, Inferno shoved sheets of rough drawings under her nose. She set down her cup and made a quick study of the design.

"This is amazing, Inferno."

"Isn't all me. The Elf here made a few improvements."

She grabbed her cup and moved to the side. The men returned to their work, heating metal, hammering, and bending it to their will, sometimes arguing over this and that, then shoving the piece into a barrel of water and starting over again.

Halfway through the process, a soot-smeared Inferno turned to her. "Lass, would ya get the blades?"

"Sure. Be right back." She faded in a blue shimmer.

In the bedroom they shared at Laugharne, a flood of memories rushed in. How safe she felt cradled in Dar's strong arms. She closed her eyes remembering the warm touch of his fingers as they trailed over her skin. "I'll have you back soon."

She found the black-bladed scimitars at the side of the bed in their leather scabbards. "Come with me, my pretties."

Back at the forge, she handed the swords to Inferno. The men became absorbed in their task to the exclusion of all else, including Etain. She lost herself in the hypnotic repetition of their work and soon felt her eyes droop. Rather than give into the urge for a nap, she headed into the house to see what distractions Spirit could offer.

Etain sent Seth and Molly off to school, helped Dylan and Tegan get dressed, and threw herself into menial household chores to keep her mind off the interminable wait for Inferno and Linq. It wasn't until the grandfather clock struck one that she realized the morning had come and gone. After lunch, Etain lay the little ones down for an afternoon nap to give Spirit her own quiet time, and returned to the forge.

She found Linq trussed up in leather straps crisscrossed over his chest. Inferno carefully inserted the swords into leather sheaths on the Elf's back. "How's it feel?"

Linq shifted the weight on his shoulders.

Inferno beamed at Etain's approach. "Look, lass. We've done it."

She circled the Elf, inspecting their handiwork. "What happened to the metal piece you were working on?"

Inferno shrugged. "We whittled it down to links and reworked the leather of what Dar had. Ya can link 'em together to carry on yer back or sling 'em on yer hip."

She eyed the dual hilts peeking over each shoulder. "Is it comfortable?"

"Takes getting used to but I can move easy enough." Linq flexed his arms and twisted his body.

Inferno waved at him. "Draw the swords."

He reached for both hilts at the same time. "It takes practice but once you have the feel for how they move, you are good. Inferno, there is a drag on the lower scabbard."

"Hmm. Take it off and we'll fiddle with it."

Etain held the swords as Linq unstrapped the leather belts. "Perhaps you should let me try it on before you change anything. I'm gonna be the one wearing it."

"Aye, guess I got carried away. Sorry, lass." She handed him the blades. "I hope the two won't be too heavy for ya."

"You will need to get accustomed to the extra weight but as they are scimitars, it should not be difficult." Linq showed her where the two scabbards linked together. "You see? I think Dar will like the design as well." He helped her strap on the dual scabbards and tightened the leather straps across her chest.

Inferno handed her one scimitar. "Pull the leather up a bit and slide the blade in." After one was situated, he handed her the other.

"They aren't as heavy as I'd expected," she said, adjusting the straps, and waving her arms as she twisted and turned. "Wow. This is great!"

"Is the weight too much?"

"Not bad." She rolled her shoulders.

"Drawing the swords is tricky," Linq said.

She grabbed both hilts and tried to draw at the same time. One hit her in the head and the other stuck halfway in the sheath. "You aren't kidding."

"Now you know what to watch for." Linq moved closer. "For the moment, work with one sword at a time."

She wrapped her hand around the right hilt and drew the sword easily. "I feel so cool."

Linq crossed his arms. "Now sheath it."

She licked her lips taking hold of the leather, and slid the sword into the scabbard. The men exchanged a satisfied nod.

"Keep practicing, Etain. At this stage, you may not be able to draw both at the same time."

She drew the blade to her left. "It's awkward. I don't use my left hand so much." She sheathed the sword and tried again. After a few practice draws, it came much easier.

Linq stepped back. "Try both now"

She took hold of the hilts, but her movements were clunky.

"Take yer time, lass. Get the moves right. We can work on yer speed after."

The three worked late into the afternoon, watching her draw the swords and sheath them time and again, making adjustments as needed. In time, her delivery became smoother but drawing the two still gave her trouble.

"I doubt you will need both at the same time, Etain." Linq helped her unstrap the leather belts. "If you need them at all."

"Thanks, y'all."

"Just a few finishing touches and she'll be sorted." Inferno took the scabbards from the Elf. "How about you help Unknown tend to yer horses?"

Her brows lifted. "Unknown?"

"A new recruit," he said, too busy checking the scabbards to look at her. "Got him working the stables for now."

She smiled. It was Inferno's method of initiation for every "newb" who wanted to join the clan. Depending on how they handled the job and the duties, they were either accepted or rejected. If accepted, Inferno assigned them wherever he saw fit.

"I think I'll take Razz. You have any preference, Linq?"

"Blackjack."

"Sorted." She chuckled and headed to the stables.

The smell of sweet hay mixed with the tang of manure made her smile. Not only did the mucking out of the stables serve as an initiation, it was also Inferno's favorite punishment for recalcitrant clan members and children, but Etain never saw it as such. A secret she kept to herself. For her, it was an opportunity to escape a confusing world, to make sense of things around her. Despite the love and compassion shown by Inferno and Spirit, her future remained uncertain. *Today is all I have,* became her mantra.

But now her life was different.

Blackjack, a large black stallion, whinnied at her entrance. "*Prynhawn da,* Blackjack," she greeted, grabbing an apple from a bucket outside his stall. "How are you this fine day?" He snorted before accepting the gift, allowing the human to rub his nose. "Handsome as ever."

With another apple in hand, she moved to the next stall to greet her favorite, Razz. "*Prynhawn da,* Razz. How's my beautiful girl?" The mare nuzzled her hair and snorted, making Etain laugh. "Here. I have a treat for you too."

She took her time in brushing each one, all the while chatting in a soft voice, getting familiar with them again. Unknown, a young man of average height with red hair and blue eyes, showed up a short time later and helped her choose a saddle and blanket for each mount. These were set aside, ready for the morning. Together, they fed and watered the horses. Once done, Etain bid the new recruit and the horses a good night.

In the kitchen, Spirit and Etain prepared tea for the children. No one mentioned the absence of the men, but the boys squirmed and fidgeted through the entire meal. After an ordeal of overstuffed mouths, spilled milk, and general chaos, Seth and Dylan scampered around the kitchen behind their mother as she prepared food for their da and Linq. With the goodies tucked safely into a large picnic basket, the boys carried it out to the forge excited to see the famous black swords of their new uncle.

Meanwhile, the girls worked together to prepare provisions for the trip to Deudraeth.

"How long will you be on the road?" Spirit asked, wrapping each sandwich in its own square of paper, and handing them to Molly to place in a bag.

Etain stepped out of the pantry, arms loaded with bottles of water, followed by a helpful Tegan with sweeties in hand. "Linq says if we leave early tomorrow and take short breaks, we can be in Deudraeth by the evening of the following day."

"It's been a while since you traveled rough. Are you up for such a trip?" Spying her youngest covered in chocolate, Spirit stopped what she was doing and scooped the little girl into her arms. "Ya wee monkey." She set her on the countertop.

"Ummy, choc-co-wat." Tegan smacked her lips, giggling as she tried to avoid the wet cloth in her mum's hand.

"I can understand why you're not using your shimmer, Etain." Spirit grabbed at a chocolate-covered hand. "Tegan, lass, you're surely your father's child. Give me your hand." She caught the little culprit with the warm cloth. "Gotcha!" Spirit made a funny face as she wiped the hand clean, making the small girl giggle more. "Why not use the Hummer and get it over with?" Her exasperation with her daughter faded into laughter. "What am I to do with ya?" She lifted her up, planted a kiss on her chubby cheek, and set her on the floor.

Etain lowered her voice to a conspiratorial whisper. "According to Linq, we must be covert." The girls laughed at their auntie. Etain grinned and gave them a wink. "Besides, you know if there's any magic in use the Hummer will be useless."

Spirit snorted her opinion. "You're havin' a laugh. You may as well ride in on top of a flamin' pink caravan, neon lights a'flashin'." She pranced around the kitchen. "Oooo, pay no mind to me. I'm just yer average silver-haired, six-foot Amazon on holiday with me friend." She put a hand to the side of her mouth. "Who just so happens to be an Elf." She stopped in front of the girls. "Y'all like me pretty swords?" Spirit pulled the pretend weapons from her back, putting her all into a Texan accent. "Would y'all like me to show ya how they work? A Krymerian chieftain showed me the proper way to use 'em."

Molly and Tegan giggled at their mum's silly show. Etain envisioned the scene and wandered out of the kitchen, lost in thought as she walked to her room.

To the North

E tain awoke mid-morning. "Damn." Angry with herself for missing breakfast and sending the children off to school, she dressed and dashed downstairs. *Sleeping like I have all day.* She hustled into the kitchen to find it empty. Afraid Linq left without her, she rushed out the back door to the forge. As she neared, she heard voices but didn't see anyone.

"Hello? Inferno? Linq?" A scruffy-headed Inferno leaned out from behind the forge, which she noticed was not in use today. He clambered to his feet as the Elf peered over the top, eyes full of merriment. "What're y'all up to?" she asked, skeptical of their present mental state. Linq stood up next to his collaborator. "Where's Spirit?"

Inferno's face glowed. "She's gone to town for a spell and took the wee ones with her. She'll be back afore ya leave."

"Why didn't someone wake me? You knew I wanted to get an early start."

"You needed the sleep, and we needed the extra time." Linq damn near giggled.

She looked from one to the other. "Time for what?"

"For this." Inferno presented her with the scabbard complete with a new sigil.

Her fingers caressed the leather surface. "It's exquisite."

"Aye. We talked about it last night and got up at dawn. It took a little ingenuity to get 'em right but, bloody hell, we did it."

"And a fine job we did."

"Yes. You bloody well did." She grinned.

Each sheath carried its own sigil. Day Star's matched the mark she shared with Dar, the flaming sun. Burning Heart bore the VonNeshta crest, a flame surrounded by a crown of swords. Affixed to the metal between the leather sheaths was an emblem she'd not seen before - a flaming sun linked with a crown of swords. "What is this?"

Linq grinned. "Your family sigil."

Her eyes widened in admiration. "Y'all have outdone yourselves."

"Let's try it one more time." Inferno handed her the scabbards.

With the black leather straps crossed over her chest and around her waist, the twin scimitars angled over each shoulder. "The fit seems better."

"We trimmed the straps. Not too much." Linq chuckled. "It still has to work for Dar."

She grasped the hilts and cleanly drew both blades. After a twirl of each one, she tucked them away. "Thank you so much."

"Looks like ya got the hang of 'em." Inferno shrugged as he rearranged a few tools. "Go get yerself ready. Spirit should be home soon. Said she had something for ya, so don't leave until she gets here."

"I will saddle the horses, milady." Linq tipped his head. "We can leave upon Spirit's return."

As he walked away, Etain held back. "Inferno, have you had a change of heart about Dar?"

"For that demon?" he blustered, but his features softened. "He's a good man with good intentions, though it doesn't always appear so. I can see the love between ya and can't begrudge yer happiness."

She hugged him. "You're a king in your own right, Inferno of Laugharne, and I love ya for it."

"Ah, be off with ya now." He shooed her to the house. "I love ya, too, lass."

Not long after, Etain heard a vehicle pull into the courtyard and stepped out the front door. At the same time, Linq walked up with the horses behind him. Spirit jumped out of the Hummer and walked straight to her, taking her hand, "Come with me," and led her into the house. Just inside the door, Spirit presented her with a small vial.

"What's this?"

"Tis a glamour. Before you go into town, sprinkle it over you and no one will be the wiser of who you are."

Etain stared at the tiny bottle.

"You must say these words as the dust lands over you, *see me not as I am but who I wish to be.*"

"See me not as I am but who I wish to be."

"Good luck." Spirit hugged her tightly. "Come home safe."

"I will."

The women returned to the courtyard. Hugs and farewells exchanged, Etain eased up into the saddle. "We shouldn't be gone long. We'll bring the horses back, and I'll head home with my brother." She hesitated and looked beyond the outer wall, her heart heavy. With a sigh, her eyes went to Inferno. "If Dar shows up before we get back..." Razz impatiently stamped her hooves, testing the reins. "Tell him I have his blades and to go home. Let him know Linq is with me." Etain swallowed hard and forced a smile. "I love y'all. See you soon."

After two days of hard riding, Etain and Linq set up camp a few miles outside Deudraeth. A secluded cave near the *Scwd yr Eira Falls* proved the perfect base. Once unloaded, Etain built a fire while Linq hobbled the horses and toted the saddles into the cave, laying one on either side of the small space. thn They shared the last of their food and ale while they chatted about the next day.

"I'll go into town in the morning for supplies." Etain clinked her bottle to his and enjoyed a long drink. "Not much, just enough for a couple days. You okay with that?"

Linq took a drink before he answered. "I think you best be careful, milady. Remember the *Bok* we saw a few miles back."

"Do you really think they'd be interested in us?"

"I am sure word has spread of Dar's quarrel with his High Council. Couple it with news of him going to Nunnehi and I think they would like nothing more than to capture the High Lord's new love interest and use her to bring him to his knees."

"I didn't realize the *Bok* were such gossip mongers. Most of the Alamir act like he doesn't exist."

"I would venture to say most Alamir do not *know* he exists." He added more wood to the fire. "For good reason. However, the same cannot be said for other realms. There are those who love him, but more would prefer him in chains or dead."

She considered his words as she bit into a piece of bread. "Okay, so the bad people have nothing better to do than obsess over Dar. But if he's not here with me, who's to know who I am?"

He lifted a brow. "Let us follow your line of thinking. A tall blonde with dual black scimitars not to mention the VonNeshta family crest emblazoned on her back. Not *too* much of a giveaway."

She jumped up, her cheeks hot, and stalked out of the cave.

"Etain," Linq called after her. "I was not trying to..."

She stormed to the river's edge. Razz whinnied and Blackjack snorted his displeasure. "Sorry, y'all." She gave each a soothing pat.

Linq wasn't far behind her. "Etain, I am sorry. It was not my intent to embarrass you."

"I'm not angry with you. I'm mad at myself. Spirit pretty much said the same thing." Etain stroked Razz's black mane unable to meet Linq's gaze. "I *do* pay attention." She leaned her head against the strong neck of the mare. "No wonder he's in such a dither, as Alatariel would say. I fell in love with my soul mate without a thought as to who he was or the ramifications of his being involved with an impulsive half-wit."

Linq grabbed her by the arm and turned her to face him. "Impulsive, aye, but far from a half-wit. Love is one thing no one can control, not even a two-hundred-year-old Krymerian." The frown on her face prompted him to release his iron grip. "Sorry. There is nothing like losing yourself in another person, especially when they return the love."

Rubbing her arm, she gave him a small smile. "Even for a wise old Elf?"

He turned toward the water. "You control what you can." He glanced back and tapped his head. "You have to use your brain. Tap into the common sense I know comes as second nature."

"You have to know I would never let anyone use me against Dar. I'd take my life first."

"Let us talk about tomorrow." He cocked his head toward the cave. She walked with him as he outlined a simple plan. "You go into town *without* Dar's swords." He paused, waiting for a rebuttal. When she said nothing, he carried on. "You can pick up supplies while I mingle with the locals."

Back in the cave, they sat across from each other. "Tell me about your brother. What do you remember?"

She closed her eyes. "Dark hair, green eyes. He was tall for his age, about six feet, maybe more." Her hands spanned out. "Broad shoulders. He looked a bit gangly because he hadn't grown into his body yet. The girls didn't seem to mind. They noticed him everywhere he went. He could've been a football player, but he liked wrestling."

"How long has it been since you last saw him?"

She placed a hand over her heart and watched the flames dance. "Not since the night our parents died, so about five years."

"How old would he be now?"

Etain sniffled. "That's where it gets complicated." His brows came together in an inquisitive arch. She cleared her throat, swiping at her eyes. "I was fourteen. He was two years older than me."

"So, twenty-one?"

"The night I lost my family, I left my world at fourteen and stepped into the Alamir a few years older. If the same happened to Robert, he's probably closer to twenty-six. He loved the outdoors, so I expect he'll be in pretty good shape."

Linq scratched his chin in thought. "It gives me something to work with. Are you clear on what to do tomorrow?"

"Get supplies and come back here."

"Right. The less time you spend in town, the better. Did you bring a cloak?" She glanced at her pack. "Keep the hood over your head. There are not many women with your hair color and none as tall as you. The weather is cool, so it should not raise suspicions."

"I'm aware, which is why I brought it." Her curt reply had no effect on the Elf.

He stretched out on the cave floor, using his saddle as a pillow. "Try not to talk too much." He yawned and turned his back to her. "I do not know if people are aware you have a Texan accent. Best not chance it."

"Bloody hell. I could speak in the tongue of the wee folk," she quipped in a sarcastic Irish lilt. "Do ya think I'd be safe enough to market on me own then?" She waited for a response. "Linq?"

A light snore drifted toward her. "Damn Elf." She shifted her saddle and settled down for a night's sleep.

Dar dropped into a chair in front of the fireplace, tossed his boots aside, and leaned back, staring into the fire. *Why did you leave me alone here?* Memories of the past few days stole the Krymerian from the present. A warm flush washed through him, remembering their brief time at *Sôlskin*. "My heart tells me you are true, yet my mind..."

This is foolishness. I must clear my head.

He jammed his feet into his boots again and made his way through the hallways toward the palace courtyard. The magnificence and beauty of the palace always proved a delight. Perhaps it would take his mind off darker thoughts. Dar nodded to those he passed, pleased to feel in control of himself again, hopeful for a reunion with his wife soon.

Women dressed in silken robes of muted blues and greens refused to acknowledge his presence. Men in uniforms glowered as he passed. Others clothed in everyday raiment did their best to ignore the seven-foot menace. Despite the adverse reactions, no one seemed in a hurry, yet he felt they had somewhere to be. A few were seated on white marble benches, each one carved and polished to a high sheen. He noted the placement of guards throughout the palace.

Are there more guards than usual?

Dar felt like a pariah amongst the pure. Despite Alatariel's command it stay within the room, it was evident news of what happened earlier in the day had spread. He was not surprised. The gossip was too juicy not to share.

It was not the first time he had been considered undesirable and he knew it would not be the last. Instead of dwelling on it, he turned his thoughts to the beauty around him. No matter how many times he walked the halls of *Modertræ*, the sheer size of the palace proper astounded him. Hallways and passages stretched in every direction, her wide, airy stairways leading to areas Dar had not yet visited. Statues of naked Elves in proud and symbolic postures carved from polished stone adorned the halls and stair landings. A few of the statues even dwarfed Dar in size.

He wandered aimlessly for most of the day until he came across a set of large, heavy glass doors leading into a secluded courtyard at the center of the palace. The private gardens of the queen. A simple command, "*Opna mér,*" opened the doors.

Lush trees shaded paths of crushed stone with borders kissed by an array of jewel-like flowers. Fountains sculpted in the image of great waterfalls from every realm graced the outer walls, their clear waters cascading in curtains of liquid sunshine. He admired each fountain but paused at one, intrigued by the exotic fish darting about.

His eyes roamed to a darker portion of the pool where a lone black angelfish lurked in the shadows. Delicate fins flowed about its body, a black cape rippling in the wind. Dar swore it kept watch over the other fish, ready to pounce and destroy any stranger who dared enter its underwater world. After a time, he noticed none of the others approached the lone sentry. He viewed it as a show of respect rather than fear.

To see if his assumptions were correct, Dar poked a finger into the pool near a school of small fish. As they scattered, the angelfish charged out with a vicious brutality that belied its beauty. The tiny warrior held its ground, willing to fight on behalf of its charges' safety.

"We have much in common, my small friend." He withdrew his finger. "Forever watching from the shadows, determined to protect the innocent." Not sure if it would work, he sent a message to the feisty little fish gliding back and forth.

Most noble warrior, I bow to you in defeat. In honor of your bravery, I withdraw from the field of battle and leave you to your watch.

The small guardian stopped. Dar was certain the fish stared at him in contemplation. The angelfish circled several times, apparently as a warning. Seemingly satisfied with the intruder's retreat, it turned and swam back to its dark corner.

The defeated warrior moved to the next fountain and watched another school of fish dart back and forth. He tried to remember the happy moments in his past, times without the chaos of anger or battles, and realized happiness had been seldom in his life.

His children were his most joyful memories. The games they played and the sound of their laughter. Thanks to Midir, those days were lost forever.

They died simply because of who their father was. His bloodline was doomed to suffer the same fate as all the VonNeshtas, yet he dared to hope the generation he gave birth to would find peace. As painful as it was to remember his children, a new kernel of hope sparked in his heart. Perhaps the child Faux carried would break the curse.

With tear-filled eyes, he lay his hand over the mark on his chest. It represented the happiest days of his life. The trip into town with Etain, the dance they shared, the warmth he felt in his heart when she sang for him, her quirks, her love, her smell. *She is my angel.*

Two loud voices calling his name shook him from his reverie. Elfin and Wolfe pushed through the glass doors headed straight for him. Before they were too close, he wiped the tears from his face.

"I'm here."

Wolfe stopped short. "By all that's holy, man. Queen Alatariel has the whole palace searching for you. Are you all right?"

He cleared his throat and smiled. "I am well. I don't understand why the queen is worried."

"Well, let us think on it for a moment." Elfin stroked his chin, eyeing Dar as though he were a person of lesser intelligence. "If threatening the queen's life was not enough." He counted on his fingers as he continued. "One, we have a dead wizard. Two, there are other wizards who, although not dead, *are* in the infirmary. Three—"

Dar raised his hands. "I get the idea. Thank you for your eloquence. I will not ask from where you have heard all this." He caught the uncomfortable sideways glance exchanged between them. "To put your minds at ease, I have been reacquainting myself with the beauty of this incredible place."

Wolfe grinned. "Massively incredible." He jabbed Elfin in the ribs and sidestepped to avoid a responding jab. "The queen would like you to join her for dinner. She was concerned when you didn't return to your room, considering what's happened. You know..." He lowered his voice. "The stuff we're not supposed to know about."

Dar deadpanned from one to the other. "I would prefer to be alone tonight. Please convey my apologies to the queen and give her my regards. She will understand."

"With the utmost respect, Dar," started Elfin.

"She will understand," he repeated.

The young men grinned at each other. "We're no Miss Manners," Wolfe quipped.

Shaking his head, Elfin placed his hands on his hips. "Not even the Mister."

"We best let her know you aren't coming." Wolfe turned to the doors. "Feel better, Dar."

Elfin held back. "You go on and give the queen the message, Wolfe. I want to talk to Dar."

"Sure. Catch you at dinner. See ya, Dar."

"Wolfe."

Elfin watched him leave, and turned to the High Lord. "I know this is none of my business, but I am going to say it anyway."

Dar shifted on his feet, interested in what the Elf had to say.

"No *one* person can save the world. Not even a Krymerian. We all have times when we need help."

"This is not about me trying to save the world."

"Then our part of it. You have friends who are more than willing to help including your amazing lady. You should not push everyone away."

He appreciated his sincerity. "Too many have been hurt because of their association with me."

"You and me, we believe in the same things. Inferno and all the others too. You may be the only Krymerian, but you are not alone. Nor are you responsible for our destinies. We each choose our own fate. Whatever happens to us is because of the choices *we* make. It is not up to you."

Elfin may think he lifted a weight from his shoulders, but it was too deeply ingrained in him. "Thank you for your honesty. I know what you say is right, but some things are impossible to change."

"You need to relax. I find when I am stressed, a good workout in the ring helps." Encouraged by Dar's attention, he rambled on. "Wolfe and I have been invited to spar with the Black Blades. Join us. I am sure they would not mind one more."

Dar crossed his arms over his chest and scrubbed his knuckles along his jaw. "After today, I am not so sure."

"If they have a problem with it, you can spar with us. We love a challenge."

"It will not be the same without my blades, but I could make do. Nunnehi has a well-stocked armory. I will think about it."

"Good. I will see you in the morning."

"Good night, Elfin, and thank you for speaking your mind."

A few hours later, a knock on his door interrupted his quiet solitude. Dar opened to a cart laden with food and drink surrounded by a sea of smiling faces.

"Good evening, High Lord." Alatariel pushed her way into the room.

"Good evening, Your Grace." He leaned out the door and saw what appeared to be the entire Elven community spread from one end of the hall to the other. "What's all this?"

Trident bowed his head as he stepped past him. "We are family here, milord. Family does not allow family to eat alone."

Dar moved aside to allow the cart to be wheeled into his room. "I thought I was relegated to black sheep status."

One by one, the citizens of Nunnehi, each with a plate, cup, and eating utensils in hand, filed into his room. When space ran short, they continued to squeeze in, spilling out the door and into the hall. Wolfe and Elfin, plates proudly displayed, were in the mix of smiling faces.

A tug on his arm found him peering into Alatariel's emerald eyes. "Now is not the time to be left on your own. Let us be here for you." She turned to a woman at her side. "Dar, this is Moira, Shalen's partner." The queen motioned to a boy and a girl who looked to be in their mid-teens. "And these are their children, Garrick and Renme. They wanted to be here for you."

His heart swelled. Elfin had been straight with him and now this. From the first moment he came to Nunnehi so many turns ago, these precious people accepted him as one of their own. Even now, after all the damage inflicted and the trouble he caused, they gathered around him in support. *How is it I ever considered myself alone?*

He lay a hand over his heart and bowed his head. "My deepest apologies—"

Moira touched his arm. "High Lord, apologies are not required. Our gracious queen explained the circumstances and what prompted your role in Shalen's passing." She paused, her bottom lip quivering. Garrick and Renme gathered around their mother. "Forgive me, High Lord. Although I understand we are all victims in this tragedy, my heart is broken." Her tearful gaze met his. "Mourn his loss, but do not take on the responsibility of his death. That weight does not belong on your shoulders."

Dar lay a hand over hers, tears burning his eyes. "*Þú heiður mig, milady. Megi guðdómurinn blessa þig fyrir alla daga þína* (You honor me, milady. May the goddess bless you for all your days)." He gave her hand a comforting squeeze. The forgiveness afforded him lifted his heart and his mood. He turned to the others. "I believe we are going to need a few more chairs."

DEUDRAETH

After a breakfast of grilled trout and cold spring water, Etain saddled Razz in preparation for her trip into Deudraeth. Once she was in the saddle, Linq handed her the Elven cloak. Spinning it through the air, she draped it over her shoulders and fastened the silver clasp at her neck.

"Remember to keep your words short, your hood up, and be quick about it. You let me deal with finding information about your brother. Once we locate him, there will be plenty for you to do."

"Aye, aye, captain." Etain pulled the hood over her head and nudged Razz.

Well away from the campsite, she veered off the main path into the shelter of the tree line and dismounted. She reached into one of the saddlebags, her fingers touching on everything inside except the item she needed.

"Figures." Ready to give up, she finally came across the small vial given to her by Spirit. "Aha! Found you." She held it up in the sunlight and marveled at its glittering contents of red, purple, and orange. "What a pretty spell." She poured a small amount into the palm of her hand. "No need to worry, Linq. This little glamour will keep my identity quite safe."

She tossed the magic into the air and turned around and around, saying the words as instructed while the sparkles showered over her. "See me not as I am but who I wish to be." She looked down her body. "Hmm, nothing's changed. Maybe I said the words wrong."

Spirit's instructions rang in her head as she reached into the saddlebag again. Eyes closed, she held the mirror in front of her face. One blue eye opened to see a violet one looking back at her. Her bottom lip between her teeth, she slightly moved the mirror and saw brilliant copper curls with a light splattering of freckles across the bridge of her nose.

"I say, Lady Etain. You're rather foxy."

For curiosity's sake, she moved the mirror down her body. The white gauze shirt was now pale green and her leathers black denim. The cloak remained unchanged.

She shifted the mirror to her left hand. The Tiffany Stone on her right remained unchanged and her nails appeared longer and painted black. "Way to go, Spirit." Etain laughed. One more check showed her no change in her sword. "I guess the magic can only do so much. I must tuck you away, my beautiful blade." She removed *Nim'Na'Sharr* from her hip and placed it in the pack behind the saddle.

Twenty minutes later, the copper-haired vixen rode into the village. Although the town boasted modern conveniences, the townspeople paid homage to their ancestors by keeping the village as close to original as possible. Light posts now powered by electricity lined the main roads. Cobblestone streets ran between whitewashed Tudor buildings. Except for the clothing worn by the people she passed, Etain felt as though she'd stepped back in time.

The warm fragrance of freshly baked bread lured her down one charming street. With Razz tethered in an area set aside for such use, she wove between displays of fragrant produce. Apples, bananas, mangos... Every fruit and vegetable imaginable made her mouth water. A basket on her arm, she chose a little of each, and entered the store. The shop owner greeted her with a huge smile. She purchased a fresh loaf of bread and a block of hard cheese to go along with the fruit, and remembered to pick up a few bottles of ale.

Etain asked the owner about a local apothecary. She happily gave Etain directions to the shop located in the next block. "Whatever you need, it'll be the best of the best. Bert's proud of his stock, he is, and keeps it fresh."

Since she wasn't familiar with the layout of the town, she returned to Razz, slipped the bags over the pommel, and followed the directions given to her. True to her word, the apothecary was on the far corner.

Inside the shop, Etain breathed in the exotic smells of spice, incense, and scented candles, giving her eyes time to adjust to the dimness. A dark-haired young man behind the counter welcomed her into the shop.

"Welcome, milady. How may I help you?"

"Are you Bert?"

"No, miss. I am Piran, his assistant. Do you know Bert?"

"Nice to meet you, Piran. No, I've not had pleasure. The lady at the market mentioned his name." She fumbled for the paper in her pocket as she approached the counter. "Do you have damiana?"

His head bobbed as he perused the list. "Yes, fresh in this morning. I believe we have everything on your list. If you'll excuse me, I'll get your order together."

Floor-to-ceiling shelves containing bottles, jars, and boxes in an array of colors lined the wall. A rolling ladder affixed to a track gave easy access to the items stored up high. Etain watched the clerk search the rows of bottles on display behind the long glass counter.

"This is a lovely shop. Have you worked here long?"

Busy in his search, he spoke over his shoulder. "A few weeks. Bert's great." He jumped down from the ladder. "Took me in when I had nowhere to go; gave me a job. He even gave me my name."

She thought it odd and apparently her expression told him so.

He chuckled. "I'm sorry, miss. I tend to talk too much. Bert keeps telling me I need to be careful. Seems like I lost more than my memory."

His admission piqued her interest. "You've lost your memory? How awful."

"It's not so bad. Bert watches out for me."

"He sounds like a generous person."

"Yes, miss. I'll be right back. Gotta slip into the back for a few of these items."

"Thank you." Etain turned to check out the rest of the shop. On the opposite wall, she found a variety of items required for the mixing of herbs, pestles and mortars, vials, small bottles, beakers, and books of spells.

One title in particular drew her in. The small red book boasted a red sash tied in a neat bow. She took it off the shelf and eased into a comfy chair. Scanning the table of contents, she hoped to find something that might help with Dar but wasn't having much luck until she came to the last spell. Love Potion #9. She flipped to the page—red wine, basil, and rose petals.

If this is what it takes to win back his love...

Lost in thought, she happened to glance to her side and discovered a display of brightly colored, polished stone amulets. One suspended on a sterling silver chain caught her eye. A circular black onyx encased in a simple setting of two silver dragons affixed nose-to-nose and tails intertwined. The ruby eye of each dragon glittered, and the links of the chain sparkled like diamonds. She carefully lifted it from the peg, dangling it between her fingers.

"The onyx protects against black magic and evil spirits," the clerk said. "It's a lovely piece, but if you don't mind me saying, far too masculine for such a delicate neck as yours."

She smiled at him in the mirror. "It's not for me."

"Your husband then?"

Her heart skipped. "No." Were she in the town of Laugharne, she would have blamed Inferno for putting him up to it. But even for him, Deudraeth was too far. "I am not married."

"I'm sorry if I assumed wrong. It's just, well, the necklace should be worn by a man with great presence. Otherwise, the piece overwhelms and is no longer an accessory."

"I *do* have a special man in mind."

"A *potential* husband." Piran smiled as he stepped from behind the counter and joined her at the display.

Etain grinned. "Perhaps."

"Shall I add it to your other purchases?"

"Yes, please." Her heart fluttered in anticipation of presenting the gift to Dar. "I think he is the just the man to pull it off."

With the sun's movement toward the western horizon, Etain decided it was time to go. She turned Razz south and meandered the way they'd come. Outside of town and halfway back to camp, the chestnut stopped, nostrils flaring, head high in the air. Etain nudged her on, and while Razz did take a few steps, she merely made a circle, refusing to leave the area.

"What's the problem, girl?" Etain loosened the reins and waited, curious to see where the mare would take them.

Razz stepped off the dirt path into the tall grass and colorful autumn wildflowers. As they continued through the vegetation, her nose picked up the scent. She patted Razz on the neck.

"Sorry, girl. My thoughts were a thousand miles away."

Now she and Razz were on the same page, she heard the rushing water of the river. The big horse pushed through the grass, but Etain pulled her up short of the riverbank. Razz snorted.

"Shh, girl."

She watched a bronzed, broad-shouldered god rise from the water. Waist-deep in the current, his hands slicked over his dark, shoulder-length hair. She couldn't be certain of the color, but black came to mind. As he shook his head, droplets of water sparkled in the sunlight like tiny crystals.

He waded through the water onto the riverbank unaware of his audience. Etain bit her bottom lip watching the water trickle down the curve of his naked, well-defined torso, to an equally impressive nether region. No amount of lip biting could curtail her gasp or soften the stamping of Razz's hooves.

He cleared his throat. "Can I help you?"

"Oh, uh..." Caught in the act, her gaze came up to his. "Aye. No. Well... We've been out for a ride and Razz, my horse, got thirsty." She sneaked a quick glance, catching his naked profile as he turned and picked up a pair of jeans. "We weren't... I mean... I wasn't expecting to see anyone. We were on our way back to town. She just stopped in the road." Razz stomped, shaking her head. Etain stroked the horse's neck hoping to calm her. "See? She's rather headstrong. I let her go where she wanted and," she gave a nervous laugh. "Here we are. With you. And me. And Razz. My horse." His laughter made her face burn. "I'm sorry for the intrusion."

"Let's get your horse a drink before she bolts in a thirst-driven frenzy and drowns you both."

The horse snorted and pulled back when he touched the reins, but a few soft words convinced her to follow. She snorted again as her mistress dismounted, and dipped her head for a long drink.

The amused young man peered at her from over the saddle. "No one comes out here at this time of day. You're the first I've ever encountered. You're definitely the first with such a brazen stare."

Embarrassed and angered by his comments, she quipped, "You surprised me, that's all."

He cocked his head. "Deepest apologies for my shameless afternoon swim and blatant disregard of your peaceful ride."

She grabbed the reins. "I'll leave you to your shamelessness."

He walked around Razz, his green eyes twinkling. "Only if you'll join me."

She stared at him for a moment, and turned as though in search of something.

"Are you expecting someone?"

"No. I'm looking for a white jacket."

"I don't recall seeing a white jacket."

"Come now." Her gaze came back to him. "Surely you jest, milord."

"Not this time."

Etain slipped her foot into the stirrup and eased up into the saddle. "It's out there. And it's yours if you think for a moment I'd do anything with you."

The twinkle returned to his eyes. "We've only just met, and I already adore you, milady."

"My *husband* will be elated to hear of your adoration."

"Husband?" His frown was playful. "What a disappointment. I'd hoped you were my ladylove come to whisk me away to your secret realm." He placed a hand on his chest. "My heart is broken."

"One of many, I'm sure." She tossed her copper curls and wheeled Razz in the opposite direction.

"With more to come," he called out.

"Miscreant." She jerked the reins to the side. Razz balked at the rough treatment, biting at the bit. In the next moment, they were in a full gallop.

At the campsite. Etain dismounted in a fury, murmuring disgruntled expletives as she relieved Razz of saddlebags, packages, and saddle.

"I should have slapped the smug look from his stupidly handsome face," she muttered, toting bags and packages to the cave. "Or a short burst of my charge. No. A long, leisurely charge. Fry his precious hair off his fat head. To see him writhing in—" She stopped mid-step, inhaled, and exhaled. "But that was the old Etain." She returned for the saddle. "The new Etain is responsible and considers the consequences of her actions."

With everything tucked away in the cave, she joined Razz at the water's edge. "It's not just me anymore, girl." She tossed her boots to the side and slipped her toes into the cool water. "I have Dar to consider."

She leaned back onto her hands, her thoughts on her love, and realized she had no sense of him. In the past, no matter how far apart they were, she could tap into their connection and be comforted knowing he was only a thought away.

Could something have happened? She sat straight up and pushed the hair from her face, an emptiness gnawing at her insides.

Aye, something happened, you idiot. He threw you away.

She shook her head. *No. Midir did, not Dar. Once Rie gets through to him, he'll come for me. I know he will.* Too anxious to sit still she got to her feet. *He has to.*

Etain closed her eyes and envisioned the man she loved. She sent a mental message, unsure if he would hear. *"You know me, my love. Please, you're the one person I need to see me as I am. Come home to me."*

She opened her eyes and turned toward the waterfall, unbuttoning her top as she walked toward it. Dropping her clothes on the bank, she dove in and swam to the center of the small lake. Inspired by a sense of recklessness, she gulped a lungful of air and dove straight toward the bottom.

Down she went, farther and farther, until the clear water turned dark. Her lungs burned and the drop in temperature made her shiver. Twisting, she kicked hard and shot back to the surface, bursting from the water and gasping for air. Razz snorted and skittered farther away. After a few more gulps of sweet air, Etain laughed and lay back, floating on the surface. Cradled in the serenity of the water, and the sun warm on her skin, the worries and tensions of the past few days melted away.

He knows my heart. He'll find his way back to me.

BETTER LEFT UNSAID

L inq rode up as she stepped out from behind the waterfall, closing the last few buttons of her top. "There you are," he said. "I was worried when I did not see you or Razz."

"She must've wandered off." Etain worked her fingers through her tangled hair. "I guess I fell asleep. I'd forgotten how early it gets dark this time of year." The last rays of orange and gold peeked from the horizon.

"Let's have a chat." He dismounted and pulled her along to the cave. "I have not seen my friend, Alaster, in a long time. He has been here for several years and knows the locals well." He chuckled. "It did not take long to end up at the pub. My work was easy after that. They tell me there is a new arrival in town."

"Piran." She explained her trip to the apothecary. "He said he suffers from amnesia and the shop owner gave him the name." At the cave, she grabbed a couple of ales, popped the caps, and offered one to Linq.

After a tap of bottles, he enjoyed a long drink. "You were to go to the market and come straight back."

"I know." She swallowed, not meeting his steady gaze. "But I promised Spirit I'd get her some rare herbs. She can't always get to town."

"Was there any recognition on his part?"

"Well, no." Suddenly, her bottle of ale seemed quite interesting. "Excellent brew, don't you think?"

"Not bad," he agreed. "What are you not telling me?"

The words rushed out of her mouth. "He didn't recognize me because I cast a glamour before I went into town."

He swigged a mouthful of ale. "Spirit, I suppose? Is that why you two disappeared before we left?" At her sheepish grin, he looked away and back. "Did it work?"

"Aye. I checked myself in a mirror. Hair, eyes, clothes, everything was different. No one would ever suspect the redhead from this morning to be the silver-haired love of Lord VonNeshta."

"Mmph," Linq grunted. "You kept it short and sweet? No lingering in places you should not?"

"I assure you there was no lingering."

"I hope so." He finished his drink. "Will you start a fire whilst I unsaddle Blackjack?"

"Sure."

While Etain set a blaze, Linq stored his gear in the cave. Razz rambled into camp as he poured a healthy portion of oats.

"The sooner we find your brother, the better. Alaster can ask around but too many questions and the *Bok* might get wind of it."

"Maybe a couple more of these," she held up two bottles of ale, "will speed up the creative process."

"Mind if we sit outside? After being in a pub all day, I would like to enjoy the fresh night air."

"As you wish."

Outside the cave, Linq shared more of his day while Etain set out bread, cheese, and fruit. With another round opened, his stories moved to how he'd met Alaster in a *Bok* raid.

"Did Dar ever meet him?" She tore off a couple of pieces of bread from the loaf and handed one to Linq.

"No. Dar was not as settled in those days." He pulled a dagger from his boot to slice the cheese. "Alaster wanted to meet him, but the time was never right. We were always in opposite directions."

"Maybe we can invite him to our home someday." She accepted the offered cheese from the tip of his blade and stacked it on her bread. "He sounds like an interesting fellow."

"He is."

"You know, maybe we should keep it simple tomorrow. I'll go to the apothecary in the morning, explain the circumstances to the clerk, and tell him who I believe he is. Then we can leave and get back to Inferno's."

Linq wiped his mouth on his sleeve. "Who do you think he is?"

"My brother," she said, thinking the answer obvious.

He enjoyed a swallow of ale. "Why?"

She clenched her jaw in conjunction with the grip on her bottle. Losing her cool with the Elf wouldn't get her anywhere. "Well, it's several things. His hair is dark, like my brother's, and he's about the right size."

"What about his face? Do you not remember his features?"

Her gaze matched his in intensity. "He was sixteen the last time I saw him. He could look different by now."

"He would not have changed so much."

"I'm nothing like I was at fourteen." The silver orb that transformed her from a child into a young woman flashed in her mind. "Who knows how living with Midir has affected him?"

"Yet you continue to pursue him." Linq leaned forward. "Sixteen is an impressionable age. Surrounded by evil, I am sure your brother is nothing like he was when you knew him. What color were his eyes?"

Again, she blinked. "Are you talking about my brother or the man in the shop?"

"It does not matter. The clerk is not your brother."

"How the hell would you know?"

"You would have recognized something. If not his face, then his voice or his body language. These things do not change much." He added a few sticks of wood to the fire. "You are not thinking straight, Etain. Since learning he is alive, have you thought about anyone else, or how bringing him into our midst might affect the balance of things?"

She jumped to her feet waving her hands through the air and sloshing ale onto the ground. "I witnessed the slaughter of my family, and had to find my own way in a world as foreign to me as the human one is to the Elves."

Her anger gave way to deeper revelations better left unsaid. "I've been expected to marry a man who saw fit to fuck my sister, leaving her pregnant, and now expects *me* to be the better person and rise above it."

She narrowed her eyes. "I have suffered the assaults of his twisted brother not only when he was alive, but even now. Then I'm told it would be best if I leave my intended in the hands of people I've never met or ever knew existed." The bottle of ale, held tightly in her hand, burst.

"And those same people waited *five* years to tell me my brother, who I thought was dead..." Her voice on the edge of a scream, she paused and pointed wildly in the air. "Lives only a few miles up the road. Well, bloody fucking excuse me if it seems a bit selfish to want to see my goddamn brother!"

He came up fast and threw down his bottle, shattering it against one of the random stones littered across the countryside, hollering in his native tongue. "*Við sjóinn og stjörnurnar! Hefur þú ekkert vit í því ljósa höfuð* (By the sea and stars! Have you no sense in that blonde head)? *Þú ert ekki sú eina sem hefur orðið. Þú ert Alamir, takast á við það* (You are not the only one who has suffered. You are Alamir. Deal with it)."

She stomped her foot. "If you're going to curse me, at least do it in a language I understand."

"*Á!* You will be the death of me, girl." He walked off.

"You sound like Inferno."

He stormed back to the fire. "I know what you mean to do. You cannot go in there as yourself. The *Bok* are everywhere."

"Linq, if it *is* him, I have to be myself to convince him."

He paced to the water's edge.

She softened her voice. "You know I'm right. If he sees me as I am maybe it will bring back a memory, a thought, something."

"What if it is a trap? I will not allow it."

"Who are *you* to tell me what to do? This is my *brother*. I have to try. Dar and I have lost too much family already."

He stalked toward her, making her step back. "I am the *Megiltura of the Cala'quessir* (Swordmaster of the High Elf). I fought side by side with Dar VonNeshta, Prince of Krymeria, during the clan wars and saw the sacrifices he suffered. I will not see him suffer more from your impetuosity. If the *Bok* takes you, nothing will stop him from coming to your rescue. If not for yourself, can you not see the danger it imposes on *him*?"

"Impetuosity?" Etain furrowed her brows. "Is that even a word?"

"Lives are at stake, and you make jokes."

"Holy crap, Linq. Dar would do the same if he were in my place. You have to know I'll do everything in my power to keep him safe, but I can't do that for him and not for my brother. If they come for me, they'll soon know who he is and none of us will be safe."

His shoulders slumped as if in defeat. "Damn if you are not right." He plopped down next to the fire, shaking his head. "We have brought this on by coming here. If we leave without him, he will become another pawn in their wretched game." She released her breath and offered him a fresh drink. "You should tend to those cuts. Are there any shards in your skin?"

Etain raised her brows at the blood on her palm. She went to the water's edge and gently washed it away. As she walked back to the cave, she held up her hand. "All clear."

"We will go in from the north end of town and leave the same way. Once we know we have not been followed, we can veer south."

Etain smiled and launched herself at the Elf, throwing her arms around his neck and planting a kiss on his cheek. "Thank you, great *Megiltura of the Cala'quessir*. I swear, I'll make you proud."

"Do not get caught." He removed her arms from his neck and set her away from him. "We must sleep. I want us both sharp tomorrow."

Early the next morning, after Etain packed the saddlebags and Linq saddled the horses, he helped her strap on the dual-sword scabbard and watched her run through a routine with her *Nim'Na'Sharr*. Her muscles warmed, she tucked away *Nim*, and drew Day Star and Burning Heart as she'd practiced at Laugharne. It took several more moves but she soon had it down.

She pivoted to her right and to her left. "I could get used to these, they're so light."

"Dar is a true master."

Etain sheathed one sword, and the other. "I hope he can master Midir's trickery. I need him to come home to me."

"I have every faith in our Krymerian. He is most resilient."

A faint smile touched her lips. "I'm gonna hold you to that."

"You will see. Shall we go?"

On their mounts, they walked a few feet from the site and stopped beneath an old oak tree. Linq reached overhead, cut a large limb from the tree, and walked his horse around the campsite, dragging the limb behind him, sweeping away all prints. He continued to drag the limb behind him as they followed the river further upstream where he tossed it into the water.

They veered off the main road nearer to Deudraeth and skirted around to the north end of town. Linq stayed put. "Should trouble occur, you leave immediately, brother or no brother."

"Aye, aye, Capitan."

Etain walked Razz down the quiet street and was somewhat comforted by the *clip-clop* of the mare's hooves as they headed toward the apothecary.

At the shop, she dismounted and loosely tethered her horse. She stepped inside but left the front door open. "Hello? Piran?"

The shop appeared to be unattended. She knew life in a small village differed from the city, but not so much that a shop owner would leave a well-stocked store unmanned. The hairs on the back of her neck prickled as her hand slipped to the hilt of her blade. At the same time, a familiar burn she hadn't felt in a while rose in her blood.

She checked the back room and found it empty except for a desk and chair. When she turned, something else caught her eye.

"I don't remember a window." She stepped out and back into the office. *A two-way mirror*. Satisfied all was well, she walked toward the front door.

A loud commotion from the back room shattered the silence. She whirled around and faced the black-haired water god from the lake.

"You must leave now, milady. You shouldn't be here." He reached for her hand, but she avoided his grasp.

"Where'd you come from?" She backed away toward the front door.

"You must come with me. Piran isn't the one you seek."

"What do you know of it? Where is he?"

The earth rumbled beneath her feet. She turned toward the front window.

The young man grabbed her arm. "He is safe. You were here yesterday and spoke with him."

"Let me go." She slapped at his hand. "How did you know I was here?" The sound of pounding hooves explained the rumble.

Outside, Blackjack collided into Razz in a flurry of mane and tails. Razz whinnied and sidestepped. Linq grabbed her reins. "Etain! We must go *now*." Blackjack reared up, nearly throwing the agitated Elf out of the saddle.

The young man pulled her attention back to him. "A magic man knows a glamour when he sees it. I knew who you were the minute you stepped into the shop yesterday."

"Yesterday?" Her mind raced. "You were in the office."

"*Etain*! There's not much time, girl! Come!"

A strange calm came over her as she glanced at Linq, and back at the young man. "Bert?"

"Yes. Now, will you please go?" He pulled her toward him.

She yanked free from his hold. "Why did you say Piran isn't who I'm looking for?"

"God! You're as infuriating as when we were kids." He took her arm in an iron grip. "Bert, Robert! I'm your brother. Now *come*."

"You? No way."

"It's a long story, little bit. Please."

She blinked, the blood pounding in her head. It was as though she was fourteen again. The last time she'd seen her brother, he'd called her *little bit*, and yelled in her face.

"Run!"

Shaken from her thoughts, her gaze followed his to the south.

A band of wild-eyed soldiers dressed in the muddy brown uniform of the *Bok'Na'Ra* set her in motion. "If you *are* my brother, you aren't safe, either. You have to come with us."

"Etain!" Linq called out, trying to control the horses.

She pulled her brother toward the front door. "I hope you can ride." Her next words were for the Elf. "Take my brother with you."

"Get up here with me, *nú.*"

With Robert safely seated on the horse, she screamed, "Go! I'll catch up."

Linq checked the progress of the approaching soldiers. "Camp!" Blackjack shot to the north, Razz in close pursuit. Etain watched until they cleared the edge of town.

The earth trembled beneath her feet as her focus turned inward. She stepped into the road and drew *Nim'Na'Sharr*, extending the talons on her left hand. Her wings proved not as cooperative. With a glance over her shoulder, she tried again. "Shit." The scabbard so ingeniously created by Inferno and Linq made no allowance for her wings.

The *Bok* stormed toward her, their eyes ablaze and spiked teeth gleaming in anticipation of their prized catch. Etain retracted her talons, sheathed her sword, and faced the oncoming assault. Amidst howls of victory, they aimed their horses at the rebellious warrior. She waited until the last possible moment and disappeared.

The lead riders yanked their reins sharply, their mounts snorting and rearing in protest. The screams of men and horses filled the air as those in the rear struggled to avoid running into their colleagues.

"Togor, where did she go?" the man in the lead yelled.

"I don't know, Kromok, sir. She just disappeared." Togor turned his dapple-grey mount to keep from hitting a fellow rider.

"Cloud, start the chant to prevent the shimmer. She won't get away so easily," Kromok ordered. "Cromorth, take your men after those two. Escape is not an option." Led by a man around six feet tall with hair the color of iron, a troop of soldiers separated from the mélange in pursuit of Linq and Robert.

A boy no older than twelve slid from his saddle and squared his thin shoulders. A cool wind blew through his long, white hair, making him shiver, despite the wool cloak around his shoulders. He faced the spot where the woman last stood, closed his eyes, and began to chant. His hands rose into the air, calling on the dark powers of the *Bok'Na'Ra*.

"Pwerau tywyllwch mawr, gwrandewch arna i. Amgylchynwch yr un sy'n rhedeg, peidiwch â gadael iddi ffoi. Clywch fy nghais, dewch i'm cymorth, Casglwch o amgylch yr un y mae'n rhaid talu ei ddyled. Mewn llygedyn o las bydd yn gwneud iddi ddianc, Trowch ei phwer yn ei herbyn, datgelu ei siâp (Hear my request, come to my aid. Gather round the one whose debt must be paid. In a shimmer of blue she will make her escape. Turn her power against her, reveal her shape)."

Etain made it into the shop just as she reappeared. Further inside, she lit her body in another blue shimmer. Unfortunately, Cloud proved a glowing testament to his teachers of enchantments. She could shimmer but not travel. "Bloody fuck!"

With it no longer an option, she loosened the straps across her chest and repositioned the scabbard to allow for a proper wingspan, but she couldn't reach the blades.

"Damn."

She ran into the back room and watched through the two-way mirror as the leader and several of his men moved on the shop. She aligned the scabbards to the center of her back and beckoned to the Krymerian blood coursing through her veins.

"Great Krymerian warriors of the past, I am not of your kind, but your son has shared his blood plenty of times. Unite your strength with mine; give me your power. For the High Lord of Kaos, please let this work."

She tapped into her demon again. Wings of white tipped in crimson spread out. She hastily repositioned the blades between her wings.

Kromok stepped into the shop. "Quickly, men. Out the back. Don't let her get away."

Help me, Krymerian warriors of old, so I may protect his legacy.

As Togor rushed into the room, Etain tightened the straps and ran through the back door.

Her great wings lifted her from the ground with a single flap. The dark-haired soldier lunged, catching her by the foot. Suspended in mid-air, her gaze locked with his deep blues. For a moment, she glimpsed the man he'd been before the *Bok* - strong, handsome, innocent. She cocked her head, sharing an inexplicable camaraderie with him.

When more soldiers poured out the door grabbing at her other foot, Etain flapped her wings and kicked at her would-be captors. Unable to break free, her talons extended from both hands. She freed herself in two grand swipes amidst the spray of blood, screams, and severed arms. Buoyed by a rush of adrenaline, she soared into the air, and swooped down, forcing those beneath her to duck.

"See ya, boys."

Charged with the duty of pursuit and capture, Lieutenant Cromorth gathered his small band of men and headed east out of Deudraeth. His second-in-command, Dex, a small man in stature, rode at his side. "I trust you know what you're doing."

Cromorth grunted. "Inside information from a very reliable source, Dex. They went north, but they'll turn soon enough. The woman has connections in the south. You watch. We'll run right into 'em."

The second lieutenant licked his lips. "I heard talk about her. Is it true?"

"Depends on what you've heard."

He lowered his voice. "That she's the Krymerian's woman and..." he scratched his nose, "there's a reward for whoever brings her in."

Cromorth cocked a brow. In reality, it had nothing to do with the Krymerian but why share valuable information with a minion? "Sounds like you have an insider of your own." The other man laughed. "It's true, but there's no reward if she's dead. He wants her alive."

"He?"

"Forget it. I like my head right where it sits, and as ugly as it is, I'm sure you like yours too."

"Fair enough, but can Kromok be trusted? He's the one with the prize."

"Well, now, the man's gotta catch her first, don't he?" The lieutenant urged his mount forward with a cluck of his tongue. "If she's as good as I've heard, she'll slip through and come straight to us to save her buddies." He glanced over his shoulder. "I figure this lot can handle a little girlie."

ROADIES

Faux threw back the covers and made a beeline for the bathroom. She rested her head on an arm stretched over the cool porcelain and moaned, wondering why she was suddenly sick every morning.

Freeblood wet a cloth and sat on the floor next to the toilet, dabbing her face. "Better now?"

"Yes. Thank you."

As he helped her up, she swayed into him. He scooped her into his arms and carried her to the bed, spouting admonishments in his best imitation of Dar. "You tread a dangerous path, milady."

By the time they reached the edge of the bed, she felt better.

"Can we get out of this house for a while?" She gave him her best pout. "Go out with me?"

"You were just puking up your guts and now you want to go out?"

"Once it's over, I'm okay." She batted her eyelashes. "Please? I found Dar's stash of cash. We can go anywhere we please." She softly blew into his ear as her hands strategically roamed over his body. "We can do anything we want, anywhere we want, for as long as we want."

"We won't be going anywhere if you keep doing that," he said, taking hold of a delinquent hand. "Where did you have in mind?"

A provocative leer in her eyes, she kissed his neck, her other hand slithering down his back to a firm butt cheek. "I know a great little place off the coast of Mexico where the margaritas and *chile rellenos* are to die for." Her tail slinked around him in an embrace far more effective than her lustful hands.

"Mexico? You mean that little place Etain tried to make me forget?"

"Mmm-hmm," she mumbled, nibbling his earlobe.

"I told you to stop." He playfully swatted at her and pushed her back onto the bed. "If we go, no margaritas for you."

"But—"

"Nope." He waggled a finger in her face. "No alcohol for you, Mama. Maybe a virgin drink, but that's it."

She thrust out her bottom lip. "Virgins are no fun."

Freeblood laughed and gave her a thorough kiss. "I wouldn't know. I'm too busy having fun with you."

She laughed as he rolled onto the bed and pulled her close.

"Me, too, but I *would* like to go somewhere, just for a little while? Take our show on the road?"

A mischievous smirk appeared. "We can do that." He pulled his cell phone from the pocket of his jeans and tapped the screen. "Come to think of it, we'd be in time for a killer rock festival going on in L.A. at a bar called The Bone. Does that fancy your suit?"

"How can they have a festival in a bar?"

"Not my problem. Are you with me or not?"

She made a grab for his phone. "First you have to tell me how you get your phone to work here."

He rolled away and onto his feet, dangling it in front of him. "Magic. Watch." With the cell phone in one hand, he extended his index finger on the other. His brows lifted in a *wait for it* moment. The screen came to life with a mere touch. He wiggled the finger and touched the screen again. Faux rolled her eyes and laughed. A video clip of the festival played, its musical riffs blaring through the tiny speakers.

"I know how to work it, dude." She snatched it from his hand and showed off her finesse with the keyboard. "They usually don't work *because* of the magic."

He cocked a brow. "If there aren't any cells here, how is it you know how to use one?"

"Human toys," she murmured, her attention on the phone. "Their sense of superiority comes in handy." A new video played a savage tune.

"Do you go to the human realm often?"

"As often as I want. Are you gonna tell me how you keep it working?"

"It could have something to do with this." He held his hand out, palm up.

"Yeah, yeah, the magic finger," she said, not impressed.

"Give it a second." A tiny blue orb appeared in his palm and gradually grew into a gem, giving off a blue glow.

"Wicked shit," she whispered. "I saw it in action when you fought that ugly recruiter."

"Yeah. I woke up in Japan in the middle of a concert and found it doing this to 'Dir en Grey.' When I went to make a call, the phone was dead. I didn't have a charger, so I got creative."

"What else can you do with it?"

Freeblood chuckled. "How about the music festival?"

"Sex, drugs, and rock 'n roll?" At his doubtful expression, she sidled closer to him and snaked her arms around his neck. "Sex and rock 'n roll at least. Let's go."

"Wait. Isn't the human realm forbidden unless it's official business?"

Faux eased a knee over his crotch. "You wanna play or not?"

The two appeared in a golden shimmer amidst sunshine, music, and tons of people who paid them no attention. Feet stomped in rhythm to ritualistic drums, their hands clapping at the riffs of smoking guitars. The heady fragrance of premium pot drifted through the crowd.

"Snack?" Freeblood disappeared into the mélange but was back in a flash with food and drinks.

Faux grabbed a hot dog and bit down just as a hand landed on his shoulder. The two turned expecting a fight but were met with a huge grin.

"What're you doing here, mate?" An Aussie with a woman on each arm smiled at Freeblood, and gave Faux an appraising eye. "How did I miss this little sheila?"

Faux smirked at her partner in crime. "Another one of yours?"

"Faux, meet Ian. We're here for the concert, man." The men shook hands as he told her of how they met during a fight in the Australian sector. "Ian liked my guitar playing and came to my rescue when a bunch of soul-sucking assholes decided they wanted my guitar. Why're you so far from home?"

Ian bobbed his head toward the stage. "This isn't an ordinary concert, mate. It's a competition. Anyone who can beat Tristania's guitarist in a solo gets ten thousand dollars."

Faux draped an arm over Freeblood's shoulder. "Please tell me you know how to play."

Before he could reply, Ian was pushing him through the crowd. "He's a natural. He'll blow you away. Speed on up and show the locals what you're made of." Ian fell forward when Freeblood rushed out from in front of him and climbed onto the stage.

"We have another challenger!" The man with the microphone didn't seem surprised to see him. "Where's your guitar?"

Freeblood grabbed a microphone in one hand and flashed his blue gem in the other. "I have it here." He grinned despite the boos and hisses from the crowd. He'd done this trick a few times. It was what first caught the attention of the Aussie and his rogue crew. When the gem flared with blue light and formed into a blue-gemmed guitar, the crowd was his.

The announcer laughed. "What's your name?"

"Freeblood."

The audience cheered. Faux glanced at Ian, who laughed and shook his head. "Sheep to the slaughter."

Anders, one of the guitarists in the band, stepped forward and gave him the once over. He smiled half-heartedly and pulled a few chords from their latest song as a test. Freeblood raked off a quick, simple riff of his own, and gradually increased in speed and complexity. Not to be outdone, Anders dove into a song that incited the crowd from roaring to ecstatic.

Freeblood smirked and cracked his knuckles. He built on the beat he played before, taking it through an intense series of strokes, toned it down a notch, and popped the frets with one hand, the other marching up the strings. Caught up in the execution, he poured his heart and soul into the performance and finished in an ear-piercing scream of strings. With the final stroke, his hand came up in a salute.

"Faux!" he yelled into the crowd.

Ian patted her on the back, a huge grin on his face. The crowd cheered. The grandiose show of recognition for a girl made him a certified favorite. With an elaborate bow, he turned to his opponent.

The Goth metal embraced Faux in its primitive darkness. Freeblood's ability to tap into the emotions of the crowd awed her. The pure eroticism of his notes invoked a passion she had never before experienced. Other guitarists mounted the stage to challenge him, but his excellence, his speed, and his sheer charisma shamed them all. Although she knew he was proud and self-assured, this show amplified those attributes. She liked this new Freeblood and thought of how interesting it would be the next time they saw Dar and Etain.

That'll be worth the price of admission.

Determined to grab her fair share of the spotlight, Faux flamed into a golden shimmer, forcing those nearby to turn aside. Anders and his bandmates, surprised by her sudden appearance onstage, kept playing. Mariangela owned the stage when she added her powerful voice to the mix.

Faux twisted, turned, and undulated in sync with Freeblood's challenging chords. As he cranked the music up another notch, she slinked behind him, rubbing her body against his. Her hands slid underneath his shirt, raking her nails over his erect nipples and down his belly while her licentious tail snaked between his legs. She flipped around so they were back-to-back and kicked out a long shapely leg, rolling her body toward the audience. Freeblood spun behind her to the other side, his blue gem guitar blazing. As Faux shimmied away, he followed, belting out riff after ear-piercing riff.

Center stage, she twirled into a hypnotizing undulation of hips, belly, and chest, her tail swaying and snapping to the beat. She stroked her body, tweaking her nipples until they stood rock hard against the fabric of her skimpy top.

Freeblood took it down a few notches and set an erotic, gut-pulsing tempo. The drummer followed his lead and added a heartbeat thump. The bass player intensified the seduction by adding a crotch-lubricating rhythm. Faux's moves rivaled those of any accomplished belly dancer. Her still flat belly rippled as her chest heaved. Intent on Freeblood, she slipped a hand into the front of her jeans and threw her head back, the music adding a delicious hum to her already vibrating fingers. The people screamed in appreciation.

A voice in the back yelled. "Suc-cu-bus! Suc-cu-bus!" Like a massive wave, the crowd united into one loud voice chanting over and over.

Faux gyrated past her guitar-playing lover, who lifted his guitar, snaring her between his instrument and his hot body. She stroked his lips with her wet fingers. Freeblood sucked them into his mouth. She recognized the lust in his eyes and appreciated the confirmation pressed against her own ache. Her fingers trailed down between his legs as she claimed his mouth with hers.

The *avant-garde* musical warriors stole the show and took the prize.

Flashes of light sparkled in the dark like cameras shooting at a concert. Problem was, this was a bar, and the lights weren't from cameras. The stage *did* have lights used when local bands played but these were too random and flashed in places where they shouldn't. Jackie was dead sure she heard footsteps that weren't her own.

She'd inherited the place from a favorite uncle upon his passing. Her being a native Texan, she'd never been to L.A. nor had she worked in a bar and had no idea what it entailed. However, at the age of forty-five she figured it was time for a change and decided to keep the bar rather than sell. Life had been a crash course ever since.

Jackie ducked behind the bar and inched her way to the end, doing her best to be as quiet as possible. She sucked in her breath, smoothed back a few stray auburn curls, and focused on what she'd learned in self-defense class the day before.

Float like a butterfly, sting like a bee.

She bit her lower lip.

Idiot, that's Mohammed Ali, not Master Kaosu.

Still, the words lowered her rattled nerves to a low hum.

The sound of approaching footsteps scattered her thoughts. Her lips moved in silent prayer as she dared to peek around the corner of the bar, one whisky-colored eye and the other. She snapped back out of sight. *I will not scream. I will not faint.* She was certain her banging heart could be heard three blocks down the street.

It was an eventful day, and the bar was closed. To bring more business in, she'd agreed to participate in a traveling music festival. The bands played at different venues during the eight-week tour and tonight was her turn.

By now, most of the crowd should have cleared out and moved on to late night clubs in the area.

She'd personally locked the doors and checked every window after her staff had gone home. *Why break-in now?* The day was busier than usual, but her bar manager deposited the bulk of the cash on her way home, so there wasn't much on site. *What do they want?* She looked above at the rows of bottles prettily displayed on glass shelves along the back of the bar. *Surely they aren't that desperate.*

Jackie reached for her handgun tucked under the bar, carefully flipped the safety, and held it close to her chest. After the count of three, she pushed up from her crouched position, and turned with the gun in the lead. A Smith and Wesson M&P9 pointed at her head surprised her. Although her heart beat like a Neil Peart drum solo, her expression revealed nothing.

She guessed the man behind the gun to be around six-foot-two, well over her own five-foot-ten, and admired the broad shoulders beneath a black pullover. A set of bright whites gleamed in the faint light.

Tall, dark, and lethal.

Jackie held her stance, a flush of anger making her scalp tingle. She knew the grin, had seen it many times at the shooting range, even admired it a time or two. The man ogled the pistol in her hand.

"Nighthawk Lady Hawk..." The laughing dark eyes slid up to meet hers. "Impressive. How does she handle?"

"Glad you asked." She squeezed the trigger.

The arrogant smile faded from his lips as he staggered back, raising his right hand to his chest, and aimed with his left. Jackie spun and ducked just as the mirrored wall behind the bar exploded, destroying glass shelves, bottles, and hours of hard work. She covered her head with her arms as shards of tinkling glass rained down.

Another male voice yelled. "Kane! Stand down!"

She scurried to the other end of the bar hoping to make it to the nearby hallway for a quick exit out the concealed door in her office. As fate would have it, she found her way blocked by the muzzle of a Glock 19.

"I'm not as curious as my brother. Put it away."

Jackie peered into a pair of light-colored eyes made even more remarkable by his dark skin. While his resemblance to the other man was apparent, she knew he was the older of the two, more from his presence than anything else. This one was inherently confident and commanded attention without the hustle and flash his brother relied on.

She raised her hands and slowly stood, placing her Lady Hawk on the bar. Curious to the outcome of her shot, she turned her head and found the younger brother on his feet, a hole through his shirt and a glare in his eyes.

Kevlar.

"I am Krz," the light-eyed man said. "You've met my brother, Kane." Suddenly, several other black-clad figures stepped into the light. "This is our clan. We are Haluci."

"Clan?" She laughed, using her best rendition of a Scot's accent. "Have we somehow been transported to bonny Scotland? Are ye wee Highlanders now?"

Krz cracked a smile. "My great-grandmother used to tell a story about an ancestor who came from the Highlands. She blamed him for the stubborn streak." He actually laughed. "We should be in L.A. in a bar called The Bone."

She eyed him from head to toe. "Right place. Wrong time. No cash on hand."

He returned the scrutiny as he tucked away his weapon. "Do we look like thieves?"

Jackie shrugged. "Depends on what you want. The Bone is a great bar and does a fair amount of business, but if you want to rob me, it doesn't require all this artillery. That little pea-shooter your brother carries would do the job."

Krz ignored the snort from his brother. "If we were here to rob you, Jackie," he laughed at her raised brows, "we wouldn't be talking." He picked up her handgun, engaged the safety, and handed it back to her. "You'd be scratching your head, wondering what the hell happened."

She replaced the Lady Hawk in its holster under the bar. "Or *you'd* be scratching your ass with a stump." Krz laughed again not in the least intimidated by her tough talk. "I've seen your brother at the shootin' range, but we've not been introduced. Care to tell me how you know my name?"

Kane rubbed his chest as he stepped forward. "You've been highly recommended by Mr. Ian."

"Mister..." Jackie had to think. She was sure she didn't know a Mr. Ian, then it came to her. "Are you talking about the Aussie who owns the shootin' range?" The gleam in Krz's eyes told her she was right. "Hmph. We'll have to have a little chat next time I go for target practice."

"Don't be too harsh on the man. He's just doing his job."

"Selling information?"

"Keeping an eye out for talent and opportunities."

"He can't be one of yours. He doesn't blend in with your crew."

"Clan," he corrected. "He's not of the Haluci clan, but he *is* our kind and quite the entrepreneur." Krz pulled up a barstool. "We'd like to make you a proposition, a business deal if you prefer. Something that should prove lucrative for you as well as us."

"I don't know you," Jackie said, reaching for her gun again. "I don't know how you got in here and I certainly don't have any intentions of getting involved in gang business." She shoved the gun in Krz's face. "Get out."

Ten barrels glinted in the dim light, each one aimed at Jackie, Kane's being the closest. She didn't flinch.

Krz raised his hands. "We are not a *gang*. We are a clan."

"I don't give a shit if you're the Jackson Five. Get out."

"Not until we talk."

She released the safety. "Get. Out."

"Krz, this lady's crazier than you," Kane said. "We'll find another portal, one not as hostile."

Krz held Jackie's gaze as he spoke. "No. It has to be here. The coordinates are perfect and people coming and going at all hours won't raise a lot of questions. We need this place."

"Not if everyone has to worry about getting shot!"

Having watched the back and forth between the brothers, Jackie huffed. "What the hell are you talking about? Are more lights gonna flash out of nowhere?"

"There! See?" Kane nearly lost his shit, pointing his muzzle more enthusiastically at the woman. "How do you explain the lights to a person who has no clue who we are?"

His hands still in the air, Krz shrugged. "I'll explain."

"Explain what?" Jackie asked.

"We are Alamir, and your bar sits in a spot something akin to a black hole."

"Honey, I'm forty-five, not four *or* five. Black holes only exist in space, and last I heard, they don't have revolving doors where you come and go at will."

"*Akin* to a black hole. It's the simplest way to describe it without going all scientific on you."

"Scientific." She shook her head. "Then let's start with the Alamir part."

"Now Jackie..." Krz gave her another toothy smile as he lowered his hands. "Why ask me to explain what you already know?"

She raised a brow. "Which is?"

"James Rhys. You two were involved..." He paused and almost giggled when her other brow lifted. "In business a few years ago."

Her doubtful expression turned haughty. "My business doesn't concern you or any of your kind."

He gave her a cool eye despite the gun barrel in his face. "James did business with the Alamir."

"What the hell do you want?"

"First, I'll tell you what I *don't* want, so maybe you'll put away that piece. We're not here to rob you or hurt you or your business."

"You *do* realize there's a live one in the chamber, right?"

Krz sighed, and looked at his brother. "Why don't you get the job done while me and Jackie have a chat?"

"You sure, bro?"

"Yeah," he turned back to her. "We're going to come to an understanding."

She watched the interaction between the brothers and eyed the rest of the clan tucking away their weapons, some already headed toward the exit.

"Like hell you are!" She dashed out from behind the bar past Krz, running to cut them off. "You're not leaving here to bring more back with you. I'm not having it!"

The clan stopped. Kane approached her, empty hands held in front of him. "Lady, you really think we need backup to deal with you?" He laughed and snatched her gun while kicking her legs out from under her. In seconds, she was on her back, staring up at a circle of amused faces. Kane cleared the chamber, set the safety, and handed the Lady Hawk to Krz. "You have a half-hour, bro. *Don't* get shot." Kane and the rest of the Haluci clan stepped around her and out the front door.

"Shall we have a civilized conversation now?" Krz offered her a hand up.

"If I thought saying 'no' would make you go away, I would." Although she felt like a complete idiot by losing her gun and being manhandled, she accepted his hand but seeing the fool smile again grated on her nerves. Whether it was due to his irritating confidence or the fact she was starting to admire the man, she wasn't sure, but if he thought she was going to go easy on him, he had another thing coming.

She followed him to the bar and slid onto a stool as he stepped behind the counter. "I hope you don't mind."

Jackie shrugged. "Stranger things have happened."

"Surely not." Krz laughed. Along the back, he found a couple glasses intact, wiped them down with a towel and placed them in front of Jackie, then groped beneath the bar. She sat back and waited. He squinted into the darkness at his feet and reached in again.

"Aha! Never fails." Krz came up with a bottle of thirty-year-old scotch. "Barmen always keep the best hidden for personal consumption."

Jackie couldn't help but grin. "Know your way around a bar, huh?"

He rocked the cork back and forth. "My granddad's. He'd take me and Kane on Saturday mornings, give my folks a rest, and we'd clean his place from top to bottom."

"Kids cleaning a bar? Wouldn't you'd rather been outside, playing?"

Does the man ever stop grinning?

"Hell no! We couldn't wait for Saturdays. It was the best fun we ever had, crawling on the floor, jumping onto the bar, arranging all his pretty bottles, dancing and singing to music from the jukebox." He poured three fingers worth into each glass. "By the way, sorry for the mess. My brother gets a little trigger happy when people shoot at him. We'll make it right." He lifted his glass and waited for her. "To a future of stranger things."

Although not one word had been discussed about this proposed business opportunity, Jackie's gut told her it was something worth considering. "You're damn right you will." She lifted her glass. "Skål."

A Strategic Move

Dar's days were filled with swordplay, Elven martial arts, archery, and anything else Elfin and Wolfe could think of to keep him occupied. Between the banter of the two Alamir and the time spent with the Black Blades, the fog in his mind began to lift.

As Dar wiped down his blades one afternoon, Elfin shared a tidbit of information about an upcoming Blade Masters gathering. "We should enter."

Wolfe looked from Elfin to Dar. "I'm up for it. What is it?"

"You boys enjoy yourselves. It is time to find my lady," Dar said.

Elfin grinned. "It is mostly warriors, but sometimes others join in. The gathering pits blade against blade to determine who is the best. You ought to join us, Dar." He propped an elbow on Wolfe's shoulder. "Surely it would make the gathering more exciting if the High Lord were a contestant."

Wolfe crossed his arms and stroked his chin. "I, for one, would like to see him in action. See if the stories are true or are just stories."

"The past few days have not been enough, Wolfe?" Dar gazed down the length of his sword. "I'd not taken you for a masochist."

There was a twinkle in Wolfe's eyes. "Sounds like a challenge to me. What do you think, Elfin?" He winked. "It's as much as a slap across the face, wouldn't you agree?"

"Aye, a serious slap," Elfin said.

Wolfe attempted a solemn expression. "One that must be resolved in the ring, I'd say."

Dar raised a brow and eyed the two from over the hilt of his sword. He could hear the whine of the line as he was reeled in. "When is this gathering?"

"Tomorrow," Elfin said as straight-faced as possible.

The Krymerian shook his head at the skill of their play, but he was not beaten yet. "Entries have to be in weeks before the event. I doubt they will accept us on the day."

Wolfe snorted. "Like they'd turn down the High Lord. Besides, we entered the three of us a week ago."

Elfin didn't give him the chance to respond. "Consider this, Dar. It is a way to show Alatariel and the wizards you are back to your old self."

"And, when you lose, a way of showing penance for your sins," Wolfe threw in for good measure.

Checkmate.

"When *I* lose?" Dar could not help but laugh at the good-hearted smiles plastered on their faces. "Give me time to think about it. I will be in my room." He slid the blade neatly into its sheath and placed it next to the others on a nearby table. "I trust you will ensure I am given the privacy needed?" Without another word, he left the training hall before the boys had a chance to reply.

Wolfe called after him. "See you in the morning, Dar."

Alone in his chambers, Dar considered Elfin's proposition as he examined the books lining the far wall. *He is right. To participate would prove I have regained my control and presence of mind.* Halfway through the bottom shelf, golden letters across the spine of a black leather-clad book gleamed. VonNeshta. He opened the cover with a gentle hand. Page after page contained names of the VonNeshta family accompanied by the date of their birth and the day they died.

It has been a long time since my last gathering.

Comfortable before the fire, he was soon lost in the pages. The hours passed and sleep eventually overtook him. Not long after he drifted off, the nightmare returned.

Etain grabbed his arms, swearing what he saw was a lie. Alatariel tried to stop his frantic lady, speaking words he could not hear. Etain framed his face with her hands, but he ignored her pleas and tossed her across the yard. When she dared to come back to him, he struck her down.

His body jerked.

Despite the accusations hurled in her face, his beautiful love came to her feet and wiped the blood from her lip, watching him turn his back and return to the window.

The book slipped from his lap.

He forced himself to peer into the cottage window. His gaze landed first on his love's black leathers puddled on the floor. At the sound of a feminine gasp, he held his breath, and dared to look. Across the bed were he and Etain, bodies intertwined, murmuring words of love. His heart always knew she was true despite what his mind told him. The betrayal was on his part by not believing her.

He woke on the cold stone floor. "What have I done?" His left fist slammed onto the hard surface. *My precious lady. No wonder you left.* He swung his right fist down. *Dar, you bullheaded oaf.*

He battered the stones repeatedly, berating himself for acting a fool and believing Midir's lies, until his anger was spent. He flexed each swollen and bloodied hand with great care. The pain was excruciating, and in his mind, deserving. The Krymerian climbed to his feet and shuffled to the en-suite.

He inventoried the damage as the cold water washed away the blood. Not only had he broken fingers on both hands, the skin along the outside of each resembled minced meat.

"Even with a healing spell, it will take time."

He rifled through the cabinets and found a box of bandages. With patience and determination, he dressed each hand, and turned to the task of cleaning the blood from the floor. Unable to get an effective grip on the cloth, he tossed it onto the spatters of blood and attempted to rub at the spots using his forearms and elbows but ended up frustrated by the effort. He rested against the chair and inspected each hand again. Ever so gently, he tested his fingers one at a time, his teeth clamped on his bottom lip.

After what I put her through. Will she ever forgive me? Should she?

Questions left unanswered, he dragged his tired body to the bed and collapsed into an exhausted sleep.

❦

A knock on his door startled him awake. "Who is it?"

"Elfin. I have come to get you for breakfast before we head to the gathering."

Breakfast?

"Let me get dressed," he called out, wondering where the night had gone. Dar swung his feet over the edge of the bed and noticed he still wore his clothes from the night before. "On second thought, I will meet you in the dining hall."

"All right. See you downstairs."

In the bathroom, Dar took inventory of his face in the mirror. Blood-shot eyes, his hair a tangled mess. *Not a good sleep.* He stared at the stubble on his chin. *No time for a shave. I would probably cut my throat if I tried.*

The basin filled with cold water, he gave himself a good dousing. His appearance was not much improved, but the chill brought a touch of color to his cheeks. He pushed the hair from his face and fumbled with a leather strap, tying it back as best he could. Blood seeped through the wet bandages on his hands, but there was no time for fresh ones.

Before going to the dining hall, other business sent the High Lord in search of the palace steward. Eventually, he found the man's office on one of the lower levels of the great tree. After a hearty exchange of "*Maith ar maidin,*" Dar asked the steward for a pair of gloves made of the softest leather possible and preferably lined with silk. The Elf disappeared into his inventory closet for several minutes before emerging with a pair.

Dar frowned. "No. These will not do."

The steward scowled. "Pardon, High Lord. You will not find a softer or more durable leather and the lining is of the finest silk."

"Please, check again."

He shrugged and after a noisy rummage of his inventory again, called out from the closet. "Ah, found another pair." Dar sighed in relief. "They must have fallen between the shelves with..." Once in the light, it was blatantly obvious the gloves were too small. "Oh, apologies, High Lord. These are for a child."

Dar eyed the first pair. "These are all you have?"

"I have a shipment due in next week, but this is it right now. Everything I had was taken by those competing today." The steward regarded the gloves. "These were made by the best in the business, High Lord. They may be a little tight at first, but your body heat will eventually loosen them up."

"I am off to the gathering myself." Dar scooped up the gloves. "Thank you, Steward. I shall be the belle of the ball."

The High Lord sidled down the hallway until he came to a private niche where he ducked in to work the gloves over his battered hands. The unquestionable quality and superb fit surprised him. "It could be worse," he mumbled, resigned to the fact it was the best he could hope for this close to the gathering.

By the time he entered the dining hall, most who gathered for the meal had finished or were almost done. There was no sign of Wolfe or Elfin, which he considered a stroke of good luck.

"Dar," Alatariel called out.

He approached the queen's table. Gloved fist over his heart, he bowed at the waist slightly. "May the light forever grace your kingdom and you forever rule in peace."

"May evil be smitten by your blades and forever contained within their deadly embrace." She motioned to the seat next to her. "Please, join me."

"It appears I have missed breakfast."

"Nonsense." At the clap of her hands, two servers appeared. "Quickly. Breakfast for the High Lord." They bowed and rushed from the hall. She leaned back in her chair, amusement sparkling in her eyes. "Nice choice of gloves. I know you to be a great connoisseur of leather goods, and they *are* a lovely pink, but I believe your complexion could handle a shade darker."

A server set a plate and silver before the High Lord. "They were not my first choice, especially for a gathering, but..." He flashed his boyish grin. "There are other things of this color that suit me fine."

The queen chastised him with her eyes. "Elfin told me you agreed to take part. Your new garb will certainly prove a distraction."

"All part of the grand plan, milady." With his breakfast served, he reached for the silver, anxious to appease his grumbling stomach. First round went to the knife and fork, proving their dexterity in avoiding his fumbled attempt to acquire them within his grip.

"It will be good for you." Alatariel watched as he wrestled with the silver.

"Perhaps." The hungry man went for round two, acquired the fork, but the irascible knife refused to be roused.

She covered her mouth with her hand. "Might I make a suggestion, milord?"

"No." Round three began with the sharp ring of silver against silver as Dar employed the fork to pry his knife from the table. The utensils subdued, he set to enjoying his breakfast. After a few bites, he asked, "Why did she leave?"

She shifted her chair closer to his and lowered her voice. "I told her to go." Her admission cut deep, but he maintained a calm façade. "At the time, our greatest concern was your wellbeing. Her presence seemed to be a hindrance."

He accepted it with a nod. "Did she go to Inferno?"

"I cannot say." She hesitated at his concerned reaction. "I would assume she would go there first."

Dar's raised brow prompted her to continue.

"For provisions." She paused. "To travel to Deudraeth and find her brother."

Curiosity turned to skepticism. "As Inferno would say, 'Yer takin' the mick.' Her brother is dead."

Alatariel pursed her lips. "She thought the same thing, but we have recently discovered he is alive and living north of Inferno's."

"And the bad news?" he asked, watching her throat bob with a hard swallow.

"He has been with Midir all this time," she said quickly. "Why? We do not know. How he came to be in Deudraeth, we do not know either. All we *do* know is he is alive."

A low growl rumbled from his chest. "You let her go? Alone?"

"I know what you are thinking, but he was sixteen at the time. Surely the influence of his parents counts for something."

"Have you lost your mind?" His fist crashed on the table. The fresh wave of pain increased his growing anger. Those few diners in the hall quickly finished their meals and left the queen and High Lord to argue in private. "You know as well as I if Midir had anything to do with that boy, he is as vile and evil as my brother."

Her glare matched his. "Then I suppose *you* are vile and evil, too. Midir was a part of you, no?"

"Do *not* try me. You know this is completely different. Sixteen does not offer the strength of mind the boy would need to resist Midir's influence."

Her voice rose to meet his in volume as she stood. "He is her *family*. We had no right to stop her."

"You had no right to manipulate my memories either." He fought the urge to bang the table again. "That boy is as dangerous as Midir if not more so."

Alatariel sat with a casual air and smoothed the folds of her gown. "She is not alone. Linq is with her."

He sighed. "You do not understand."

"Dar, you have had a hand in their training. Etain is quite capable of protecting herself and Linq is certainly able to keep her in check."

"No disrespect to him, but if Etain's brother has half the power she had before the blooding, Linq won't have a chance and neither will she."

"Do not be ridiculous," she scoffed. "Have faith in your lady."

Dar flexed his hands and grimaced wanting to hit something. Instead, he leaned into her face. "Know this, Queen Alatariel. If any harm comes to my lady, you will answer for it. And not just you. The entire kingdom."

He straightened. "Midir did not take that boy in for his welfare."

"So is it off to rescue the fair maiden from the evil brother?" Once said, she realized her error.

He shoved the table over as he came to his feet, scattering food and dishes across the floor. A red-eyed glare erased all trace of sarcasm from the queen's demeanor. "Etain has every right to track him down. I know she can handle herself, but do not for one second think the boy is not evil. It *is* within him. For the sake of my lady, my friend, and your kingdom, I pray the bond with his sister is stronger than the bond with my brother. I have a gathering to attend."

THE BLADE GATHERING

D ar strolled into a central square filled with Elves. Amassed for the games were two groups he knew all too well. The first being the Royal Guard, thought to be the greatest weapons masters ever known, each selected for his or her superior skills and willingness to lay down their lives in the protection of the Royal family. The others, known as the Black Blades, second only to the Royal Guard in ability, were a band of ruthless warriors, trained well in the art of war.

Dar approached a group of young Blades. "Excuse me, friend. I am in need of a blade or two. Would you be kind enough to lend me yours?"

"Why don't you run down to the market?" The Blade turned. "I hear—" Face-to-face with the High Lord, the young Elf tucked his swords under his arms, dropped to one knee, and placed a fisted hand over his heart. His fellow Blades followed suit. "Forgive me, High Lord. I-I was not expecting..." He offered his blades. "My swords are yours."

Dar eyed the kneeling Blade. "What is your name?"

He kept his head lowered. "Er, Llyr, High Lord."

"Are you in the tournament?"

"Aye, High Lord." Llyr dared to lift his head. "My first."

He admired the Blade's boldness and appreciated the significance of what it meant to the boy. His own performance in his first tournament had been less than stellar, but no less intoxicating. "I will not take that privilege away from you, Llyr. Anywhere else I can obtain blades this late in the day?"

Llyr jumped to his feet and snapped his fingers. Several younger warriors came running. "Two of you, hand your swords to the High Lord. Quickly!" Without hesitation, Dar received an array of black-bladed swords to choose from.

Dar accepted two broadswords with thanks and tested each one with an individual spin. His moves were awkward, due to his injured hands and unfamiliarity with the blades, but he continued working until his delivery felt smooth enough to compete, even though his timing and speed were not where they should be.

"Not quite my scimitars but they will do nicely. Are you not participants in the gathering?"

"This is our first year as official Black Blades, High Lord. We have not yet earned the right to take part, but we hope to qualify for the next one."

"It will be a great honor to see the High Lord in battle using our swords."

"I am privileged to use the weapons of a Black Blade, no matter his status. I shall endeavor to do them proud." He saluted the young Blades with a fisted hand over his heart. "Watch closely. Perhaps you will learn a few tricks even the old-timers do not know. They may help you qualify next year."

Their eyes widened in unabashed worship. "We will, High Lord."

"Now, where do I check in?"

One pointed across the playing field. "Hueil is the Master of Names today."

Another added, "We hope one of the Black Blades will take the title this time."

Dar turned to his companions. "Sorry to disappoint but I shall do everything within my power to ensure it does not happen."

The young Blades shuffled their feet, their eyes darting to each other.

Dar grinned. "Laugh, boys. It is a joke."

The nervous young Elves smiled. "Oh! Of course, High Lord."

He laughed as they hurried away, and turned to an older Elf with a clipboard in hand and scowl on his face.

"Name?"

"Halló, Hueil. Do you not recognize me?"

"Aye. I know who ye are," he said, giving him a narrowed eye. "Do ye not recognize protocol? Or have ye been off so long, ye lost all sense of propriety?"

Dar raised a brow. "Pardon me, sir. Dar VonNeshta, dual black blades."

"Hmph!" Hueil placed a tick next to Dar's name. "Bloody show-off," he muttered, walking on.

Dar spotted Wolfe and Elfin across the ring and walked toward the two. Out of the corner of his eye, he noticed an Elf maiden, who seemed to keep pace with his every step.

Wolfe grinned. "Looky here. The man's broke out his besties for this one."

"Mate, sometimes it takes a woman's touch to win the day." Elfin's grin turned into a giggle.

"Wolfe, Elfin." Dar graciously accepted the humor at his expense.

"I've always seen you more as 'love me lavender' than 'baby butt pink'." Wolfe laughed, his eyes reduced to mere slits.

Elfin chimed in. "This pink is far too delicate to be 'baby butt.' It reminds me of a lass I once knew, tits dipped in pink frosting."

"Laugh all you want, boys. I intend to take the prize."

"Which prize would you be referring to, Dar?" Elfin nodded toward the dawdling maiden.

Dar glanced over his shoulder. "A stray I seemed to have acquired along the way. Do you know her?"

Elfin winked at the girl and waved. "Zysha is not one who is easily swayed from what she wants."

"She is in for a big disappointment. No one compares to my Etain."

"You speak true, Dar." Wolfe chortled. "But I don't think Zysha got the memo."

Not long after, the Ringmaster called muster and made known the names of the combatants. Hearing theirs, Wolfe and Elfin left Dar on his own.

Zysha pushed her way through the crowd and tugged on his sleeve. "Milord." She curtsied. "I have a request." Her tongue seductively slid over her lips as she reached in between her full breasts and pulled out a scarf. "Would you do me?" Her eyes widened and she giggled. "Oops! I mean, would you honor me by wearing this scarf whilst in battle?"

"It would not be appropriate, milady." He tried not to notice the ample bosom barely held in by her scanty dress, but she moved closer, breasts first, and ran a suggestive hand down his arm. He pushed it away. "I am happily married."

Sensuous lips pouted. "Is she watching us? Point her out to me."

Tartarus. "M-My wife is not here today."

Zysha winked and wrapped the scarf around his neck. "Of course not."

A light breeze blew the ends of the scarf into his face. It was a valiant struggle to keep his opinion of the matter to himself as he swatted it away and dug even deeper for the semblance of a smile.

"It is merely a show of support. I want you," she licked her lips again, "to win." Batting her eyelashes, she added, "It would be rude to refuse."

Hearing his name called, he pulled away. "I have to go or they will not allow me to compete."

"Luck is with you, handsome. My scarf compliments your gloves." Zysha blew him a kiss.

"They are not *my* gloves," he muttered. With his first step, a sharp pinch to his buttocks caused him to turn his head. A gratuitous foot from the crowd made him stumble forward.

Wolfe, Elfin, and the others laughed.

"Nice ensemble, High Lord," someone shouted.

More teasing drifted his way as he righted himself and stormed across the ring.

"Damn woman."

Zysha called out, "After you show them how to fight, I will show you how to celebrate."

More laughter broke out when Dar stumbled into Wolfe. "*Tartarus.*" He glared at the two. "I swear, if either of you say anything about this to Etain, I will gut you both like river trout."

They zipped their mouths shut and threw away the key doing their best not to laugh.

"I have a plan for this little contest. If we work as a team, we should take most of them out, leaving the three of us to decide who will be the Grand

Master. From what I hear, it is time someone other than the Royal Guard takes the honor."

"Aye. It has been a long time coming," Elfin said.

"But when it's us three," Wolfe said, "no more alliance. May the best warrior win."

The three moved around the arena until they found a suitable spot, and faced the other participants as a united force. Wolfe and Elfin drew their swords and took defensive positions on either side of Dar, who scoped the competition.

"Let them come to you, tire themselves out. The rest should be easy."

A ray of sunshine illuminated the dais from where the queen commanded her audience, flags of the Elven houses represented in the event flying behind her. With the promise of a warm day, she wore a gown of green, accented by a sash of sparkling gemstones sitting just beneath her breasts. The fabric shimmered in the light like the waters of the southern seas. For today's festivities, she wore a tiara to complement her sash, the fire of each gem sparkling against her rich auburn tresses.

"Welcome to the Blade Masters Gathering, an ancient tradition we have upheld for many turns. This game promises to be the most exciting one yet. Our High Lord of Kaos has agreed to participate." She waited for the cheers and clapping of hands to subside. "He is certain to deliver an interesting show." Laughter rippled amongst the audience. "Thank you for your attendance. May your favorite warrior be the one to take the prize."

Accolades and best wishes washed over the combatants.

At the queen's raised hand, a gong sounded, and the competition began. Dar's trio formed a tight circle, back-to-back. Protected on either side by Wolfe and Elfin, his handicap became a mere inconvenience. The pain from his broken fingers merged with the spin of his blades and spurred him on.

Steel on steel reverberated through the arena turning it into a small battlefield. Booted feet lunged, while others fell back. One warrior spun and struck as her opponent blocked. Factions formed to weed out the weaker warriors.

Dar took a hit but a well-placed kick to the belly sent his attacker out of the ring.

Wolfe elbowed his comrades. "Duck!"

All three dropped at the same time just as a barrage of claymores flew over their heads. They glanced at each other, grinned, and rose up, their swords crossed overhead. In a single step, they slashed down and out. With a twist of each wrist their blades came up and down again stabbing forward. The claymores being the heavier blades could not match the speed at which the lighter swords moved. Their wielders soon found themselves on the wrong side of the qualification barrier.

Vendors passed through the crowd hawking a variety of refreshments and souvenirs. Onlookers cheered with every successful hit delivered by a favorite and cursing with every miss. A swirling breeze cooled the sweat on the brows of the flushed warriors but at the same time churned the dust beneath their feet.

As the numbers in the ring dwindled, the trio's circle loosened slightly. They ventured farther away from one another to achieve individual victories yet remained close enough to group together should a united force come against them.

The fight raged until those left could be counted on two hands: Dar, Wolfe, Elfin, three Royal Guards, and two maidens. Dar volunteered to face the women, leaving his accomplices to deal with the Royal Guards.

With a respectful bow of his head, Dar made his introduction. "I am Dar VonNeshta. I am here to take the title of Grand Master." He twirled his swords. "Will you dance the blades with me?"

"The Silent Warrior," said one maiden.

"In some cases."

The other bravely stepped forward. Dressed in armor of red leather, amber eyes peered out from her matching helm. "I am Illiana. I seek the title of Grand Mistress. I would dance with the devil to take the game."

Dar raised an appreciative brow. "You are not an Elf."

"Neither are you, High Lord." She smirked and lifted her sword.

Dressed in the deep blue armor of the dark Elves, the Elf maiden made her introduction. "I am Myanis. I seek the title of Grand Mistress. I too am ready to dance, although two against one hardly seems fair. Shall we wait for your friends?"

Dar lifted the tip of one blade and tilted the other over his head. "Where would the fun be in that?" A small trail of blood trickled down one of his wrists from inside his glove. The women exchanged subtle hand signals ignorant of the Silent Warrior's extensive experience with the code.

"Shall we see how silent you are in defeat?" Illiana called out as her sword searched for an opening.

Dar backed away and waited. To the seasoned warrior, their pattern of attack was obvious, but he knew he'd have to take several blows to land a few of his own. With the left sword, he jutted out toward Myanis and took a hit from Illiana. Dar met her blade with his right, his blade traveling the length of hers, and came up to deflect a blow from Myanis. He followed through with his left, but Illiana blocked the attack. The women worked together to push him back.

His arms snapped out, one to the left, one to the right. The side of one blade slapped Illiana on her side while he brought the other up to deflect another hit from Myanis.

Anger blazed in Illiana's eyes. "Dirty play, High Lord."

"Were it dirty, you would be in pieces."

Myanis took advantage of Dar's distraction and slammed into him. The impact carried enough force to push the big man back a step. Illiana shook off her pain and joined her cohort, pushing Dar closer toward the edge of the ring. He leveraged his powerful legs against the dual steam engines and stabbed his swords into the dirt, cursing himself for letting them get the best of him. He peered over his shoulder. His rear foot rested just inside the outer edge of the disqualification line.

He also noticed how close Myanis stood next to him. Ready to finish the game, he reared his head back and bashed her on the side of her forehead. She staggered back. Illiana danced away before he could move against her, slicing her blade at him. Dar dropped to one knee. As her sword passed over his head, a loud crack echoed when the sides of his blades connected with the armor around her rib cage. Myanis returned, a bruise forming on her forehead and whipped her sword down connecting with Illiana's.

Dar heard the weapons collide, rolled out of the way, and came up with a boot to Myanis' backside sending her out of the ring. He turned to Illiana, who was on the ground. Dar held the tip of his sword at her throat. "Yield."

Her bloody grin faded into a grimace. "It appears to be the only option."

"Aye, unless you can pick yourself up and raise your blade."

"Give me a day or two." She took in a slow breath. "Then maybe we can discuss it."

Dar chuckled. "Is that a yield?" She groaned and painfully raised two fingers in assent. He removed his blade. "You fought well, milady."

"Not well enough." Her hand fell to her side. "We will meet another day, High Lord, and I will not fall so easily."

"I hope not." After a bow, he turned to Wolfe and Elfin. "Let's do this."

No sooner did the words leave his mouth than the two came at him. Their blades dipped and slashed from both sides. With a mighty swing of a black blade, Dar shattered the sword in Wolfe's hand, leaving a razor-like point. As he pivoted to block Elfin's attack, he heard his name called. Zysha laughed as she pulled up the skirt of her dress exposing far more flesh than decorum allowed.

Elfin laughed. "Someone is anxious. Shall we end this now so you can get to real business?"

"Boy," Dar led with his right, "watch out, or I will send her to *your* room."

"O-ho!" He blocked the move. "Threats, is it?"

Dar swung up with his left. "A promise."

Again, his name came from the crowd. This time there were declarations of a good time and lack of sleep. Fire in his eyes, Dar turned. Elfin pressed the advantage and knocked him on the head with the side of his blade. Black spots danced before Dar's eyes. When Wolfe slammed the side of his broken blade into him, he doubled over, and his black blades slipped to the ground.

In a rush of inspiration, Dar grabbed the scarf from his own neck and wrapped it around the neck of his opponent, pulling it tighter and tighter until the man could no longer breathe. When Wolfe dropped to his knees, Dar picked him up by the seat of his pants and tossed him out of the ring.

The Krymerian spun into a crouch and only had time to retrieve one blade before Elfin charged in with a flurry of blows pushing him back. His dogged attack allowed Dar no time to plan his retreat. With one last step, he heard her warning gasp just as he tripped over Illiana. A whoosh of air rushed from between his lips when he landed in the dirt outside the barrier of the ring.

Elfin's surprised expression matched that of the fallen warrior, but he recovered more quickly. With a grin from ear to ear, he lifted his sword into the air to the cheers from the crowd, relishing in the adoration as he strutted within the circle. Flat on his back, Dar laughed, amused by the strange twist of fate.

Zysha rushed to Dar. "High Lord, you are wounded." Her nimble fingers set to work on the buttons of his shirt.

He swatted at her hands. "It is nothing. I am fine."

She ignored the rebuke. "I must see how bad it is. You will come home with me so I can properly take care of you."

With a huff, he sat up and inadvertently knocked Zysha onto her ass. He stood, turned his back on the insufferable woman, and stepped into the arena.

Still on her back, Illiana struggled to breathe. "Come to finish the job?"

He grinned as he held out his hand. "I achieved what I set out to do."

"Another trick?"

"It would not be to my advantage this time, milady. We have both lost the prize."

She accepted his hand and with his support came to her feet. "We underestimated you, High Lord."

"Aye. I hope you have learned a lesson." With a good-natured wink, he added, "Never underestimate your opponent, milady, especially an injured one."

She bowed her head. "Thank you for the reminder."

Still holding her hand, he perused her face more closely. "Have we met before?"

Illiana pulled her hand free. "I am confident in saying no, High Lord. We have never met." She saluted him with her sword and turned.

There was something about the woman that niggled in the back of his mind. He knew she spoke the truth about their having not met yet he could not shake the feeling. Dar caught her by the arm. "If you are not Elven, from where do you come?"

A cold amber gaze met his. "If you do not mind, I would like to get cleaned up. We can talk tomorrow if you insist." She shrugged from his grip and limped out of the arena.

Dar watched her leave and turned with the intention of joining Wolfe and Elfin for a quick congratulatory handshake.

"*She* would not make you happy." Zysha watched the maiden warrior leave the arena, but her demeanor softened as her eyes moved to his face. "Now me, on the other hand..." She ran her fingers down his chest. "I will—"

"You will not." At his wits' end, his pure white wings spread out and lifted him in a single flap.

A Solar Moment

Linq rode hard to the north, mentally daring the young man beside him to lag in any way. Etain would get to the camp long before they would. He did not want her to be alone for long should trouble come calling.

After several miles, he veered in a wide arc to the east, and turned south, keeping close to the trees. He slackened their pace upon hearing the rush of the river, and with little provocation, the animals turned toward it. As much as he hated to stop, the horses needed water. The men dismounted to stretch their legs while the horses quenched their thirst.

A soldier stepped out from behind a tree. "You bloody Alamir are so predictable. Men, take their weapons."

Linq recognized the *Bok* uniform of a lieutenant and stepped in front of Robert. "He is a shop owner. He has no weapons."

"Check him anyway and tie 'em up. We'll wait here."

One roughly bound Linq's arms behind him, and pushed him to the ground with a brain-rattling thud. "Wait for what?"

Robert grunted as he landed on his knees beside him.

A backhanded slap from the lieutenant split Linq's lip. "Shut up! You'll know soon enough."

A soldier, smaller in stature, spoke, "No sign of anyone, sir."

"Be patient, Dex. The bitch will show."

"The *bitch* is here. Cromorth, isn't it?"

The man smirked and turned. "Pretentious cow. You think you're going to take all of us?"

"Let's find out." Etain lifted *Nim 'Na'Sharr* in front of her. As the soldiers moved into position, her eyes cut to Linq. A brief nod exchanged between them acknowledged the plan.

Her body grew to her full height of seven feet and her wings fanned out. With a single beat, she soared into the sky, turned, and did a freefall toward the soldiers, who scattered.

Linq pushed his hands out as far as he could manage. The avenging angel slashed the bindings around his wrists as she swooped past, and dropped her sword next to him. Linq grabbed the blade and freed Robert.

The moment she landed, Cromorth raised his sword and ran at her. She drew the black-bladed scimitars, crossed one over the other, and pushed forward. Committed to his advance, the lieutenant ran straight into the path of the crossed swords and lost his head, the smirk frozen on his face.

"Pretentious dick." She darted into the patrol, slashing and jabbing her way through the *Bok* soldiers.

Linq fought his way to his blades. "Robert!" He tossed *Nim'Na'Sharr* in his direction and joined Etain in the fight.

She pivoted out of a double attack and bent low, slicing through the lower leg of one soldier. The other, unable to alter his move, brought his blade down and cut deeply into the fallen soldier's neck. She turned and came face-to-face with the one still standing. She deflected his furious assault and blocked his underarm dagger jab. Another twist saved her from the edge of his sword to which she answered with a slash at his head. The soldier ducked and jabbed again. This time he hit flesh. She staggered back.

"The bitch bleeds!" The soldier laughed as his cohorts surrounded the High Lady.

She glared at the advancing men, but something made her look beyond them. Linq followed her gaze. Robert was slumped on the ground, his arm bathed in blood and *Nim'Na'Sharr* inches from his hand. A guttural scream made Linq turn in time to see her launch into a fresh attack, ruthlessly cutting through the *Bok*.

He tried to work his way toward her, but a voice spoke in his mind.

Get Robert out of here.

Although stunned by her ability to communicate with him in that way, a war ensued within him. Leave a comrade in the heat of battle or save an innocent? His frown reflected his opinion of the command, but he changed direction and fought his way through the mélange to her injured brother.

The day suddenly erupted in a white light. Linq recognized it for what it was. He had seen Dar's *ultimá solar* decimate entire platoons of *Bok*, and while not as bright, he knew this light would prove just as lethal. He lunged toward Robert and knocked him to the ground as the beacon passed over them.

Once the light faded, Linq raised his head. Etain lay crumpled in a heap, her wings outstretched and Dar's blades in her hands. He jumped up and ran to her.

"Etain!" Robert struggled to his feet and followed.

The two checked her injuries. "Make sure her wings are not broken." Linq attempted to release the straps of the scabbard but a strong grip on his wrist stopped him.

"Leave it," she whispered. "Sheath the blades. I will not part with them until I see Dar."

Her gaze was clear and intense as she sat back on her heels. Linq and Robert returned the swords to their rightful places. Accompanied by guttural grunts, she retracted her wings.

Robert reached to pull her against him, but she resisted.

"I'm okay. Let me see the cut on your arm."

"It's just a flesh wound," he replied. "You be quiet and rest."

She relaxed against him. "It's nice to have my big brother back."

Linq did his best to clean her multiple cuts and scrapes with water from his canteen, and dressed Robert's wound. Once done, he scouted the area to make sure they were alone.

On his way back, he picked up *Nim'Na'Sharr*. "This is strange."

"What is?" Etain opened her eyes.

"The runes still glow."

She pushed against her brother to sit up, but he held onto her and asked, "Is it significant?"

"Dar forged this sword with his own hands and instilled his magic into its creation to make sure his protection was always with her. They glow as a warning of evil." He offered the blade to Robert and was certain the young man flinched. He moved *Nim'Na'Sharr* even closer as he pointed at the center rune. "See how it glows red and the blade glows white?"

Robert's eyes were for Etain only.

"Maybe it's the aftereffects of all this." Her gaze darted around the site. "Where are the soldiers?"

"Don't you remember?" Robert asked. "You lit up like a Christmas tree and blasted 'em all to hell."

She turned to Linq. "Oh no."

"Aye. Dusted every last one of them."

"The solar flare." She closed her eyes. "Great. As if it weren't bad enough already."

"What is done is done." Linq crouched next to her. "Rest a few minutes while I gather the horses. We must go."

By the time he returned, Etain was on her feet.

Robert chose a dapple-grey gelding with mane and tail of pure black. "You don't mind if I ride this one, do you?"

"It makes no difference to me as long as you lead a few back." Linq eyed Etain, thinking her too pale, but knew his concern would fall on deaf ears. "Think you can handle one or two?"

She did not respond, only stared at the horse Robert chose to ride.

"Are you okay, Etain?" Linq asked.

"Uh, no. I mean, aye. I'm good." She glanced his way for a moment but turned and stashed a sheathed *Nim* into the pack on Razz's rump. "I can take as many as you need me to."

They followed the river south until Linq decided it was safe to make camp for the night. "No fire," he said as they dismounted.

With the horses secured, the three shared a light meal, huddled close together to ward off the chill, and went over the events of the day.

"They knew you'd go that way and waited," said Etain.

Robert's gaze darted back and forth between the two. "We rode north for a long time. How could they know?"

"An excellent question," Linq said, stretching out. "One I have been trying to sort out since we were detained by our *Bok* friends." Hands behind his head, his eyes closed. "I suggest we take turns keeping watch. Wake me in a couple of hours."

After another day's ride, the three arrived at Castle Laugharne late in the afternoon, turning heads as they rode in. Etain refused to stop until she found Inferno, who was in the forge hammering on a piece of metal.

"Gods, lass!" He tossed the hammer aside and strode toward her as she slid off Razz, wrapping her in a bear hug. "Let me have a good look at ya."

Her arms tightened around his neck. "Don't let go. Please, hold me a little longer." He obliged her desperate plea and held her close as she cried on his shoulder. "I can't tell you how happy I am to see you, to know y'all are okay." She lifted her tear-stained face. "How are Spirit and the kids?"

"They be fine. We're all fine."

"Where's Ruby and Felix? They usually act as escort for anyone coming in."

Inferno sighed and released her. "They're around here somewhere."

"Have you seen Dar?"

"Haven't seen hide nor hair of the man." He squinted an eye at Linq. "Have ya not had news?"

"We came straight here from Deudraeth. "

Inferno eyed the stranger. "Aye, well, they've been busy all over. We called in the clan. Been gettin' messages from other clans all week. Some of the chieftains and a few of the Council are coming fer tea." He motioned toward the additional mounts. "Where'd ya find the strays?"

"Gifts from the *Bok,*" said the Elf. Inferno raised a brow.

"Is Spirit here?" Etain asked.

"Nay, lass. I sent her and the kids to her family's place. Kids and hob-knobbing brass don't make fer good company. They'll be back to-morrow. Swee's stepped in, been cooking and getting ready for tonight."

Right on cue, the healer stepped out the back door. "Etain, welcome back."

"Swee." Etain eyed the young woman. "What're you doing here?"

She paused for a moment, We swallowed as she met the blue-eyed glower. "Oh, well, the fresh air and change of scenery convinced me to stick around a little longer."

"Are you here to keep tabs on Dar for the Council? Give them a signal when his guard is down?"

Swee blinked. "I-I guess you didn't notice my absence at what I'm sure was a free-for-all the day they left. I resigned from the clan."

Etain raised a brow. "Savage?"

"I couldn't take it anymore. I don't know why Dar puts up with her." She shrugged. "I guess his strength is on the battlefield, not in public relations."

"Dealing with her *is* a battlefield," Etain muttered.

Swee laughed. "Etain, you're such a gem. I hope we can become friends."

"Since you're here of your own accord, maybe we can."

The healer gave her a good once-over. "I hate to say this but you look horrid. Come into the house and talk to me. We'll have you fixed up in no time."

"First, let me introduce my brother." She pulled him closer. "Inferno, Swee, this is Robert. Robert, this is Inferno, he's family, and this is Swee, a new friend of the family."

A blush in her cheeks, Swee smiled sweetly. "Welcome, Robert. I wasn't aware Etain had a brother."

"Neither were we," Inferno said, offering his hand. "Welcome to me home. I hear ya were raised by Dar's black-hearted brother, Midir."

Etain felt the blood rush from her face. "Inferno."

Robert gave Swee a slight smile but stared at the man.

Inferno noted his avoidance of the offered handshake and lowered his hand but held the hard gaze. "There'll be no funny stuff while yer in me home or when yer with our girl here. We watch out for our own and don't tolerate any—"

"Inferno," Swee interrupted. "I'm sure Robert will behave, especially with the likes of you around." She took Etain by the arm and pulled her toward the house. "Why don't you two come with me? I think you both could use a cold drink and a warm bath."

Inferno waited until the back door closed. "Tell me what ya can about that one. A glint in his eyes makes me balls twitch."

Linq walked with him into the forge. "The sooner I talk to Dar, the better I will feel."

"Nothing on his condition yet?"

"I have not heard from Alatariel."

Inferno grunted. "He'll find his way back. I've never seen anyone so full of fight and fire. Unless ya wanna talk about our lass. Heaven help anyone who steps betwixt those two or they'll be burned alive." Taking up the sledge, he set to hammering the metal piece again. "Now tell me how ya came by the extra horses."

Linq stared at the house for a moment. "Do I have a tale to tell you, my friend."

In the kitchen, Swee sat brother and sister at the island and drew an ale for each. "If you two are okay, I'm going to make sure your room is ready, and prepare one for Robert."

Etain watched her leave the room and turned to her brother. Unnerved by his stare, she blurted, "Well, here we are. I hope we can have a chat later tonight."

"I'm sure we can find a quiet spot to rendezvous after things die down." His eyes never left hers. "Looks like we caused quite a stir."

She shifted and ran a hand through her hair. "I'm sure everyone's on edge with the *Bok* on the move."

He gave her a lazy grin. "This Dar I've heard mentioned, is he the husband you referred to at the river?"

"He's not *actually* my husband."

"Is there a chance he might be one day?"

Not prepared to talk about her relationship, she avoided the question. "Shall we go upstairs? A warm bubble bath is what I need right now."

"Lead the way, milady."

Guess Who Came to Dinner

Alone in her room, Etain breathed in Dar's lingering scent and closed her eyes, giving herself a warm hug. "I will see you soon, my love."

She tossed her filthy clothes aside as she walked into the bathroom. While the tub filled, she poured in a good half bottle of bubble bath, brushed out her hair and pinned it up. Moments later, she immersed her weary body into the water and sighed in heavenly bliss. A light knock came at the door.

"I'm in the tub."

Swee stepped into the room. "You look at home in all those bubbles."

"Mmm, I am." She patted the side of the tub. "You have time for a chat?"

"Everything's under control downstairs; I can take a break." She sat facing Etain. "Your brother isn't so hard on the eyes."

"Aye, he *is* handsome." Etain reclined against the back of the bath. "I want to hear about you. I'm not surprised you've become friends with Spirit and Inferno, but I have to admit, I'm surprised to see you here."

Swee gave her a nervous smile. "After the Council left, I came by to see Dar but you were already gone. I offered to help clean up and get things back in order. It gave me and Spirit a chance to talk about different things and found we have the same interests in healing and herbs. She came to visit me in town one day and offered me a room, which I thought was a little weird, but when I met the kids, I fell in love. Especially with little Tegan. She is so cute."

"She's a darling. I think it's wonderful, Swee." Bit by bit, her aching muscles relaxed. "You'll never find better people."

"So true." She tilted her head. "I didn't want to say anything downstairs, but I was surprised to see you without Dar. Spirit said he's not been feeling well. How is he?"

Etain frowned and concentrated on soaping the bath sponge. "I don't know. I hope the Elves can help him."

"Don't worry." Swee's voice was a comfort. "He's too stubborn to let anything keep him down for long. Trust me. He'll be back." She leaned forward and touched Etain's shoulder as she stood. "I best let you get your bath and me back downstairs. I hope you don't mind but I've laid out an outfit for you. It's one less thing you have to think about."

"Thank you, Swee. I'll be down soon."

Etain lounged in the bath until the water turned lukewarm, pulled the plug, stepped out, and went to the shower to wash her hair.

Her thoughts on Dar, she worked the shampoo through her long tresses. The sweet fragrance whisked her away to a lazy afternoon spent in an open field of flowers. It was a beautiful spring day filled with sunshine, the flowers in full bloom. Dar surprised her with a picnic basket full of goodies. But the bigger surprise was how he let down his warrior guard and revealed the sensitive, intelligent man behind the façade. She fell in love with him that day.

Funny how I never recognized it before.

She twisted the water from her hair and stepped out of the shower. A movement out of the corner of her eye made her turn. Robert's brazen stare took her by surprise.

"What the hell are you doing?" A nearby towel rescued her modesty.

He crossed his arms over his chest and leaned against the door. "You saw mine. It's only fair I see yours."

"That was an accident." The towel wrapped around her securely, she walked to the vanity. "I didn't know you were swimming in the river, and I *certainly* didn't know you were my brother."

"As I recall, your modesty was somewhat lacking." His infectious smile was hard to resist but Etain managed. "Stop giving me the evil eye." He lowered his arms and stood next to her at the mirror. "It's not like you have anything to be ashamed of, sister."

"Exactly. *Sister*. Obviously, Midir didn't teach you any manners, not that he had any himself." She opened a drawer and reached in.

A small tug of war commenced when he made a grab for the comb in her hand. In the end, his firm grip twisted her wrist, and the comb was his.

"Midir taught me more than manners. Sit, *sister*. Let me turn this mess into a thing of beauty." With a huff, she sat and watched him in the mirror as he worked the comb through her hair with great finesse.

"For instance, some situations require a gentle hand." He picked up the heavy mass and yanked back, locking his gaze with hers in the mirror. "But there are times when a man must take control."

She tried to jerk out of his hold. "Are you trying to piss me off?"

He pulled her head farther back. "Just a little brotherly love." After a kiss on the forehead, he released her. "Swee says the guests are starting to arrive." He placed the comb on the countertop and edged toward the door. "Don't be too long."

"I won't be if you leave now." She walked with him to the door. "By the way, where'd you find those fancy duds?"

He preened under her attentions. "I found these in the wardrobe in my room. I gotta say, whoever they belong to must be some man. I'm no shrinking violet by any means, but wearing these clothes makes me feel like a kid playing dress-up. I fill 'em out pretty good, don't you think?"

"They aren't a bad fit." Thoughts of Dar brought a melancholy tone to her voice. "You look very handsome."

He winked and opened the door. "I hear a few of the oldest clans are coming tonight. Don't keep them waiting."

The door locked, she returned to the bathroom to dry her hair and add a light touch of makeup. The memory of Robert's shameless stare made her shiver. There wasn't a shred of respect in his eyes.

She remembered him as a considerate, thoughtful kid who knocked on her door, even if it were open. But this... This *man*... He was much different. She didn't know what to think of him.

Satisfied with the reflection in the mirror, she strolled into the bedroom. Like Swee had said, an outfit lay on the bed. "Wow, it must be some shindig."

Smooth, luxurious silk flowed through her fingertips. She turned toward the full-length mirror and held the chemise-style dress in front of her, admiring the shimmer of the blood-red fabric against her fair skin, and slipped the bit of decadence over her torso. It molded nicely to her curves, the flirty hem dancing just above her knees. She turned and raised a brow at the daringly low back exposing her down to the lowest curve of her back.

"Holy crap. Really, Swee? Let's hope I can live up to your expectations." Next to the bed sat a pair of strappy heels in the same shade of red.

After one last check in the mirror, she shrugged and headed out the door.

Familiar voices drifted toward her as she descended the back stairs. Inferno's boisterous laugh outshined them all, and brought a smile to her lips. In the hallway, her brother slid up to escort her into the main room.

"You're going to knock 'em dead, *mon petit*."

A chill ran down her spine and she stopped.

The smile on his face faded. "Did I say something wrong?"

His apparent remorse helped her relax. "No. No. I'm sorry. I'm a little nervous about meeting all these important people."

"I'll be by your side all night."

Heads turned when the dark-headed god in black entered the lounge with the silver-haired woman in red on his arm. Robert quietly whispered, "Breathe."

She inhaled as her gaze roamed over the group. There were a few familiar faces, but most were people she'd not met, some friendly, some not so much.

Inferno saved her from her thoughts. "Come here, lass. There's a few people I want to introduce ya to."

Robert relinquished her to his custody but stayed close. Names swirled through her head as she met the chieftains of the strongest clans in the

Alamir—S-A-F (Stand and Fight), COL (Creatures of Light), FWH (Fight with Honor), and UKElyte.

Fortunately, the call to dinner cut short any further introductions.

Etain found herself seated between her brother and Aramis, chieftain of the Dragon clan. At the head of the table, Inferno and Linq sat on either side of a man in unusual garb. She leaned toward her brother and quietly asked if he knew the strange man in red, white, and blue robes.

"Cappy. He's an Alamir Ambassador."

"Really? How do you know him?"

She caught Cappy's eye and flashed a dazzling smile. He tipped his head but a man on the other side of Inferno drew his attention away. She recognized Thoric dressed in his signature black.

"In my business, it's important to know who is who," Robert said.

On the other side of Aramis was a beautiful young woman dressed in robes of blue. Etain couldn't tell the color of her hair from the blue scarf wrapped around her head, but her brows were dark and her eyes turquoise. She politely asked the Dragon chieftain for an introduction.

"Etain, may I introduce the Lady Ambassador Rhapsody. Rhaps, this is Etain of the LOKI clan."

"Nice to meet you, Lady Ambassador. Welcome to Laugharne. But I'm afraid the LOKI boat sailed a long time ago."

"Sorry, Etain. I hadn't heard." Aramis raised a hopeful brow. "Perhaps I can finally convince you to join the Dragon clan." The chieftain leaned toward Rhapsody. "I've been trying to entice this young lady our way for a while now."

Rhapsody chuckled. "From what I hear, she would be a valuable asset. Etain, lovely to meet you." She offered her hand. "Please, call me Rhaps."

Etain accepted the gesture. "I didn't realize I had a reputation."

The man seated on the other side of Rhapsody leaned forward. "We're Ambassadors. It's our business to know the Alamir, especially those in close contact with our Krymerian friend." His robes of white surged with electric light.

"Oh, stop it, Ohms." Rhapsody waved him off but introduced the fourth and final Ambassador. "Etain, this is Ohmslaw, He may not sound like it, but he and Dar have been friends for many years."

"Hmph." Ohms grunted. "I don't know if I would call our relationship friendly."

Rhaps raised her brows. "Then shall we call it cordial?"

His dark eyes focused on Etain. "Good to meet you, Lady Etain. Where *is* the big man? Don't tell me he's already run off on a new adventure."

She chuckled. "I'm afraid it's the other way around. We were away on business, and I decided to leave him to it. It gave me the opportunity to catch up with my brother." She motioned toward Robert. "We haven't seen each other in a while."

A cough came from further up the table followed by a muttered, "Typical," said loud enough for Etain to hear. She turned but everyone appeared engrossed in other conversations.

Ohms seemed not to have heard the remark. "He must have lost his mind to leave your side. I see what attracted the man but for the life of me I cannot fathom the reverse."

An uneasiness crept over Etain. "Deeper than you can imagine, milord. Thank you." He raised a brow at the unusual response, but another conversation pulled him away. She leaned toward Robert. "All these dignitaries, I feel out of place."

He gave her hand a comforting squeeze. "You fit in fine."

"This girl will never fit in," a boisterous voice declared. Robert shot a virulent glare at a wall of a man who loomed on the other side of the table. He grinned at a stunned Etain. "A damn sight for any sore eye."

Her brother came to her defense. "Who are you to insult Lady Etain?"

"Me?" The big man laughed. "Why I'm—"

"Master G!" She vaulted out of her chair. "I didn't know you were coming."

He watched her graceful dash around the table with an appreciative eye. "Need to know basis, E."

Her eyes sparkled, drinking in the six-foot-five frame of her former chieftain. "It's been ages." Memories of her early Alamir days with this impossible man and her first clan, Darth, rushed in.

"It has been a helluva long time. It looks like it's been good to you."

"I can say the same for you, Master G." Etain grazed a hand over his nearly bald head. "Keeping it close to the cuff these days. I like it." She was certain there was a hint of a blush in his cheeks.

His laugh rumbled throughout the room. "Glad you approve. It keeps the kiddies in line. But you... Hell." His green-blue eyes appraised the once ragamuffin duckling. "There's nothing left to the imagination tonight. Good thing you didn't dress like this when with the clan. I never would've let you run off."

She frowned. "I didn't run off. Besides, I knew you weren't interested."

"Hmph. Dirty jeans and T-shirts. Yeah, not a big turn-on."

She lovingly punched his muscular arm. "I would've kicked your ass anyway."

"Not in a million years, E." He laughed. "Not in a million years."

"How is the ragtag bunch of heathens?"

"We're damn near respectable nowadays with a good-sized base of operations. I wish they could see how well you're doing. You've been missed."

"It would be good to see the boys and Angel again. Come, sit with us." She pushed him down into a chair across from hers. "You stay right there." She joined her brother and made the introductions. "I guess you know everyone else."

"We are all well acquainted."

During the meal, Master G entertained those nearby with stories of the early days, interspersed by many a teasing joke. Etain laughed and made sure he didn't exaggerate too much.

With dessert served, the conversation moved to serious matters. The various chieftains expressed their concerns and offered opinions in the hopes of gaining a solution to the *Bok'Na'Ra* issue. The Ambassadors did what they did best and kept everyone on topic and tempers in check.

Thoric brought to light a new development. "I've heard rumors the Haluci Clan have discovered a static portal in the L.A. area. Can anyone verify?"

Angel, the chieftain of the FWH Clan, smirked. "Have you been dipping into Cappy's spirits again, Thoric?"

He lifted his chin with a disdainful glint in his eyes. "If I had, the news would be far more interesting than a new portal. Unless someone else has anything to say, I'll take your silence as a no." His gaze touched on each of the chieftains as he spoke. "Let's discuss the security for the stones. It is crucial they be protected. Have precautions been taken?"

Etain leaned toward Aramis. "What're they talking about?"

"The stones of the Alamir," he whispered.

"They must be awfully important."

Rhapsody overheard her. "They're extremely important, Lady Etain. Without them, the Alamir would not exist. They are the source of our powers."

"Seriously? All this is based on a bunch of rocks?"

The Ambassador smiled. "They're more than that. Actually, the stones they speak of are all pieces of one."

Etain lifted her wine glass, fascinated by the story. "Where'd it come from?"

"It was given to the original Alamir ages ago," Aramis said. "No one knows from where it came. Only that it was given to Leictreacha."

Rhapsody picked up the story. "In the beginning, it was passed from clan to clan every five hundred days to avoid any one clan claiming a monopoly. It remained whole for many years, but when the clan wars began to rage, it was broken into pieces in an effort to weaken the storm. Not long after, the Council was formed, and the pieces entrusted to the five strongest clans for safekeeping."

"What happened to... What was his name?" Etain asked.

"Leictreacha," Robert said.

"Leic-tre-acha. What happened to him?"

"He died."

Etain furrowed her brows. "How?"

Master G leaned forward. "Some believe he died when the stones were broken apart. Others say he lives in the pieces of the stone. The red is the fire of his heart." His gaze went to Rhaps. "The blue represents the windows to his mind." The green-blue eyes moved to Aramis. "Brown is the earth that grounds the body." He came to Robert. "Green represents the wind that breathes life into the soul." The last bit he saved for Etain. "Then there is the fifth piece, the silver shard, the unknown."

She squirmed under his gaze. "I-I didn't know you were so well-versed in the history of the Alamir."

He shrugged. "It became a necessity."

Etain leaned forward on her elbows. "You seem to have gone beyond mere common interest. Why haven't I heard all this before?"

Rhaps spoke before Master G. "Although we are Alamir, we are still human. Only those in possession of the stones know of their existence these days. Too many have defected to the *Bok* and would love the opportunity to destroy them and the Alamir. I must impress upon you that whatever you learn tonight be kept in the utmost confidence."

"You said the pieces were given to the five strongest clans." The Lady Ambassador nodded. "So why are Dragon and Darth here? Sorry, Aramis, Master G. Where is LOKI? Even *I* know they're one of the five."

Ohmslaw joined in the conversation. "Lady Etain, Inferno explained the situation between Dar and his clan. We felt it best Aramis act as liaison to avoid complications."

"And Master G?"

His eyes roamed from Etain to her seemingly disinterested brother, and back to her. "Circumstances demanded an historian for the Alamir, someone to chronicle our past in order to better understand our future."

She sensed there was more to it but knew this wasn't the place or time and pushed her chair back. "Sounds like politics to me. If you don't mind, I think I'll retire for the evening."

"You make sure what was said tonight stays here." It was the same gravelly voice she'd heard earlier.

Etain turned toward the top of the table. Unfamiliar with the voice, she wasn't sure who'd spoken. "Excuse me?"

A rugged man with dark, close-cropped hair who sat next to the FWH chieftain stood. "Personally, I think we should follow the Krymerian's selfish example and watch out for ourselves, leave the humans to their own demise. They have no appreciation for our intervention. But as it seems to cause such distress among my colleagues..." He motioned to the others around the table. "I play the game. However, I believe they will all agree it's best to keep Alamir business amongst the Alamir."

"Tonos. Not cool," Thoric said. "We're not here to—"

Tonos turned to the Ambassador. "It is the perfect time to address the failings of a man who struts through life as though he's not responsible for the deaths of hundreds of Alamir."

"What does that have to do with me?" Etain asked.

"It's no surprise why he's not here tonight to face the five clans. He knows all too well the reception he would receive. Instead, he sends his girl to spy and report."

A flush of anger warmed her skin. "Are you talking about Dar?"

Inferno came to his feet. "Our lass is no spy."

Etain's hand lingered over the steak knife at the side of her plate. "Who the hell are you to insult Dar?"

Aramis touched her arm. "Etain..."

The arrogant man laughed. "I am Tonos of the *.com* clan, and my point of view is shared by many in the Alamir. Even his own clan demands his extermination. If you ask me, we would all be better off."

The knife's wooden handle felt smooth, cool to the touch, and fit comfortably in the palm of her hand. "Dar has never killed an innocent."

"Tell it to my dead sister and her family," he retorted.

She gauged the distance between herself and the hateful man and considered the obstacles in her way. In a blue shimmer, she disappeared only to reappear behind him. "Your clan isn't part of the five. Why are *you* here?"

Arrogance shone in his eyes. "And you have *no* clan. Why are *you* here?"

"This is my home." How she would love to use her solar against the impudent man. "*Why* are you here?"

Angel turned in her seat. "It has been a long journey for some of us. Tonos was chosen as my escort to ensure my safety."

Etain eyed the woman with honey-blonde hair. "One of your own wasn't good enough?"

Indignant, she answered, "If you paid closer attention to your own kind you would know *.com* is one of the best clans when it comes to combat."

Etain's fingers twitched around the knife. "Maybe we should see how good he really is."

Tonos laughed. "You going to prick me with your little stick, girl?"

She glanced at the weapon in her hand, cut her eyes back to Tonos, and lunged.

"Etain!" Inferno yelled as he and Linq scrambled around the table.

Robert shot out of his seat. Master G, the closest of them all, reached for Etain. The knife spun in her hand, light gleaming off the sharp tip as it neared Tonos's heart. Linq pulled Angel out of the way.

Tonos sidestepped just as the blade breezed past his chest, Etain slamming the knife into the tabletop. "*That* was for effect." Her breath rasped in his face as five talons extended from her knuckles. "*These* are for you."

Master G leaped forward as Robert yanked Tonos away. The deadly talons stopped centimeters from G's face, Etain's wrist caught in his fierce grip. "I think it's time you called it a night, E."

"Let. Me. Go."

Tonos continued his taunts. "The murdering bastard's taught you well, *girl.*"

A blue charge shot from her free hand, hitting Tonos in the chest. The blast threw him and Robert into Inferno, forcing the men into the other guests. Chairs, people, and dishes clattered across the floor.

"Shut him up," Master G yelled and tightened his already firm grip. "Release these things, E."

Her focus was on the big-mouthed man struggling to get to his feet. "Dar is not a murderer."

"Neither are you." Master G squeezed harder. "Now put 'em away." The lethal projections slipped out of sight. "Where the hell did those come from?"

"Will you be here in the morning?" she asked, too wired to answer his question.

"If Inferno doesn't kick us out."

"I will see you before you go." She turned to her former dinner companions. "Rhaps, Ohms, it's been a pleasure. Aramis, it was good to see you again."

Each murmured a good night in turn. She opened her mouth to utter a general good night when a new face stepped through the doorway. Dark brown eyes held hers for a long moment as he walked into the dining hall. Etain felt strange, like nothing she'd felt before not even with Dar. She watched the young man approach Master G and whisper into his ear.

"Alamir, we have a problem," Master G announced.

Flashes of Light

All heads turned when two young men dressed in black appeared in the doorway of the dining hall.

"Krz," Angel said. "What're you doing here?"

"Pardon the interruption, folks, but the situation is critical. We've acquired a new entry that will get us into the human realm faster and should prove a lot safer for our people."

"Where?" Tonos asked.

"No time to explain now." Kane stepped next to his brother. "We have to move."

Inferno shot Tonos a warning glare as he passed by the man. "What the hell is it now?"

"*Bok* agents have been spotted in the human realm and in too many locations to be random," Kane said.

"How long ago?" Thoric demanded amidst the bustle of people hastily preparing to depart.

"Within the past hour," Master G said.

"Hour?" Thoric motioned to Ohms and Rhaps to join him.

Cappy took over command. "Angel, Tonos, how soon can you get people on the move?"

Angel snapped on her utility belt equipped with throwing stars, nunchaku, a set of sai, and two butterfly knives. "We have a bigger problem. The COL fortress has been breached."

Tonos pressed the communicator in his ear. "Ant and Tim are on their way with a crew."

"Is anyone hurt, Natas?" Thoric asked the COL chieftain.

"Too early to confirm. The Don says the east wall has fallen. It's total mayhem."

"Let us know if you need more."

"Will do," he said on his way out the door.

UKElyte and S-A-F advised they had teams on standby.

"Kane can meet UKElyte and take them through," said Krz. "I'll go to S-A-F—"

"By the time you'd get there, they could already be in place," said Thoric. "Get UKElyte. If your location proves itself, we'll consider it for future use."

Etain approached Thoric. "I can be changed in five."

"No, lass. Stay here with yer brother." Inferno lifted a hand at her intended rebuke. "Ya had a long few days and need yer rest. Linq, make sure she stays put."

Thoric shrugged. "Sorry, Etain. If it helps, we Ambassadors are staying here too."

"Keep us informed on all fronts," said Ohms. "In the meantime, we'll contact those clans closest to COL to send in reinforcements."

"I'll get in touch with some of the smaller clans to help in the human realm," Rhaps said.

Cappy turned to Master G. "Anything in the LOKI area?"

He conferred with the dark-eyed young man at his side before he answered. "I wouldn't count anything out."

"Aramis, contact Savage. Put them on alert," the Ambassador ordered.

"Ra is on his way to the castle as we speak," Aramis said, headed for the door.

"Good." Cappy addressed his fellow Ambassadors. "The entire Alamir realm should be on high alert."

Etain stepped out of the way while the room cleared. Her gaze came around to Master G, who smiled and tipped his head. "Maybe next time, E."

She shrugged, her slight smile disappearing when she noticed intense brown eyes set on her. The strange young man cocked a curious brow as he followed Master G out of the dining hall. Angel followed by Tonos was close behind.

Tonos smirked, muttering as he passed Etain, "When all this is over, it's you and me in the arena, *girl*."

The Mobius Arena, a sacred dome where the Alamir met to settle their differences. Two would walk in but not necessarily walk out.

Etain's scalp tingled. "With no one to save your ass."

"Are you okay?" Robert's voice made her jump.

"Hey. Care to take a walk with me?"

Outside, sister and brother watched from the shadows as the last of the chieftains departed. They remained hidden until the Ambassadors, Linq, and the others went back inside. Robert offered his jacket against the chill of the night as they walked along the smooth path at the edge of the graveled courtyard.

"Is it true what the man said about LOKI wanting the Krymerian out?"

"Can we talk about something else?"

"Sure." Robert slid his hands into his front pockets. "These people take the *Bok* pretty seriously, huh?"

"They *are* serious. Attacking COL is a bold move, but I don't want to talk about that either."

"Right."

They walked along in silence for a short time.

"Tell me how it was living with Midir."

"Midir?" He shrugged, his hands still in his pockets. "Life was good. He gave me everything I needed, a good education, nice clothes, a safe place to live. He took care of me and opened my eyes to a different way of life. He even set me up in business once my talents became apparent."

"A different way of life. I'm sure," she murmured, shaking her head. "So what *are* your talents?"

"You were in my shop. I have a knack for the organic. I've created many a magic spell. Midir used a few in his business."

She stopped and faced him. "Have you any idea what his business was?"

"I knew enough."

She rolled her eyes. "He murdered our parents."

"A *mercenary* killed our parents," he said. "Midir arrived in time to stop him from killing me. If only you hadn't run..."

She shot him a narrowed glare. "*You* told me to run. You have no idea how many nights I spent scared and alone, asking myself why it happened. Midir planned the whole thing."

"Etain, you have it all wrong."

Her hands balled into fists. "He told me himself, Robert. Midir hired the demon because he wanted *me*. He wanted *my* power."

"Aren't we full of ourselves tonight?" He scoffed. "He saved *me* and never showed a moment's interest in you."

"Are you sure?" She placed her hands on her hips. "There's so much you don't know about him."

"I think you'll find it's the other way around." He turned away.

She sighed. "Damn. I've just gotten you back and here we are already acting like brats. I'm sorry I upset you."

"Midir was good to me," he said from over his shoulder. "I won't have anyone bad-mouthing him, even my sister."

"It's been a long day. Why don't we get back to the house?" She touched his arm. "Tell me how it happened for you while we walk."

"How what happened?"

"Your initiation into the Alamir."

"What makes you think I am Alamir?"

"How else could you live in his realm or be in this one?"

"I have no idea, but I assure you, I'm not Alamir."

She frowned and pinched the bridge of her nose. "My head hurts and I'm too tired. I'm going to bed. We can talk tomorrow." She kissed him on the cheek and left him alone in the courtyard.

Once through the front doors, Etain bypassed the living room and headed for the stairs. Before going up, she removed her heels, her mind elsewhere. When she stepped onto the landing, she found the young men in black pacing back and forth.

The one with light eyes spoke. "Hello. You're Etain, right? Etain Rhys?"

She stepped back. "Who's asking? What're you doing up here?"

The two men exchanged a glance. "Forgive me. I forget we've not been introduced. I'm Krz." He motioned to himself, and to the man at his side. "This is my brother, Kane. We are of the Haluci clan."

"What do you want?"

"She doesn't believe you, Krz," Kane said. "Look, if we weren't who we said we were, you really think we would've made it past the front door?"

"Easy, man. Etain, we're a small clan who operate on a covert basis."

"Yet you show up here today."

Krz breathed in. "Covert in the human realm. Thoric and the other Ambassadors are familiar with our work."

"Forget this, bro. We haven't the time."

Krz concentrated on her rather than his brother.

Etain thought for a moment. "Thoric mentioned an Haluci clan earlier and a new portal."

"He did?" The man appeared proud of the mention. "Good. I overheard your conversation with him. Do you want to help? Will you go with us?"

She retreated a step. "Why would I go with you?"

Kane stepped in front of Krz and turned his back on Etain. "They could already be closing in on the family. We have to go!"

Etain recognized the communication between the two. She shared the same with Dar. Kane stepped aside and crossed his arms over his chest. Krz turned his gaze on her. "Your father was James Rhys."

She considered the handsome, light-eyed man and his brother. "My father?" Etain stepped onto the landing. "Did you know him?"

"No, unfortunately, but we know a woman who did. It's her place we've acquired as a portal. Would you like to meet her?"

Etain bit her bottom lip. First, she found her brother, who she thought dead, and now, an opportunity to speak to someone who knew her father. Was it too good to be true? Should she trust these men? They seemed sincere. Their auras were good; one blue, the other orange.

She turned to Kane. "You mentioned a family."

"Who could be dead by now, thanks to you!"

"Give me five minutes."

"Kane..." Krz said, "Get UKElyte. We'll meet you there."

Tiny explosions of light sparked in the dark of night as the Alamir stepped into the human realm. Teams appeared wherever there was the most *Bok* activity—Boston, Rio de Janeiro, Tokyo, and Perth.

Etain and Krz appeared in a bar in L.A.

"I swear. I'll never get used to your lights," said a woman coming out from behind the bar. "I duck and run for my gun every time!"

Krz laughed. "A burst of cardio's good for you, Jackie."

"Stop it," she said, laughing. "We need to tweak the plan a bit. Appearing in the main bar area isn't gonna keep your operations covert."

"You have a point. We can alter it to the storeroom if you're on board with it."

Kane and members of the UKElyte clan sparked in. Jackie nodded in their direction, but her whiskey gaze widened.

Krz cleared his throat. "Um, Jackie, meet—"

"I'd know this girl anywhere." Jackie's smile faded as the women stared at one another.

Dressed in leather pants and a "Rock or Die" T-shirt, she appeared to be acceptable by aura standards. Etain had no recollection of the older woman but suffered her scrutiny. If this were a trap, she'd be damned if she'd be the one to give anything away.

"As I live and breathe," Jackie said, giving her a good once over. "You're the spitting image of your mama, but I'll be damned if I don't see the same steel in your eyes as your dad."

Etain blinked, hearing her own words repeated.

"You're a far cry from the girl I last saw." She glanced at Krz. "She was always pretty, but could Aurelia ever get the girl into a dress?" Jackie beamed at Etain with what she interpreted as pride. "Hell no! The little sprite insisted on living in jeans and T-shirts. A girl after my own heart." If possible, her grin widened even further. "But the worst part for Auri..." Jackie looked down and laughed. "Nice boots, Ms. E. You've certainly grown into 'em."

A familiar spark lit in Etain's mind. A memory, fuzzy, yet warm, began to take shape. Only one person ever called her mom Auri. "Jacleen?"

Kane smirked at Krz. "What're the odds, bro?"

"Not anymore, babe," Jackie said.

Etain wrapped her arms around the woman and squeezed her tight. "Holy hell, Jacl..." She pushed her back to arm's length, "Jackie!" Despite the woman's business dealings with her dad, she'd proven a good friend to the family. "With all that's gone on. Holy crap." She laughed, pulling her close again. "I worked so hard to put things behind me. I'm sorry—"

Jackie patted her on the back. "Don't you worry about it, Ms. E. I'm glad to see you're alive and well. *I'm* sorry I wasn't there for you."

Etain swiped the tears from her eyes. "You couldn't have known where I was. Hell, *I* didn't know where I was for the longest time." She let out a nervous chuckle. "What brought you to L.A.? And a bar? I mean, I didn't know your business with dad, but... A bar?"

She laughed. "It belonged to an uncle who passed away a while ago. I thought about selling but decided it was time for a new life, so I packed up and moved out here. If I'd known it'd bring you back into my life, I'd have moved sooner."

"Excuse me, ladies," interrupted Krz, "but we have more pressing business now."

"Sorry, Krz," Jackie said. "They're in Beverly Hills for a fancy campaign dinner. I'll get you the address." She headed to the bar. "It's just up the road a spell. Won't take long to get there."

Etain turned to Krz. "A politician?"

"She's a Presidential candidate."

"Since when did running for President become dangerous?"

Kane answered this time. "Since her opponent decided to hire a *Bok* assassin to level the playing field."

Jackie returned with a piece of paper. "Here you go, Krz." She eyed Etain. "Come with me, girl."

She pushed her onto a barstool, went behind the bar, grabbed a couple of shot glasses, and a bottle of Patron. The glasses set in front of Etain, she filled each one to the rim.

"What's this for?"

"You're whiter than a sheet, Ms. E." Jackie picked up one of the shots. "This'll help." She winked and downed the tequila.

Etain ran a hand through her hair, picked up her glass, and slammed the amber liquid down her throat. A warm glow blossomed out from her belly. "One more," she gasped.

"Make it quick," said Krz. "We have a lot of ground to cover."

"No time." Kane grabbed Etain by the arm before she could pick up her glass. "Gotta go now."

She pulled from his grip. "You asked me to trust you. Now it's your turn to trust me." Etain finished off her second shot. "I know a really quick way. Show me a map of where we're going."

"The general direction is northwest of here," Krz said. "Beverly Hills."

"Can you zero in on the address?"

"Here." Jackie slapped a piece of paper on the bar. "I've been following the campaign. I never trusted the asshole she's running against."

Etain grabbed Krz by the arm, who made a grab for the paper, and shoved him into his brother. "Meet us there," she yelled at the clan. At impact, the three lit in a blue shimmer. "I'll be back, Jackie!"

The three materialized in the middle of Rodeo Drive. Etain turned her head. "Which way, Krz?"

Kane clung to his brother, his eyes the size of half-dollars. "What the hell was that?"

Krz shook his head and laughed. "Whatever it was, I wanna do it again."

Etain rolled her eyes. "I thought time was of the essence. Which way?"

"Um, oh. The Four Seasons is..." Krz turned until he came back to his original position. "This way."

Sirens waled and flashing lights cast alternating reds and blues over the face of the hotel. The three took off in a dead run toward the hotel. People too busy looking over their shoulders ran at them, terror in their eyes. The hotel was in chaos with policemen yelling, children screaming, people running away, and emergency techs heading into the fray.

In the middle of the fracas, Krz leaned toward his brother. "We have to split up. Find the family. Get them out."

Kane sneered at Etain as he spoke to Krz. "If it isn't already too late."

"Just find them." Krz set him on his way with a push and turned to Etain. "Are you okay?"

She stared at the entrance to the hotel. "I can feel it. Them."

"The family?"

"The *Bok*. They're still here. We may have a chance." She shoved her way through those exiting the main doors.

"Wait, Etain!" he yelled. "You don't have a weapon."

Etain kept to the outer walls of the corridor, making her way through the onslaught of humans who were desperately trying to distance themselves from whatever evil lurked within the hotel. She heard whispers of "shooting" and "terrorists." It was forbidden to interact with humans while on their terrain but with all the chaos around her, finding the right room was difficult.

Damn the consequences. She decided to ask just as a set of double doors burst open at the end of the hall. People in formal evening wear poured through them and joined the other fleeing guests. Etain inched her way to the open doors and slipped inside.

The large banner across the back of the stage confirmed she'd found the right place. A movement to the left of the stage caught her attention. There she saw a girl with dark hair about fourteen years old. Etain followed her frightened gaze toward the stage. A man and woman were on their feet, staring in the same direction as the girl. She could tell they were the girl's parents, her hair being the same color as the man's and her profile similar to the woman's.

Etain looked further to the right and staggered at the undulating dark form. The years since her parents' deaths melted away. Much like that day, she was mesmerized by the sense of evil radiating from it.

A gunshot snapped Etain out of her paralysis. The woman on the stage touched her head, blood flowing down the side of her face. Etain thought the bullet must have grazed her scalp.

The girl's scream set her into motion. Etain ran between the tables, her great wings extending when she stepped onto the platform. She dove for the woman as another shot breezed past, just missing her head, but hit the woman in the shoulder. Etain wrapped her wings around her and the two fell toward the floor. Although her wings softened the blow for the candidate, Etain grunted from the impact.

"Oh my god. Are you okay?" the woman asked, her eyes wide.

"I'm good. Don't worry about me. How are you?"

"Oh, I've had better days. Feeling a bit woozy." She blinked. "Where are we?"

Etain furrowed her brows, and noticed what the woman spoke of. Instead of the stage floor, they lay on the front lawn of a familiar house. "Well, it appears we're at my house. In Texas."

"What?"

Etain sensed the woman was near to passing out. "You're doing great. Stay with me, okay?"

"I must be hallucinating. My head hurts." The woman closed her eyes but opened them suddenly. "My daughter! Where's Chloe? Where's Ed?"

"They're safe. My friends are watching out for them."

"Am I dead?"

Etain smiled. "Definitely not."

"Oh, well, I'm Caroline. Thank you for helping me."

"I'm Etain. How about we get you back now? I'm sure the EMTs will be there by now."

In a blue shimmer, the two reappeared on the stage floor. The young girl Etain saw earlier was on her knees, holding Caroline's hand. "I'm here, Mom," the teary-eyed girl said, Krz behind her. "I'm okay. Dad's here too."

"I'm here, Caroline," her husband said, Kane at his side.

Both were oblivious to the guardians who watched over them.

Caroline smiled at each one including Etain. "Thank you all. Thank you."

"It's a pleasure to meet you, Caroline," Etain whispered. "Shall we keep this between us?"

The woman gasped, the pain finally registering with her brain. "I've just met my guardian angel in the flesh. Who would believe me?"

Etain laughed and looked at Krz, who nodded. "Caroline, the EMTs are coming." She grimaced as she released her wings. "These brave young men will ride with you to the hospital to ensure your safety. You take care of you and your beautiful family."

Chloe squeezed her mother's hand. "Mom, are you sure you're okay?" Her father kneeled next to her, placing an arm around her shoulders, and his eyes on his wife.

"I am, thanks to..." Caroline turned her head. "Where did she go?"

"I'm right here, Mom," Chloe said, tears trickling down her face. "Dad's here too."

"The blonde in black. With wings?" Their wide-eyed expressions reminded Caroline of what her angel said. "Never mind, I must be in shock."

Back at the Hacienda

Swee was up early the next morning to get her usual chores out of the way so she could spend time with Etain, and hopefully, her handsome brother. With most things done, she noted the lateness of the day and realized she'd not seen the young woman. She ventured upstairs and tapped on Etain's door. With no answer, she tapped again as she slowly opened the door.

"Etain?" The covers were tousled, the corner of a silken sheet casually draped over a leather-clad derriere. *Why're you dressed?*

A teacup on the bedside table caught her eye. *What's this?* She stepped into the room, picked it up, and sniffed the liquid. "Root of asphodel." She dipped in a finger and brought it to her lips. "With a wormwood infusion. Where would you get a concoction like this?" She returned the cup to the table and shook the sleeping girl. "Etain, you must wake up. It's afternoon." With no response, she shook her a little harder. "Etain. Spirit should be home soon. Come on. Wake up."

The girl still didn't respond. Swee pushed her onto her back and leaned into her face. Relieved to hear her breathing, she grabbed her by both arms, and gave her one more inspired shake. "Etain!"

Her head lolled as she mumbled incoherently.

"Get up and talk to me. It's a beautiful day."

Etain peeked out from heavy lids and leaned against the headboard. "What time is it?" Her words dissolved into a cough.

"You need water." She hurried into the bathroom and returned with a glass. "Drink it slowly."

Etain sipped. "I must've drunk more than I thought. My head feels like a rock." She placed the glass next to the teacup.

"It wasn't the amount you drank, hon. It was that." Swee pointed to the cup. "Where did it come from?"

"What? I don't know. It was there when I went to bed last night. What is it?"

"Draught of the Living Dead." Swee sniffed the cup again and wrinkled her nose. "Not your run-of-the-mill sleeping potion."

"It sounds familiar." Etain slumped over onto her side. "My whole body feels like a lead brick."

"I have something for you." Swee pulled her into a sitting position. "You need to stay awake, Etain. Maybe a bite to eat will help too."

"Oh, breakfast. Aye." Her head jerked up and down in a nod. "Now you mention food, I'm starving." She licked her lips.

"Good." Swee took her by the arm and coaxed her off the bed. "I need to see you on your feet though." Etain wobbled but was able to stand on her own. "Splash water on your face and change your clothes."

She gave Swee a sheepish grin. "Oh. Well…"

Swee snatched the cup from the nightstand. "We can chat while you eat. Be right back." Before she stepped out the door, she said, "The clothes I laid out for you last night are in the wardrobe. I don't know where you found that killer dress you wore, but you made an impression on our guests. If they didn't know you before, they sure know you now."

Etain blinked at her. "It was on the bed."

Swee shrugged. "I laid out a pair of black leather pants, a white shirt, and your boots. Be back in a bit. Keep moving."

"Mystery of the red dress." Etain mused, sinking back onto the bed. "Five more minutes."

Her mind drifted to the events of the previous night, particularly Jackie P. She'd not had contact with anyone from her old life since coming to the Alamir. It felt strange. It felt right. Jackie was one of the good ones.

After saving Caroline and her family, Etain returned to the bar. Dressed in black leathers, she blended in well with the crowd, just another metal fan. She inched her way to the bar through the mass of people, relieved to find her friend tending.

Jackie motioned to one of the barmaids chatting with her for a few moments, and grabbed a bottle of tequila and two glasses. "Come with me."

Etain followed her toward the back into a small but efficient office. A desk spoke of the business side while the two-seater sofa and two easy chairs showed another side of the entertainment business. It was quieter in here but there was no getting away from the thump of the music.

Jackie placed the glasses and tequila on the glass coffee table and sat on the sofa. "Have a seat." She patted the spot next to her. "Tell me how James Rhys's daughter came to be an Alamir." She popped the cork on the bottle and poured out two golden shots.

Etain hesitated. "You make it sound like a bad thing."

Jackie shrugged. "Can be. I'm sure you know the score by now."

"Yeah…" She ran a hand through her hair, taking in the office. "I totally know."

"Come on. Join me." Jackie offered her a shot.

It helped soften the edge a bit. After three more, the edge was well off.

"I guess you heard about Mom and Dad?"

"I heard they disappeared along with you and your brother. No details were ever given. I thought James had finally..." She shrugged again. "Seeing you with those Alamir, it tells me things didn't go according to plan."

"What plan?"

"Things had gotten too heavy, even for James. He wanted to get out of the..." She hesitated. "Well, er, the consulting business."

Etain shook her head. "He didn't have a chance. They were assassinated."

"Oh my god." Jackie teared up and leaned forward taking Etain into her arms. "I'm so sorry, baby girl. Since I never heard anything, I'd hoped for the best."

The women held each other for a long moment, sharing their tears. Jackie pulled away, walked to the desk, and grabbed a box of tissues, setting them on the coffee table. For Etain, the years fell away as she told of the night she lost her family and of her initiation into the Alamir. The fear of the unknown and the pain of loss engulfed her, reminding her of how alone she'd felt for so long.

"I can't tell you how sorry I am." Jackie popped out a couple more tissues and handed one to Etain. "James and Auri didn't deserve... Well, none of you deserved it." She blotted at her eyes and blew her nose. "You didn't mention your brother. Where's he in all this?"

Etain closed her eyes and lowered her head into her hands. "I thought he died too. But..."

"Please tell me he didn't."

"No," she whispered. "He's alive and well."

"Etain." Swee was shaking her awake. "Let's get this tea down you. It'll help."

"What?" One eye cracked open.

The healer poured a cup and handed it to her. "*This* will make sure you're one hundred percent. After that, you can eat and change."

"Tea?"

"It's a special brew, so drink it all."

Etain pushed up and leaned against the headboard, opening the other eye. She took the cup and sipped.

"Make sure you drink the whole cup. The sleeping potion was a heavy one." Swee set a tray in front of her. "Although, I don't think you drank much."

"I didn't drink any of it. It was cold by the time I came home." She attempted a grin. "Iced tea it was not."

"Did you and Robert go out last night?"

Etain closed her eyes. "No."

"Did you ignore Inferno and go out on your own?"

She opened her eyes and finished the tea. "Something like that."

"Well, as long as you're back in one piece. I hope it was successful."

"It was." She tried a forkful of egg and a bit of toast. "Oh, you know what? I know why the potion sounds familiar. The Elves used it on Dar."

"I can't imagine what he did to make them use it on him."

"Trust me, they had plenty of reason." Etain enjoyed a few more bites but noticed a sadness suddenly come over the healer's face. "Is there more news on last night's raids?"

"Yes. FWH, *.com*, Dragon, and LAVA showed up at COL and helped pick through the rubble of what was once the east wall. There were injuries but no fatalities, thank goodness. Natas had a thorough search done. Aside from the wall, the only thing amiss was an open door in the lower portion of the fortress."

"Nothing too serious then. Good. Are the Ambassadors still here?"

Swee shook her head. "The last of them left about an hour ago. They monitored what came in well into the night. Some reported bombings, others sent reports of riots and general unrest. One clan claimed they were barely able to avoid the lynching of an important human dignitary and his family. The Haluci clan, the ones who showed up toward the end, said their ops were successful, albeit their target suffered injuries. The Ambassadors agreed it was imperative the full Council meet with the chieftains of every clan and make some hard decisions."

"Damn." She ran a hand through her hair. "You mentioned the Haluci clan. Who are they?"

Swee took her hands in hers. "Etain."

"Swee. Are they trouble?"

She closed her eyes, cleared her throat, and tried again. "Wolfe and Elfin have returned."

"Really?" She pulled her hands from Swee's and sat up straight. "Holy crap, I must look a mess." She rolled out the other side of the bed but she no sooner stood than she was on her bottom.

"Etain! Are you okay?" Swee rushed to her side. "Here, let me help you. Please take it slow."

Etain laughed, holding onto her arm as she stood. "I'm not good at the weakling thing. Thank you. I'm good now. I don't know what's in that tea but it's amazing." She straightened her shirt and tried to smooth her hair with her hands. "Is he going to surprise me? Should I wait here and act like I don't know?" She laughed like a daft schoolgirl. "No, I should go downstairs. Save him the trouble." She hurried to the door.

"Dar isn't with them." Swee's words stopped her cold.

Her hand on the knob, her sharp intake of breath was the only sound in the room. After a hard swallow, she asked, "Did he stay in Nunnehi?"

"I don't know."

"Where are they?"

"Downstairs. They want to talk to you in private."

Etain turned, walked across the room, and out onto the balcony. "Send them up."

SAFEKEEPING

Dar landed in the courtyard of the Elven palace to find Alatariel waiting for him.

"I hear you met our Zysha."

"That woman has no concept of the word *no*," he said. "Rie, I must go. My lady deserves an apology and to know I am well."

"Yes, she *does* deserve your apology, but more importantly, she deserves a husband who is whole and of sound mind. You have been through so much, Dar, and you need time to heal. Etain knows you love her."

"I am well, Rie. Being here has helped me immensely, but it is time to get back to my life. Before I leave... There was a woman in the tournament—"

She raised a brow. "A wandering eye, sir?"

Dar chuckled. "No. She was not an Elf."

"The tournament is open to all races, you know that."

"Aye, I am aware, but this one... Something about her seemed familiar."

The queen shrugged as she turned away. "I do not know, Dar. Perhaps you should check with those in charge of the tournament. They would have a list."

"Her name is Illiana."

Alatariel stopped and slowly turned. "Apologies, High Lord. The name does not ring a bell."

"Dar, there you are." Elfin made an untimely appearance with Wolfe at his side.

"Congratulations." Dar gave him a warm handshake. "You fought well. Wolfe—"

Wolfe cut off whatever Dar intended to say. "Zysha's been singing your praises and probably will for days."

Dar shook his head and closed his eyes briefly. "Let her sing. We are leaving." Elfin and Wolfe glanced at the queen and back at Dar. The High Lord clapped his hands. "Let's move."

Wolfe jumped, and bowed. "Glad to have met you, Your Highness. Nunnehi has been glorious."

Elfin bowed. "Thank you for your generous hospitality, Majesty."

"Such brave knights are always welcome in Nunnehi."

Alone with the queen, Dar gave her a stern eye. "Something is going on here, milady. Luckily for you, the desire to see Etain outweighs my curiosity." A smile lit his face. "Thank you for all you have done for us, although I question your methods. The important thing is Midir is gone once and for all."

"You are an extreme man, Dar, which occasionally calls for extreme measures. I would do it again in order to keep you safe."

He chuckled hearing his own words recited back to him. "Sage advice, milady. I will keep it in mind."

Alatariel held his hands in hers. "She loves you, Dar. Never take her love or her for granted. None of us knows the future."

A momentary pang for a lost family pierced his heart. "Aye. Despite what has happened, I trust her above all others and will not give up until she knows it." He lifted her hands for a light kiss across the knuckles. "Be blessed, Your Grace. May the light be your guide and the dark nothing more than a moment to rest."

She pulled him in for a warm hug. "Be blessed, High Lord. I love you like my own family. Please take care and come back soon with your lady." With a kiss on his cheek, they parted.

The Alamirs' return ended any further conversation. "Ready to go, milord," said Elfin.

"We picked up a few rations from the kitchen in case we get hungry." Wolfe nodded at the pack slung over his shoulder.

"Good thinking, boys." Dar noticed he was still wearing the pink gloves. "Alatariel, please tell the steward I will return these on my next visit."

She laughed. "I doubt they will be missed but I shall convey the message."

Before long, the three stood at the point where they entered Nunnehi from Laugharne. Elfin scratched his head. "I hope you know how to open this thing because I do not."

Wolfe draped an arm over his shoulders. "I've always wondered."

"What?"

"What kind of Elf you be. Now I know."

He gave his friend a sideways glance. "What kind?"

"The kind who doesn't know how to open a portal." Wolfe danced away, laughing.

"You are a sod," Elfin declared but shared in the laughter.

"Fortunately, *I* know the words," Dar said. "*Komdu aftur til Laugharne.*"

Upon speaking the magical words, a slim line quivered in front of them, and expanded, revealing the world on the other side. The trio stepped through into a sunny afternoon in the Alamir realm.

Wolfe and Elfin headed along the path, ready to get back home but noticed halfway down that Dar remained at the top of the hill.

"Are you okay, Dar?" Wolfe called out.

The man appeared to be confused. His head turned to his right and left, then straight ahead toward the horizon.

Wolfe leaned toward Elfin. "You don't think he's had a relapse, do you? Because if he has, I think we're all fucked."

Dar went down to a knee and bowed his head.

Elfin shrugged. "I do not know, my friend. Perhaps he says a prayer of thanks for his safe return."

In the next moment, they overheard him mutter, "I will destroy them all," before getting to his feet.

Wolfe glanced at Elfin. "Should one of us..."

After a game of rock-paper-scissors, Wolfe blew out a breath, shaking his head. "Damn. May the gods be with me."

At his approach, Dar growled. "Do not."

The Alamir froze, carefully turned to his friend, and cocked his head toward Dar, his eyes wide.

A silver spark appeared above Dar's head and slashed toward the ground. "I will lay waste to the entire castle."

Elfin rushed to his friend, both of them craning their necks to see through the portal.

"It does not look like Nunnehi to me," Elfin said. "Why would he go back?"

The young men bobbed and dodged one another to peer through the rift. "Elfin, those golden doors are bigger than Nunnehi's."

"Let me see." He pushed Wolfe aside, but a bright light made them shield their eyes.

Dar stepped through the portal.

⁘

On the other side, it closed with the snap of his fingers as he approached the golden doors. A hand on each one, he contemplated whether to simply obliterate them or use a more covert approach. With wings spread, he was airborne in a single thrust.

The LOKI chieftain passed over the castle several times before choosing the perfect location—the East tower. Along his way, an unexpected sight came into view. Shera, alone on the ramparts. *This could be an opportunity.* He invoked a cloaking spell and landed behind her, silent as death.

By the time she realized something was wrong, a clawed hand covered her face and dragged her into the shadows. His grip tightened against her struggles, cutting off her air supply. Dar could taste her fear. He relished it. Fed on it. She collapsed in his arms.

The woman tossed over his shoulder, he made his way to the deserted East tower through hidden passages where he could or kept to dark hallways when he could not. No one knew the layout of the castle better than its creator.

Dar came to the uppermost room of the tower where he dumped Shera's inert form on the floor. He left for a moment but soon returned with a length of rope, threw one end over the rafters, and tied the other around her wrists, pulling until her toes barely touched the floor. With a single talon, he cut away her clothes but left her undergarments, and retreated to a dark corner to wait.

When Shera roused, shadows decorated the walls with supernatural patterns. She found herself suspended from the rafters, embarrassed by the fact she was nearly naked. Her struggles against her restraints made the ropes tighter.

Remember your training.

She slowed her breathing and scanned the room for an escape route. The door wasn't far. She looked up the length of the rope.

From the darkness came a laugh that made her flesh crawl. She turned toward the hideous sound. Her heart nearly exploded at the sight of red eyes peering at her from the corner.

The others will come for me. She tried to assure herself.

"Who are you?" Despite her best efforts to remain calm, a cold sweat covered her skin. "What do you want?"

"Where is she?"

The shock of hearing her chieftain's voice sent her into a spin. "Dar?" She grunted in her effort to stretch her toes toward the floor to still herself.

He stepped into the fading light, his wings tight around his body. "Where is Etain?"

She gasped at the change in the man. "W-What's happened to you?"

"Where. Is. Etain?" He grabbed her face with a clawed hand. "I have to commend you on the spell that keeps her presence from me. When I find her, you will share the recipe." The tip of a talon slid down her throat. "Or I will rip you apart one piece at a time and bathe in your blood."

Shera fought to control her shivers. "D-Dar, I-I don't know what you're talking about. She isn't here."

His tongue lashed out and licked the blood trickling down her chest. "I want her back. Now."

She'd never heard his voice so cold, so vicious. "Please, I swear. I don't know. We've been busy with other things."

"You lie," he hissed. "But by the time I am through with you, I will have the answers I seek." Dar paced the room, his eyes on her the entire time. Eventually, he walked back to her, standing too close for her comfort. "What do you hope to gain by taking my lady? I ask again. Where is she?"

Shera saw the red eyes change to gold with green flecks dancing in their depths. Desperate, her mind searched for any way to stop this from happening or possibly delay it. "D-Don't you know? The *Bok* have launched attacks on the human realm."

He paused, a talon only a hair from her flesh. "It is what they do."

"No, t-this was different. All the clans have sent teams to deal with them." She fought to keep the panic at bay. "We've been put on alert, but LOKI hasn't been called."

"LOKI will not be called." His eyes followed the trail of the talon down her belly. "There is too much unrest within the clan. We are considered unreliable." An evil grin curled the corners of his mouth. "Do not be concerned with the *Bok*, little Shera. You have other things to concern yourself with.

"Every moment beneath my blade will be more exquisite than the last, right to the end." She squealed, shivering all the more. "After all, a corpse does not beg for mercy, does it?" His hellish laughter filled the room.

Fear won over her warrior training. "Dar, I swear on my life, I don't know where she is." She cried as the tip of his talon grazed down her arm, drawing a fine line of blood. "S-Savage would know. If she's here, Savage would've given the order."

"Where would I find the witch?" He pushed his face into hers. "If you lie to me, I will come back and finish this."

"No! Please don't leave me here. S-She'd be in the throne room, waiting for further orders from the Ambassadors." Dar let go and disappeared into the shadows. "What are you doing? Dar! Please, please don't leave me here. I swear, you'll find her in the throne... No, you'll find her *on* the throne. She's obsessed with it." Shera tried to catch a glimpse of the demon in the dark. Suddenly, a thin line of light appeared, widening to a small town.

"You will leave this place. Am I clear?"

She nervously eyed the portal. "W-Where is that?"

The talon returned to her throat. "Am. I. Clear?"

"Y-Yes, Dar. I will leave."

He cut the rope. "Good."

She landed on the floor with a grunt. He tossed the remnants of her clothes through the portal. "Get out of here before I change my mind."

On shaky legs, she inched toward the opening, but stopped before the final step. "I was always loyal to you—"

A hard push knocked her through the portal. "Thank you for your service."

The portal closed, he picked up a knife from the floor and slid it into his boot. His first thought was to open a new portal to the throne room, but his evil smirk returned as he closed the gateway. The intrigue of a cat and mouse game cooled his demon blood and cheered his heart. It was a perfect opportunity to practice his stealth, a skill in which he always excelled.

Clan members seemed to be in short supply along his way through the dark castle, far less than he would have liked. Maybe Shera told the truth and the clan was in the throne room, waiting for the call from the Ambassadors.

In no time, he stood in the circular main entry, the last rays of the sun shining through huge glass windows set in the ceiling thirty feet above. A hallway stretched in every direction, each one on a separate path with its own end.

To his right was the hallway of the Judicial Caste, established to uphold fairness and justice within the clan. Banners hanging along the hall represented their different charges; blue for integrity, white for purity, and grey for authority and strength of character.

Are they part of this as well?

To his left was the hallway that led to his healers and wielders of magic, the Magi Caste. Their banners in the earthy colors of brown and green bore the symbol of power - a staff flowing into a spiral tail. It also served as a haven for visiting honorary members of the clan, Ambassadors, fellow chieftains, and whomever else the High Council deemed worthy.

In the Northeast corner was the hallway of the Warrior Caste, where new recruits began their journey in the clan to become highly trained soldiers as protection against the *Bok*. Their banners donned a sword and shield in grey on a field of red and white. *Do they have any idea what they defend now?* Most of the clan belonged to the Warrior Caste but there were those who rose to greater heights.

The BloodCore dwelled in the Northwest portion of the castle, its hallways lined with banners of black and red bearing a golden snake swallowing its tail. Considered to be among the deadliest warriors in the Alamir, they were battle-hardened gladiators held to a higher standard than the Warrior Caste. The mere mention of them struck fear into the hearts of those they opposed. Like the other castes, their charge was the protection of the clan, but should a mutiny occur, much like what was happening now, the BloodCore was the chieftain's last defense. He wondered on whose side they would stand today.

Only one hallway called his name today. Habit had him reaching for his scimitars. "*Tartarus*. Plan B," he muttered as he marched the path to the throne room, his wings settled on his back.

Upon his approach, the grand doors opened. He expected to find the clan gathered in the great hall to witness his fall as chieftain in a show he was certain had been perfectly choreographed by his second-in-command. Instead, he was surprised to see Savage alone, looking quite comfortable upon the throne, clad in the dark green armor she wore for special occasions. She was quite becoming with her blonde hair braided and piled on top of her head, but it was not her usual style.

"What are you doing here?" she growled as she straightened her back and leaned forward.

"Are you not happy to see me, Savage?" Dar closed the doors behind him and strolled into the throne room. "Was it not you who claimed I go more than I come? Well…" He spread his arms. "Here I am, in the flesh. Where is Etain?"

Savage rose from her seat. "We have more important matters to deal with than your bitch. The Alamir are on high alert. Who granted you entry?"

"*I* am the chieftain of this clan. It is my right to come and go as I please." Her dramatics would not distract him from his goal.

"Maybe your bitch isn't as simple as I thought and has gone to find someone who can better please her. A *Bok*, perhaps?

"Are you certain this is how you want to play it?"

"What I *want* is the clan and the stone."

"Stone?"

She curled her upper lip. "*The* stone, Dar. The one entrusted to LOKI for safekeeping. Where is it?"

"What does a stone have to do with any of this? I have come for Etain."

Savage glared down her nose as she descended the dais. "The stone and this clan are more important than a woman." Something in his eyes made her stop a few steps above the floor. "You really don't know?" In an uncharacteristic show of camaraderie, she jerked her head toward the rear of the hall.

He knew of the stone she spoke about and where she was going. What he could not understand was the sudden concern over the LOKI piece of the original Alamir stone. During the early years of the clan, he locked it away deep below the castle. Only those he trusted most knew of its existence. The room was impenetrable, even by him. The stone door could only be opened with the use of two keys. One he carried with him. The other was hidden within the throne.

He followed her to the rear of the dais and watched her touch the center of the LOKI insignia engraved into the wall. An invisible door opened and the two stepped into a passage carved from the very rock upon which the castle stood. Steps of stone spiraled down into the earth. As they descended deeper below the castle, torches blazed to life, lighting their way. Dar smelled the dampness seeping through the walls and felt the air turn cooler. The stairs spilled into a long corridor that split into three more corridors and carried on for miles beneath the valleys and mountains of the terrain above. Their trek ended a few feet from the bottom step in front of a black door.

Dar raised a brow at the key Savage removed from inside her shirt. "Could you not secure the key in a more appropriate place other than your—"

"Tits?" Savage laughed. "Who would dare breach such a formidable fortress?"

"Indeed." Dar leaned against the rock wall for support, lifted a boot, and ran a single finger from the front to back. An unseen pocket along the side opened. The twin to the key in Savage's hand appeared.

"Hmph," she grunted. "Probably best for you."

Both keys inserted, the chieftain and his second-in-command turned the locks. The door opened without a sound. As soon as Dar entered, a torch set well above his head flared to life initiating a chain reaction around the circular room. Within moments, thirteen torches set the space aglow with their warm light.

Dar immediately went to the single column in the center of the room. The walls, floor, column, and extended ceiling were of a single boulder. Even with his ability to manipulate the rock with a wave of his hand, it took days to chip the room into the shape he envisioned. He had set the red stone of Leictreacha on the column for safekeeping from lustful eyes and sticky fingers.

"What have you done with the stone, Savage?"

Her eyes widened. "Me? I was asking you." She pointed to the door. "The door was locked, and I have only the one key. You have the other."

She had a point. "How could you know it was missing?" He circled around the column, his mind awhirl with possibilities of how the room may have been breached.

Savage retreated toward the door to stay out of his way. "Our Magi felt a shift in whatever it is they feel. Once they brought it to my attention, I felt something was missing."

He stared at her from across the cavern. "I feel nothing unusual."

She cocked her head as though listening to a faraway sound and shrugged. "Nor do I, but neither did Natas."

Dar raised a brow. "What does the COL chieftain have to do with this?" The smirk on her face gave him an uneasy feeling.

"The COL castle was attacked." Savage clucked her tongue. "Why am I not surprised you know nothing of it? There's only one Alamir who holds your interest now." She shook her head. "Poor, pathetic Dar. So misguided."

"What does Natas have to do with the LOKI stone?"

She casually inched closer to the opening of the doorway. "Upon their first inspection, nothing was amiss." She cast a conspiratorial gaze at Dar and practically purred. "Within a few days, his version of Magi told him there'd been a shift of energy within the castle. After a new investigation, they found the sapphire left in COL's protection was gone."

Dar inspected the column more closely. "And there has been nothing suspicious here at LOKI?"

Savage emitted an amused grunt. "Other than our chieftain's sudden reappearance?" Dar shot her a warning glare. "Perhaps in our case, the shift wasn't caused by the stone, but the lack of your presence. Either way, the stone is not where it should be, and neither are you." She slipped out of the room.

Dar lunged toward the door, making a futile grab at the smooth surface as it closed with the finality of a crypt.

"Savage! What the hell are you doing?" The last sound he heard was the click of the locks as she turned both keys.

"Once the clan has cast you out and voted me in as chieftain, you'll be released." He heard the victory in her voice. "Afterwards, you and your bitch can go to hell for all I care."

Golden Doors

The door was open. Another game of rock-paper-scissors ensued. Wolfe rolled his eyes and walked into the room first. The High Lady was on the edge of the bed, lacing her boots.

"Hello, Wolfe, Elfin. I hope you've had a safe trip."

"Aye, Lady E.," said Wolfe. "We got here as fast as we could. We were surprised to find you here."

"Oh? Where else would I be?" Her boots secured, she stood with an air of authority. "Did things not go well in Nunnehi?"

Wolfe glanced at his friend. "Nunnehi was great. We even participated in the Blade Masters Gathering. Dar, too."

Etain stared at the man.

"Aye." The ice-blue gaze slid to the Elf. "He would have won too, if he had not tripped over Illiana."

"I don't know," Wolfe teased with a straight face. "You gotta admit he was a little rusty."

"Rusty or not, it was an honor to compete with him."

"True, true." Wolfe nodded. "But—"

Etain placed her hands on her hips. "He was well the last time you saw him?"

Wolfe was taken aback by the interruption. "Oh, aye. Definitely."

"Well, until we stepped through the portal," Elfin added.

"He came with you then?"

Wolfe scratched his head. "He came with us but as soon as we stepped through, well, he fell to his knees, mumbling."

"We thought he was giving thanks for a safe return," Elfin continued. "But—"

"*Gentlemen*! Where is Dar?"

"That's just it, Lady E. We're not sure." Wolfe stepped back at the flash in her eyes and hurried on with the rest. "He opened another portal and vanished."

"Another portal?" She eyed the two. "Where would he go?"

Wolfe shrugged. "We saw big golden doors. Kinda like what they have in Nunnehi, but different."

"With a crest," Elfin added. "He was muttering about laying something to waste."

She disappeared into the wardrobe and emerged a few moments later, scabbard in hand. Wolfe and Elfin exchanged nervous frowns when she drew the blade.

"Was the crest like this?"

The two blinked, caught off guard by the blade in their faces. When they finally focused on the sword rather than her, they recognized the insignia.

"Oh yeah, that's it," Wolfe confirmed. "But bigger."

"Right, bigger," Elfin agreed.

"Thank you, boys. Would you do me a favor and ask Swee to come back?" She tucked the sword away. "Alone. Do not tell Inferno, Linq, or my brother. Do not tell anyone. You speak to Swee only. Understood?"

"You're going after him?" Wolfe asked.

"Please, keep it to yourself and give me time to do what I need to do."

Elfin nodded. "Be safe, Lady E, and bring him home."

"Aye."

As soon as the door closed, Etain returned to the wardrobe to put on her breastplate, and strapped Dar's twin blades onto her back. A glowing *Nim* rested in a golden scabbard on her hip. "We're among friends here. Why do you still glow?" She slipped on her dragon helm.

"Are you mad at me for leaving you here last night? I wasn't sure how effective you'd be in the human realm."

I am as effective as you allow me to be, milady.

Etain bowed her head. "Forgive me, *Nim*. I will not doubt you again."

Swee hesitated at the door seeing Etain dressed for battle and pacing the room. "Wolfe said you wanted to see me?"

"Ah, thank goodness, you're here. Aye." Etain stopped and motioned her into the room. "Dar has gone to Castle LOKI. I don't know why he thinks I'm there, but it doesn't matter."

"What're you talking about?"

"Dar came through the portal with Wolfe and Elfin, but left through another. He's gone to deal with the High Council. I'm sure of it."

Swee remembered her last day as a member of the Council. "They *did* threaten you, Etain. What do you need from me?"

"I need someone to know where I'm going, just in case things turn sour with the clan."

"Surely Dar can handle them."

"No." Etain slowly blew out a breath. "Things didn't go so well last time. I can't take that chance."

"O-Okay. Before you go..." Swee reached out for Etain's wrist. "I'm checking your pulse." After a moment or two, she asked, "Would you mind taking off your helm?" Etain slowly removed the headpiece. Her forehead felt warm, but not feverish. "Look into my eyes. Any headache or fuzziness?"

"No."

"You wouldn't lie to me, would you?" She poked and prodded the warrior's neck for any swelling.

Etain dropped the helm into a chair and caught the healer's hands. "I'm fine, Swee. I can't let him face them alone."

"You shouldn't go on your own. It isn't safe."

"I may have no faith in the High Council, but I believe in the clan. They won't betray their chieftain." Etain let her go and slipped on the helm.

"I have to say, you are incredible in your armor. Part of me wishes I were going with you just to see their faces."

Etain grabbed the black circlet of Dar's breastplate. "Remember, not a word to anyone."

Swee mimed zipping her mouth.

"We'll be back soon."

Robert knocked on Etain's door and waited. He knocked again. With no one else about, he turned the knob, stepped inside, and locked the door behind him. The bed was made. His gaze went to the bedside table. The teacup was gone.

"Etain?"

He noticed the open wardrobe and peeked inside. The red dress he'd laid out for her last night was there but the leather breeches and white shirt he'd put away were gone. "Then she *has* been here. The tea should have..."

In the corner of the wardrobe, he spotted what he believed to be her crystal sword. As he started to close the door, he realized it no longer glowed and brought the blade into the light. It was not made of crystal, but the pommel was decorated with a clear, round crystal. A cackle, sounding eerily like Midir's, wafted through the room as he brandished the sword toward an unseen opponent.

Five double barbs popped out from the hilt, digging deep into his palm and fingers. Robert threw the blade to the floor. "Fuck!" Blood dripped from ten tiny punctures that burned like hellfire. Tears stung his eyes as he rushed into the bathroom and shoved the hand under the cool water from the tap. "Foul piece of shit."

With a small towel wrapped around the wounds, he returned to the bedroom, but the sword was not where he'd dropped it. Instinct told him to check the wardrobe. There, in the corner, sat the blade tucked away in its scabbard as pristine as the day of its creation.

"Bewitched." He slammed the door of the wardrobe shut. "Let's see how much damage you do from your dark corner." Robert left in search of the healer, his new *friend*. "Maybe she can tell me where the hell my sister is."

Halfway to the stairs, Swee met Robert coming toward her. "Swee. Are you all right?"

"Yes." She put on a brave smile. "I popped into my room for a quick tidy up."

"Has someone upset you?"

She felt like his green eyes could see into her soul. "N-No, of course not. I think the excitement from yesterday has caught up with me."

"Do you know where Etain is?"

"Sorry, Robert. I've been so busy all morning, I haven't seen her. Maybe she's in the back garden."

"Will you go with me?"

She shrugged. "If you like."

As they walked down the stairs, she asked, "What's your story, Robert? Etain never talked about her family."

"We haven't seen each other in a long time. My business keeps me out of Alamir intrigues."

Swee chuckled. "Are you a magic man?"

Robert smiled. "I guess I am."

"What *is* your business?"

"I own an apothecary in Deudraeth, a small town north of here."

"Your own apothecary?" Visions of *Swee's Apothecary* added a dreamy quality to her voice. "If I had my own shop, I'd spend hours mixing potions and concocting new spells."

"Sometimes I dabble but I've been very busy as of late. My assistant Piran has been a godsend."

"You have an assistant too?"

"He runs the shop, which allows me the freedom to do research and develop new resources. Customer demand keeps me on the go."

"Are most of your customers Alamir?"

A sly grin spread across his face as he wagged his index finger. "*Non, non, mon petit*. The secret of my success rests on two principles—resourcefulness and discretion. My resourcefulness brings in an array of clients, but discretion keeps me alive. I don't discuss my clients. However, I encourage them to talk about me at every opportunity." They walked through the empty kitchen and out the back door. "Who is this?"

Swee followed his gaze. "It looks like one of Inferno's hounds. You aren't afraid of dogs, are you?"

"Of course not. I didn't know there were dogs on the grounds. Where would the others be?"

"He only has the two, Felix and Ruby." She waved to the dog. "Hi, Felix! Ruby's probably not far. Hmm. That's odd."

"What?"

"He usually comes to me."

Robert watched the hound. "Are you sure it's Felix?"

"Yes. Why is he just standing there?" Swee took a step toward the dog.

Felix lowered his head, his ears laid back and teeth bared.

"Oh." Swee stopped. "He's never done that."

Robert placed an arm in front of her. The fur along Felix's back raised up and his tail stiffened, his growl menacing. "Maybe we should go back inside."

"I don't know. I'm afraid if we..."

Felix stepped toward them.

"Do you have a knife, Swee?"

"A knife? Why?"

"If he attacks—"

"He won't attack. We've only caught him off-guard. He'll settle down in a minute."

"I don't agree."

"Felix, boy! Where are ya?" Inferno came around the corner, Ruby at his side, and stopped. "Ruby, stay." A tense moment passed before he released a shrill whistle, getting the dog's attention. Felix's stance seemed to relax but his gaze remained on the couple. Inferno approached the hound and placed a hand on his head. "*Tá na páistí ag iarraidh ort. Gadewch i ni fynd yn ôl i'r tŷ. Dewch* (The kiddies are asking for ya. Let's get back to the barn. Come)."

They watched the man and his dogs walk away.

Swee shivered. "Let's go to the courtyard and see if Etain's there. But after that, I better get busy. Spirit's due home any minute."

As they approached the corner, she heard the fading giggles of children, but saw the Hummer. Inferno and his hounds were in the distance headed toward the barn, chasing after his wee ones.

Swee laughed and pulled Robert along with her. "Let me introduce you to the lady of the house." As expected, she found her in the kitchen. "Welcome home, Spirit. I'm glad you're back. How was your trip?"

Spirit held a cup in her hands, blowing away the steam. "No one's happier than me. Children are *not* the best traveling companions."

Swee turned to the man at her side. "This is Etain's brother, Robert."

He bowed his head. "Pleased to meet you, milady."

Spirit lifted her cup for a sip as she eyed him from head to toe, but set the cup on the countertop. "So you're the brother?"

His eyes sparkled with a touch of mischief. However, Swee stole her attention before he could answer. "Let's celebrate your homecoming. We have plenty of food left from last night's dinner. I heard the kids outside."

"Sounds a plan to me, lass. I'm cream-crackered from the trip." Spirit shifted on the barstool. "I sent the wee devils outside to play and burn off some energy."

"Well, you don't have to do anything. Robert can be my sous chef."

The duo worked in concert, chopping, blending, and sautéing leftovers to create an innovative new meal.

"I hear Etain made an impression," Spirit said.

"Oh, my goodness. I wish you could've seen her in the red dress." Swee took over the duties at the stove. "Robert, can you make a salad?"

"I believe I can manage." He relinquished the spatula to the chef.

"A red dress?" Spirit seemed surprised.

Robert paused. "Is it so unusual?"

"If you knew our girl, you'd know she doesn't do dresses and never wears red."

"Her favorite color was red when she younger." Robert sliced a large head of lettuce in half. "She was always in a dress."

Spirit raised a brow. "Do you know *why* she only wears black?"

A heavy silence blanketed the kitchen. Confused by the sudden change, Swee turned from the stove.

The knife poised over the split head of lettuce, Robert stared at Etain's guardian. Spirit challenged him with her steady gaze, her eyes alight with something Swee had not seen in the mage before. She wasn't sure whether it was a protective fire burning within the hazel depths or the promise of a lethal response. Swee opened her mouth to speak but the back door opened.

Inferno stopped just inside the kitchen, his eyes on his wife. "Ya all right, love?"

Spirit lowered her eyes before raising them to her husband. "Aye, me love. I could do with some fresh air though." She slid off the barstool. "Let's take a walk."

"Anything for me lady." He held out his arm for his wife and afforded a quick glance at Robert. They passed through Linq and the UWS clan members who came with him.

Swee noticed an indiscernible nod pass between the Alamir chieftain and the Elf. She cleared her throat and stole a glance at Robert, who hadn't moved an inch. *I don't understand what happened here.* She called out, "Don't go far. Tea should be ready soon."

LONG LIVE LOKI

From the top of the dais, Savage watched the LOKI clan file into the spacious throne room. Although she sat upon the throne in the presence of the High Council, she was not so arrogant as to do it in front of the entire clan yet. There would be plenty of opportunities once they appointed her chieftain. This was her time and she planned to luxuriate in it. With Dar locked away and having no means of escape, she could take all the time in the world. Therefore, with a patient heart, she waited until the entire clan filled the great hall.

She loved the order she brought to the clan. No more mingling of the castes. Warriors stood with warriors, clad in their grey armor. The Magi dressed in robes of greens, blues, and browns, kept to themselves. The Judicial Caste looked their part in robes of blue or white. Finally, the BloodCore, *her* BloodCore in their red armor, filed in and surrounded the dais.

Pyro, *Nae'Blis* of the BloodCore, and Warden, *Machin Chin* of the Warriors, stepped forward and stood alone in the gap between the clan members and the BloodCore, who faced them from the base of the dais.

Savage frowned when she noticed her Council was not complete. "Where is Shera?"

Warden answered. "She's not been seen since this morning."

Savage muttered under her breath. "Incompetent idiot." Then graced all in the room with a rare smile. *She'll be the first I replace.*

"Welcome, my clan family. Today is an important day for LOKI, for us." She paced back and forth as she spoke. "It is a day in which we as a clan will unite and determine a new future. A future of our own choosing. You're all aware of the recent quest made by your High Council in search of our chieftain." She stopped, turned her face to the heavens, shook her head, and addressed the clan with a forlorn expression. She even managed to shed a tear. "It saddens me to bring you this news."

The clan watched with expectant faces. She maintained the sad mask, but her heart danced knowing she had them in the palm of her hand. Delighted to deliver the killing blow to Dar's reign, she opened her mouth to speak, but the floor suddenly trembled. Savage steadied herself with a hand on the throne.

The great columns vibrated, cracks lacing up the mighty pillars. Tiny fragments of glass sparkled as they showered down from the shattered windows above. The doors rattled in their jambs. Those nearest scattered only moments before they exploded from their sturdy hinges and sailed through the air. Several of the BloodCore, including Pyro, fell to the floor to avoid one of the wooden missiles. Its twin embedded into the throne itself, just missing Savage.

Everyone checked their neighbors for injuries. Assured no one was hurt, each head turned toward the ruined doorway. A concerted gasp ran through the clan. Even Savage was taken aback by the seven-foot, silver-helmed dragon with wings extended above its head.

The creature's sword shone with a light as bright as its eyes. "Honey! I'm home."

Savage clenched her jaw. She knew that voice.

Warden recovered first and stepped in front of the intruder. "You will answer for this trespass."

Savage cracked her whip. "Pyro, do your duty."

"BloodCore," he called out. Seven of the red-armored caste immediately surrounded the stranger. The remaining BloodCore filled the gap in front of the dais.

Etain recognized the soldiers. They were some of the first to join the clan when Dar made the announcement. He trained them, fought with them, and trusted them with his life. It would hurt his heart to see them standing against his lady and his wishes.

She sheathed *Nim* and removed her helm as she softly spoke the name of one in particular. "Jstmad."

With the threat contained, Savage continued her speech. "Do you see?" Her gaze moved from person to person as she spoke. "Do you see?" She turned and pointed the end of her whip at Etain. "He insults us by sending his *mistress* to do his bidding. I am a better leader than he ever was."

Etain narrowed her eyes as she stepped toward the dais, but the Blood-Core brought up their shields, partially drew their blades, and tightened the circle.

"It is time we take our future into our own hands," Savage carried on. "The High Lord has proven his disregard for the clan. He has left us here to rot while he pursues personal interests, none of which includes us, his clan, his family. It is time for a new leader, a strong chieftain who will make a strong clan."

Etain hissed through her teeth, whispering just loud enough for those close by to hear. "Surely you don't believe this load of crap." She turned her head to speak over one shoulder, and the other. "You know Dar. He would not forsake the clan for personal interests. I know he's here. I can feel him. Help me find him and stop this insanity."

The whip snapped over her head, bringing her attention back to Savage. "I am the law within these walls. Dar is a traitor and a coward. Why else would he send you instead of coming himself?"

Etain returned the glare and lifted her chin. She was no speechmaker but had to say something. "You are a liar, Savage."

Greatly amused by the simple words, the woman laughed loudly. "I give you the chance to speak and that's all you have to say?"

"She *is* a liar," spoke a voice from the destroyed doorway. All eyes turned to a boy of fifteen, dressed in black jeans and a white shirt, boots riding low on his thighs. He wore his blond hair long and in a braid down his back. Etain blinked. She'd not seen this boy before. His resemblance to Dar was uncanny. The boy repeated himself, pointing a finger. "*She* is the liar."

Savage continued to smirk. "Even a child can see her deception."

Etain realized his eyes weren't on her. She followed his gaze and laughed. "Look again, sister. He ain't pointing at me."

Dar paced the circular room, berating himself for letting the woman get the better of him. In spite of his predicament, he found *some* solace in the fact he had taught her well. Still, the missing stone was a serious matter, but the puzzle would have to wait. He must find a way out of this prison first. Since he had personally excavated the space, he knew the walls were far too thick to phase through.

He went back to the stone door, racking his brain for a chant, a spell, anything to breach its solid surface. He investigated the seal where the door met the rock wall.

"You are too much of a perfectionist for your own good, Dar." He sighed and pressed his forehead against the black stone. It was then he recognized the tingles in his gut. A warm flush followed, making him sweat. *Etain.* To feel her in his blood again was a great relief.

The High Lord of Kaos delved into a mental meld with his wife. Through her eyes, he saw her surrounded by BloodCore, their shields raised and blades ready.

"Jstmad." A snap over her head made her look up. He saw the power-crazed woman on the dais spewing her disease.

"This ends today."

Dar held his pink-gloved hands before him and called to the demon within. He battered the center column, breaking it down so he could stand in the center of the room. With the gloves removed, he smiled to see his hands had healed enough to manage the task, and cupped them together, moving his lips in a silent chant. A ball of air formed in the space between his palms. It soon widened and lengthened into a tower of swirling wind. Its thickness gave the illusion of stone yet was as transparent as glass. Within its walls was serenity while outside was total chaos.

His raised hands extended the power farther into the gap above his head. The winds swirled in a frenzied tornado, drilling through the solid rock. To quicken the process, he engaged his *ultimà solar* to compromise the rock.

Etain was here and nothing was going to keep him from her any longer.

It was only a slight rumble, like what she felt when a hot rod idled next to her little red sports car at a light or how you felt the power of a Harley long before you saw it.

Definitely a Harley.

The top of the dais exploded, the throne careening into the air. A bright light shot out from the resulting crevice and blasted it into pieces. At the explosion, Etain put on her helm, ducked her head, and crouched. The BloodCore, who imprisoned her, tightened the circle, lifted their shields overhead, and joined her in a crouched position.

The Warrior Caste also lifted their shields and ran to those in the clan who had no protection. Before the pieces of stone rained down on their heads, they pushed as many Magi and Judicials out through the great doors as they could, and lifted their shields to cover those who could not escape. Pyro and Warden shifted their own shields to protect themselves. Savage, having been thrown from the dais, lay exposed to the falling debris.

Without a second thought, Etain aimed an electrical charge through an opening in the wall of BloodCore, hoping it would be enough.

Shards of stone showered down, several penetrating the protective shields. Bits of rock pock-marked the walls while larger projectiles embedded into the floor. Dirt pattered everywhere and dust settled over everyone and everything.

Etain checked those closest to her. No one was hurt. When she heard footsteps crunch through the rubble, she dared to lift her head from the shelter of the shields.

"My lady," said Dar.

No two words ever sounded as sweet. He was a welcome sight, his blond mane falling freely over his incredibly broad shoulders, framing his handsome face. Those fathomless gold eyes, so intense, made butterflies flutter in the strangest places. She couldn't read his aura or connect with his emotions, and the expression on his face was unreadable, but she stood, feeling as though her heart had stayed in her boots.

At least he didn't call me a whore this time.

"My lord."

He eyed her from head to toe. As uncomfortable as she felt under his scrutiny, she refused to shift or give into the fear that he lured her here to further her degradation. She breathed through her nose and relaxed her shoulders, prepared for whatever came next.

A bright smile came to his face. "What are you doing here?"

"Huh?" The man sounded as if they'd run into each other on the street rather than amidst total chaos. *Did his lips twitch?* Still, she couldn't read him. "I, uh..." She remembered the scimitars. "Your swords." The air crackled from the surge of power between them.

His eyes twinkled as he held her gaze. "Beauties from my beauty."

His smile lit the room and assured her he was her Dar. "I-I brought this too." She removed the circlet of his breastplate from around *Nim's* scabbard and handed it to him. "Something told me you might need it."

"My lady, my lady." He almost sang the words. "You are most wondrous indeed." The moment he clasped the circlet around his throat, black armor spanned out, sweeping over his chest and back, encasing each arm down to the wrist. With his armor in place, he commanded his BloodCore to their feet. Those who faced Etain, including Jstmad, performed an about-face. When the BloodCore drew their blades, she removed her helm, and reached for her *Nim*. There was no way she could get Dar's blades to him in time.

Rather than attack, the seven BloodCore held their swords before them in a show of respect. Dar acknowledged their loyalty with a nod. The warriors stepped past him and formed a protective shield between the High Lord and the other BloodCore. Dar extended a hand to Etain.

He pulled her close and caressed her face. "Thank *Tartarus* you are safe. I thought you were..." He let it go with a sigh. "I have missed you, *a chuisle*."

Caught in his gaze, she had to explain. "You have to know I would never—"

He swallowed the rest of her words with a passionate kiss.

When he pulled back, an emotional struggle showed in his eyes. "As incredible as you are in your armor, I would rather have you naked." Lustful hands grasped her rounded bottom. "Let's put an end to this sad chapter of our lives, my precious lady, and go home."

"Aye," she whispered, grateful to have him back.

Pyro helped Savage to her feet. "The bitch tried to kill me," she snarled, appalled by the reunion on display. "Did you see her attack me?"

Warden stumbled up. "Savage, no one has willingly raised a hand to our cause. They watch and wait. Even now, Dar's BloodCore is loyal to him."

"Like sheep, they wait to be led. Once Dar has been defeated, the Blood-Core will be ours. Pyro, finish this."

Wariness filled the eyes of the *Machin Chin*. "No, Pyro. We can't win. They see him as their chieftain."

"Have faith, Warden," Pyro whispered, his eyes on the High Lady. "Once she is out of the way, we will work together to bring him down. I have bested her many times in our arena. This will be no different."

Savage licked her lips.

"She's not the same as she was, Pyro," Warden argued. "He has changed her. They're too powerful."

The man paid no heed to her warnings and drew his red blade. "You are wrong. *She* has changed *him*, made him weak. Now is the time to strike."

Dar watched the fool come toward them. "Watch my back," he whispered to Etain. "Stand down, *Nae'Blis*. Put away your weapon and walk out. No one will think any less of you."

Pyro rolled his shoulders and cracked his neck to one side, and the other. "I disagree. You abandoned your clan and now you come here to destroy our home. It is down to me to see you answer for it."

Dar looked past Pyro's shoulder at the real traitor and motioned toward the BloodCore, his veterans facing the new bloods. "You have taken this too far, Savage. You have torn this clan apart. Set brother against brother. Leave while your head is still attached."

"It's you who has caused this, not me!" she screamed. "Even with your rabid bitch in tow, you're no match for the LOKI clan. Once you're gone, we *will* be whole again." Savage twirled her whip over her head.

When Etain's backside brushed against his, he knew she was in position. His armor rippled like a second skin as he reached back for Day Star and Burning Heart. The twin scimitars slid from their leather sheaths with ease. He brought them forward, one crossed over the other and sliced the whip into pieces.

Savage staggered back. "You shouldn't have come back, Dar. You have shamed yourself before the entire clan and proven you're no longer fit to rule."

"LOKI deserves a leader, not a ruler. If you think you are the one, come and take it from me. Prove your own worth. Stop hiding behind others and fight me for the honor of leading this clan."

"Do you expect me to quake and cry like a little girl?" Savage threw her ruined whip to the floor and reached for the axe at her side. She pushed Pyro out of her way and came at Dar, backing him toward the wall with an onslaught of relentless swings and jabs. Strike after strike, her personal hatred of the chieftain bled deeper into her attack. Dar blocked from one side, sweeping up to parry a strike from the other.

Savage reversed the axe and poked out with the handle, hitting Dar's ankle. The Krymerian, having caught the move too late, fell on his backside. She raised the axe and swung at Dar's head. He rolled to the side and was on his feet with lightning speed. Sparks flew when the blade hit the stone floor.

He turned to Pyro's advance and set the black scimitars into motion with such speed and force it took the man by complete surprise. Day Star cut in low followed by Burning Heart's high move. In an animated series of advances, Pyro took several blows to his shoulder and side, the blades cutting through both armor and flesh. He stumbled back and fell to the floor, gasping for breath.

Savage jumped in with a series of quick jabs and hit her mark several times before Dar turned with his blade high. She lunged into the opening at the armpit of his armor. He followed through with Daystar, knocked the axe from her grip, and hit with a hearty sidekick. The impact propelled the woman toward her clansmen. Those in her way, parted. The self-appointed ruler careened into a wall and slumped to the floor.

With Dar distracted, Etain moved at the same time as the *Machin Chin* made a run at him with her katana. She slammed into the woman, knocking them both off their feet, and sent the katana skittering across the floor.

Warden recovered enough to catch Etain's fist in her hands, and after a power struggle, wrapped her strong legs around her. With a flip, she was on top. Etain's wings rendered useless beneath her, Warden placed an arm over her throat, cutting off her air. Etain bucked and twisted, trying to break free but the arm pressed harder. Black spots filled her vision.

Mistress.

Not now, Nim.

Warden reached for the katana just out of her grasp, loosening her hold on Etain. It was enough. Etain breathed in and called to her sword. Warden's eyes widened realizing her mistake. She screamed and arched her back when *Nim's* hilt jabbed into her kidney. Etain pushed her off, raised up and rammed a fist into the woman's belly. A punch to the face knocked her out.

"You should've stayed on the porch," Etain rasped. Her gaze shifted between the sentries and the BloodCore, and noticed the unconscious Savage sprawled on the floor. She glanced across the room. All eyes were on the LOKI chieftain as he walked amongst the clan. There were several injuries, but he took the time to reassure and speak a healing spell over those who suffered.

Embraced within the obscurity of the moment, she pushed to her feet, picked up *Nim* and her helm, and went to stand over the heretic, Savage. *To kill her now would end this insanity. Cut out the cancer and let the healing begin.* The tip of *Nim* pressed into the leather armor over Savage's heart.

Words from another time echoed in her mind. *Push it in. That's all you have to do. Just push it in and all this will come to an end.* Dar knew no other way to end the agonizing push and pull between them. *We circle around each other, taking pieces here and there, never accepting what the other offers, yet never letting go.* Words spoken before her eyes had opened to what lay between them.

The clash of metal on metal brought her back. Her eyes cleared as she turned to check on Dar. It was not his sword but those of his original BloodCore in answer to the inexperienced imposters Savage surrounded herself with. So far, no other clansmen moved against their chieftain.

So, Miss Too Big for Your Britches, I leave you to the fate of his choosing. You don't deserve a quick death.

With the mutinous element of the BloodCore subdued and corralled around their misguided ringleader, the High Lord returned his swords to the scabbard worn by his chosen High Lady of Kaos and stood at the base of what was once the throne. On the floor next to his foot, Dar picked up a golden crown of laurel leaves with swords scattered among them. Most of the sharp-tipped swords pointed down to dig into the head of the wearer as a reminder of the weight of duty. Dar raised the crown over his head.

"You no longer have the right to wear the Crown of Kaos," Savage croaked, now on her feet thanks to the help of Pyro. A battered Warden joined them.

"Silence." Dar's voice was twice as cold as his gaze. "This is the crown of my forefathers. Only those born of Kaos, *my* bloodline, can bear the weight of such a responsibility." He lowered the crown onto his head. Etain stood next to him, her head held high. "*I* am the Master of this castle, and you *will* kneel before me."

"I will not kneel to a man who has no honor." Savage spat.

"Kneel," his voice boomed throughout the hall, "or lose your head."

Pyro dropped to one knee. "Long live the High Lord of Kaos."

Savage watched the BloodCore follow their *Nae'Blis*. In a domino effect, the entire circle of the LOKI clan fell to a knee.

"Get off your knees! If we work together, we can beat them!" Aside from Dar and Etain, she was the last one standing. "I will *not* swear fealty to you."

Etain made a move toward the woman, but Dar halted her with a touch. "Any fealty sworn by you would be a lie, Savage. Whatever honor you once had no longer exists. However, you *will* kneel."

His gaze of golden fire met her red rage. In the end, she bent the knee.

"I, Dar VonNeshta, the High Lord of Kaos and chieftain of the LOKI clan, strip you of your position as my second-in-command. You are exiled forever. I should have your head for your crime of mutiny but since my lady has been returned to me unharmed, I feel somewhat charitable."

Savage jumped to her feet. "I will see you dead for this and no one," her grey-green eyes slid to Etain, "will be able to stop me."

"Get out of my sight before I change my mind and strip you of more than your status."

The angry woman stormed through the shattered doorway.

Warden was next to voice her opinion. "This clan is not what it once was. Savage stood beside you and led in your absence without any guidance or help from you. I cannot follow someone I do not respect."

Dar silently watched her trail after Savage.

He turned to the *Nae'Blis*. "I suppose you agree."

Pyro waited until the women left the hall. "She speaks the truth, milord. The clan is not what it once was. However, the blame does not fall on the shoulders of just one. We are all at fault." He motioned to those around him. "Every last one of us."

"I should have put my foot down long ago." Dar removed the crown from his head and held it before him. A flash of energy shattered it to dust. He then faced the remnants of the LOKI clan lining the great hall. "We have all forgotten our roots. What was once a noble clan, honor-bound, has turned into a pack of snarling dogs. The lust for power has corrupted the blood and spread its disease through the clan."

His eyes slid to the BloodCore imposters. "Our vows to one another have been broken. I am as much at fault by not governing my Council as I should." Dar took a contemplative breath. Etain interlaced her fingers with his in a silent show of support. He said the words before he could change his mind. "From this day forward, the LOKI clan will be no more." Etain squeezed his hand.

"But, High Lord," one called out from the clan. "Where will we go? This is the only home some of us know."

"I know how it feels to lose your home. It may feel like the end of the world but it is not. It is merely the end of a clan. There are other clans in need of your varied talents. Gather your things and leave this place. As our family has been destroyed by the lust for power, I will destroy this castle. It will no longer stand and shall not rise again." A stunned silence filled the room. "I suggest you get moving."

The *Nae'Blis* was the first to move. He and his fellow BloodCore ensured the great hall was cleared quickly. Senior members of each caste took on the responsibility of assisting others to gather their belongings. Dar and Etain watched and listened to the quiet whispers, some harsher than others.

She leaned into Dar. "Are you sure?"

"I built this place with my heart and soul." His gaze lifted, taking in the elaborate walls and ceiling of the great hall. "It was no less than what LOKI deserved. My clan was my life. I thought it would live on forever."

"I know what these people mean to you, my love."

"Nothing in life stays the same." He squeezed her hand. "It was my intention to pass the clan into the hands of a strong Council. However, without my guidance they have lost their way. It is best we all move on."

"But if your heart and soul are here, how will you feel once this place is gone?"

The corner of his mouth twitched. "They have found a new home, *a chuisle*. The past is the past, aye?"

"Aye." Her voice was barely audible. "But there are clan members still loyal to you. Remember the BloodCore who stood with you."

"Loyal to my face when it suited them. Where was their loyalty during my absence?"

"Speaking from experience, I'd say they've probably wondered the same of you."

Her words stung but he knew she spoke the truth.

With the all-clear given, Dar pulled her to him. "Stay close to me."

The High Lord and High Lady proceeded to the outer courtyard. In his final act as chieftain, he drew on the power of Kaos, infusing it into every fiber of his being. The sun faded to black, and the skies darkened. White wings spread and his powerful arms extended at his sides, forcing his muscular chest out. The white light of Kaos set him aglow. The walls cracked, any remaining windows shattered, and the ground shook as the power poured from his eyes.

Etain gritted her teeth against the dull roar of the wind and sounds of rendered stone. Many covered their ears. Parents hovered over their children to protect them from flying dust and debris. Husbands, wives, lovers, and friends clung to one another. Several cried, others screamed, still others accepted the travesty in mute resignation. A barrage of pure power reduced the stone and glass to piles of rubble. With the castle destroyed, the ground gave way. The remains of the once proud LOKI clan stared in bewilderment at the place they had called home.

Once the aftershock subsided, the only thing left was a great pit where the castle once stood. The High Lord made a final decree. "LOKI is dead. Any who try to resurrect the clan in this name will answer to me. Remember what you have seen this day, and should you seek a new clan, do not repeat the same mistakes. Leave this place and never return."

TAKEN WITH THE TAKING

Dar waited until he and Etain were alone before opening a portal to their room at Laugharne. "I hope I did the right thing," he whispered, tears in his eyes.

Etain stroked his cheek. "They will find their way, my love."

"It was their home. It was *my* home with the Alamir."

"They'll find new clans. Some may even start their own. You have infused life into a dead people."

"Perhaps."

"Besides," she took his hands in hers, "you have a *new* home with me."

"I owe you an apology, milady. I know you would not betray me. Why I let—"

"I knew you'd find your way back to me. What we share is unbreakable."

"*A chuisle*—" She stole his words with a kiss. He wrapped his arms round her and held on like a drowning man at sea would cling to a lone piece of driftwood. "I have missed you, sweet lady," he breathed into her ear. "You are my reason, my life."

"Let's get out of this armor. I want to feel your skin next to mine." She gasped, watching his second skin armor slide into itself until only the circlet remained at his neck.

With a single command, "*Scaoileadh* (release)," the ring disappeared. "Now, shall we get you out of yours?"

Together, they released the straps of the scabbard. Dar removed it from her back casting a keen eye over the workmanship. "Where did you find this, my love?"

"Inferno and Linq made it for your new swords, at my request."

"But I already have a scabbard—"

"That fits you. I asked them to make one I could wear." At his raised brow, she confessed, "After what happened in Nunnehi, I needed some part of you close to me."

Guilt stabbed at his heart. "I am sorry—"

Her hands covered his. "I'm not telling you this to make you feel bad. Having your swords with me gave me strength and comfort, and believe me, they came in handy."

He cleared his throat and turned his attention back to the scabbard. "Aye. Well, I recognize the sigils for our families but what is this one in the center?"

Etain smiled softly and stood next to him, her fingers caressing the symbol. "It's *our* family sigil. You and me. Do you like it?"

His voice low and respectful, he said, "It is perfect," and placed an arm around her shoulders. "We are quite fortunate to be surrounded by these incredible people, *a chuisle*."

"Aye. Quite fortunate."

"Now, back to business." Dar set the scabbard aside and loosened her breastplate, holding onto it while she wriggled free.

From the moment he set it down, she was in his arms again. "Thank you for loving me the way you do."

His tongue tickled along the length of her neck. "I love you naked in my arms, wet and hot for my cock."

Her eager hand between his legs gave testament to her agreement.

"*Tartarus*, woman," he groaned, leaning into her. "As much as I want you now, it must wait."

"Am I so easily tossed aside?"

He touched his forehead to hers. "My lady, never again. Tonight will be ours but for now Inferno should know of my return and we are well."

"I doubt either of us is on his mind right now."

He smoothed the hair from her face. "A father's children are always on his mind. He loves you very much."

She tilted her head. "And I love you all the more for seeing it."

"He should hear of LOKI's dissolution before the rumors start."

Etain chuckled. "There's my mighty warrior. Business before pleasure."

He brought her in close and kissed her on the ear. "I will not tolerate any interruptions. I want to take my time," his lips whispered along her jaw, "love you slowly," hovering over her mouth. "Savor your sweetness." He claimed her in a soulful kiss.

Covered in gooseflesh, she held onto him. "Let's be quick about it then."

Voices drifted up the stairs as they descended, hand in hand. Dar stopped halfway down. "Do you know who is here?"

"Don't worry. Inferno called in the clan because of recent *Bok* activity."

"You should have said earlier, Etain."

She sighed. "Of course, what was I thinking? Should that have been before or after Savage tried to take your head? Or maybe—"

"Point taken."

Before she stepped into the dining hall doorway, she placed a hand on his chest. "You wait here a minute." The moment she showed her face, a barrage of voices spilled from the room.

One rose above the rest. "Etain! Where have you been?"

Dar heard a chair scrape across the stone floor, followed by quick footsteps. The next he saw, a dark-haired young man held her in a far too intimate hug. "I've been manic with worry."

"Put me down, silly. I'm perfectly fine." He set her on her feet, but a possessive arm slipped around her waist. Dar raised a brow. She quickly glanced at him, and turned her smile on whoever else occupied the room. "Look who I found remodeling the LOKI castle."

She reached for Dar's hand and pulled him into the doorway amidst gasps and wide-eyed stares. The room became a clamor of cheers as people rushed to welcome him home, pushing the strange young man farther away.

Dar bowed to accept a hug from Swee. "Welcome back, Dar. I've missed you terribly." His large hands engulfed her tiny waist and set her back.

"I am surprised to see you." He scanned the room. "Did the others come—"

Inferno bulldozed his way through the throng, Spirit close behind. An audible intake of breath echoed through the room as the two men faced one another.

Dar squared his shoulders for the berating sure to follow. "Inferno." He dipped his head to the lady. "Spirit."

When Inferno engulfed him in a hug, Dar gave Etain a puzzled grin. "Damn! I thought we'd lost ya. Welcome back." Laughter filled the room again. Inferno turned and embraced Etain with the same fervor. "Lass," he whispered into her ear, "I been sick with worry." He let her go and turned to Dar again. "Are ya sure yer back to yerself?"

Dar placed a fisted hand over his heart. "Damn sure."

Inferno eyed Etain. "I don't know how ya did it, but ya done a bloody fine job." He swiped at a sudden tear. "Ock, damn dust gets me eyes ever' time." Another round of laughter erupted through the hall.

Spirit hugged Dar. "I had faith in you the entire time."

He kissed her cheek. "It is what got me through."

Eyelashes fluttering, her face turned as pink as the gloves he had worn in the tournament. "Your havin' a laugh." She chuckled and nodded toward Etain. "It was her stubborn determination what did it."

Dar pulled Etain close. "How could I not come back to this beautiful lady? My love. My life." He lovingly stroked her hair, drinking her in with his eyes. Her arms went around his neck and gave him a kiss full of unspoken promises.

"Enough of that," Inferno huffed good-heartedly. "We've just sat down to eat, and no matter from where ya came, Dar, me belly's hollerin' to be fed."

Dar flashed his boyish grin. "I have done many things in my life, Inferno, but never let it be said I stood between a man and his dinner."

With a light-hearted air, the clan returned to their seats while two more places were set. Elfin and Wolfe, their usual jovial selves, told the tale of the Blade Masters Gathering.

Etain tugged on his sleeve and leaned toward him. "Yes," she whispered.

He furrowed his brows. "Yes to what?" The sparkle in her beautiful eyes made him all the more curious.

"Everything that's happened. All we've been through."

He thought his heart would stop when she lowered her eyes and breathed in.

"What we have between us doesn't require a ceremony." Her ice-blue gaze came back to him. "But I want *every*one to know you belong to me and I to you. We are a packaged deal. If anyone messes with you, they will answer to me, and vice-versa."

He took her face in his hands and kissed her as though he had never kissed her before. "Are you certain, *a chuisle*?"

"Oh, aye."

Wolfe and Elfin's story closed with the details of Dar's mishap with the fallen warrior maiden, ending with his disqualification.

Dar turned to the room, a grin larger than life on his face. "All great stories at my expense. But none compare to the one I have to tell." He lifted his mug to Inferno and Spirit, and the rest of the table. "She said yes!"

The room quieted.

"We are to be married!" Dar emptied his mug and beamed at the woman by his side. The quiet erupted into a spectacle of cheers and congratulations.

Accompanied by a fine wine brought up from the cellar, conversations varied between an appropriate wedding ceremony to who would be invited, aside from those at the table.

With dessert served, Inferno broached the topic of when. "We'll start first thing in the morning. The two of ya should go into town and find yerselves proper clothes."

Etain choked on her wine. "Tomorrow?"

"Oh, aye. No need to wait. The two of ya have wasted enough time."

Dar laughed. "I wonder at your urgency, Inferno."

"We could use good news for a change and with all the clan here, why not? Do ya have anyone not here ya want to invite?"

Dar glanced at Etain. "Alatariel?"

"Do you think she would?"

Linq pushed from the table and stood. "Consider it done. I will extend your personal invitation to the queen."

"A queen?" Spirit exclaimed. "Goddess of us all! I can get a proper wedding together but to entertain a queen? What do I do with the children?"

Etain's eyes widened. "The kids are here?"

"Aye. Upstairs." She narrowed her eyes. "But don't get any ideas. We've not the time for visiting. You can say your hellos after you're married."

"Do not fret, Spirit." Dar topped off her glass of wine. "Alatariel is a gracious lady and would not expect anyone to go to extra lengths on her behalf."

"Queen or no queen, we can't leave Spirit to do it alone," Etain said. "It's *our* wedding. We should help."

Spirit waved her hand. "Your mission is to find a dress. The planning part is my pleasure, love. Aeval and the faeries will help make it extra special. They'll know what to do. Accept it as our wedding gift."

"We all will be happy to pitch in!" Wolfe exclaimed.

"Aye!" shouted the rest of the clan.

Linq lifted his half-filled glass of wine. "I will return in time for the festivities. Thank you for the exquisite meal and entertaining company."

"Safe trip, my friend." Dar and the others lifted their glasses. Linq downed his wine, bowed, and was gone. Dar turned to Etain. "I would like to toast my beautiful wife-to-be. Inferno, pass the wine."

"Ya won't be finding any in this one." He laughed, turning the bottle upside down. "But I'll be happy to open another." He reached for a fresh bottle from the sideboard and refilled every glass, but raised his before Dar. "A toast to the bride and groom. May joy and peace surround ya, contentment latch yer door, and happiness be with ya now and bless ya evermore."

Later in the evening as they luxuriated in a warm bath, Dar's first question involved the stranger who greeted his intended with too much familiarity. She smiled at him from across the mounds of bubbles.

"That was my brother, Robert. I wanted to introduce you, but he disappeared and once you made the announcement..." She shrugged. "The rest was a blur."

"He is not what I imagined. How does it feel to have him back?"

"We haven't had much time to talk but having him here feels good, and weird." She laughed and blew at a mound of bubbles. "It's hard to believe he's real. On the other hand." She paused. "He's different, almost scary."

"Rie told me he was raised by Midir."

"Mmm, aye." She poked a toe out of the cloud of suds and ran it along his cheek. "Maybe that's why he scares me."

He caught her foot in one hand. "Midir was not what I would consider a father figure."

"Not even in an *Addams Family* way." She tried to wriggle free of his hold.

His other hand trailed along her shapely leg. "Addams family? I am not familiar with this name. Are they significant?"

"That tickles!" She laughed and splashed him with her other foot. "No, never mind. It was a random reference to another time."

He reached for her, splashing water over the edge of the tub. Amidst squawks and laughs, he caught her around the waist and pulled her on top of him. "Speaking of another time. When I returned from Nunnehi, I could not find you. I thought you had left me for good and found a way to block me. Then I remembered the threats made by the High Council. I was certain they had taken you to punish me."

She touched his cheek. "I don't know why you couldn't feel me, but I wouldn't leave without a word. I couldn't do that to you." After a soft kiss, she leaned back. "Come to think of it, I didn't know you'd come back until I spoke with Wolfe and Elfin. Do you feel me now?" At his raised eyebrow, she chuckled. "My blood."

He remained pensive. "Aye, its burn is a welcome heat. It has been so since you found me at LOKI. Whatever blocked you is gone." He brushed back a stray silver lock. "And you? How is it with my blood?"

She sighed deeply and touched her forehead to his. "I didn't realize how much I missed it until now. No wonder I felt so strange those days away from you."

"Tell me about your adventure to find your brother."

She turned and made herself comfortable against his chest, recounting the days spent in Deudraeth, their near capture at the apothecary, and quick escape. "When we got to Inferno's, it was mayhem. Ambassadors, chieftains, all different sorts of Alamir had come for a discussion of the *Bok*."

"Was anything decided?" he asked, distracted by her slippery, wet skin.

She shrugged, soaping a bath sponge. "Not that I know of."

"Perhaps I should meet with Inferno before we retire to discuss the defense of the castle to be sure everyone is safe. And he needs to know of LOKI. Time seemed to slip away earlier." As he absently fondled her breast, his warrior mind rummaged through strategies. Names of those he knew he could count on in the event of a skirmish ran through his head.

A sudden twisting of his thumb scattered his thoughts. "Ow! What was that for?"

She turned to face him. "Where are you?"

"I am here with you."

"Your body is but your mind's running around this bloody castle."

"Sorry, *a chuisle*." He gave her a sheepish grin. "Shall we get to bed? We have a busy day tomorrow."

"Maybe I should go to my room across the hall." She stood in the tub, her skin shimmering from the mix of bubbles and water. "You know, to be on the safe side."

Dar rested his arms on the sides of the bath and licked his lips. "Five more minutes."

"But you just said—"

He pulled her down on top of him. "Ten, then." *Tartarus, her body pressed to mine is all I need.* His lips met hers in a fiery exchange of shared passions. "Never let me go, beautiful lady."

"You will never be free, my sexy savage."

"Are you sure this isn't too much, Spirit?" Etain asked for the tenth time. "I feel guilty leaving you to make all the arrangements."

"If it was, I wouldn't be doing it, would I?" Spirit shooed the couple out the front doors. "Go find a beautiful dress for your wedding."

On the front steps, the door slammed in their faces. The couple blinked.

"She is a small thing, but I would not want to cross her."

Etain chuckled. "You'd think it was *her* wedding day."

Dar turned and held out his arm. "Shall I escort thee to town, milady?"

Arms linked, she agreed with a Texan version of a British accent. "I say, milord. I would like nothing bettah."

Dar nearly pulled her off her feet as he turned in one direction and she the other.

"Where are you going?" She pursed her lips. "Town is this way."

He laughed as he reached into his pocket and pulled out a set of keys. "No walking today. Inferno has offered up his vehicle."

He reminded her of a kid in a toy store. She raised a brow. "Inferno? Gave *you* the keys to his Hummer?"

"Oh, aye." He opened her door and offered his hand as she climbed in. She watched him walk around the vehicle and settle in behind the steering wheel. The doubtful expression on her face made him say, "I didn't do it."

"I'd like to know how you wrangled this deal."

His grin returned. "He must want us married real bad."

Etain laughed, shaking her head. "I guess so. But how is it the High Lord of Kaos knows how to drive?"

He shifted into gear and winked. "Dar VonNeshta, man of mystery."

"Seriously, Dar. Where did you learn to drive?"

After another shift of the gears, he drove in silence for a time. Etain sensed his inner turmoil and waited. "It was a long time ago, my love."

"Everything was a long time ago with you. Tell me now or we can go back to Laugharne and you can deal with Inferno." He gave her a sideways glance. "And Spirit."

"There is no need to get nasty." He smirked at her raised brow and crossed arms. "I was not the man you know today when I met the Alamir, but neither were they. My heart was dead, filled with remorse and the need for revenge. I had not confirmed who murdered my family."

"You told me it was Midir."

"Back then I was not certain and refused to lose another member of my family without irrefutable proof. Yet the desire to make someone pay became stronger every day."

She stared out the window, her mind drifting to the days after the loss of her family. "Yeah. I get it." *But it was long ago, too.* She pushed the thoughts away. "Is that when you started LOKI?"

His laugh was more of a grunt. "My interests were far more sinister." He down-shifted for a sharp curve in the road. "I hired out as a mercenary."

"I remember when we first met." She shrugged. "*Officially* met at your home in Krymeria. I'd heard stories of you but didn't realize it was *you*."

He raised an inquisitive brow. "Did I scare you?"

To which she grinned. "Not in the least. You were far too kind and respectful."

"Darknight?" He frowned. "Kind and respectful? I am glad we did not meet during those days. No mercenary needs a tarnished reputation." He gave her a wink.

"Well, if it helps, I *did* have a lamp to hand as protection."

"Thank the gods I had better things to do." They laughed together. "I know you do not like to admit it, but you were fragile, Etain. You had lost so much. I believed your learning I was a part of LOKI was difficult enough."

"Which reminds me. Did you tell Inferno about what happened?"

"We are here."

With the beast of a vehicle parked at the edge of town, they ventured on foot to explore the shops they missed on their first visit. Etain remembered the excitement she felt that day, the sweetness of a newfound relationship with a man she thought would never be hers and the pivotal moment their relationship moved to a new level. She secretly glanced at her handsome love, her fiancé, and swallowed. There was so much she didn't know about him.

"So, did you tell him?"

He took her hand in his as they walked. "We had a discussion that ended with his keys in my hand."

"Okay. I won't push it. Why a mercenary? Did you learn to drive then?"

He released her hand and tucked her arm around his. "All I wanted was to destroy. The Alamir were not organized and were prime targets for the *Bok*. My experience as a Krymerian served me well in hunting them down and ending their miserable lives. Sometimes our agenda would take us to the human realm. Although there are static portals between certain spots, we were unable to open random portals to travel. At that point in time, I preferred not to share my ability with portals, so we learned to drive. Pyro can fly a plane."

She stopped. "No kidding? Pyro was a mercenary with you?"

"Oh, aye. A damn good one too."

"Wow." She ran a hand through her hair. "It must hurt to see him side with Savage."

"It is his way of showing me how far things have gotten out of hand."

"Why didn't he just talk to you?"

Dar sighed. "As the Alamir say, easier said than done." He nudged against her. "You know better than anyone."

"Oh, aye. I know quite well. You're so busy with stuff."

The couple strolled along sidewalks constructed of rose-colored pavers that lined both sides of a cobbled street. Quaint little shops with large windows arranged their wares in bright displays, tempting those who walked by to come inside. Goods spilled out from open doorways onto the sidewalks.

"But when we met, you said you were a member of LOKI. Had you quenched the desire to destroy?"

A pharmacy at the top of the street neighbored a small fruit and vegetable market. The sweet fragrance of strawberries melded with the scent of juicy oranges, coalescing into the heady bouquet of freshly baked bread.

"Not then. It became a part of me but something stronger made me focus on more productive methods of helping the Alamir. I noticed several new initiates who struggled to adapt. Many were left to their own devices and paid a price they did not deserve to pay. It is why I created LOKI." He lovingly squeezed her hand. "I will share a secret if you promise not to tell anyone."

"How many of *my* secrets have I shared with you?"

He raised a brow. "Are we talking voluntarily?"

With a playful slap to his arm, she pulled him close. "I won't tell anyone."

"My BloodCore, they were my fellow mercenaries."

"Well, I have a secret I will tell *you*, voluntarily. I'd always heard LOKI was a *clan* of mercenaries. After meeting you, they didn't seem as scary, but it did take a while to get the skills and backbone to request an audience."

"Then I must share one last secret."

"I don't know if I want to hear it."

"You are a fearless warrior, Etain. Do not be faint at heart."

She rolled her eyes. "I'm not afraid, more like I'm not sure if I'm ready."

"You were ready. The moment I saw your name on the list, you were automatically approved."

"Hmm. It explains a lot. You should've told me."

"Nonsense. It was within my powers as chieftain to approve whomever I wanted in the clan. I did not go against clan edicts."

"Did you ever approve anyone else?"

"None I can recall. Look here," he pointed to a window farther down the street, "there is a dress over there."

Etain knew the subject was closed and there would be no further discussions about it.

They walked past a charity shop toward another with a dress display in its window, but she decided it was too old-fashioned.

A men's shop, a shoe store, a small furniture and appliance store, and a discount shop were passed by at the prospect of another window filled with dresses. Etain smiled and pulled Dar in.

Once inside, he frowned at the assault of estrogen that met them at the door. He politely greeted the ladies, but whispered into Etain's ear, "I think I will wait outside. You don't mind, do you?"

"Do *not* wander off."

"Of course not." He tipped his head. "Ladies," he murmured, making a quick exit as an eager salesclerk swept Etain deeper into the fabricated jungle.

Free for the moment, he breathed in the fresh air. His confessions to Etain seemed to have lifted a weight from his shoulders. *She is my soul mate. I must learn to trust her with my past as she trusts me with hers.*

With the decision made to inspect other nearby shops, he turned and collided into a cloaked figure. By the size, he judged it to be a woman which was immediately confirmed by a string of colorful words uttered in a feminine voice. Elven words. She crouched to recover her basket of goods now strewn over the sidewalk.

"Apologies, milady. I did not see you there." Dar retrieved several oranges rolling toward the street. "Are you all right?"

She continued to gather her things, muttering under her breath.

He crouched and placed the fruit into her basket as he tried to get a glimpse of her face. "Are you hurt?"

Dar straightened when the woman came to her feet. Although the hood hid her features, he did get a peek of dark hair and pale skin. Amber eyes met his. Disconcerted, he stepped back. "Illiana?"

"Keep her safe and beware the dark son, brother."

"Excuse me?"

He heard Etain call his name from within the shop and turned his head for a second. When he looked back, the woman was gone. Dar searched down and up the street. There was no sign of a cloak anywhere. The only proof of her existence was a stray orange rolling toward the doorway of the shop where Etain stood, ready to step out.

"Stop," he said with such authority, she froze mid-step. He strode to her and scooped up the lone fruit. "An escapee on the lam."

She laughed and accepted the orange. "Where did this come from?"

"You would not believe me if I told you."

"Hmm. Well, thank you, my shining knight, for protecting me from the evil plot of the vile orange."

He bowed low. "My life for yours, milady." He straightened and noticed her lack of packages. "I see you have no dress. Did nothing suit you?"

"Nothing." She searched the other side of the road that boasted a butcher, a baker, and just short of a candlestick maker, a candle shop.

Dar sensed her frustration. "Tell me again why we came to town."

"Mainly to keep us out of Spirit's hair, but I'm not finding anything to my taste."

A lascivious grin turned up the corners of his mouth. "What *would* be to your taste, my warrior vixen?"

Preoccupied, Etain missed his attempt at humor. "I don't know. I've never even thought about a wedding much less what kind of dress I would wear."

"Do not worry." He drew her close. "It is just a dress. We will find something."

She pushed him away and placed her hands on her hips. "And you're just a Krymerian."

Her sharp words had no effect. "Etain, you are perfect with or without a dress."

"If your blasé attitude is what I have to look forward to, you can count me out. I'll go home and we can be done with it."

Dar ran a hand over his face. "Where you are concerned, *a chuisle*, nothing could ever be blasé." She crossed her arms over her chest. "I am sorry it came out wrong. Tomorrow is a most important day for both of us. Our marriage tells the world we are united, a show of force if you will."

He dared to gaze into the steely depths of her eyes and rested his hands on her shoulders. "As you said, it is not needed between us. To *know* you love me, words cannot convey the joy in my heart. I can hardly believe you have agreed to be my wife. So please forgive me if a dress falls low on my list of priorities. For me, it is you who is most important."

She uncrossed her arms, a glimmer of a smile on her lips. "Stop it. You really make it hard to stay mad when you say things like that. Even though it's never been a priority, I want it to be perfect."

"It will be." He grinned. "You have me." As they kissed, the clock in the town square struck the hour. "It is noon. Shall we get a bite to eat and rest our feet? Perhaps the break will give us a new perspective."

Not long after walking into a nearby pub and placing their order, they found themselves blessed with the company of Wolfe and Elfin.

"What are the odds we would end up in the same pub at the same time?" Elfin laughed, beer in hand.

Wolfe slapped him on the back. "Aye, it must be fate."

"Aye," Etain mumbled. "It's a bloody mystery considering there's only two pubs in the whole town."

"A fifty/fifty shot, Lady E." Wolfe lifted his mug in a mock toast and downed the contents. "Ah, ice-cold beer! Another round." He was off to the bar before anyone could protest.

Dar grinned. "How is it you two were able to slip through the Inferno wedding net?"

With a beer in one hand, Elfin pulled up a chair with the other. "We are doing our part," he said with a wink.

Wolfe returned with four golden pints. "Inferno knows we are more effective if left to our own devices."

Etain nodded toward the pints. "Have you left your devices for a grander purpose?"

Wolfe laughed. "Our devices are well in hand, milady. Now is the time to celebrate."

Several cold beers provided by the cheerful duo followed a sumptuous meal of crispy fried cod and chips. The men enjoyed an afternoon of swapping stories, which proved entertaining not only for their small party but for the other patrons of the pub as well. Somewhere along the way, news of the forthcoming wedding slipped out, instigating a stream of congratulations, toasts, and a lot more beer.

Late into the afternoon, Etain brought the revelry back to reality with a reminder of her need for a wedding dress.

Elfin placed his fresh brew on the table. "You have not found a dress?"

She frowned. "Not yet."

"Bloody hell." Wolfe turned to Dar. "The shops close early around here. You best get to it!"

"I told her I would marry her dress or no dress," Dar laughed, finishing off his beer.

Elfin grinned. "I highly recommend a dress. Otherwise, one of us randy blokes may abscond with your fair bride."

"Like a dress would make any difference," Wolfe threw in.

Dar did his best to keep a straight face. "Aye, it only gets in the way."

Etain rolled her eyes and stood but grabbed hold of Wolfe's strong shoulder to steady herself. "If you will excuse me, good sirs, I'd prefer to be dressed."

Dar winked at the others. "There is a challenge, mates." He slipped from his chair and slapped both men on the back. "We shall see you at Laugharne."

"Aye, you will, milord." Wolfe and Elfin tapped glasses and swigged their beers.

As they exited the pub, a boy rushed past Etain, pushing her into Dar. "How rude," she grumbled, glaring after him.

Her sexy savage wrapped his arm around her waist. "Dress first, milady. Then we can commence with the taking."

Again, she rolled her eyes, the rude boy forgotten. "You're quite taken with the taking bit, aren't you?"

"Aye, milady. 'Tis me favorite part."

His steady gaze turned her legs to rubber and set the butterflies aflutter in her belly. He suddenly glanced across the road and pointed. "I see a shop we have not scandalized with our presence."

Mná Cumasacha

B lack eyes watched the couple cross the road. A slim figure slithered up next to the hooded observer. "I caught 'em at the pub. They're getting married."

Sparks flashed in the black depths. "Anything more?"

"Nah, unless you like blabbing about the old days."

Red lips parted in a sinister grin. "What tales did our lady have to share?"

"She didn't say much. It was mostly the men talking. She's looking for a dress."

"Of course, a dress."

"Your lady is very pretty."

A low chuckle issued from the hooded figure. He was amused by the ownership so easily afforded him. "Yes, my lady is exquisite."

"Want me to follow them?"

A red-skinned hand ruffled the boy's white-blond hair. "No, you have done well, Cloud. Go see Raum. He will reward you for your services."

"Sure. Anytime." The boy disappeared down the street.

Dathmet remained hidden in the shadowed doorway. *A wedding. How can I resist?*

Upon the engaged couple's return to Laugharne, Inferno came around the corner into the courtyard. "Dar, for fuck's sake. It's about damn time."

"Sorry, Inferno. I did not realize I was in high demand." He chuckled with a wink at Etain.

Inferno gave the two a good once over. "I'm not seeing any packages."

"It's not easy finding the right dress, you know. Laugharne isn't the most fashion savvy town."

His doubting eye went to the groom. "And what's yer excuse?"

"Me?" He glanced at Etain. "I have something in mind."

"Hmph. If it isn't up to my standards, I have an old suit what belonged to me great grandda. It might just fit yer oversized bones. Ain't so fashionable but it'll do the job."

Etain sighed, her gaze sliding to the man at her side. "It better be spectacular."

Dar laughed. "I will not disappoint."

"Well, then..." Inferno attempted to drape an arm over the towering man's shoulders but settled for a hand on his upper arm. "Lord Groom, yer spending this fine evening with me and me boys. A stag do, of sorts. There'll be no rest for the wicked tonight."

Etain pursed her lips. "I guess I'll go find Spirit and see what we can do about me. Y'all don't get too crazy, okay?"

"No promises there, lass." The two disappeared around the corner.

"Now to create a dress from thin air." She headed into the castle in search of an answer to an insurmountable problem.

Etain stepped into the Laugharne foyer to find everything in a bustle, faeries twittering here and there carrying this and that. A tiny one dressed in pink landed on her nose. Her voice, like a small chime tinkling in the wind, assailed her with the current disaster.

"*Oíche mhaith* (Good night), pretty lady. Are ye here to help? I certainly hope so. Lady Spirit says there's no proper gown to be found. Terrible it is with the wedding for the morrow."

How does Spirit know?

The faerie stopped long enough to take a small breath. "Not to worry. Ms. Spirit's a clever clog." She lowered her voice and placed a hand at the side of her mouth as though sharing a secret. "Herself offered her own weddin' gown." Her giggle made Etain laugh. The small faerie slid down her nose, but her wings fluttered to the rescue. Etain offered her a safe place to continue her story in the palm of her hand. "Everone's busy doing alterations."

Etain merely smiled as she headed up the stairs toward the sounds of women at work.

"The ladies are doin' a fine job. The dress might be a tad short, but they won't know until the bride herself shows up. By the time they're finished, it'll be as if it was made just for her. *Mná cumasacha* (Talented women), they are. Have ya ever met them?

"Oh, you must meet them. See." The faerie pointed to the far corner of Spirit's bedroom. "There they are now. I would love to be a seamstress, but they tell me I've no the patience fer it. Can you imagine? I think I have patience aplenty. Oh, look..." She turned in another direction. "There's the ones who will make the circlet to sit on her silver locks. I hope her hair is the color of yours, milady. It's very pretty."

A larger faerie, aglow in green, buzzed up to Etain, hands on her small hips. "Liadan, ye've no time to be gossiping with the bride. Get yerself back down the stairs and to the kitchen. It will take us all to meet this deadline." Her serious blue eyes landed on Etain. "Milady, we need ya for a few fittin's."

The pink faerie's eyes widened as she listened to her elder. Standing in Etain's palm, she curtsied to the older faerie, and turned to her new friend. "*Leithscéil* (Apologies), milady. I didn't know it was you. I have duties to tend to." With a tinkling laugh, she flittered out the door.

Spirit eyed the bride. "It's about time. You must've gone to every bloody store in town."

Swept into the activity around her, Etain felt lightheaded. "You *do* remember who's driving the train? It's not like I have time to shimmer off to Paris."

"I've come up with a solution, just in case." Spirit dragged her to a table covered with fabric, spools of thread, needles, and other sewing necessities. "We're going to have to work late to get the dress ready for tomorrow."

"The little faerie told me you've donated your own wedding dress. Are you sure? Shouldn't you save it for Molly or Tegan?"

"You're as much family as the girls. Now get out of those leathers and let's get to work."

Etain's heart beat an unsteady rhythm, a warm rush sweeping over her skin.

"Get her water," Swee ordered, stepping in and guiding her to a nearby chair. "You look like a deer caught in the headlights," she laughed, accepting a glass from one of the larger faeries. "Thank you." She pushed the glass into Etain's hand. "Drink it before you pass out."

Feeling further disconcerted by the smiling eyes, Etain put the glass to her lips and sipped. "So you're in on this too?"

Swee placed a comforting hand on her arm. "There are some very determined people in this place."

Etain's heart slowed. "You're telling me." She watched the pandemonium for a few minutes, took another sip of water, and set it on the floor. "Let's figure out how the heck we're gonna get a tiny little dress to fit an Amazon."

"You ladies get on with the measuring," Spirit said as she walked to the door. "I have a bit of business downstairs. Swee, I could use your help."

"Okay. But wouldn't I—"

"We won't be gone long." Spirit cocked her head toward the door. "Come on."

Swee glanced at Etain and shrugged as the mage dragged her from the room.

Twenty minutes later they were back with an entourage of trays loaded with snacks, bottles of spirits, and enough crazy hats and fascinators for every lady in the room. Spirit laughed at Etain's furrowed brow. "What's a wedding without a hen-do?"

"While we work on my dress?" She grabbed a musketeer-styled hat with a large feather in its band.

"A party with a purpose." Swee laughed, donning a pink fedora. "Ladies, come and get some refreshments and a hat."

Laughter filled the room as the women changed and exchanged headwear, enjoying the company and a few minutes of relaxation before digging into the real work.

Well after midnight, the exhausted group parted company. Spirit and the others headed off to bed, leaving Swee and Etain to their own devices.

"Mind if I escort you home, milady?" Etain grinned.

"Thank you, kind warrior. You never know what lurks in the dark corners of a castle."

The two laughed as they walked from one end of the second floor to the other.

"I hope I can sleep tonight," Etain said as they approached Swee's bedroom.

"I bet you're out the minute your head touches the pillow." Swee yawned, and laughed. "Sorry. It's been a busy day."

Etain yawned as well. "So it has. Thank you for your help today."

"I'm glad I could be here for you and Dar."

Etain gave her a heartfelt hug. "Sleep well. See you in the morning."

"Night, Etain. It's going to be beautiful."

⁓ ⁘ ⁓

Upon receiving news of Dathmet's impromptu visit to the town of Laugharne, Thamuz tossed aside all vestiges of protocol and stormed into the young man's private chambers.

"Have you lost your mind, compromising our plans with your stalker tendencies?" At first, it appeared he spoke to an empty room. He turned toward the sound of footsteps from the direction of the en-suite. Dathmet stepped out, a bath towel around his hips, drying his face with a smaller one as he sauntered across the room to the bed. Thamuz blew out a heated breath. "If VonNeshta picks up as much as a whif—"

"VonNeshta is too enthralled with his future wife to notice anything else. Relax, Thamuz." He threw the small towel onto the bed and picked up a fresh shirt. "He suspects nothing." He turned with a nonchalant air, buttoning the shirt. "To see how he moves was enlightening. Neither seems to be much of a threat."

"How many times must I remind you to not underestimate your target? VonNeshta is far and above anyone you've tracked in the past. He can be every bit as deadly as your father and has been known to exceed Midir's brutality."

Dathmet let the bath towel drop. Thamuz caught the challenge in the black eyes and averted his gaze. "Don't ruin my good mood, Thamuz." He jammed one leg and the other into his trousers. "Otherwise, you will pay for your insubordination."

Hearing the zipper, Thamuz's gaze returned to the intense young man now appropriately dressed, his crisp shirt tucked in.

"Let me remind you of something you seem to have forgotten." Dathmet crossed the room to an oversized highboy, opened a drawer, and pulled out a pair of dark socks. "VonNeshta hasn't met the likes of me."

New Beginnings

Happy with the way things were going downstairs, Spirit grabbed Swee. "Come with me. It's time we checked on our girl."

They found her sitting on the side of the bath wrapped in a towel, staring into the mirror. "What're you doing, Etain?" Spirit bustled in. "It's nigh an hour till you're to be wed and you sit here like a lost soul."

"I-I don't know what to do."

"Ah, lass, did you never go to a wedding?"

Etain shrugged. "Maybe. I don't remember."

Spirit sat next to her and put an arm around her shoulders. "No worries. We'll have you pretty as a picture in the blink of an eye."

The women escorted the bride down the hall to Spirit's bedroom. Amid brushes, pencils, and makeup, they set out to transform Etain into a glowing, ethereal goddess. Swee combed her silver tresses while Spirit worked on her nails.

Etain watched the mage tame the rag-tag edges. "Spirit?"

"Aye, lass?"

"Don't people usually rehearse before the actual wedding?"

"I suppose they do in some places, but not here."

Etain sighed. "I don't know what to do or how to do it. I don't even know what to say."

"Don't you worry." Spirit patted her on the arm. "We have a plan."

"I have another question."

"Aye, lass."

"Shouldn't we have a preacher to marry us? Do we even have preachers in the Alamir?"

"Of a sort." Spirit held the emery board in mid-air. "For someone who doesn't remember, you have a lot of questions."

Etain shrugged. "Sorry."

"All done." Spirit smiled. "If I didn't know better, I'd think these were the hands of a lady."

Etain admired her handiwork. "For a day at least. Thank you, Spirit." She furrowed her brows. "What do you mean by 'of a sort'?"

"I'll take this one, Spirit, if you don't mind," Swee offered.

"It's all yours, milady. I'll work the tangles out on this side."

Swee caught Etain's eyes in the mirror. "Our powers, our strengths, come from nature—earth, wind, fire, water, and the unknown. Each one ties into a part of us—body, spirit, soul, mind, and the unknown. Some of us take a more spiritual approach toward being Alamir. They remind us to honor nature, to appreciate her generosity and gifts, and to take nothing for granted. In the beginning, I've heard they were called by a name no one could pronounce." Swee chuckled. "Not even them. Nowadays, we call them priest or priestess."

Etain accepted the explanation with only one question. "Which do we have? A priest or priestess?"

"Ah, lass, we want this one to last," said Spirit. "It has to be a priestess."

Etain wasn't sure how it made a difference, but if Inferno was happy with a priestess, she was good enough for her. "What happens after I'm all done up?"

"The two of us will go out the front doors and around to the back garden. Inferno will meet us, and he'll escort you down the aisle."

"Is he afraid I'll run off at the last minute?"

"Blessed be, lass." Spirit laughed. "Where do you get these ideas? It's traditional for the father of the bride to escort her down the aisle and present her into the safe hands of her groom."

"Oh. Sounds rather draconian to me." Etain admired her pretty nails to hide her embarrassment. "Not to be rude, but shouldn't my brother escort me?"

Spirit closed her eyes and sighed. "We hadn't thought of him. I'm sorry, lass. Have you seen the lad?"

"Not since the other day when we came back from LOKI."

"Let's stick to the plan we have for now. If he shows up at the last minute, we'll adjust."

Etain lowered her voice to a whisper. "I wish they were here."

"I know it's not the same without them, love." Spirit covered her hands with hers. "But we're proud to stand in for your mum and da. We love you like one of our own."

"I'm sorry to be such a baby." A tear escaped down her cheek. "You've been a blessing, and given me so much. I love you too."

"It's a big day, lass, and a lot to take in."

Swee wrapped her arms around the two women. "Your parents would be happy for you, Etain."

"Thank you, Swee. I think they would love Dar as much as I do."

"Aye, they would." Spirit broke the group hug. "Are you all right now?"

Etain grabbed a tissue from the dressing table and dabbed her eyes. "Aye." Spirit brushed and braided her hair while Swee added a touch of makeup. "Will the kids be there?"

"In a way. They'll be watching from a room upstairs, under guard." She winked at Etain. "I'll not have them messing about, especially with a queen on her way."

Etain frowned. "But I want them to meet Dar."

"There'll be plenty of time *after* the festivities."

With a dab of gloss to her lips, she was ready to slip into her gown. When Spirit removed the sheet from around the dress form, Etain and Swee gasped at its fragile beauty.

"Spirit..." Etain touched the delicate bodice. "It's stunning."

Beautiful hand beading crisscrossed the scooped bodice of the ivory gown. Down the front, transparent silk chiffon edged with eyelet lace covered silk satin, while silk lacings drew the gown in to accentuate her curves. Placed over the cleavage were intricately hand-beaded and embroidered silk georgette angel wings. The rest of the dress carried a soft sheen that reflected the light, giving it an ethereal air.

Etain carefully stepped into the gown. Swee and Spirit lifted the delicate dress up to her shoulders. Silk chiffon sleeves gave the gown a light, angelic quality. Not to be outdone, the back of the gown, split from the shoulders to the top of her tailbone, was held together by silk lacings, exposing her muscular back.

She twisted and turned in front of the mirror. "How did they add the length? It was at my ankles last night."

"'Tis a secret of the faeries, love. Not even I'm privy to their magic." Spirit's eyes sparkled. "You are a vision."

"One more thing." Swee placed a delicate silver circlet on the bride's head, a perfect white pearl at its center. "There. Dar will be speechless."

"It'll be the first time ever." Etain laughed to keep the tears at bay.

Swee helped Spirit into a gown of deep purple velvet made similar to Etain's but with a more modest neckline and enclosed back. As she ran a comb through Spirit's hair, the sounds of a fiddle drifted in through the open window.

Spirit turned to Etain. "It's time, lass."

Her heart pounded. *Am I ready?* After one last look in the mirror, she smiled. *Yes.* The women made their way downstairs.

"Remember to breathe," Swee reminded her before ducking into the kitchen.

Etain and Spirit went in the opposite direction toward the front. Before they stepped outside, Spirit took the bride's hand in hers and squeezed.

So far, it was a good day. Everything was in place. The bride was dressed and ready. The food was prepared. The altar stood at the point where the front courtyard and back garden met beneath a white canopy of fluttering canvas decorated with small white roses and baby's breath. Elegant white ribbons tied to tree limbs performed a dainty dance in the wind and tiny white lights hugged the trunks in wait for sunset. Even the weather cooperated by clearing out the overnight clouds and allowing the sun to shine.

As she worked her way to the front, Swee recognized most of the guests as UWS clansmen. Felix and Ruby, one black and one red, had white ribbons tied round their necks, tugging against the hold of Wolfe and Elfin, who grinned like Cheshire cats. She waved to the faeries sitting along the tree branches and witnessed the arrival of a group of Elves who filled the seats near the back. Beyond the Elves, she spotted a tall figure in a black cloak. Although she couldn't see a face, she guessed it to be a man by the broad shoulders and the way he carried himself.

Dar stood at the altar dressed in a black leather vest over a white shirt with billowing sleeves closed at the cuff, his blond hair neatly plaited down his back. Black leather boots finished with silver accents along their tops rode low on his powerful thighs over black leather trousers. On his hip was a beautiful scabbard, the hilt of the sword inside just visible. From those sitting nearby, she overheard the sword was named Day Star, made in honor of his bride. Swee sighed at the striking groom. *Etain, you are a lucky woman.*

Next to the groom, and nearly as tall, was an Elf clad in a tailored jacket of deep blue velvet. Although they'd been introduced when he and Etain returned from Deudraeth, she'd not had much interaction with him. She thought Linq rather unusual and savage, mainly due to his hairstyle. Most of the Elves she knew wore their hair either loose or plaited, much like Dar's. However, Linq wore his blond hair in a wide strip from his forehead to the base of his skull and streaming down his back in a banded tail, the sides of his head shaved. Seeing him today, she thought it was time to get to know him better.

Beyond the groom and his intriguing best man stood the priestess, ethereal in airy layers of pale blues and purples. The one person missing was Etain's brother.

Melodic strands of Bach's "Cello Suite No. 1 in G Major" filled the air. Dar turned with the others. All eyes watched as Spirit rounded the corner followed by Inferno, dapper in his own leathers and purple shirt, his arm intertwined with a vision.

A collective gasp ran through the audience. Dar's heart skipped and beads of sweat formed on his forehead. When his eyes met hers, the world fell away. He sent her a heartfelt message of love and reassurance. Etain answered with her beautiful smile.

At the altar, the music faded, and the priestess blessed the couple with a warm greeting. "You are Etain," she stated, her voice pitched so only they would hear, and turned to the groom. "And you are Dar. I am Anu. I usually do not perform this ceremony on such short notice." She held out a hand to Etain and one to Dar. "But as Spirit is a dear friend and Inferno so insistent," she winked, "I have agreed with provisions. Please, join hands with me and each other."

Dar gave Etain a wide-eyed look. She bit her bottom lip and squeezed his hand.

Connected within the circle, the priestess closed her eyes and spoke in a language neither Etain nor Dar understood. Her energy meshed with theirs—exploring and testing their bond—but her presence was not invasive. She did not judge, nor did any trace of her energy remain when she withdrew and opened her eyes. Her smile reflected the love they shared.

"The history between you is rich and full. Your future will prove even more so. Never doubt one another for it is the love you share that makes you strong, will *keep* you strong, and binds you together."

She raised her voice to address their guests. "We have come together in celebration of the joining together of Lady Etain and Lord Dar. The law of life is love unto all beings. Without love, life is nothing. Without love, death has no redemption. If we learn only one thing in life, let it be this.

"As with any aspect of life, marriage has its ups and downs, its trials, and triumphs. With full understanding of this, Dar and Etain have come here today to be joined as one. Etain, do you come of your own free will to be joined with this man?"

She smiled at her groom. "Aye. I do."

"With who do you come and whose blessings accompany you?"

"She comes with me, Inferno, her guardian, and her family's blessings."

"Inferno, thank you."

He shared a smile with the couple and joined the other guests.

The priestess continued. "Above you are the stars. Below you are the stones. As time doth pass, remember... Like a stone should your love be firm. Like a star should your love be constant. Let the powers of the intellect guide you in your marriage and let the strength of your wills bind you together. Let the power of your love and desire make you happy, and the strength of your dedication hold you together. Have patience with one another for storms will come, but they will pass. Be free in giving affection and warmth. Have no fear and let not the ways of the unenlightened give you unease."

"Dar, only you have the right to bind yourself to Etain. If it be your wish, say so at this time and place your ring in her hand."

He looked at the priestess, who smiled in expectation, and at Etain. "It *is* my wish. But I have no ring."

"The bloody rings," Spirit muttered with a glare at her husband, who was in charge of the small detail.

A feminine voice rose over the mutterings of the group. "Perhaps I can be of assistance."

Ruby whimpered and Felix barked, both dogs straining against the tight holds Wolfe and Elfin had on them. The wedding party turned. A tall, slim woman with long auburn hair wearing a gossamer emerald dress walked down the aisle. By her side was a small boy with the same color hair, carrying a package topped with an ivory pillow.

"Greetings, High Lord and High Lady." The woman's voice was warm and low-keyed.

"Alatariel, this is an honor," Dar said.

Etain smiled, happy to see her new friends. "We're so glad you came. Hello, Raff. You're very handsome today."

The small boy's cheeks turned pink as he gave her a shy smile.

"We could not miss your special day." Alatariel bowed her head in a show of respect. "I have come with gifts. I hope you do not mind." The queen frowned at Dar. "I am not surprised you forgot the rings. You were never one for such details." She tilted her head toward the Elf at his side. "Be sure to thank Linq once this is over."

The cherub-faced boy beside her lifted the pillow. "These rings I give as a blessing on your union. Each platinum ring has three stones embedded in its surface." Alatariel pointed to the stone on the far right. "This is the birthstone for Lady Etain. A perfect peridot symbolizes love, truth, and loyalty."

Etain said nothing but wondered at her source of information. Birthdays were not a subject she and Dar ever discussed, nor had she discussed it with anyone else in this realm, not even Spirit or Inferno. Due to the circumstances of her induction into the Alamir, her birthdays—the date of her human birth as well as her Alamir birth date—were sad reminders of her lost family.

"The one to the far left is Lord Dar's birthstone. An exquisite mul-ti-faceted diamond symbolizes love, purity, and fidelity. The stone in the center represents the two as one. A rare gem created by the union of these two magnificent stones." Her attention returned to the couple. "Each carries its own beauty and strength and can easily stand alone. However, when bound together, the strength of two join as one. May this unique pairing represent the love you share and serve as a reminder that together you are the strongest you will ever be."

Dar picked up the larger ring. "Thank you, Rie." He lifted Etain's hand and placed the ring in her palm. "It is my wish."

The priestess resumed the ceremony. "Etain, only you have the right to bind yourself to Dar. If it be your wish, say so at this time and place your ring in his hand."

Etain grasped Dar's right hand and placed the smaller ring in his palm. "It is my wish."

Alatariel bowed her head, and with her small escort in tow, returned to their seats.

"Dar, if you wish Etain to be your wife, place the ring on her finger." He slid the ring onto the third finger of her left hand. "Repeat after me."

As the priestess spoke, she paused every few moments to allow Dar to recite the words to his beloved. "I, Dar VonNeshta, by the life that courses within my body and the love that resides within my heart, take you, Etain Rhys, to my hand and my heart as my chosen one. I promise to love you wholly and completely without restraint, in sickness and in health, in plenty and in poverty, in life and beyond, where we will meet and love for eternity. I will not seek to change you in any way. I will respect you, your beliefs, and your ways as I respect myself."

The priestess thn addressed the bride. "Etain, if you wish Dar to be your husband, place the ring on his finger and repeat after me."

Etain slid the ring onto the third finger of his left hand and recited the vows as instructed.

The priestess lifted a crystal chalice, blessed the wine within, and handed it to Dar. "Two come together as one to drink from the vessel of love."

He lifted the chalice to Etain's lips, who hoped she wouldn't dribble on her beautiful dress. After a sip of the heady red wine, she took the chalice and held it to Dar's lips. With a wink at his bride, his hand covered hers. "Just to be sure." Etain rolled her eyes as he finished the wine, and handed the chalice to Anu.

Linq pulled a dirk from his belt. Etain watched her husband offer his left hand to the Elf. The point of the blade scored across his wrist, leaving a dark line of emerging blood. She soon felt the burn of the blade on her left wrist. Dar pressed hers to his as Linq bound them together with a strip of white linen.

"Say the words as I say them, *a chuisle*."

Her gaze shifted between his eyes and his lips as she echoed his words. "Two come together, blessed in the blood. My body, my spirit, and my heart are yours in every way. My love I give to you forever and a day."

Bound together in heart and blood, they turned to their guests as Anu declared, "I pronounce you husband and wife. May your love be the guiding light for all your days. Blessed be."

Dar pulled Etain to him, kissing her as though they might never kiss again. She melted into him, her heart beating like a bass drum. The wedding guests jumped to their feet and gathered round the couple, hooting and hollering.

Alatariel approached once again, the auburn-haired boy a step behind. "Dar, Etain, congratulations! You must come to Nunnehi once you have settled into your new life." A small motion of her hand beckoned the boy closer. "I would like to bestow one more gift to each of you." Raff lifted the package. Alatariel untied the ribbon revealing a fabric in constant change. "I give you these cloaks. They are made of a chameleon fabric that will match their surroundings. Their power transfers to all dimensions and will protect you no matter what you may face."

The couple thanked her warmly. "Are you able to stay a while longer?" Dar asked. "We would be honored to have you celebrate with us."

"I would be happy to." Her gaze went to the couple who stood behind Etain. "Hello, you must be Spirit and Inferno. Between Etain and Linq, I feel as though I know you already."

"Your Highness." The mage dipped into a curtsy. "Thank you for your kindness."

"Welcome to me home, Yer Majesty." Inferno bowed. "We're damn proud to have ya here." Spirit pinched him on the arm. "Ow."

"Don't offend the lady first thing, love."

Alatariel laughed. "Linq prepared me, Spirit. It is my pleasure." She held her hand out to the small boy who stood behind her. "May I introduce my nephew, Raphael. He is a most helpful young man."

"Aren't ya a wee sprite." Inferno shook his hand. "Welcome, Raphael."

"Nice to meet you, Raphael." Spirit smiled at the boy. "I wish we'd known you were coming with your auntie, I would've brought the kids down."

The queen raised a brow. "What do you say, Raphael?"

Etain thought he may be intimidated by the new faces and was prepared to whisk him away. Just as she made a move, he spoke, "Nice to meet you fine people. You may call me Raff."

Dar chuckled, giving his new bride a sideways glance. Inferno laughed. "Would ya like to meet me hounds, Raff?"

"Are they the ones back there?" He glanced back at Wolfe and Elfin.

"Aye. Felix be the black one. Ruby's the red. Do ya like dogs?"

A big grin spread across his face. "Mother tells me I may have one when I am older. Maybe if I tell her about Felix and Ruby, she will not make me wait so long."

Inferno addressed the queen. "Ya don't mind, do ya, Yer Majesty?"

She gave the boy a sideways glance and raised a brow. "I believe it will do him good."

The chieftain scooped Raff into his arms, making the boy squeal with delight. "Felix! Ruby! Come meet a new friend." With the hounds in tow, Inferno walked toward the window where his children were congregated to watch the festivities. "Hello, my wee ones. Come down and meet Raff, keep him company whilst we adults chat."

Eyes bright, the children laughed and waved. "Hi, Raff! I'm Seth. We'll be right down!"

Raff waved in return, his cheeks red with excitement. "You may put me down, milord. I would not want to keep you from the celebration."

Inferno chuckled. "Aren't ya the polite one. Think ya could teach me kiddies a few manners whilst yer playing?"

Seth, Molly, and Dylan raced out the kitchen door, straight for their Da. Overcome by hellos and introductions, Raff had no time to answer. Tegan waddled up from behind the others and reached for his hand. "*Bore da, Raff. Me Tegan.*"

The rest of the bridal party walked toward the white-draped tables set in the back garden. Spirit gave the queen her seat next to Etain.

Alatariel glanced around the garden. "It is lovely." Her gaze came to the bride. "You shine like a star today, Lady Etain, and Dar, you are most handsome."

"Thank you, Rie." Dar reached for a bottle of wine. "Not even the stars compare to my beautiful wife."

"Well said, High Lord." Alatariel raised her glass. "To the High Lord and High Lady VonNeshta, may your days be happy and full of love."

Those at the table clinked glasses and drank to the toast.

Alatariel leaned toward Etain. "Linq tells me you found your brother. I am surprised you have not introduced him yet."

Etain pursed her lips and set her glass on the table. "Apologies, Rie. I'm embarrassed to say I've lost him again. He was here the other day but has since disappeared."

"Perhaps he does not approve of your choice?"

Etain scoffed. "He hasn't even met Dar. When I *do* find him, he better have a damn good reason for not being here."

The queen laughed. "Perhaps urgent business called him away." One of her Royal Guard approached and whispered into her ear. "Thank you, captain. Gather Raphael. I will be with you in a moment." She turned to Etain and Dar. "We must be on our way."

"So soon?" Etain took hold of her hand. "You haven't been here long enough."

"You will come to visit me, aye? And bring your enterprising brother. I would like to meet him." She stood and kissed Etain on the forehead, then Dar. "Be well."

"And you, Rie." Dar hugged his wife close as the others bid their farewells. Alatariel, Raff, and her Royal Guards walked toward the main gates and faded in a warm glimmer. The bridal party breathed a deep sigh, glanced at one another, and laughed.

On his feet, Linq lifted his goblet. "A toast to the bride and groom." He grinned at the couple, and addressed the guests as he spoke. "May the light of friendship guide your path. May the laughter of children grace the halls of your home. May the joy of living for one another trip a smile from your lips and a twinkle from your eye." His smiling gaze returned to Dar and Etain. "And when eternity beckons at the end of a life heaped high with love, may the Creator embrace you with arms that have nurtured you the whole length of your joy-filled days." He raised his goblet. "Skál!"

Everyone cheered as they lifted their glasses. "Skál!"

Inferno waited until each guest was replenished with more wine and raised another toast. "May the goddess be with ya and bless ya. May ya see yer children's children. May ya be poor in misfortune and rich in blessin's. May ya know nothin' but happiness from this day forward. Slainte!"

At this point, Elfin and Wolfe decided to offer their blessings. Elfin toasted first. "There are four things you must never do—lie, steal, cheat, or drink. But if you must lie, lie in the arms of the one you love. If you must steal, steal away from bad company. If you must cheat, cheat death, and if you must drink, drink in the moments that take your breath away."

Not to be outdone, Wolfe followed with one of his own. "Friends, I hope you do four things in life—lie, steal, cheat, and drink." He winked at Elfin. "When you lie, do it to save a friend. When you steal, steal someone's heart. When you cheat, cheat death. And when you drink, drink with me!"

Laughter and the clinking of glasses filled the garden.

"Oh-ho," exclaimed Elfin. "May you be welcomed in Heaven at least an hour before the Devil knows you are dead!"

Wolfe narrowed his eyes. "May those who love us, love us, and those who don't, may the Creator turn their hearts. If he can't turn their hearts, may he turn their ankles, so we'll know them by their limping."

Inferno stepped around the table as Elfin opened his mouth again. "Boys, *ta* for the colorful blessings. I'm sure our guests would like to eat before they're too drunk to realize they're hungry."

The two grinned and raised their goblets. "Cheers, boss!"

The afternoon passed in a tapestry of laughter and well-wishes. Platters of roasted meats garnished by a colorful assortment of grilled vegetables sat at the end of two long tables. An array of hot meat pies, Cornish pasties, and sausage rolls encased in flaky shells of puff pastry enticed even the staunchest dieter with their delights. An English favorite, golden fried chips, took center stage, flanked by fresh fruits and cheeses. At the opposite end was an array of freshly baked breads, fruit pies, and puddings that demanded a slathering of rich cream. Chilled kegs of beer stood ready, and bottles of wine adorned each table. For those too young or not of the alcoholic persuasion, an array of fizzy drinks, tea, and coffee awaited.

The High Lord and High Lady VonNeshta made it a point to thank every guest for coming on such short notice. At one point, Linq slipped up beside Dar for a quick chat while a distracted Etain conversed with other guests.

"Congratulations on your speedy marriage, High Lord."

"It was rather unconventional by Krymerian standards, but it will do. Regardless of Etain's initial resistance, I doubt Inferno would have appreciated a two-year wait."

"No, I do not imagine he would."

Dar walked a few steps away from the group. "We have known each other a long time." The Elf nodded but held his tongue. "In all my days since Alexia, I never once considered being with another woman. After what happened to her and my children..." The travesty of Midir brought back the terrible anguish of losing his wife and family. "I could not, did not want, to share my life with another. When she passed, I thought I would not love again. But Etain..." He searched for the right words. "Etain, well..."

Linq grinned. "I never thought I would see the day when the High Lord of Kaos was made speechless. That alone is worth a mention in the history books."

Dar laughed, relieved no further explanation was required, although there was not one when it came to his relationship with Etain. He draped an arm over the Elf's shoulders and lowered his voice further. "If I hear one hint of this conversation in a book or even as hearsay, it will be followed by lamentations of what was once a glorious, yet short life of an Elf."

Linq met his comment with laughter. "Far be it from me to expose our High Lady's power over the High Lord. I am glad to see you happy."

As afternoon faded into evening, Zorn brought in a local band for the night's entertainment. With the flip of a switch, Inferno transformed the garden into a faerie wonderland.

Etain finally convinced Dar it was the duty of the newly married couple to have the first dance. When the band played a slow Celtic ballad, Dar was uneasy at first, but soon lost himself in his new bride's smile and relaxed into the simple steps. It wasn't long before others joined them on the dance floor. Warmed by the drink and the easy company around him, Dar even tried a jig or two.

"Faux," a deep voice whispered into her ear.

Fast asleep, she rolled onto her back.

"Faauux."

"What?"

"Do you remember me?" The voice was soft, hypnotic.

A wicked grin lifted the corners of her mouth. "How could I forget you?" Her blood thrilled at the thought of the blood-skinned demon. "Your hair is like fire. So sexy."

His sensuous laugh gave her a delicious shiver. "You are pure sex, *mon petit*, and your tail is quite talented. Did you enjoy yourself at the club?"

A growl came from deep in her throat as she arched her back and rolled onto her side. "Mmm. It was just what I needed."

"Do you remember what *I* need?"

Her brows knitted together in thought. "You want the source of the protection spell, but I don't understand why. They aren't worth your time."

"None of your concern, little demon." His exhaled breath lifted tendrils of her hair. "Freeblood cannot be deterred from going to Laugharne."

Her lips turned in a frown. "But we're having fun here. I don't want to go."

"It's what *I* want. We will make them pay for what they've done to you."

"But not Freeblood, right? He's cool."

"Freeblood must not know of our plans." His tone was sharp. "Dar can read his thoughts."

"He can read mine too. After all, we have a link stronger than the blood."

The fire-haired apparition laughed. "Don't worry. Placing a veil between you and the Krymerian will be child's play. Much easier than what I conjured with his precious bitch. He'll never know a thing." He trailed a possessive hand over her body. "Now, tell me one more time, sweet Faux."

Her eyes opened, staring into his red gaze. "Get to the castle, locate the source of the spell, and destroy it." She stroked his blood-red cheek. "Now, tell me what *I* get in return."

"Power. And your Freeblood."

AFTEREFFECTS

S wee found herself swept onto the dance floor by a stranger dressed in black. "I hope you don't mind, milady. I believe you enjoy dancing as much as I."

Her head swam as they turned about the floor. "What gives you that impression?"

"By the tapping of your feet. I was certain you were about to break into a solo act."

She almost smiled but thought better of it. "Whether I was or not, I prefer to be asked."

The dark-haired man laughed. "And I prefer not to be turned down." Coming close to the happy couple, he turned and whisked Swee toward the other side of the floor. "Summons or invitation?"

She blinked. "Excuse me?"

He guided her around the edge of the dance floor, his demeanor as light as his feet. "Were you summoned or invited to this prestigious affair?"

Despite the heat permeating from the man, she shivered. His face was handsome enough, but the emptiness of his black gaze left her with a hollow feeling. "Are you a friend of the bride or the groom?"

"Merely a disinterested traveler passing by."

She felt like she was floating on air, but his smirk brought to mind things she would rather not consider. "Not many come out this way just in passing." Others on the floor drifted by shrouded in their individual auras - blues, whites, greens, pinks. A power gifted to her upon her transition into the Alamir. "I think it would be the last place for a disinterested person." Swee shivered again, noticing how his aura shifted between black and black ringed in red.

"You have me, milady." He twirled her around. "I am the lowest of the low, a charlatan, a wedding crasher." His tone mocked her concerns. "Do you think it's true?"

The more he said, the less she liked the man. She forced her gaze back to the magnetic black holes. "Think what is true?"

"Their happy faces."

Swee stopped the dance, but her brain continued to spin. Afraid she might fall, she held onto him.

"Are you not enjoying yourself?" He acted concerned for her welfare, but his smirk told her something different.

A flush of heat dried her mouth. Her tongue darted out, licking her lips. "You don't belong here. Who are you? What do you want?" Swee scanned the crowd in search of Inferno or Linq, anyone who might know what to do.

From across the dance floor, Zorn stroked his violin in time with the band watching the interaction between the healer and the stranger. He didn't like the man. Maybe it was the slicked-back hair or the way he moved. Zorn checked the others in the garden. Inferno and Linq were preoccupied in conversation. Wolfe and Elfin were engaged with ladies on the dance floor. No one seemed to notice the unusual man except Swee, and now him.

Step by step, Zorn slowly distanced himself from the band. The strokes on his violin did not give away his preoccupation with the dancing couple. Once at the rear, he tucked the instrument behind a large speaker. He was certain she was in trouble.

The mass of dancers made it impossible to cut across the floor, so he skirted around to the other side. Hidden in the shadows, he listened to the hissed conversation between Swee and the man.

"Do not make a scene, milady. It will only get someone killed."

She struggled against his grip. "I believe it's your intention. It can't be me. I'm no one."

His guttural laugh made the hairs on the back of Zorn's neck rise. "Don't underestimate your value, *mon petit*."

"Swee." Zorn stepped out from behind a tree as the two neared the back gate. "You promised me a dance. Surely you aren't leaving before I've had the pleasure."

"Zorn."

He recognized the fear in her eyes just before she cringed at the tightened grip on her arm.

"Take my hand." His eyes darted to the man behind her. "Today is such a special day. I'm sure your friend wouldn't mind." He beckoned with a wave of his fingers. "Come on. One quick dance." She bit her bottom lip, caught between danger and salvation. "Take my hand, Swee."

She stretched her hand toward him. Zorn grabbed her by the forearm, but the stranger jerked her back. For a moment in time, Swee served as a conduit for the evil thing holding her captive. His darkness coursed through her, threatening to consume Zorn's soul, but if he let go, she would be lost forever.

"Swee!" Zorn tugged with all his might.

She crashed into him, forcing the air out of his lungs when they hit the ground.

"Zorn."

"Are you okay?"

"Yes."

"Stay here." He jumped to his feet and ran through the gate into darkness.

Swee clung to the wall as she struggled to her feet. She peeked from behind the large tree in search of Dar and spied him laughing in the arms of his beloved Etain. It seemed no one noticed her scuffle with the stranger.

Her body shaking, she attempted to smooth her hair and noticed the bruises forming on her arms. She slumped against the wall. *I won't let this ruin their party. We can discuss it when Zorn gets back.* Without a word, she quietly made her way to her room.

Ruby's ears pricked, a low growl in her chest as she lifted her head. Felix came up on all fours, tail as stiff as the hairs on his back.

Inferno noticed their strange behavior. "What's got yer dander up?"

Linq scanned the grounds. "Maybe there is a stray outside the wall hoping for a handout."

Ruby's lips peeled back. White fangs glistened in the faerie lights. In the blink of an eye, the red-haired menace was on the table, poised for attack, her gaze on the back gate. Felix jumped over the table and pushed off with his powerful hind legs when he hit the ground. Ruby in close pursuit, knocked the table into the seated guests. People scattered as the two cut straight across the dance floor and dashed through the gate.

Inferno fell back and sprawled on the ground. "What the bleedin' hell?"

Linq scrambled from his chair right before the table crashed over. Heads turned and people gasped as goblets, dishes, and silverware flew everywhere. He laughed, offering a hand to Inferno. "Woe betide the game they chase."

"To hell with the game. Woe betide the wee devils when they come home," Inferno grunted, dusting off the dirt.

"Shall we go in pursuit?"

"If they aren't home by morning, we'll go looking for 'em."

Etain called out, "Are y'all okay over there?"

"Aye. Nothing bruised but me bleedin' pride."

Later in the evening as the guests departed, Inferno clasped Dar's hand in his, giving him a wink. "There's a small cottage about two miles up the back road. Has all the modern stuff. With four kids, ya can't always afford to get away, and ya can't go too far when ya do." He pulled Spirit close. "We renovated the place as an escape when things get out of sorts."

Dar opened his hand and showed Etain.

"The linens are fresh, and kitchen stocked," Spirit said. "It's not much of a honeymoon suite, but it'll give you time alone."

Etain hugged them both. "It will be perfect. Thank you."

"Thank you, Spirit, Inferno." Dar took Etain's hand in his.

"Yer family now, Dar, but if I hear even a squeak about our girl being mistreated, I'll be all over yer arse."

Dar bowed his head. "She is in safe hands."

"Be off with you now." Spirit shooed them toward the front courtyard. "We have cleaning to do and don't need the likes of you in our way." After one more hug, the bride and groom strolled out of the garden.

"Alone at last." Dar wrapped her in his arms as she draped hers around his neck. "Do you mind if we travel by horseback? I think the feel of your bonnie arse—"

"I have a better idea. How about we forget the horse and we shimmer? I have an itch needs scratching, and you have the only scratching post that can soothe it."

"*Tartarus*, woman, why are we still *here*?"

In a blue electrical flash, they stood wrapped in their lovers' embrace before the thatched roof cottage. The two shared a quiet moment of appreciation of its quaint beauty. Sconces on each side of the door softly illuminated the entrance while warm light from inside gave them glimpses of a cozy interior. Dar smiled at his bride as he unlocked the front door, turned and picked her up.

She linked her arms around his neck. "Sentimental old fool."

"I am no fool." A glance at the door had numbers and dimensions ticking through his head.

She laughed. "Do we have a problem?"

Clearly, the door would not accommodate people of their stature. "A slight change of plans." He called upon his version of a shimmer to bypass the small opening.

In the living room, he set her on her feet. "Stay right here. I have something for you." Dar dashed out and around the side of the house to the small garden he had seen from the front. The sweet scent of flowers, roses in particular, lifted his spirits even higher as he searched for the perfect bloom under the full moon. At last, a magnificent rose stood out from the rest.

The stem in hand, something moved out of the corner of his eye. He reached for the dagger in his boot, doing his best to appear nonchalant and unaware. Moonlight flashed off the blade as it twirled between his fingers and made a clean cut of the stem. He brought the flower to his nose in a show of enjoying its perfume while his senses scanned the area. Whatever he thought he'd seen before was gone.

He laughed and attributed his moment of paranoia to a crazy day. With a wave of his hand over its dark red petals, and a few whispered words, the rose faded into ice blue, its center deepening to violet. *To match her beautiful eyes.* Happy with the results, he returned to the cottage.

"A gift for my bride."

Her eyes wide, she gasped. "It's exquisite."

"*You* are exquisite." He kissed her mouth unable to resist another taste of her sweetness. "I will grow you an entire garden of roses at *Sólskin.*"

"As lovely as those you grew in Krymeria?"

A tiny shock ran through him. "You remember?"

"Of course." She gave him a soft smile. "It wasn't *that* long ago. They were the most beautiful roses I'd ever seen."

My queen of surprises.

Covetous hands slid up her arms. She looked over her shoulder as he turned her, an expression of uncertainty on her face. "Do not worry." He took his time in unlacing the silk ribbons down the back of her gown. She once described his hands as elegant. Seeing them immersed in their current task, he had to agree.

He gently pushed the dress from her shoulders careful of the delicate fabric and kissed her fragrant skin. "I love your smell. So soft, so seductive." His lips brushed the back of her neck and along the curve of her shoulder. Her soft moan and the goosebumps on her skin attested to her enjoyment.

The gown slipped to her waist. A moan from deep inside him vibrated against her silver mane as his hands ventured into another exploration of her provocative curves.

"My intrigue," at her hips, he jerked her hard against him, "I cannot solve." The dress puddled to the floor as she drew his head down, taking his mouth. Dar circled his open hands over her taut nipples, enjoying the sensuous tickle of the hard nubs against his palms.

Another soft moan from his love emboldened him further. He rolled a pink tip darkened by desire between thumb and forefinger while his other hand explored the heat between her thighs. "You are pure intoxication." Fingers damp with her juices trailed up to her lips.

Etain turned to him, her eyes heavy with desire, and took his hand in hers, kissed his palm, and lowered it to his side as she pressed her lips to his, trailing her fingers down the front of his shirt. From the bottom up, she slowly released each button. Dar tried to assist.

"No." She batted his hands away. After the last button slipped open, she pushed the fabric over his broad shoulders. A shrug finished the job, shirt and vest falling to the floor. Appreciation for his lean, muscular frame, sculpted to perfection by years of wielding a heavy blade shone in her eyes.

His belt came next, left to dangle from its loops as each strained button of his leather trousers slid through its mated opening. He ached to get on with it but realized he still wore his boots. "A moment, milady." He sat on the floor and undid the laces on the back of each boot. Etain laughed as she helped pull each one off.

She grabbed his hands before he could remove his trousers and shook her head. "Do not take away my pleasure." He shrugged and stood. She guided the leathers to the floor, helped him to step out, and cast them to the side.

Naked before one another for the first time as husband and wife, they basked in the magnificence of their spouse, yet did not touch. Anticipation vibrated between the couple as though it were their first time to make love.

"My husband." Etain traced the outline of his strong shoulders and trailed over the mark on his smooth chest. Her tongue soon followed, teasing him with light flicks over his erect nipples, making him shiver each time she pushed the small bud back and forth between her teeth. Greedy hands traveled south, her touch light, electric. This time, the gasp came from *his* lips.

She whispered into his ear, her breath hot and teasing. "You are a beautiful man in every way, my love."

When she kneeled before him again, his knees nearly gave way from the tremors bubbling up into his belly. Her mouth was hot, hungry, her swirling tongue driving him to near madness. Helpless, his hands dove into the silvered mass of her hair.

"My lady."

As delicious as the sensations were, he pulled back before he lost all control and guided his fiery vixen up to him to claim her lips in a savage takeover. Strong hands strayed to her backside and lifted her, coaxing her long legs around his waist, their mouths consuming one another. He carried her to the bedroom and lay her on the bed. After a loving gaze, he began an assault with tender kisses along the inside of her thighs. At the silver-haired nexus, his tongue delved into a long, luxurious exploration between her lips.

She breathed out his name. "Dar..."

The silent warrior blazed a trail across her flat belly to the rise and fall of rose-tipped breasts. Light, airy kisses tickled along her shoulder to her delicate neck, and to an ear, where his soft breaths made her shiver. "My wife." He traveled along her jaw to a final takeover of her mouth as she took him into her private domain.

Content in each other's arms, Dar placed a kiss on Etain's forehead. "I am sorry about the rings, my love. In Krymeria, we did not exchange rings as a sign of our union."

"It's okay. We weren't given much time, were we? I didn't think about rings until Anu mentioned them." She intertwined her fingers with his. "If you didn't exchange rings, how was the marriage confirmed?"

"We were bound by blood. The ceremony usually lasted three days."

She sat up. "How long does it take in Krymeria to bind two hands?"

Dar chuckled. "It was a nod to the actual ceremony. Alas, there are no longer any who can perform it."

She rolled her eyes and snuggled close to him again. "Alas, if that were the case, I'd be satisfied as friends with benefits. If the blood we've shared between us isn't enough by now, then to hell with whoever's left to care. Like you said, this is *our* marriage."

"You are right. Our marriage, our rules."

"So what's next for this dynamic duo?"

"Dare I say sleep?"

At the mention of the word, Etain yawned. "I think we've earned it."

Linq and Inferno sat back, each with a fresh mug of ale, watching as the faeries tidied the garden. "Not that I'm an expert on how weddin's ought to be, but I think me wife did a fine job."

Linq clinked mugs with him. "She outdid herself. I did not see a glitch anywhere."

"Ah, me Spirit knows how to throw a do."

"The newlyweds looked to be happy too."

"Aye, I believe they are."

"I believe there is one even happier." Linq lifted his mug.

Inferno's laughter filled the back garden. "I did me best to hide it."

The Elf laughed. "Your grin gave nothing away."

A weary Spirit and several faeries came out from the kitchen. While the small ladies fluttered toward the large tree to join their kinfolk, Spirit plopped down in a chair across from the men. "What're you giggling gerties on about?"

"Enjoying the evening quiet is all, me gorgeous love."

"It was a grand day, Spirit."

"Aw, *ta*, love." She sighed. "It was fun, but I'm glad it's behind us."

"I have been wanting to ask all day, Inferno. How is it you have a rare Krymerian sword?"

"This little thing?" Inferno laughed as he picked up the claymore-size sword at his side and unsheathed the blade to show to his friend. "A gift from the groom."

"An appreciation of your efforts?"

"More like a bribe." He winked. "Dar said it's been upstairs since his bloody Council came to visit but with everthin' what's happened, he hasn't had the chance to give it to me."

"It was an impressive addition to your wedding attire. What plans for the blade now?"

"This beauty will be hanging on me study wall. She's too heavy for the likes of me to wield on a daily basis." Inferno eyed the other two. "Speaking of a beauty, has anyone seen the backside of the prissy brother?"

Linq shook his head and sipped his ale.

"No one's mentioned it." One of the faeries brought Spirit a cup of tea. "*Ta*, love. Just what I need." She blew at the steam rising from her cup. "Not even Etain's seen him."

"Could the bloody wanker have run back up north? He didn't seem too happy with Dar's appearance the other day."

Linq rested his mug on the arm of his chair. "It would be risky on his part. The *Bok* are probably on high alert after what happened."

Inferno merely nodded.

Spirit's gaze moved from one man to the other. "Well, what happened to cause a high alert?"

Linq lifted his mug for another drink, his eyes wide as he glanced at Inferno. The Alamir shifted in his seat. "Er, well, 'tis a long story me love and—"

"Inferno Gallimore, you best start talking unless you want to sleep in the barn tonight."

He briefly closed his eyes with a sigh. "It isn't me story to tell."

"Then whose is it?" Her gaze slid to the Elf. "You better not say Etain. What happened whilst you were in Deudraeth?"

Linq licked his lips. "The day we left, Etain insisted her brother go with us, so we returned to the apothecary. Someone told the *Bok* of our presence. She put her brother on Razz and said she would meet us on the road."

"Did she?"

"Aye." Linq lowered his mug. "She did and there was a fight."

"How bad was it?"

"She obliterated the entire troop with her *solar*."

"Oh, dear goddess." Spirit covered her mouth with her hand. "Does Dar know?"

"He has been busy since his return. We have not had the chance to talk."

Her gaze slid to her husband. "And I don't suppose you've mentioned anything to the man?"

"Spirit, love, he no sooner showed up with Etain and they're talking about getting married. When the hell am I gonna slip in something like that?" He raised a brow. "I wasn't about to ruin the stag-do or the weddin'."

"I suggest one or both of you tell him the next time you see him. If the *Bok* are on high alert in the north, it's only a matter of time before it spreads to the south." She sipped her tea. "Whoever told the *Bok* of her presence would know from where she came. Dar needs to know before they show up here."

"Bloody hell, love. If ya aren't right. We'll give 'em at least a day or two of married bliss before we blow everthin' apart."

Dar awoke just as the skies lightened. "Wake up, my love. I want to share our first sunrise as husband and wife."

A sleepy eye opened. "*Why* are you awake?"

"How can I sleep when I am married to the most incredible woman I have ever met?" Dar flashed his boyish grin. "Come now." He tugged on her arm. "Let's watch the sunrise."

She threw her other arm over her eyes. "You don't get out much, do you?"

He leaned against the headboard, crossed his ankles, and stated in a matter-of-fact tone, "As I see it, you have two choices."

"Hmph."

"You can get up, get dressed, and accompany your loving husband into the garden to view the spectacular sunrise of our first day as husband and wife..." He paused with a devilish purpose.

Etain sighed, her arm still over her eyes. "Or?"

A thrill ran through him to hear the perfect word come from her perfect lips. "Or..." He twisted off the bed, ripped the comforter from her delicious body, and dragged her to the edge. "You can be carried," he licked his lips, reveling in her shrieks, "naked and delectable by your loving husband."

She kicked at him and twisted away to free her ankles from his grip. "All right! I'm up." Begrudgingly, she crawled out of the bed and stretched. As much as he enjoyed her naked, he offered her his shirt. With a grateful smile, she slipped into it and hugged herself. "Mmm. Your smell makes me feel warm and sexy."

Dar smiled at the erotic sight she posed with the tails of the shirt at mid-thigh.

She frowned. "Although your behavior is somewhat less desirable."

Dressed only in his leather trousers, Dar laughed and linked his arm with hers. "I am afraid it is too late, milady. You are stuck with me now - behavior, smells, and all that goes with it."

"At least you're easy to look at," she conceded, laughing with him.

Secure in his arms, she rested her head against his shoulder as they watched the first rays of the new day peek over the horizon. "Even the beauty of the dawn pales in comparison to you, my precious one." His hands came to rest on her belly. "When the time is right, we can start our family."

Her hands covered his. "Aye, when the time is right, my sweet husband." She turned in his arms. "I love you."

It was all he needed.

Once the brilliant shades of morning began to fade, they strolled back into the cottage, hand in hand. "Let's take a shower," Etain said, pulling him toward the bathroom.

"Dare I accompany you, milady? My last attempt did not fare well for me."

"Well, your last attempt was to take advantage of a naïve, young virgin. Serves you right."

"Hmph. Certain aspects of that statement are debatable. But for my own good, I shall not protest at this time."

"A very wise man, I'd say."

"Not so wise if you are able to keep talking." He gave her a playful push and followed her into the shower.

As he soaped her back, he admired how it tapered down to a firm, round bottom, his hands slipping along her curves. After a thorough rinse of his hands, he pressed her body against the glass with his, and slipped a hand between her thighs.

Their bodies moved in symmetry. He gritted his teeth in the hopes he could control himself and not climax too soon as he eased his cock into her heat, her sighs making the effort more monumental. Her body bucked against his as he stroked her, matched only by the powerful thrust of his hips. In time, ragged screams of pleasure filled the small cottage.

Unfortunately, the glass proved less robust than the lovers pressed against its transparent skin. Vibrations rocked the supports from the wall. Consumed by their lovemaking, the couple didn't notice until the glass gave way. Dar clasped Etain tight to him with one arm and cast a protective shield of invisible air around them with the other, then twisted his body so she would land on top of him.

Suspended centimeters above the floor, Etain grinned. "I didn't do it."

Dar released the cushion of air. The dangerous shards scattered, leaving a clear area beneath them.

"I didn't do it alone." He laughed. "Shall we finish our shower and get dressed, my delicious wife?"

"Only if you keep your hands to yourself, my handsome savage." On her feet, she offered him a hand.

"Damn. Married one night and already whipped into submission."

"You love it." A mischievous light in her eyes, she reached for a towel and made a sad attempt at popping his naked butt cheek.

Dar caught the end of the towel and pulled her into the shower, careful of any stray glass shards. With a spin, he turned her back toward the running water, giving her a thorough kiss as he sneaked out a hand and turned off the hot water, leaving on the cold. He ran out of the shower to her indignant shrieks.

"Dar VonNeshta!" she yelled. "You're racking up a long list of paybacks!"

"Which I shall await with great anticipation," he laughed and grabbed another towel. In a flash, he disappeared into the bedroom.

He heard the water turned off, and by the subsequent sounds, imagined her wrapping herself in a towel. Not long after, she shimmered into the bedroom, a violet glare in her eyes.

"Your fine ass is mine, mister."

"Anytime you please, milady," he challenged, slapping a still naked butt cheek.

Laughing together, they turned to the oversized wardrobe and discovered an array of clothing Spirit had seen fit to provide. "Makes you wonder how well the woman knows us."

Etain picked out a set of black leather top and trousers. "How hard can it be? Black leather on black leather, accentuated by black leather. Besides, most of my clothes are actually mine."

Once dressed and the broken glass swept up, the newlyweds shared a light breakfast and spent most of the morning in the gardens. Dar pointed to each of the plants, sharing their common and Latin names. They exchanged ideas on the manor - changes Etain would like to see, the hiring of staff, and the prospect of children. Dar was quick to assign the duty of finding staff to her. Such things were not his forte. Delegation was where his strengths lay.

She rolled her eyes. "Like I have any experience."

"You have a good judge of character, milady. You will do a fine job."

"You really think you're getting off that easy? I expect to be plied with more than just pretty words, milord."

He raised his brows with a glint in his eyes. "Bribery, is it? What form of payment do you have in mind?"

"Not what you're thinking." She laughed, taking a step back. "*That* is not considered payment between husband and wife."

"How would you know what I am thinking?" He moved forward and trailed a finger down her arm.

She shrugged away beyond his reach. "The hungry leer in your eyes, for starters."

"Do not change the subject." He moved closer.

"I'm not changing the subject. You are." Another step back.

"I think it is best." He followed.

"What is best?" She slid back another foot.

"Changing the subject." Dar stepped forward.

Determination shone in her beautiful blue eyes. "No, we are negotiating."

"Negotiating, is it? I thought we were discussing bribery."

At this point, she came to the end of the garden path, her backside pressed against the stone of the cottage.

A grin spread across his face. "Oops. It appears our negotiations have come to an end. Checkmate."

"Only the path has come to an end, *not* our negotiations."

"Did I not tell you this," Dar indicated the cobbled path on which they were standing, "is the path of negotiations? When two people have walked the path of negotiations to its end, which you and I have, negotiations also come to an end."

"That was not a negotiation."

"Oh, I beg to differ. I think I have negotiated with great skill." He bridged the gap between them in a single step. "I will take my bribe now."

She pressed her hands against his chest. "We were discussing *my* bribe."

Dar shrugged, his body close to hers. "A win-win situation." He dipped his head, trailing the tip of his tongue up to her ear. "My fiery vixen."

She sighed and closed her eyes. "Winning is good."

Along Came a Bloody Man

The next morning, a bloody Zorn led by an equally harrowed Felix stumbled into the Laugharne courtyard. He collapsed onto the gravel path and closed his eyes, thankful to be home and in one piece. Felix sat at his side, panting as the man took slow, deep breaths. Gravel crunching beneath small feet was as welcome a sound as the tiny voices fading when they ran away, yelling for their father. Soon, he heard heavier footsteps and deeper voices.

"Zorn, laddie." Inferno crouched next to him. "Where ya been, boy? What's happened? Dylan, go tell yer mum to bring water. Be quick about it."

"Aye, Da."

Zorn heard the crunch of gravel as the little boy ran off.

Tegan, having come with her brother, wrapped her chubby little arms around Felix's neck. "Good, Fewix. Good boy."

Inferno turned an eye on his hound. "Ya look like the back side of a cow, Felix."

Zorn's dry lips attempted a smile. The sight of Inferno and BadMan, a fellow clansman, made him want to jump up and give each one a kiss. He tried to speak, but only managed a cough.

"Be still, boy," BadMan ordered. "Water's comin'."

At the sight of Spirit, water bottle in hand, BadMan tried to ease Zorn up into a sitting position but stopped at his pain-filled cries. Bloodied mud covered his back. "Fucking hell, Zorn."

A bowl of water for Felix in his arms, Dylan peeked from behind his mother, unsure whether to carry on or cry. The dog's lolling tongue made his decision for him, and he toddled a wide, cautious berth around the injured man.

Zorn tried to hold the bottle, but it proved too heavy. Inferno unscrewed the top and put it to his lips. "Take it slow."

Several sips later, he croaked, "*Ta.*"

"Let's get him to the house." Inferno and BadMan got him to his feet but had to carry him. The gravel beneath where he'd been lying was wet with blood. The men shared a glance. "Kitchen."

"I'll stay here with Felix, Da." Dylan squatted next to the exhausted hound.

"*Ta*, son. Come get me if anything changes."

"Sure, Da."

"Sure, Da," Tegan echoed.

They lay Zorn face down on the cool granite of the kitchen island. His eyes closed as he breathed in familiar scents of home - the wood fire, the lingering aroma of bacon and fresh coffee, the sharp tang of blood and sweat.

"Ugh, I stink."

"Bleedin' hell, boy. Who's done this to ya?"

Bleary eyes squinted. "Ruby," he whispered before he passed out.

"Someone get Swee," Inferno hollered and turned to his wife. "Love, do ya know where the girl is?"

"I'm here," Swee said from the doorway, headed toward the sink and pushing up her sleeves. "What's happened to him?" she asked over her shoulder, washing her hands.

"He stumbled in a few minutes ago. He didn't say much," BadMan said.

"I need a good look at the wound."

Inferno grabbed the tattered ends of the shirt and made short work of removing the filthy rag. Zorn's body jerked in reaction, but the young man did not wake. Swee bit her bottom lip at the bloody gash from his right shoulder to left hip. "Sweet goddess of us all," she muttered. "I'm going to need everyone's help."

Spirit filled a large pot with water and set it on the stove to heat. "There's herbs in my room that will help. I'll grab sheets and towels on the way."

"I'll need a needle and something for sutures too," Swee yelled after her.

"Can ya handle this without me, lass?" Inferno asked.

"As long as BadMan stays." She set to washing away the dirt and blood from the outer areas of Zorn's back. "Go check on your hound, Inferno. Your man is in good hands."

His eyes on the wolfhound, Inferno knelt between his children. "Now then, boy. Let's have a look at ya." Felix whimpered as his master began a careful inspection, checking eyes, teeth, and ears.

"Fewix is sad, Da," Tegan said, her tiny brows knitted together.

"Aye. He's had a rough few days, *mi cariad*. Come on, boy. On yer feet." Inferno urged the dog up. Felix licked his master's face as his experienced hands ran along his backbone, over his hindquarters, and down each leg. "No broken bones."

"He's bleeding, Da." Dylan pointed at Felix's head and chest.

"The blood on his head isn't his," he said, prodding through the matted fur. He found the flesh intact, but the same exploration of chest and belly produced a high-pitched yelp. "Easy, boy," Inferno cooed. "*Fachgen da. Byddwn yn mynd â chi sefydlog i fyny* (Good boy. We'll get you fixed up)."

Tegan's bottom lip quivered, her eyes bright with tears. "Poor Fewix." She reached out to touch him, but her father caught her hand.

"Leave him be for now, *merch fach yn.*" Instead, she patted her da on the shoulder and slipped a thumb into her mouth.

Inferno located several gashes, the blood now clotted or dried. "Easy, boy. Good boy." He patted Felix on the head. "Where's the red wagon, Dyls?"

"I think it's at the stables. Can I pet him, Da?"

"Aye. Gently, on his neck. It'll help settle him." Dylan placed a soft hand on the dog's head. Tegan, thumb firmly set in her mouth, reached out with the other hand, and tenderly stroked Felix's neck.

"Go get the wagon, Dylan."

"Aye, Da." The little boy scrambled to his feet and disappeared toward the stables.

Tegan's thumb came out of her mouth with an audible pop. "Is Fewix gonna wide in da wagon?"

Inferno chuckled and hugged her to him. "Aren't ya the smart girlie? Aye. He needs doctoring, and he's too big to carry."

She nodded, stroking the black fur. "Fewix a big boy."

Dylan returned, a large red wagon rattling behind him. Inferno got to his feet and lifted the dog that weighed at least one hundred and fifty pounds into the wagon.

"Da?"

Inferno wiped his sleeve across his forehead. "Aye?"

"Where's Ruby?"

Tegan whimpered at the reminder of the russet dog. "Wuby."

He considered his two youngest. Their sweet faces, so innocent and trusting, twisted his heart with an almost unbearable pain. He feared the worst, but until Zorn woke and told them what happened, all he could do was hope she would show up soon. Inferno peered toward the estuary.

"She'll come home when she's ready." He crouched and hugged his children to him. "What's say we get Felix fixed up whilst we wait?"

"Okay." Dylan pushed away, trying to be the big boy.

Tegan smiled. "Make him hansome for Wuby, Da."

"Aye, *cariad.* We'll make him handsome for our Ruby."

Hours later, Swee stopped by Zorn's room for another check. She smiled at finding Inferno next to the bed, a bandaged Felix at his feet. The hound raised his head at her entry, snorted, and returned to his dozing. "Good to see you, too, Felix."

"Never mind the wee devil. He's not been himself since he's come back."

She bustled to the bed. "None of us have. Is he healing okay?" She checked Zorn's vital signs. Pulse was steady. Pupils looked good. Lungs sounded clear.

"Aye." Inferno patted Felix on the head. "He's a good boy, doing what he should, getting' well and watchin' over Zornie. Wish he could tell us something about Ruby, though."

At the mention of the female hound's name, Zorn's eyes fluttered open.

"Zorn?" Swee touched his forehead. "Zorn, can you hear me?"

Inferno leaned over the young man. "Zornie, lad, can ya talk to us? Do ya remember anything?"

He looked from the woman to the man. "Ruby." Tears slipped from the corners of his eyes.

Swee held his hand in hers. "It's okay, Zorn. You're safe. You're home."

"Felix is here. He hasn't left yer side. Do ya know—"

"Red."

Inferno shared a look of uncertainty with Swee. "Aye, Ruby is red. Do ya know—"

"No." He shook his head slightly, his sights on another place. "Him."

Inferno and Swee turned their heads to the door expecting to see another visitor.

"Him?" Inferno echoed.

"Do you mean the man from the wedding?" Swee asked, unsure of what prompted her to think of him. Probably because the last she saw, Zorn was chasing the man who attacked her.

"What man?" Inferno asked.

"I'll explain later," she muttered out of the side of her mouth. "He definitely wasn't red."

Terror filled the young man's eyes as he squeezed her hand. "He. Burned." His breathing became erratic, beads of sweat covering his forehead and upper lip.

"Inferno, try to keep him still. It won't do him any good to rip his stitches. I have a mix to help him sleep."

Swee dashed out of the room and returned within moments, a small vial in her hand. "Zorn." Her voice was soft and melodic, "I need you to drink this, okay?"

The cork squeaked as she worked it from the neck of the bottle. Zorn struggled against his captors, his eyes wide and wild.

"You have to rest." With one hand on his forehead, she brought the vial to his lips. "Dammit. Zorn. Stop fighting us."

Felix raised his head and whined, his blue eyes shifting from Inferno to Swee.

"Felix." Inferno clicked his tongue. "Up. There's a good boy. Lie down." On the bed, the hound gave him a wary eye. "Don't ya worry, laddie. Go on. Lie down. Right across like that. Good boy." Inferno shrugged at a doubtful Swee. "Making use of all our resources, lass." He slapped a hand over Zorn's forehead and held him down. "Slip the wee bottle between his lips before he gets a fresh wind."

Swee pinched the young man's nose closed, shoved the vial between his lips, and didn't let go until he swallowed. Zorn was asleep within seconds.

She stepped back with a loud sigh, pushing the hair from her face. "Phew! Thank you, Inferno. Thank you, Felix." She scratched the hound under the chin. "I couldn't have done it without your help."

Inferno moved aside to give Felix room to jump down, and fixed a serious eye on the healer. "Now, tell me about the man at the wedding."

Come the following day, an urgent knock accompanied by a muffled voice awoke the newlyweds. Dar grabbed his dirk on the bedside table and came out of the bed.

A squinty-eyed Etain sat up. "Who could that be?"

"Someone not long for this world." Dar wrapped a towel around his hips on his way to the door. "What the hell is it?"

Elfin staggered back. "Sorry, Dar. I know, uh, well... Sorry to intrude, but..."

"What is so damn important?"

"Inferno sent me."

Dar lowered his voice and joined him outside, closing the door. "Spit it out, Elfin."

"Ms. Spirit says evil is coming this way. Inferno thinks it is the *Bok* and wants everyone at the castle."

Dar placed a hand on the Elf's shoulder. "Take a breath. Tell him we are on our way." He turned to the door, and back to Elfin. "Do you know if any of the other chieftains are still in town?"

"I do not but I will ask Inferno."

"No. I will ask him myself."

With that, Elfin raced up the road back to the castle.

Dar found Etain dressed and lacing her boots. "What if it *is* the *Bok*? The clan isn't big enough to handle what may be coming."

"I will not let anything happen to them, *a chuisle*." Dar quickly dressed as Etain strapped on *Nim'Na'Sharr*.

"So much for the honeymoon."

"Let's see what we are up against first." He took her in his arms. "It could be they have no intentions of coming here and we can finish what we started."

As he turned to go, she caught his arm. "Wait a minute." Etain grabbed one of the cloaks gifted from Alatariel, shook it out, and fanned it over Dar's shoulders. "It's cold out there." Closing the clasp at his neck, she pulled the hood onto his head. "So handsome."

"You feel the cold more than I. You must wear the other." He picked up the remaining cloak and placed it over her shoulders, fastening the clasp. "My beauty."

After another kiss, Dar grabbed the scabbard with both his blades, and they headed toward the door.

Dar and Etain found Inferno, Linq, and several UWS clan members in the courtyard, staring intently at a makeshift table. She gave Dar a quick kiss. "I'm gonna find Spirit."

Inferno waved him over. "Sorry to interrupt—"

"Think nothing of it." Dar viewed the map spread before the men. "How long do we have?"

"Not a clue. A few of me men are scouting the area. Wolfe's gone into town to see if any chieftains are still kicking around."

"I could take to the skies. It would be much faster than anyone on horseback," Dar offered.

"I need ya here. We'll know what we face soon enough. I got the clan checking fer faults in the walls and making repairs."

"It makes no sense," Dar said. "Why would the *Bok* show themselves?"

The missing stones came to mind. UWS was a strong clan but too small to be given the responsibility of keeping one of the pieces. Dar dismissed the idea as another came to him.

"Does this have anything to do with Deudraeth?"

The Elf stared at the map as though he had not heard the question.

Dar knew better. "Linq?"

"It may have to do with Deudraeth." Linq glanced away. Inferno cleared his throat, taking his turn to stare at the map.

"Feel free to explain, Elf."

Linq sighed. "How much do you know about our trip?"

Dar did not like where it was going. "I know the *Bok* showed up and the three of you made a miraculous escape." He crossed his arms over his chest. "Spit it out."

"I can sum it up in one word."

"Then please do so."

Linq glanced at Inferno.

"Now, Elf!"

"*Solar.*"

Dar breathed in and blew out slowly, his eyes on the house.

Linq stepped into his line of sight. "She was not aware of what she did. It was not her fault."

"Whose fault would it be, Linq? Yours?"

"She was protecting us."

"If this were a new power, I might be more forgiving. But it is not. She will be held accountable as expected with any Alamir warrior."

"Not until you cool down. The last thing we need is a spat between the two of you."

"A spat is not what I had in mind."

Inferno joined the Elf in his blockade. "He's right, Dar."

Dar frowned at the men.

"Did she tell ya about the dinner?"

"Aye."

"Did she mention what happened *after* the dinner?"

Dar's expression darkened.

"Hmph. Thought not. Ya been way too calm." Inferno told of the barrage of *Bok* infiltrations into the human realm, plus the attack on COL.

Dar waited for a mention of the missing stones. When nothing was said, he considered it could be one of two reasons. Either Savage lied, which was not outside the realm of conceivability, or Natas contacted only those clans who held them. Dar thought it a sound strategy. No need to alarm the entire Alamir realm. There was one sticking point, though. The LOKI stone had disappeared with no apparent intrusion. Once he dealt with the immediate problem, he must speak with Natas and the other three chieftains.

Several riders came in, interrupting his thoughts. BadMan's feet hit the ground in a puff of dirt. "They wear the armor of the *Bok* and there's a lot of 'em."

"How long do you think we have?" Dar asked.

"Considering the size and the fact they weren't in any hurry, I'd say a day, maybe two."

Inferno whistled. "How do we fight a company of *Bok*?"

"We do not. At least not alone." Dar's mind already at work, he glanced at Linq. "Black Blades."

The Elf nodded. "Will you be going then?"

Dar held up a hand before Inferno could object. "No. Etain will go. It will be best if she is not here."

"Do ya hear what yer saying?" Inferno blustered. "We need all the fighters we can muster."

"She could do more harm than good should she light up again. We will all be safer with her tucked away in Nunnehi."

Linq asked the obvious question. "How do you propose to get her to stay *there* when she knows what is going on *here*?"

"Swee, Spirit, and the children will go with her. She will stay if she thinks it is to protect them. Then we can concentrate on the battle knowing our women are safe."

Linq snorted. "Choose your words carefully when you speak to her."

Dar smirked and headed toward the back door. "I know how to handle Etain."

He walked through an empty kitchen and down the hallway to the front rooms. With no one about, he bounded the stairs two at a time. She met him on his way up the stairs to Spirit's herb room.

"What do you need me to do?"

"Go to Nunnehi and request the services of the Black Blades and the War Wizards. Rie will gladly lend them to us for a few days."

"Good idea."

"And you will take Spirit, the children, and Swee with you, for their protection. I will give you the words for the portal."

She frowned. "I understand Spirit and the kids but why Swee? She's been through plenty of battles and knows the score. If it gets ugly, you'll need her skills as a healer."

"The War Wizards are far more experienced at both."

"Okay." She shrugged. "And when I get back—"

"No. You must stay there." The pretty pout on her face melted his anger. "It is important for me to know you are safe."

"I'm not helpless." He heard the steel in her voice. "I know how to fight."

"You *are* a fighter, one of the best I have seen, but you have not been completely honest with me, Etain. In this situation, I think it best you be somewhere else."

"I didn't tell you everything for this very reason. I can hold my own against the *Bok*."

What the hell. Let's go there.

"Your blaze of light will not deter them, no matter how many you turn to dust." He gained a sense of satisfaction from her attempt to hide her surprise. "Aye. I know. It is the reason why I am sending you to Nunnehi. The *Bok* have seen enough already."

"I had to protect my brother and Linq." Her voice grew louder with every word. "If I hadn't, I'm pretty damn sure they would both be dead."

Dar's voice rose to meet hers. "If *you* had waited for *me* to go with you to Deudraeth, all of this could have been avoided."

"Are you serious?" She stared at him, fisted hands on her hips. "After you called me a *whore*, the last person I wanted to wait for was *you*. I was damn happy to have a place to go without any bloody Krymerians."

Dar clenched his jaw and grunted.

"It came down to *me* to save what little family I had and I did it without you *whooshing* in to save the day." She poked herself in the chest as she spoke. "*I* did it. *Me*. I can take care of myself."

Spirit poked her head out the door at the top of the stairs. "Crikey, lass, what in the world's gotten into you?"

Etain huffed and pushed past Dar. "I'll let the master of the universe give you his orders."

Etain stormed outside and walked straight up to Inferno and Linq still at the makeshift table. "I guess you both know I've been relegated to sitting on my ass."

The two tried not to smile but failed miserably.

"Yeah," she huffed. "I thought as much. Bloody man."

"Don't be too mad with him, lass."

"He will not take chances with your life, Etain."

"But he takes them with his. How am I supposed to just sit in Nunnehi?"

"Do not worry." Linq grinned. "Alatariel will find plenty for you to do."

"If protectin' me wife and kiddies doesn't suit ya, what if I told ya Zornie and Felix stumbled in yesterday?"

She felt properly chastised but equally curious. "I didn't know they'd left."

"Swee tells a crazy story about a stranger who was at the wedding. She says Zorn chased after him and the dogs chased Zorn. I didn't see anyone out of place, so I don't know how true it is."

"Well, the dogs *did* raise a ruckus. I'll talk to her. Is Zorn okay?"

"Nay, lass. He has a nasty gash across his back. Felix suffered a few himself."

Her stomach suddenly turned. "What about Ruby?"

"I'm hoping she'll show up soon."

"Oh, Inferno." She touched his arm. "Do you want me to take Zorn with us?"

"He should stay put. I'll get the healer from UKElyte to check on him."

"Don't bother. Dar has a group of War Wizards on order. They can do any healing needed."

His eyes widened as he glanced at Linq. "So we're gettin' some of them, are we?"

"And Black Blades." She pressed her lips together, hesitant to ask. "Should we tell Dar about Zorn?"

Inferno shook his head. "It's clan business. We take care of our own."

"I agree," Linq said. "Let the High Lord concentrate on the *Bok* until we know more about what happened."

Etain eyed them both. "Just make sure I'm not around when you tell him."

While Spirit and Swee rushed off to round up the children and pack their bags, Dar went in search of his wife. He found her outside with Inferno and Linq. Between her steely-eyed glare and their smirks, he realized his luck remained in a downward spiral. Back straight, he soldiered into the fray. "Etain, may we have a word in private?"

She raised a blonde brow. "A warning to play nice with the Elves? I assure you, *they* aren't in any danger."

Linq kept his eyes on the map with a grin on his face. Not so polite, Inferno kept a keen eye on the couple.

Dar sighed. "You will need the chant to open the portal."

Her eyes widened in mock surprise. "You're going to entrust *me* with your sacred chant? You *do* live on the edge, High Lord."

"As you will find out, High Lady, if you keep this up." Dar motioned toward the back garden. "It must be guarded for the sake of our Elven friends."

"By all means. For the sake of our Elven friends. Linq, Inferno, I'll see you before I go." She stalked past Dar.

He ignored the quiet snickers from the men and caught her up underneath the large tree at the back gate. "Put down your walls, Etain, so I can transfer the words directly into your memories."

She crossed her arms and shifted her hips.

Once the sacred words were hers, he attempted a truce. "My sending you to Nunnehi has nothing to do with your abilities." His gaze never left her face. "I can*not* lose you. I will do whatever it takes to keep you safe, even if it means suffering your wrath."

She let her arms fall to her sides. "Before I go, let me give *you* a warning."

"Please, Etain…" This was not how he wanted them to part.

"Listen to me, Lord VonNeshta." She gripped the front of his shirt and brought his face to hers. "If any harm comes to you, no matter how insignificant, no matter how slight, I will be here. No one, not even you, will keep me away. You are the most important person to me."

His shoulders relaxed as his hands trailed down to her hips. "Fair enough. You make sure to behave yourself."

Her lips crushed his in a powerful kiss, and leaned back with a face of pure innocence. "Like a saint, *a chuisle*."

TROPHIES

Commander Crom stood at the main gates of the Elven palace, patiently waiting for the "oohs" and "aahs" to subside. Etain also admired the city thinking it more beautiful than the last time she'd been here.

"A single tree, you say?" Spirit and the kids looked straight up.

Tegan tugged on Etain's trousers. "Pwetty twee, Tain."

She scooped the little girl into her arms. "Very pretty. Do you want to go inside?" Tegan grinned and nodded, her eyes bright. Etain eyed the other children. "Do y'all want to go inside, too?"

"Aye!" said the three in unison.

"Blimey. A city in a tree." Spirit laughed. "These Elves must be a friendly lot."

"Most of the time." Alatariel joined them in the courtyard. "Every family has a tiff now and then. Would you not agree?" Her small entourage of Elven women fanned out at the main doors.

"Your Highness." The mage dipped into a curtsy. "Children, do as I taught you."

Seth and Dylan bowed as grandly as any courtier. Molly curtsied like a lady. Tegan, still in Etain's arms, slipped a thumb into her mouth and stared at the queen.

Alatariel wrapped the mage in a warm embrace. "I am so glad you could come, Spirit. Are these your children?"

"Aye. Seth's the oldest, then Molly and Dylan."

"And this is Tegan." Etain tilted her head and whispered, "Alatariel is the Queen of the Elves."

Tegan pulled her thumb from her mouth with a loud pop. "'ike Ink?"

Alatariel smiled but furrowed her brows at Etain, who chuckled. "Aye, like Linq."

The queen also chuckled. "Welcome to Nunnehi, little ones. I am sorry we did not meet at your Aunt Etain's wedding. I think you will have a wonderful time." She turned to a dark-haired maiden dressed in a blue gown. "Raven, please ask Raphael to join us."

Alatariel turned to Swee, who followed Spirit's lead with a curtsy of her own. "Thank you, Y-Your Highness."

"It is good to see you again, Swee. How have you been?"

A pink blush colored her cheeks. "Quite well, thank you."

The queen turned to her final guest. "Not quite the reunion we had hoped for." She welcomed the High Lady with a hug. "But it is always a pleasure to see you, Etain. Dar has told me what is happening at Laugharne."

"Of course." She smiled on the outside but her eyes rolled on the inside. *Why trust the little woman to deliver your bloody message?* "It's good to see you too, Rie. Thank you for taking us in on short notice."

"I could not turn down an opportunity to spend time with you and get to know these lovely women. It has been too quiet around here as of late, has it not ladies?" Titters and giggles from the small entourage affirmed that it had. "We could use a touch of livening up." Alatariel waved a hand. One young lady with white hair worn in a plait down her back broke from the group. "Erudessa, please show Ms. Spirit and Ms. Swee to my apartments. The High Lady and I will be along shortly."

"Yes, milady." Erudessa curtsied with a shy smile. The pink of her gown set off her deep blue eyes. "If you will follow me, miladies."

"What about me wee ones?" Spirit asked.

Raphael ran up with a huge smile on his face. "*Bore da*, Alamir."

An out of breath Raven followed close behind. "I am sorry, Your Grace." She curtsied to the queen, and shot a narrow-eyed glare at the boy. "The moment I opened the door, he flew down the hallway like a hawk after its prey."

The women looked at one another and laughed.

"You are not to blame for our Raff's willful ways, Raven."

Upon seeing the small boy, Tegan wiggled in Etain's arms. "Down, Tain."

Seth and his siblings absorbed the small Elf into their ranks, the boys sharing arm punches with one another.

"Do you want to see our *Modertræ*?"

"What is a *Modertræ*?" Dylan asked.

"She is where we live!" Raff held out a hand to Tegan, who accepted without hesitation. "You will love her." The two turned and led the way.

Spirit gave Etain and the queen a wide-eyed smile. "Puts me in *my* place."

"Please come with me, miladies." Erudessa led them into the palace followed by the other maidens leaving Alatariel and Etain alone with Commander Crom.

Once the courtyard cleared, the commander bowed. "We will be at Laugharne within minutes of stepping through the portal, High Lady. Our Black Blades are accomplished warriors and will help even the odds."

"Thank you, Commander Crom." Etain bowed her head. "Please be safe and please keep him safe."

"Always, milady." Crom saluted the women and swung into the saddle.

Alatariel leaned toward Etain. "The Blades are at the portal. Commander Crom wanted to reassure you himself."

"How thoughtful." She smiled, touched by the gesture. "Thank you, Rie, for taking us in and for helping Dar." She shrugged. "For everything."

"It is small repayment for what your generous husband has done for us." She linked an arm through hers. "Shall we join your friends and get to know one another better?"

Sequestered in the queen's private apartments, Alatariel asked Spirit how she determined trouble was on the way.

On the edge of her seat, the mage took on a serious air. "Swee and I were working on strengthening the protection spell around the house. It was hanging on by a thread. Scary to think if the little bit hadn't been there, I couldn't have cast at all. Something was eating up me spell."

"Do you know if it is the *Bok'Na'Ra*?" the queen asked.

Etain coughed. "Sorry."

Spirit dismissed her with a turn of her head. "I doubt it could be anything *but* the *Bok*."

Alatariel leaned forward. "But why a sudden attack on a homestead?"

Etain coughed again. The queen snapped orders for a drink as Spirit went to pat her on the back. When an assistant appeared with a glass of cool water, Alatariel shoved it into Etain's hand.

"Are you okay, lass?"

Etain took a drink, her eyes watering. "Thank you. It *is* the *Bok*."

"How could you know?" Spirit asked.

"I guess no one told you what happened during my trip to Deudraeth."

The mage narrowed her eyes. "I heard the tale from me husband and Linq."

"Oh." Etain lowered her gaze.

Alatariel placed a gentle hand on her arm. "Perhaps you should tell us. How does a visit to your brother cause such havoc?"

"On my first visit to Deudraeth, I went to the apothecary shop to pick up a few herbs for Spirit." She turned to the mage. "I have the damiana you requested. I'd forgotten about it until now." Spirit nodded impatiently and motioned for her to continue.

Etain explained how the clerk was new to the town and of his claim of amnesia, then told of their return to the town the next day and the inopportune appearance of the *Bok* but stopped short of telling them about her *solar* decimation of the patrol.

Alatariel came out of her seat. "Is the clerk your brother?"

"No. It turns out he's the owner of the shop." Etain ran a hand through her hair. "My brother, not the clerk."

"Could Linq have done something to tip them off?" asked Swee.

"He would not be that careless," Alatariel said, circling the seated group.

"Very true." Etain picked at the arm of the chair. "Linq doesn't make those kinds of mistakes."

"Well," Swee stated the obvious, "someone betrayed you to the *Bok*."

Alatariel stopped. "Could it have been your brother?"

"He's the one who warned me. It wasn't him."

"It was merely a question, Etain." Alatariel's gaze swept to Spirit. "He has lived in the town for a while. We must explore every angle to learn what we can."

"They chased after him and Linq too."

The queen laid her hands on Etain's shoulders in a show of support. "If it were my brother, I am sure I would react the same way. I cannot imagine how you must feel right now."

"Tell her what happened when you found Linq and your brother," Spirit said.

Alatariel felt the young woman stiffen. She came round and sat in the chair across from her. The lack of color in her face concerned her. She took her hands in hers. "What happened, Etain?"

She glanced at Spirit, and Rie. "They injured my brother. There were so many. I couldn't fight them all. My anger took over and I... My *solar* fried them to dust."

Alatariel breathed in and squeezed Etain's hands. "Well, that explains it."

Etain suddenly turned to Swee. "Inferno said something happened to you at the wedding."

"Uh, well... What did he say?"

"Not much. I don't think he believed you."

"I'm sorry to hear it." Swee shifted in her seat and narrowed her eyes. "There *was* a man. I saw him at the ceremony, and again at the reception. He said he was a wedding crasher just passing by. Who just passes by Laugharne?"

"Well," Etain glanced at Spirit, "people around there are pretty friendly. Maybe he thought it was okay."

"You weren't right next to him." She leaned forward. "He swept me onto the dance floor and said rude things. He definitely isn't a fan of Dar or you. If Zorn hadn't noticed, he would've swept me right out of there."

"For what reason?"

Swee crossed one leg over the other and crossed her arms over her chest. "Maybe he thought I was a magic princess and wanted to steal me away. How should I know?"

Etain placed a hand on her knee. "It's not that I don't believe you. I don't understand why no one else noticed. What could he possibly want to achieve by kidnapping you?" She stood and walked a few paces. "You didn't recognize anything about him?"

Swee lowered her arms. "No. At first, I thought him rather charming." She focused on her hands in her lap. "But the more he said the more I knew he didn't belong there. Zorn's lucky to be alive."

Etain stared at the three women.

"What is it, lass?"

She walked toward the door. "I have to go back."

"Wait, Etain," Alatariel called out.

"No. My brother may be at risk. I didn't think to look for him before we left. Besides, I can't sit here while Dar and the others fight on my behalf." It would drive her crazy knowing the sacrifices they would make because of her spontaneous combustion. Plus, she had no idea if her brother could defend himself. He'd proven himself rather ineffective when it came to a fight. "It's my fault they ride on Laugharne."

She opened the door and ran into a tall Elf, well over six feet, dressed in a dark blue uniform trimmed in silver. Etain gawked at eyes the color of amethyst framed by silky black hair. Full, rosy lips added a touch of whimsy to his otherwise elegant features.

His speculation turned to amusement. "Surely this cannot be *the* Lady VonNeshta."

She stepped back and lifted her chin. "I am."

He raised a dark brow. "A VonNeshta admitting responsibility?" He held her intent gaze as he entered the room. "I have always heard the family motto to be 'I didn't do it'."

The smirk on his face angered her. Her gaze darted to the queen, who appeared to be just as amused. *How dare they insult Dar!* She turned, prepared to give the impudent man a piece of her mind.

Alatariel didn't give her the opportunity. "Etain, this is Rana, our *Megiltura* of the Black Blades. Rana, not everyone in the family shares Dar's indisposition to accepting blame. I assure you, she is definitely our Lady Etain, High Lady of Kaos."

Etain studied him more closely. Either the man knew Dar quite well or... *He doesn't look like an idiot.*

The *Megiltura* respectfully bowed his head. "It is a pleasure to meet you, Lady Etain. Please, forgive my humor. I have the greatest respect for our High Lord. He has taught us many valuable lessons." His deep voice reminded her of honey on freshly baked bread, warm and comforting, but his gaze was as sharp as the blades he carried.

Etain blinked. "Rana is *Megiltura*?"

"Yes, of course," Alatariel said as though it were common knowledge.

"But Commander Crom is leading the Black Blades to Laugharne. I thought *he* was *Megiltura*."

The queen raised a brow at the High Lady's knowledge of their history. "We have had to make certain adjustments through the years. These days, the *Megiltura* of the Black Blades has the esteemed responsibility of instructing our novice Blades. Since you have had the good fortune to train with the High Lord, one-on-one, I think it would be a wonderful opportunity for our novices to train with you, teach them a few of the techniques you've learned from Dar. In return, I believe you will learn a thing or two from our *Megiltura*." She turned to Rana. "Thank you for your time, milord. I look forward to your progress reports."

"Your Grace." He bowed and glared at Etain.

Caught off guard by the whole affair, she returned the glare, and turned to Alatariel. "Dar needs me."

"Pardon us, milady." Spirit stepped in and pulled the stubborn warrior to the side. "Lass, I know how you feel about taking care of your own business, but this isn't just about you anymore." She squeezed her hand. "Dar needs a clear head. If you're in the mix, he'll be too distracted. Give him and the others the time they need. Use your time here to share what you know with the Elves and learn from them."

Etain hesitated, torn between her desire to protect those she loved and doing as she was told. It was a hard pill to swallow. After sharing a quick hug with Spirit, she followed the stiff-backed Elf through the door.

Alatariel sat with the other women, happy she would not have to warn Dar of his wife's imminent return. "Ladies, I have plans for each of you as well."

Spirit and Swee looked at one another. "We weren't expecting special treatment, milady."

A slight lift of a finger set several Elves into motion. "It is not a matter of special treatment, Spirit. Consider it an opportunity to expand your knowledge and ours. I hope you will forgive our lack of ceremony, but Dar did not allow much time to prepare."

An older, dark-skinned Elf with matted hair of light brown and black eyes joined the women. Dressed in animal skins, he had the appearance of a barbarian, but his speech was mild-mannered, his voice deep and melodic. "Your Highness."

"Chelri, thank you for coming." Alatariel made the introductions. "Swee, I understand you are a healer. This is Chelri, our *Frábær Heilari*. He is highly skilled in the healing arts. I thought perhaps the two of you may have a lot in common and could learn from each other."

"You are so thoughtful, milady." Swee practically glowed with excitement. "I've always heard wonderful things about the Elven healers, but to actually work with one is a dream come true. It's my pleasure to meet you, Chelri."

"Milady." Chelri bowed slightly. "If you will please come with me, I believe I have much to show you." They walked side by side, already deep in conversation before stepping out the door.

The queen turned to the last of the Laugharne threesome. "Spirit, I have saved you for last. I wanted to escort you to meet our *Nai Turamin*. Sylvan is a talented mage who has a most creative touch with her potions and spells. She will offer you valuable pointers on strengthening your magic."

"Oh, milady. Here I was thinking I'd be cooling me heels while Inferno and the others were hard at work. Do you think Sylvan can help with the evil casting?"

The two passed into a long hallway.

"I am certain she has something. I have seen her work many miracles."

After several twists and turns, they arrived at a set of doors with a carving of the Tree of Life on their faces. Spirit blinked several times. "The leaves seem to move in an invisible breeze."

"Because they do."

With an astonished laugh, Spirit followed the queen into the cavernous room. Alatariel made the proper introductions, and graciously excused herself, leaving Spirit in the capable hands of the *Nai Turamin*.

Anxious to contact the High Lord, Alatariel returned to her private rooms. Door locked, she kicked off her shoes and curled up into one of the overstuffed chairs. Within moments, she and Dar were connected. He questioned her further on Etain, asking if she mentioned her encounter with the *Bok*.

"She mentioned her brother was injured, which made her angry, and they were outnumbered. She feels responsible for this attack."

"It was only a matter of time. I should have known better than to..." He trailed off. *"Rie, I know I—"*

"Dar, not even a High Lord can predict the future. Do not worry. Rana knows how to proceed with Etain. He will ensure she is too exhausted at night to do anything more than eat and fall asleep."

"Thank you, milady. To know she is safe will allow me to concentrate on this infernal battle."

"Do you think it will come to that?"

"It is all they understand. My Black Blades have already proven their worth. The War Wizards will be a great asset, and the Dragon clan stands with us. We sent a general plea to the rest of the Alamir community. None have responded, but it is early."

"Stay safe, Dar. Keep me informed."

"Let me know should my wife get into trouble."

She laughed. *"Your lady will be much too busy."*

Dar met the approaching Black Blades at the crest of the hill. Commander Crom bent a knee, the company following suit. Dar clapped his hands. "On your feet. There is no time for this."

Crom ordered his men to form two tight rings around the High Lord. Dar made eye contact with every man as he spoke. "This will not be an honorable fight. I promise it will be a confrontation of outrageous odds. The *Bok* marches on a homestead, not an army prepared for war. Our first objective is to ensure they do not breach the castle walls."

"What do you wish us to do, High Lord?" Crom asked.

"I will take nine men with me to the north. Send scouting parties to the east and west, and dispatch one to the estuary in the south. Have the rest move on to Laugharne to prepare the grounds. Unexpected surprises are not an option." Dar recognized many of the faces in the circle but chose nine men who he fought with before and was well-acquainted with their capacity for ruthlessness, stealth, and discretion. "Let's move."

"High Lord," one of the Blades said. "Surely we can do more than hide in the dark."

"These are no longer ordinary men we fight." His posture matched the severity in his eyes. "This is the *Bok'Na'Ra,* as evil as evil can get. They have come for my wife, your High Lady. They wish to obtain her powers for their own twisted agenda. The scum will take her for their own wants, to use and to torture, to turn against us." Heads bobbed as the men listened. "I want better odds for the coming battle. Scouting the area is as important as the battle itself. We *must* know what we face."

An oath of 'death to the *Bok*' resounded through the group.

Dar continued to speak above the murmurs. "Let's take the fight to them for the honor of keeping our High Lady safe and for the glory of freeing this world from their influence. Any man not prepared to do whatever it takes should come forward now." With no response, he faced Crom. "Send the wizards to the castle. Our work tonight is not for them."

Crom saluted with fisted hand over his heart. "As you command, High Lord."

Dar addressed the men one last time. "If you come across anything out of the ordinary, report to Commander Crom immediately." He turned to the commander. "When the scouts return, go to the castle to share your information with Inferno, the UWS chieftain, and Linq. We will do the same."

"It shall be done, High Lord."

Those Blades not part of Dar's group split and faded into the landscape. The Krymerian gathered his elite Blades into a tight circle. "What I am about to ask may go against everything you have been taught as Black Blades, but we face a foe who has no honor. At the least, we will be outnumbered five to one. Listen closely." He made sure he had their full attention before saying more. "The enemy is on the move, but even the *Bok* sleep. Tonight, we slip into their camp and dispense with as many as we can before dawn."

One known as Sion spoke in a low voice. "Mayhem and confusion?"

"Aye. Hopefully, it will throw them off-kilter, make them question the viability of their endeavor."

Another by the name of Riko said, "If keeping our High Lady and the realm safe from evil means killing the enemy while he sleeps, I will, milord. I have one question, though."

"What is it, Blade?"

"May we claim trophies?"

"You may, but do it quickly. Tipping the odds in our favor is our main objective. For now, we will scout like the others."

Dar peered over the heads of his men as they prepared to leave. A familiar blond-haired Elf approached. "Mind if I join in? If we include you in the count, we will remain well within your incessant Krymerian quirk for odd numbers."

"It will not be pretty." A part of him was glad for his offer. Linq could be every bit as brutal as any Krymerian. His help would tip the scales in their favor.

"If it were pretty I wanted, I would have gone to Nunnehi with Etain." Linq gripped Dar by the shoulder. "This is not like anything we have encountered in the past. I say we show no mercy."

"Your blade is a welcome asset."

Dar and his patrol stole away into the afternoon without a sound. Coming to a small forest, they tread through the trees, every step well placed lest they give fair warning to those they sought. In time, they came upon a large *Bok* encampment. Crouched low, the men fanned out amongst the trees to observe. The camp displayed no sense of urgency. Slow and steady appeared to be the mantra of the day.

The Blades took note of the varied uniforms, easily determining who was who by the jobs they performed. The grunts, those new to the ranks, gathered wood, toted water, and performed general duties. Above them were those who raised the tents and controlled the supply lines. Cooks built their fires in preparation for the evening mess. Soldiers busied themselves with sharpening blades, while others engaged in swordplay. A small unit practiced with bow and arrow as others took turns throwing the axe. Officers, distinguishable by the gold brocades set on each shoulder, wandered through the camp.

Dar pointed to different sectors. "I count three sentry posts in the camp each with three men."

"Aye, milord. The officers' tents are to the north, closest to the trees." Riko nodded in the general direction.

A sudden scattering of small, brown birds from the treetops had Dar lifting a finger to his lips, more in reflex than in command. These men were professionals who needed no reminders of their precarious circumstance. Each man melded into the forest. A group of *Bok* passed by within a few feet carrying two large deer carcasses between them, complimenting each other on their prowess with the bow.

"The bastards are bold," Sion whispered.

"To have so many men and so few sentries, they must believe Laugharne will be an easy conquest," another commented.

"Hmph," Dar grunted. "A miscalculation on their part. We split into three groups. Each will take out the sentries, then one man from each group will stand in their place. Should an officer question the whereabouts of the other posted men, make sure you kill him quietly. That leaves six to move through the camp with me. Linq, you are our rogue."

Linq tipped his head.

"As each quarter falls, the sentry is to close in and make sure all is clear. Move with extreme caution. Start with the officers since they sit closest to cover. I will take the eastern sector. You men take the western and fan out from there. With their leaders eliminated, perhaps we can even the odds to a degree. Let's move."

Etain's Nunnehi

Her long legs easily kept up with Rana's quick pace down corridors, around corners, and past room after room. "Are we headed to the Black Blade training hall?" No response. "I'll take that as a yes."

They turned another corner.

"Uh, Rana, sir?" He shot her a caustic glare keeping his pace. "*Megiltura.*" She rolled her eyes. "What did Alatariel mean by 'progress reports'? Is she reporting to Dar?"

He appeared oblivious to her questions, no matter how many she asked. After a few more turns, he stopped before a set of grand double doors, their surfaces black, smooth, and warm to the touch.

She leaned back to take in their full height. "Is this obsidian?"

"It is not. They were a gift, carved by visiting masonry dwarves many turns ago."

Etain gawked at him, surprised he had spoken.

On the face of the doors was a tall warrior in full armor, twin scimitars poised for battle. One foot rested squarely on rock, while the other was poised on the skull of an unknown adversary. Arced above the warrior's head and highlighted in silver were words she didn't recognize. "What does that say?"

Rana stood back and placed his hands behind his back. "*Bein óvinum okkar munu glampi undir sólinni.* They are Elven. The bones of our foes will gleam under the sun."

Her fingers lightly traced the unknown warrior, thinking how much he reminded her of Dar. In need of a touch of his essence, an emotion, or anything to assure her he was well, she mentally reached out for her husband.

Rana opened one of the doors and entered the training hall. "Come, Lady Etain."

Irked by the intrusion and the inability to reach Dar, she ran a hand through her hair and followed him through the large doorway to the center of the room.

He stopped and turned. "Lady Etain. I am not personally familiar with Alamir etiquette. However, in Nunnehi it is our custom to close a door after entering a room, especially one such as this." He waved his hands to indicate the majestic proportions of the hall. "We do not wish to disturb other citizens within the palace."

Etain frowned, feeling more like a child than a High Lady, and returned to the massive doors. "Who the hell are we gonna disturb this far out?" she muttered. She braced herself and pushed at one with both hands. It would not budge. After a deep breath, she focused on her demon strength to help with the immovable objects. Neither door would cooperate.

Rana came from behind and lightly tapped one door, then the other. Each one closed with a quiet *poof*. A look of disdain on his face, he left her staring at the doors.

Amidst expectations of an explanation, she felt the tiny warning bells of gooseflesh rise over her skin. From the corner of her eye, she caught a movement and ducked just as a blade flashed over her head. Its impact with the dark doors rang through the hall.

Etain moved to her left and drew her sword in time to block another strike. She arced her blade, catching the black blade, and pushed Rana backward. As he swung again, she pivoted, kicked back, and knocked the sword master off his feet. No sooner did her foot touch the floor than Rana swept a leg underneath her, dropping her flat onto her back. He scrambled to his knees and pinned her sword arm to the floor, the tip of his blade at her throat.

"I have you, milady."

Victory faded into perplexity at the confident smirk on her face.

"Pardon me if I disagree, *Megiltura*."

A pinprick on the inside of his thigh drew his gaze down to the gap between their bodies. What he found was a menacing dagger poised between his legs, aimed at his most precious jewels. A concerted intake of breath passed through the students who clamored around the combatants. Etain's feeling of victory diminished considerably for not noticing them sooner.

"It would appear you have the upper hand, milady. I yield." Once the threat was removed he sat back on his heels. "Nice work, Lady Etain. I must admit, I am impressed." The *Megiltura* stood.

"I didn't realize we had an audience." Etain accepted his offered hand.

"You are Lady Etain?" a green-eyed Elf maiden asked in wonder.

"*The* Lady Etain?" Clarified another set of eyes, brown with gold flecks belonging to a dark-haired male Elf.

Several young Elves crowded around her but one stood out from the rest. A bronze face framed by blond hair with gold eyes that roamed over her with too much familiarity. Although dressed like the other students, he spoke with a confident authority. "So you are Etain. I am Taurnil. Welcome to the Black Blades."

"Thank you," she said, somewhat unnerved. "I'm honored to be here."

"Hallo." A stocky, browned-skinned Elf popped up in front of her, smiling from tapered ear to tapered ear. "I am Dalos, best friend of Taurnil. You are very pretty."

She laughed. "Thank you, Dalos. Nice to meet you too."

Rana brought order to the group with a clap of his hands. "A little decorum if you please. Stop crowding the lady. We are not barbarians."

"Except for Ardana and Bis," Dalos said, making the others laugh. Etain smiled, fairly certain the comment was said in jest.

Taurnil whispered into her ear, "Ardana and Bis are wild Elves or *grugach*, tribal and barbarian." He nodded toward a corner of the room.

Dressed in simple animal skins and sporting tribal tattoos on their dark brown skin, a young man, and a young woman, both with long, black matted locks, scowled at the group.

"Ha," Bis growled, showing a set of lethal incisors. "Maybe our Lady Etain can teach us a new joke."

"*Dina*!" Rana roared. All attention snapped to the *Megiltura*. "This is our Lady Etain, High Lady of Kaos, Princess of the Realm, and Queen of Krymeria. You will show her the utmost respect as required by her station. However, when within these walls, our High Lady shall be a Black Blade, no more and no less. The moment we step outside those doors, you will remember to conduct yourselves appropriately. You are dismissed."

The Elves of Nunnehi came together as a family every night to share the evening meal with no consideration of race, occupation, or rank. Aside from the Royal family, who were held in the highest esteem, the residents of Nunnehi were equals. The queen, her ambassadors, and honored guests sat at what they referred to as the high table that stretched from one side of the hall to the other. The Black Blade novices had their own table at the back of the room with benches instead of chairs and not quite as long as the high table.

Etain waved to Spirit and Swee, who sat to one side of the queen. The women motioned her to join them, but she shook her head and pointed toward the novice Blades. Then Alatariel called her over. Not wanting to offend the queen, she detoured to the high table and bowed.

"Greetings, Queen Alatariel. May the light bless you and darkness flee before your presence."

"Greetings, Lady Etain. May the light bless you and darkness flee before the might of your blade. Will you honor us with your presence for the evening meal?"

"Thank you for the honor, milady. However, may I be bold and request I be excused from the high table tonight? I've only just met the students of the Black Blades and would like to get to know them better."

"Etain, you will have plenty of time to become familiar with them."

She lowered her voice. "Perhaps, but I have a big gap to bridge between being the High Lady and being one of them. I would like to start building that bridge as soon as possible to put them at ease."

The queen held her gaze for a moment. "As you wish, Lady Etain."

She bowed her head, stepped back, and went to join her fellow students. Along her way, she noticed a group of children sitting together at their own table. It made her happy to see Seth and his brother and sisters amongst the Elven children, laughing and too busy to notice her.

As she approached the table in the back of the great hall, she searched up and down its length for an empty seat, wondering if she'd made a mistake. Maybe the gap from Black Blade to High Lady *was* too wide. Afraid she'd miscalculated, she walked past the table.

I'm not so hungry anyway.

A hand shot out and grabbed her by the wrist, nearly pulling her off her feet. "Hey," the deep voice said. "Are we too good for you?"

Taken by surprise, her eyes flashed and her hand twitched. For a split second, her heart stopped at the golden eyes smiling at her. They reminded her of another set of gold eyes.

"I-I didn't see an open seat, so I thought I'd—"

"Nonsense." He held onto her wrist as he pushed those next to him down the bench to make room. "You will sit here with me. We work too hard in the training hall for you to miss a meal."

After a quick glance toward the main table, she squeezed in next to Taurnil and smiled at Dalos sitting on her other side.

Dalos beamed. "Welcome to our humble corner of the hall."

"Made humbler by the likes of you," a silver-haired Elf quipped from the end of the table.

Etain narrowed her eyes at the young male, unsure if he referred to her or Dalos.

Another spoke before either of them could respond. "Little wood Elf, rubbing elbows with the elite. Next thing, you will be expecting us to bow and call you *Dottrinn Minn*."

Dalos continued to grin. "Well, you know, I am not one to brag," he said, accompanied by several guffaws, "but my clan *does* come from the mightiest tree in the forest. *Dottrinn Minn* would not be out of the question."

Etain furrowed her brows as she tried to sort out what the title meant.

"My Lord Hard Head," jibed a female Elf, lifting a mug. Everyone at the table laughed and joined in the mock toast.

Caught up in the humor, Etain lifted hers. "Better a hard head than a hard ass."

The laughter immediately subsided. The novice Blades lowered their mugs and looked from one to another, their faces grim. Etain kept her mug in the air. It was a strong-willed fight to keep from rolling her eyes and shoving her mug down one of their throats. *Bloody hell.* Her glass wavered. As her hopes dwindled, the Blades laughed, thumped their mugs on the table, and drank.

Taurnil tapped his glass to hers. "A worthy opponent out of the arena as well as in."

"By the stars! Royalty with a sense of humor. You are full of surprises, Lady E," said Bis with a brown-toothed grin.

Etain laughed, and enjoyed a drink, happy to know she'd made the right choice.

Later in the evening, the students were the only ones left in the dining hall and showed no signs of slowing down. They quieted once Rana appeared.

"*Kapparnir.*" His gaze went to Etain. "Valiant ones, tomorrow will prove to be a new day in more ways than one. As we have a new student among us and Nessa was promoted into the senior ranks, we must re-arrange our pairings."

"But, *Megiltura*," protested a silver-eyed Elf. Etain thought the dual streaks of silver in his otherwise dark hair complimented his eyes nicely. "Since Nessa was my partner, I thought any new student would be mine."

"Valin, I must pair partners who will challenge one another. You are not yet experienced enough to give the Lady Etain a worthy workout." Rana's unexpected gentleness surprised Etain. "Lyli, you will pair with Valin. Dalos will move to Narien. Taurnil, you will pair with Etain."

Dalos shrugged and offered congratulations to his best friend. "I guess it is only right you train with the Lady, my friend. Let me know if she gets to be too much for you."

He winked and laughed until he caught Etain's serious eye. His face pale, he coughed and ducked his head.

"Dalos." Etain patted him on the back. "You'd be a worthy adversary, I'm sure."

His chipper attitude returned. "I would, milady."

"Lady Etain." Rana drew her attention to him. "Novices train with a black blade. Please stop by the training armory in the morning and choose one to your liking."

"Thank you, *Megiltura*, but I have a sword."

His lips thinned. "Students of the Black Blades train with a black blade. You will choose an appropriate blade and be ready to train at first light." With a sharp turn, he left the dining hall.

"We shall see," she murmured.

Taurnil whispered out of the side of his mouth, "Be careful, E. He can be a nasty opponent."

"As can I, T." Her hands on the table, she pushed up and stepped back over the bench. "I've had a rather big day, my pretties. I think I shall retire now. Heaven knows I'll need the rest to keep up with the likes of y'all."

Taurnil stood as well. "May I escort you to your room, milady?"

"I appreciate the offer, but I know my way around."

He jumped in front of her and offered his arm. "Think nothing of it. I would be remiss if I should allow such a lovely lady to walk alone through these cold halls."

"Beware, Lady Etain," warned a male Elf with pale skin, long black hair, and piercing green eyes. "Taurnil is a diehard ladies' man. His charms are legendary."

She linked arms with her proffered escort. "Not nearly as legendary as my husband's."

Taurnil's eyes sparkled with a mischievous gleam. "I am still young, milady. Give me time."

The others laughed, but Etain shivered at the signals sparking in her blood. Nonetheless, she bid everyone good night with promises of an exciting first day of training.

"How long are you with us, milady?" he asked as they strolled through the hallways.

"I don't really know. The *Bok* currently march on the home of a close friend, but Dar wouldn't let me stay to fight. I suppose I'm here until things settle down."

"Were you *my* wife, I would not want you endangered, either. He has been through a lot in his life. I think he has made a wise decision."

"Oh, do you?" She stopped and turned to face him. "What do you know of my husband?"

"I have heard all the stories. He is a true legend." She could hear the respect for Dar in his voice. "I hope to meet him one day."

"Aye, he has his moments," she whispered. "Perhaps I can arrange a meeting."

At her door, Taurnil bowed and kissed her hand. "I would like that. Sleep well, Lady Etain. May your dreams be as sweet as thee."

"Thank you, Taurnil." She pulled her hand from his. "I look forward to training with the Black Blades. I'm sure I have a lot to learn. Good night."

"Good night, milady. I am sure it will be I who learns a lesson or two."

Etain woke early the next morning, dressed, and detoured through the kitchen to grab a bite to eat. Just a little something to settle her stomach. She sauntered through the halls, chewing on a small roll. At the great doors of the training room, she remembered their introduction from the day before. With a light tap, they opened without a sound. *Huh, imagine that.* Another touch and the doors closed.

She strolled about the large room, exploring this kingdom within a kingdom. The smells of metal, leather, and sweat came together in an aroma she found unexpectedly pleasant. Shields and dull-edged black blades lay in paired groupings about the hall. One wall, adorned with long and short bows, accompanied by leather quivers filled with arrows, led her to three medium-sized well-used targets at the far end of the hall. There were a couple of tables and a few chairs, but it was mainly open, plenty of room to wield a blade or ten.

She chuckled but ended up with a small bit of bread down the wrong pipe, making her cough and sputter until the bread finally dislodged. After dragging in a full breath, she leaned against one of the heavy tables, and set the piece of bread aside.

Morning sunlight streamed through the skylights lighting the room with its glory. In keeping with the rest of the palace, the white floor was of a material she didn't recognize.

Etain crouched and ran her fingers over the rough surface. "Good grip." Toward the center of the hall was a blue square about the size of a boxing ring, minus the ropes. The floor in this area was soft and spongy. "Hand-to-hand perhaps?"

Murals along the far wall drew her deeper into the room. They appeared to be depictions of various battles in Elven history, many of which included a man who bore a strong resemblance to Dar. Her fingers lightly danced over the image of the black-winged angel.

Farther down, the murals took on a darker tone both in color and subject. These depicted dragons in different stages of evolution. A battle with winged serpents blended into another where the heads of dragons sat atop human bodies, wings folded on their backs. The final mural was of two men, standing face to face. The older man wore the markings of a dragon with scaled skin, elongated snout, amber snake-like eyes, and dressed in a royal robe. The other was rather handsome, despite his dragon-like skin. Blue eyes were set into a face with a noble nose and full lips framed by shoulder length brown hair.

How imaginative.

Something shiny glinted out of the corner of her eye. At the end of the gallery was a small entrance into another space. Etain stepped inside to walls displayed with an array of weaponry. She bypassed the spears, axes, and maces without a second thought. The black-bladed swords and daggers were what called to her.

A beautiful katana sang the loudest. The hilt was warm to the touch and accented by a silver guard with a black blade. Blade in hand, she went into the large hall, working through a few paces. Although the feel was smooth and balanced, it was nothing like her *Nim*. She returned to the armory and replaced the katana in its hold. There were many versions of rapiers, colichemardes, long swords, scimitars, and even a demon shamshir. She handled a few, but none fit in her hand as perfectly as her own sword.

Voices from the outer room floated into the armory. *Time for class.* Near the doorway, she heard Dar's name mentioned in reference to the Blade Masters Gathering. Not wanting to stifle their conversation, she hung back where she could see them and if she remained still, they wouldn't notice her.

"He actually asked permission to use my sword. I could not believe it."
A tall, silver-haired Elf paced around the small group.

"The man used *two* swords at the same time. I thought he would win for
sure," said another. This one, shorter than the first, had close-cropped dark
hair and small features.

"Well, maybe if Zysha had not been catcalling and making eyes at him,
he probably would have won. She is always trying to catch herself a Blade,"
said a female Elf with cropped auburn hair.

"Does she not know he is married?" asked the one named Valin, flipping
a dagger into the air. "Or that he is the High Lord?"

"He carried her scarf into the ring," argued a squat, brown-skinned
creature, unrecognizable as an Elf except for his ears. "Perhaps she had good
reason to make eyes at him."

"Why would he want *her*?" the silver-haired one asked. "He is married
to a goddess. The man must live a charmed life."

"Charmed indeed," Etain muttered and stepped into the training hall.
Several sets of wide eyes watched her approach. "Where would I find this
Zysha?"

"Lady Etain," Valin said. "We did not know you were here."

"Does she live in the palace?"

Accustomed to obeying orders, Dalos answered, "No. She's probably
opening her father's shop, off the square." Several sets of eyes glared at him.

Etain was out the black doors like a shot.

Dalos rolled his eyes. "Yee, we're in for it now. You think maybe someone
should go after her?"

"I love a good fight," Valin said, tossing his dagger into the air and
watched as the blade stabbed into the table in front of Dalos.

"How good could it be? I believe the odds will favor—"

Taurnil walked into the hall and leaned against the table, pulling the dagger free. "What are we betting on today?" He eyed the sheepish expressions.
"What?"

"Er, Taurnil," Dalos said, "did you pass Lady Etain as you came in?"

He pushed off the table. "What happened?"

"We didn't know she was in there," Lenwe blurted. "We were talking
about the Blade Masters and Zysha—""

"More like gossiping." He stabbed the blade into the wooden surface
and headed toward the door.

Valin looked at the others. "Think we should help?"

"It *would* be fun to watch," said Dalos.

They smiled at each other and moved toward the door but stopped as
Rana walked in.

"Be alert, *Kapparnir*. Pair off with your partners and let us begin."

Taurnil moved down the hallway as quickly as he could without causing a stir. At the outside courtyard, he broke free and hurried to the main square. A large water fountain decorated with tiny forest faeries and water nymphs at play marked the center of town. He circled the fountain and peered down each subsequent row of shops in search of the silver-haired Amazon. Nothing was out of place. He circled around one more time to the road leading to the shop of Zysha's father. The maiden was busy at work and did not appear to be in any distress.

Perplexed, he tried another tactic. *Where would I go?* With a shrug, he circled the fountain with the intention of cutting through the small park just beyond the square. When he stepped on the curb, he noticed a movement to his left. Underneath a large misshapen oak tree, he saw her leaning against the trunk, cleaning her nails with the tip of her dirk, occasionally glancing in the general direction of the girl.

Taurnil joined her against the tree. "*Góðan daginn*, Lady Etain." His gaze followed her glance down the road.

"Morning."

"How are you today, milady?"

"I am quite well. Thank you for asking. And how might you be, milord?"

"I am well." His eyes came back to the beautiful face. "However, I must admit, I am somewhat curious."

She glanced down the lane once more. "Pray tell, what makes you so curious?"

"Are you here to bask in the beauty of this fine morning," he placed a finger on the dagger to get her attention, "or stalk your prey?"

The ice-blue eyes met his. "I haven't decided."

He cocked a brow. "You know, High Lady or not, Queen Alatariel would be forced to dole out severe punishment to anyone who brought harm to a citizen of Nunnehi."

She smirked. "I believe she would have to catch me first."

"Are you not familiar with the speed of an Elf?" He struggled not to smile.

"Are you not familiar with the powers of a fully transformed Krymerian?"

"Is there one in the area? I'd love to see one in action," he said, a lopsided grin on his face.

"Ha. Funny man." She slipped the dirk into her boot. "You obviously have a lot to learn." Etain pushed away from the tree, but he grabbed her by the arm. "I wanted to see what I'm competing with. Personally, I don't see it."

"See what?"

"What turned his head."

He felt the tremor run through her. "She did not turn his head. Well, not like you think. The maiden has no shame."

"And apparently, neither does Dar, sporting her scarf during the tournament." She pulled free from his grasp.

"E." He softened his voice and blocked her path. "He was not *sporting* her scarf. She threw it over him as the games began. The man was put on the spot."

"You were there?"

"I was not." He frowned. "Rana sent a few of us novices on a training mission, so I missed it. But I have it on good authority her attentions were not encouraged."

She closed her eyes and shook her head.

"Did I say something wrong?"

"No." She sighed. "It's just..." With a shrug, she opened her eyes. "This is going to sound ridiculous, but you remind me so much of Dar. The color of your eyes, the silly grin, even the way you laugh."

He stared at her.

"What?"

"How can I look like the High Lord?" Taurnil distinctly remembered him having brown hair and blue eyes.

"What are you talking about?"

"Is it not obvious?"

Etain stared back at him. "Are you serious? Blonde hair, gold eyes—"

"*I* do, yes."

She furrowed her brows. "Well, so does... Oh, wait." She covered her mouth with her hand and laughed.

Taurnil shifted his weight, his hands on his hips. "What is so funny?"

"I'm sorry, Taurnil." She continued laughing. "It's not you."

"Would you like to tell me what is?" Seeing her this way made it difficult for him to be angry but he refused to smile.

"When was the last time you saw Dar?"

He thought about it and shrugged. "It has been a while."

"So, you didn't see him the last time we were here?"

Taurnil lowered his hands, shaking his head. "No. Like I said, I was away." He narrowed his eyes. "I wish you would stop laughing."

"I'm not laughing at you, T. It's me. You know *why* we were here last time, right?" He nodded. "Well, Dar now has blonde hair and gold eyes. Except for the ears, the resemblance between you two is remarkable."

"I look like my cousin?"

"Huh?"

He laughed at her stunned reaction. "Did she not tell you?"

"Oh my god. You're Rie's son."

Taurnil exhibited an impressive courtly bow. "At your service, milady."

"Hmm." She tapped a finger against her chin as she circled the Elf. "How extraordinary. She said Dar doesn't know."

His shoulders slumped. "No, and mother will not allow me to approach him. I have read everything ever written about the man. By the stars, I feel as though I know him already." He leaned against the tree, a dreamy look in his eyes.

"Perhaps we've met for a reason, dear cousin." Her eyes narrowed in a conspiratorial way. "I think Dar would be glad to meet you. He values family over everything."

Down the road, Zysha suddenly shivered and happened to glance up the lane. She smiled at seeing Taurnil and lifted her hand in greeting, but he was too preoccupied with his companion to notice. She poked one of her assistants. "Who is the woman with the prince?"

The small Elf stopped his sweeping and turned. "That is the Lady Etain."

She pursed her lips. "I have never heard of her. Who is she?"

He raised his brows. "You do not know?"

Exasperated, she placed her hands on her ample hips. "Would I be asking if I knew?"

He snorted a laugh. "*VonNeshta*. The High Lady of Kaos, Etain Von-Neshta. The High Lord's *wife*." Satisfied with her paled reaction, he left her to gawk.

Unholy Hearts

The Blades shared a meal of bread and cheese while they watched the *Bok* feast on roasted deer. Dar's mouth watered from the aromas, but his appetite would not be satisfied with cooked fare tonight, no matter how rare the meat. Tonight would be a feast of warm and bloody hearts in their final rhythmic beats.

One of the men approached Dar, a bottle in hand. "Pardons, High Lord." Dar turned to eyes dark as the night. "Will you share a nip or two of grog with an old friend before we go off on our little adventure?"

"I do not drink just any grog, Elf."

The Elf's smile revealed a row of perfect white teeth as he settled against a tree. "Insults, is it? What a fine way to start a reunion." He pushed back silver strands of hair that had strayed from their bindings.

"What insult?"

His smile turned into a frown as he held the bottle between his legs and worked the cork. "How long have we known each other, High Lord?" The cork came free with a soft pop. Both men glanced toward the camp. Fortunately, the sound did not carry over the sounds of men at work.

Dar kept his voice low. "We are not here to play games, Túrë."

"I disagree, High Lord." Túrë's smile returned. "War is the greatest game there is to play."

Dar grunted a deep-throated chuckle. "That is not what you said the last time I saw you."

"Oh? And what did I say the last time you saw me, High Lord?" He swiped a sleeve over the mouth of the bottle.

"As I recall, you said *love* was the greatest game."

Túrë offered the bottle to Dar, who after a second glance, accepted but sniffed the contents before taking a deep draw.

"Then your memory fails you, High Lord. Love is the greatest game played from a *female* perspective. For men, it is war."

Dar wiped his mouth and handed the bottle back to the Elf. "How is Elisandre?"

"She is quite well. Thank you for asking, High Lord."

"Stop with the 'High Lord,' Elf. How is it you come by Krymerian grog?"

He enjoyed a drink and chuckled. "As I recall, it was a wedding present."

Dar lifted his brows. "You kept it all this time?"

"I knew we'd meet again, Hi… Er, Dar." He chuckled again, passing the grog. "Too bad our reunion is not under happier circumstances."

"Aye."

"I know. We can drink to your recent change in marital status."

"Do you old women have nothing better to do than gossip?" Dar enjoyed another drink.

Túrë's laugh rumbled through his chest. "Apparently not. I hope to meet the lady one day."

"Perhaps, if you do not die today." Dar handed the bottle to his friend.

"The same goes for you, High Lord."

The two shared the grog for a time in silence. As the evening darkened into night, the encampment became quiet, telling them the time had come. The men came to their feet.

"Would you do me the honor, Dar?"

"Aye, Túrë, but it is I who am honored." They watched as the first group of Blades moved out. Dar lowered his voice to a mere whisper. "Do not be alarmed should you—"

Túrë placed a hand on Dar's shoulder. "I have your back, milord."

The mud-smeared assassins slipped into the camp, weaving round the officers' tents, minds fixed on the first part of their task to incapacitate the night watch. Linq joined Dar and Túrë who held back.

The High Lord tuned into the sounds of his men. To his left, he heard the scrape of booted feet and the whisk of a sharp blade sliding into warm flesh followed by the soft exhalations of life. The sharp scent of death carried on the wind. Dar and Túrë headed toward the eastern sector while Linq headed out on his own.

Sion and his fellow Blade, Riko, applied a fresh layer of mud over their faces and uniforms, then swept around to the western side of the dense forest. Timing and speed would prove as valuable as their black blades.

The *Bok* sentries quickly succumbed to their blades with no alarms raised. While Riko disposed of the bodies, Sion added another layer of mud to his blond hair and took over sentry duty, his finely tipped ears listening to the sounds of his brother Blades as they moved from tent to tent. He surveyed the immediate area but saw only the shadows cast by the campfires and took advantage of the moment to step behind a nearby tree to relieve himself.

Within moments, he heard an unfamiliar voice boom from the darkness.

"Where the hell are the sentries? I swear by the devil, I will tear out your black hearts myself and shove them down your worthless throats."

"By the stars," Sion muttered, fastening his breeches. As he stepped from the dark sanctuary of the tree, he untied the leather strip holding his mud-caked hair in a tail down his back, covering his ears. "Here, sir." He recognized the man as a *Bok* officer by the shiny signets displayed across his chest.

He blustered at Sion's sudden appearance. "You worthless shit. Where's the other one?"

Sion nodded toward the forest. "Personal business."

"Piss on your own time." He cocked his head and eyed him from head to toe. "I don't know you." He came closer and pulled on the Elf's collar. "This isn't *Bok* issue." The man sniffed. "You smell funny." The officer stepped back and placed a hand on the hilt of his sword.

Sion nearly laughed at the irony. Nothing smelled worse than the stink of evil rolling off the man. He shifted and straightened his black jacket. "I come from the north, past the mountains. My brother and I joined during the march south." It was not too far from the truth.

"The north. Understandable." His tone conveyed his disgust. "You should be shoveling shit, not standing as sentries. I'll have a word with the commander." He turned toward the trees and drew his sword. "The man must be a bloody whale if it takes him this long to piss. Let's find this brother of yours."

Sion's first instinct was to reach for his blade, but he fought the urge. Once away from the camp, he would be in a better position to grab the dagger in his belt and dispatch the filth quietly. As he turned, an odor stronger than any the *Bok* could emit, something between aged carrion and raw sewage, made the hairs on the back of his neck rise. His heart stopped, knowing his impersonation of a *Bok* sentry was at an end.

Another officer stood with the first, accompanied by a dark green, long-faced goblin also dressed in an officer's uniform. Although tall and slim, they were deceptively strong and as ruthless in a fight as the smell they carried. If he hoped to get out of this alive, Sion would have to make the first move and be quick about it.

The lieutenant laughed. "Shall we leave our friend to his dinner and go find his dessert?"

"Leave the Elf's weapons untouched, Fregus," the other called out. "I'll add them to my collection." He laughed and glanced at the lieutenant. A frozen, blank stare met his gaze. The mouth moved, but only blood oozed from between the lips. The lieutenant crashed, face-first, into the dirt.

Riko stood in his place, blood dripping off his black blade. "I hear dessert is a killer." His sword came up, but the officer jumped back and blocked in time to save his neck.

The Tengu goblin impaled Sion with its yellow malevolent stare. The Elf matched the glare, hoping to trap him in an Elven trance. Gradually, inch by inch, Sion slid one foot back toward the darkness of the forest and the other hoping for a quick escape.

In time, his efforts proved fruitful. The tree behind him appeared in of the corner of his eye. He blinked. The momentary break proved his undoing. The goblin sneered, drool dripping from the deadly slit of a mouth. Its yellow eyes glittered with heinous intent as it made a move, spinning a double-bladed sword - one end serrated, the other honed to a finely curved edge.

Sion slammed a shoulder into the goblin before the blade could take his head. He spun around the trunk of the tree, reaching for the blade on his back as he moved. Coming full circle, he slashed down and nicked the right shoulder of the goblin. Fregus grunted and made a grab for the blade but missed. Sion worked fast while he had the advantage. He swung his blade down, twisted his wrist, and cut up, separating the goblin's head from its body. The head bounced off the trunk, spewing its foul-smelling, acidic yellow blood. Sion danced away several feet to avoid being saturated.

He tucked his nose into the crook of his elbow and walked around to the severed head. One powerful swing hacked off a pointed, dark green ear. He turned in time to see Riko gut the remaining officer where he stood.

"By the bloody stars," Sion exclaimed.

"Aye, they be bloody tonight." Riko cleaned his blade on the fallen officer's uniform. "*What* is that stench?"

Sion grinned. "The only thing that stinks worse than a Tengu goblin is a dead one. You had me worried."

"Sorry, brother." Riko slapped him on the back. "These officers don't travel alone. My hands were full relieving others of their duties. Nice work on the goblin."

Sion picked up the severed ear and slid it in his belt. "We should find the High Lord. He needs to know about this one. There could be more."

Dar separated from Túrë and slipped into an officer's tent. Safe from detection, he tapped into his demon, just enough to increase in size and extend his talons. He loomed over the sleeping officer, covered the face with one hand, and cut through the flesh below the ribcage. Wide eyes stared in disbelief as Dar slid a hand through the incision into the chest and yanked out the beating heart. He held it before the man, the blood pumping black and thick as oil, bathing his hand with its warm stickiness.

"Your sacrifice gives me what I need to defeat your kind." His demon fangs ripped into the muscle, blood dribbling between his lips and down his chin. Guttural grunts of satisfaction rumbled in his throat as he devoured the heart of his enemy.

His own blood felt like fire in his veins, filling him with an insatiable thirst. He slashed through the tent and saw the camp through the red eyes of his demon. The pulse of so many hearts beat a deafening tattoo, each with its own unique rhythm, united in an erotic symphony that sang to his bloodlust.

He lost count of the throats slit by blade or talon but kept track of the hearts – five, to be exact. Three for the family he lost so many years ago, one for his father, and one for his Etain. Inside the tent of his latest victim, shouts of alarm cut through his bloodlust.

Túrë's head popped in through a slit. "High Lord, it is time."

Dar shivered from the force of will it took to leash the demon. "Aye," he rasped. The remains of the final heart hit the dirt with a soft thud. As he swiped the blood from his lips, another shout, this time much closer, set him in motion. He ducked through the slit from where Túrë disappeared. Arrows whizzed past them as they made a mad dash into the trees. The Krymerian and the Elf stopped briefly, each hidden behind a birch. Dar motioned to Túrë. The Elf tipped his head and disappeared into the night. Dar slipped away in the opposite direction unseen.

At a point between the *Bok* camp and Castle Laugharne, the covert group gathered around the High Lord. To see his men covered in as much blood as he eased his conscience to know he was not alone in the bloodlust. Although he did not mention it, Dar was especially aware of Linq's absence.

"You have done well tonight. Be proud." His gaze met every blood-covered face. "Your efforts have bought our side time to prepare for battle. These animals have no honor and would murder every Elf and Alamir in their path." He opened a portal with a wave of his hand. "This will take you directly to Laugharne. Clean up, eat, and rest. We have a full day tomorrow."

His Blades on their way, Dar closed the portal and breathed in the cool night air, noting a faint scent of rain. With a slow exhale, he pushed the hair from his face with blood-covered hands and gazed at the gathering clouds.

Whatever it takes, a chuisle.

When swift footsteps came his way, he sighed, squared his shoulders, and summoned the demon again. Whatever pursued him would find a nasty surprise in their path. He spread his legs and raised his talons. The instant the figure burst out of the trees, Dar lashed down with the right and up with the left. He felt the warm breath of the being *whoosh* into his face, his target having fallen on his backside.

"By the stars!"

"*Tartarus*!" Dar retracted the talons.

Linq gave him with a wry smile. "I had forgotten how dangerous it is to hunt with you." His hair, face, and clothes were as bloody as Dar's.

"Are you hurt?"

"No." Linq accepted the offered hand. "Merely a lucrative outing."

Distant noises of pursuit echoed through the trees. "We best get moving." Dar stretched out his wings. "See you at Laugharne." In a single thrust, he was airborne and banked in a wide circle to fly over the encampment before turning toward the castle. The corner of his mouth twitched to see the *Bok* scurrying about in confusion, deprived of their leaders.

In a matter of minutes, he hovered over Laugharne and landed outside the outer wall. He was met with another unwelcome sight as he walked into the courtyard. Faux and Freeblood.

"Goddamn," he cursed under his breath.

"Hey, Dar." The smile on Freeblood's face disappeared as Dar passed by. "We've come to help."

Faux huffed and wrinkled her nose. "Ugh, you're disgusting."

Dar cast a wicked glare. "This is not a place for children. Run along to wherever you came from and take your boy with you."

"Like he said, we've come to help." Faux slipped an arm through Freeblood's.

Dar's hand itched to slap the grin from her face, but his eyes cut to the boy. "And you..." He shook his head and walked away.

"Wait a minute." Freeblood darted after him. "You don't own the market on honor. We heard the plea for help and came."

Dar took a moment to scan the boy's thoughts. Aye, there was honorable intent there. Yet something else lurked at the fringes. Images flooded into his mind - cravings, morning sickness. He specifically included the words in his spell to alleviate the usual ailments of pregnancy. Even with her being a demon, it should have done the job.

Experience as a king and warrior had ingrained their lessons deep. Nothing showed on his face or in his voice.

"We have done what we can to even the odds, but they will have reinforcements coming. The foe we face outnumber us."

"Then why don't you give them what they want so they'll go away?" Faux licked her lips, swaying her tail.

Dar clenched his teeth and grunted. "Get to the house."

Black eyes flashed and the pernicious tail snapped. "Luckily for you, I *do* feel a little tired." She tugged on Freeblood's arm. "Come on, baby. We'll find something to do tomorrow."

"You go on," Dar said to her, but his eyes were on the boy. "We have things to discuss."

"Like the lady said, we'll find something to do tomorrow." As they moved to walk past him, Dar grabbed Freeblood by the shoulder and spun him around. "Okay, we can do it now. Go on, Faux. I'll be right behind you."

A golden glimmer washed over her skin as she narrowed her eyes at Dar. "No prisoners, *mon petit*." She pressed her lips to Freeblood's and disappeared in a shimmer.

"You wanted to talk to me about—"

A firm hand to his throat cut off his words, but Dar's fingers tightened on thin air. Freeblood dashed away in a blur and reappeared a few steps behind the Krymerian. "You said you wanted to talk."

Dar turned. "Why are you here?"

"Like I said, we want to help."

"This is the last place she should be." Dar swung out with a brick-like fist.

Freeblood blinked and nearly lost his head. At the last second, he ducked as Dar's fist whizzed over. "Why?" Dar was quick to recover and slashed back with his left. Freeblood leaned back out of the line of fire.

"A pregnant succubus with Krymerian blood? She would make the perfect bargaining chip for the *Bok*." He lashed out again and grazed the young man's chin. "If not that, she would bring a high price in any market."

Freeblood's head snapped back. He stumbled but kept on his feet. "Hang on!" Another left hit the right side of his face. He dropped, his other cheek kissing the gravel. With a shake of his head, he scrambled away and got to his feet.

"You have risked the life of my child by bringing her here." Dar went at him again.

"Here is the safest place for her!" He danced back to widen the gap between himself and the enraged man. "Look at the muscle around us."

"Had you come sooner, I would have sent her away to a safe place. Did you not learn anything from your skirmish with the recruiter? You have no idea what it means to lose your family."

Double-fisted jabs connected with Dar's diaphragm, doubling him over. "Don't ever say that to me again." Freeblood pulled back, fists clenched. "Unlike you, I loved *my* brother. Thanks to my asshole father, I wasn't told of his death until a month after he was gone." The admission seemed to take the steam from his engines. He lowered his fists and sucked in a breath. "You'd better take your own advice and rest up, old man. You're going to need it if you want to kill more *Bok* than me."

Hands on his knees, Dar watched the boy go into the house. He did not agree with his actions where Faux was concerned, but he acknowledged the common ground they now shared. He needed time to think. With wings spread, he was airborne in seconds.

Betrayal

———

Dressed in Ambassador robes of red, white, and blue, Cappy entered the courtyard accompanied by two other Alamir, a man and a woman, who wore black leather armor. The three exchanged worried looks when they saw the winged demon take flight. A murderously wicked pitchfork appeared in the woman's hand when the demon landed in front of them.

"Greetings, my friends." The red-eyed demon tucked his wings close to his body and offered his hand in welcome. "Thank you for coming."

Thoric, the black-leathered man, tentatively accepted the offering. "You are not an Alamir," he stated, noting the blood splatters on the demon's skin and clothing.

The creature grinned. "Just the hired help."

Cappy adjusted his robes as he surveyed the area. "I know this to be the Castle Laugharne of the UWS clan. Where are her people?"

"It *is* rather late. I would say most are inside, asleep."

Thoric cocked a brow. "Rather presumptuous, don't you think?"

The demon sighed. "It has been a bitch of a day and tomorrow promises to be even more so."

"How do we know this blood all over you isn't Alamir?" Arachnia jutted the tynes of her pitchfork at the demon.

"If it were, we would not be chatting as though old acquaintances." The three exchanged uncomfortable looks. "I will send someone to wake Inferno. There is fresh coffee in the kitchen if you would like to get out of the cold."

Cappy shrugged at his companions. "How many demons make an offer of coffee? Please, lead the way."

"Cappy, you sure you want to do this?" Arachnia whispered.

"We will be fine," he replied, pulling his robes close against the chill of the night air.

"If you say so." But she kept her pitchfork at the ready.

Inside the kitchen, the demon pointed at the canisters on the counter. "Feel free to help yourself. Like I said, the coffee should be fresh. If you prefer tea, bags are in the tin. I will get a clansman to wake Inferno." He ducked out a door.

Arachnia leaned toward Thoric. "Since when do the Alamir work with demons?"

"Anything's possible these days." Thoric turned. "Is he familiar to you, Cappy?"

The friendly demon returned before he could answer. "Inferno will be down soon." He walked past the three toward the back door. "If you will excuse me, I have other business." Before he stepped out, he added one more thing. "By the way, if anyone asks, I didn't do it."

Arachnia smirked. "I guess the rumors are true."

"What rumors?" Thoric asked. "Anyone for a coffee?"

"Make mine black," Cappy piped up. "The rumors about our Krymerian friend, my young chap."

"Aye. Dar." Arachnia scowled at Cappy. "And no one was talking to you." She turned to Thoric. "I'd prefer tea if you don't mind. I ran into a few of his former clansmen not long ago. They said he'd changed."

Thoric laughed. "You really think that was Dar?"

"Who else says 'I didn't do it'? Besides, he didn't ask for identification. Why, you ask? Because he knew who we were. Trust me. He was Dar."

Thoric poured two cups of coffee while water for the tea heated in a kettle. "Anytime the words 'trust me' come from your mouth, Ara..." He handed a cup to Cappy and took a seat, "I have to hold my breath."

Her eyes narrowed. "Have I introduced you to my pitchfork lately?"

Thoric grinned and sipped his drink.

"With Dar here, it poses a problem for us." Cappy leaned back, coffee cup in hand.

"I don't agree," said Thoric. "I have it on good authority he dissolved the clan. No clan, no problems."

"I beg to differ. He has been accused of treason."

"The charge is for treason against a clan that no longer exists, not the Alamir."

"The dissolution of the clan has no bearing on the charge. Are we not the Ambassadors of the Alamir, sworn to uphold our laws?" Cappy blew into his steaming cup and dared a sip. He smacked his lips and performed the process again. "Might I remind you of the matter of the LOKI stone."

"May I remind you any action taken must be unanimously agreed upon by the Ambassadors?" Thoric glanced around the room. "I only see you and me here, so any charges against the man will be set aside for now."

"Good to hear." A scruffy Inferno shuffled into the kitchen, headed for the coffee. "A bickering clan's the least of our worries."

~ ❖ ~

In his flight to consider the situation with Freeblood and Faux, Dar happened across a small *Bok* unit tucked off the side of the road. He silently landed a few yards away and crept close enough to eavesdrop on their conversation. Gathered around a fire, the *Bok* discussed the events of the day and speculated on what was to come. Their talk came around to what they thought would be the capture of the High Lady.

"I've heard tales of her unusual strength."

"Yeah. There've been whispers about her powers too. A fierce white light is what they said."

One scruffy soldier laughed. "Who gives a damn about any light? I want a gander at her soft pussy, part them pink lips with my—"

The man next to him guffawed and slapped him on the back. "Careful what you wish for, Mick. It might be where the light comes from! Sizzle your little bit of sausage right off."

Mick good-heartedly pushed at the man next to him and spit into the fire. "Eh, won't be much fight left in her after the officers have their share."

"If the master leaves anything *to* share," another said, his evil grin revealing a row of yellow-stained teeth. "And if she survives *his* attentions," he picked up a stick and poked at the fire, "she'll be given to the most valiant soldier from the campaign. So you boys may as well go home. The bitch is already mine."

"You'll need us to hold down her puffed-up husband, Krinos. Make him watch." The laughter grew louder.

"We'll see how high and mighty either of 'em are after that," Mick snorted.

The danger lurking in the shadows never registered with the soldiers until a deadly set of talons burst through the chest of one. Dar jerked back, pulsing heart in hand and devoured it before their wretched eyes. "This is for her mother."

The men scrambled over each other, some drawing their swords, others running in terror. The demon flashed through the throng of those who stayed to fight. A slash to the left, another to the right, each one fell beneath his talons. His bloodlust rekindled, he bathed in their blood, smearing it over his face, chest, and arms. "This is for her father."

Those who ran suffered a worse fate than those who stayed to fight. Dar reveled in the chase, darting behind trees and rocks. He relished the false sense of security he allowed them when they thought they had lost him, only to be skewered with his talons and dragged up into the sky. Sharp incisors sank into their sweat-covered flesh and the warm blood flowed, raining over those below.

His dazed victims watched in horror as he ripped the hearts from their chests and squeezed them into a bloody pulp before their eyes darkened in death. These hearts he did not deem worthy of ingestion. With the flick of a wrist, each of his prey fell to the ground.

The blood-soaked mercenary returned to the courtyard of Laugharne as the sun lightened the cloudy skies. At the sounding alarm, Inferno and the rest of the small army soon appeared, weapons drawn. Everyone came to a standstill at the bloody apparition.

"By the gods, man," Inferno exclaimed. "Are ya hurt?"

Dar clenched his jaw and grunted.

"Where have you been?" Linq gave him a good once-over.

"When it comes to the protection of my family, I will cut down anyone who stands in my way, whether they be *Bok* or Alamir. We should have a full day to finish preparations. Put those Blades who did not join in yesterdays's exercise to work on the pitch." He turned to Inferno. "I need to rest. Wake me in exactly two hours, if I am not already up."

"Aye, Dar. We'll have ya up in time," Inferno said. "Ya sure yer all right?"

"I need to rest." He walked toward the main doors.

"Dar. Dar," Faux called out.

His stride did not falter. "I have no time for your games, Faux."

She caught up and stood between him and the doors. "No games, Dar, I promise." Enflamed eyes of gold made her shiver. "Uh... Where's Etain?"

"She is safe. That's all you need to know."

"But, Dar—"

"I have no time for you, girl!" His voice resounded throughout the courtyard as he pushed her aside and disappeared into the house.

Inferno turned to Linq. "Something's going on with him. I think we best keep a close eye while Etain's away. He seems ready to snap."

"I think that time has come and gone. All we can do is make sure he does not unravel. I hope Etain stays where she is."

"She won't leave me wife and Swee alone."

"She knows there is no danger in Nunnehi. If she gets any inkling how bad it is here, nothing will keep her away. You know how she is."

Inferno laughed and clapped him on the back. "Aye, I know well. We best make sure we win the fight before she finds out." Another thought crossed his mind. "Speaking of staying put, have ya seen her blasted brother lately?"

"Not since Dar returned. Think we should be concerned?"

"Maybe, but I don't have the time to be frettin' over the bloody fool. I hope he can hold his own if he runs into the *Bok*."

A handful of those from outside walked through the kitchen, including Arachnia and the two Ambassadors. An unusual couple was seated at the island, eating breakfast in silence. The girl stared as the trio passed. The men ignored her, but as Arachnia neared the doorway into the hall, she glanced over her shoulder with a guarded expression.

In the hallway, she commandeered Cappy and Thoric into the dining hall. "Who was that woman?"

"What woman?" The two asked simultaneously.

She rolled her eyes and lowered her voice. "The one with the horns and a tail, sitting at the island in the kitchen?"

"Hmph." Cappy seemed disinterested. "Sorry, dear. Didn't notice."

"You should pay closer attention, Ambassador. Something about her isn't quite right."

"Well, if you think she's important, keep an eye on her, Ara," Thoric said. "We have more pressing business."

She blocked the door and crossed her arms. "I get the sense you're not telling me everything."

Cappy gave her an unconvincing smile. "What on earth are you talking about?"

"Both of you seem distracted. No, you *are* distracted. What's going on?"

The men exchanged a glance. Thoric shrugged and nodded toward her. Cappy cleared his throat. "Well, this is not for public consumption and must be kept in the strictest confidence."

She shifted from one foot to the other.

A glint shined in his eyes, but he responded in a serious tone. "There is the matter of the missing stones."

Her gaze went from Cappy to Thoric. "Stones? You said COL's was the only one missing."

Thoric nodded. "Well, Savage recently discovered the disappearance of the LOKI stone. The other three clans have been notified and we're awaiting their responses."

She stared at the men. "Is that the real reason for this visit? To question Dar?" Her hands slid to her sides. It was all she could do to remain calm. "Do you really think he would do such a thing?"

Cappy laughed, brushing it aside with a wave of a hand. The deadpan expression on Arachnia's face dispelled his attempt at any further humor. He cleared his throat. "Yes. Well. It is merely speculation at this point. We must be thorough in our investigation for the safety of the Alamir. Dar's standing with LOKI, and as a result, the Alamir, has been in question for some time now."

"I never thought to hear it confirmed by your own lips, Cappy."

"Surely this is no surprise. You've known of our efforts to keep track of the man."

She placed her hands on her hips, her gaze moving back and forth between them. "What I can't understand is the fact you've ordained this insane belief Dar would act against the Alamir after all he's done for us. Have you lost your minds? Thoric, tell me you're not a part of this ridiculous witch hunt."

The man placed his hands on her shoulders, but she shrugged him away. "Ara, I am here to ensure Dar is treated with the utmost respect and not railroaded into anything inappropriate."

Disbelief colored her laugh. "Our reason for being here is inappropriate. Not only will I keep my eyes on the demon girl," her gaze impaled each man in turn, "I'll keep them on the two of you as well. You all make my pitchfork twitch."

Freeblood put his finger under her chin and forced her to look at him. "They have nothing to do with us. Finish your breakfast. Then I want you to go upstairs and rest."

"Stop treating me like I'm the little woman." Faux pushed away from the counter. "There's a fight coming and I intend to be in on it."

"Faux, you have another life to think of now."

"What good will that life be if the *Bok* come in here and take over? Neither my life nor the baby's will be worth anything once they find out who's it is." An inner fire flashed in her black eyes. "I *will* fight and you will *not* stop me."

He sighed. "Okay, okay. If you're that determined..." He stroked her arm. "But, please, go upstairs and rest for a little while. Conserve your energy."

"You're right. I should lie down." She caught his hand in hers and sidled up close. "Don't let me sleep through it."

"I won't. In the meantime, I'm going to find Inferno and Linq." After a long kiss, they parted. Freeblood headed to the back door while Faux walked toward the hallway. With one last look, he stepped into the yard and closed the door.

At the twist in her gut, Arachnia broke away from the Ambassadors, and returned to the kitchen but hearing the strange couple's voices, she stood outside the door to eavesdrop. It all seemed innocent enough, but something about the woman made her uncomfortable.

Faux. That's what he called her. Maybe it was the wicked smirk on her lips. Or perhaps it was the words she murmured after the young man disappeared out the door.

"Don't worry, my darling Freeblood. I *know* what's coming."

She silently followed the succubus up the stairs and hung back behind a corner of the landing as Faux moved to each room, pressing an ear to the door, and peeking inside. After investigating the whole floor, she made a beeline to a blank wall. Arachnia thought the demon was touched in the head until a hidden door suddenly appeared. When Faux stepped through, she caught a glimpse of another set of stairs before it closed. Arachnia crept closer and carefully turned the handle. Locked.

"*Scheisse.*"

A mild explosion made the breath catch in her throat. *I have to get in there.* Arachnia built up the saliva in her mouth, aimed at the lock, and spit. The metal sizzled, foamed, and disintegrated. The door swung open of its own accord.

She cautiously approached a burnt door at the top of the stairs and peered around the edge. Shelves lined one wall with various sizes of bottles, some clear, some blue, red, or brown. She watched the demon girl bypass books on herbs, plants, and magical lore for a large mortar and pestle. Faux stopped and turned her head toward the far corner of the room.

"Hello, good-looking. Glad you could make it."

Arachnia followed her gaze. There was only an empty wooden chair. *Terrific.*

Faux carried the mortar and pestle to the large table in front of a dormer window. "No, but I can feel it. Do I actually need to have it in my hands to destroy it?" Arachnia stared at the corner as Faux spoke over her shoulder. "I'm ready."

She watched the demon girl lick her lips as she turned from the table and walked to the shelves. Faux shuffled through a stack of bowls until she found the right one and grabbed a black candle from the same shelf. The items on the table, she lit the candle, dripped melted wax into the bowl, and placed the candle into the soft wax.

"Water?" Faux's head turned left and right. She grabbed another bowl and went to a small sink in a far corner. Back at the table, she spoke again. "Okay, okay! Not to the wick. Got it."

She fired the wick as she repeated directions from an unseen instructor. "Visualize the power of the protection spell wrapped around the castle. Right. Oh my god! I see it. I see the spell. It's pink." She nodded. "Yes. I feel its power. Okay. Draw it to me and the candle."

"Wait. It's changing. The mist is turning into a wall." Faux jumped. "I *am* concentrating."

Arachnia's mind ached. Everything she'd witnessed in the past few minutes was too bizarre to believe. Surely, Spirit wouldn't entrust the casting of a protection spell to another.

"It's turning to mist again and swirling toward me and the candle," the demon girl said. "The protection spell will be gone in no time."

Arachnia leaned against the wall of the small vestibule. *She isn't casting a spell. She's reversing one. I can't let this happen.* Afraid the spell might be beyond repair, she transformed into her altered form – a black arachnid with a scorpion tail – and slinked into the room.

Faux didn't turn around but her tail matched Arachnia's every move as though it had eyes of its own. "I don't know who you are, but you don't look like the type with a death wish. Come any closer and you'll never see your ambassadors again."

"You have to stop, you fork-tailed freak."

Faux glanced at the empty corner. "She's nothing but a lame ass Alamir."

"Why do you invite pure evil into this home?" She dodged a stab from the malicious tail. "The *Bok'Na'Ra* will destroy everything within its walls, including you."

"Aw, don't worry." Faux turned and lashed out again with her tail. "I'll make sure you're dead before they get here."

Arachnia charged at the girl. Flames shimmered over Faux as a fire blast rolled from her hand. Arachnia grimaced when the ball of fire clipped her shoulder, setting her on fire. A quick spray of venom extinguished the flame.

"You're already dead, succubus." An extra set of arms from her mid-section made a grab for Faux. She ignored the painful kisses of the flames from the succubus as her elongated fangs aimed for Faux's neck, but her bite closed on empty air.

The demon girl spoke from across the room. "You have the nerve to call *me* a freak." She glanced at the black candle, and at the corner. "Yes, it's working." She gave the spider-scorpion a scathing glare. "Once the water overtakes the flame, the spell will be dead and so will you."

Freeblood burst into the room and first saw Faux cringing in the corner but was caught off-guard by the spider-scorpion. He wasn't sure what to do next.

"Freeblood!" An animated Faux pointed at it. "This mutant cornered me in here. Hell only knows what she wants."

The creature turned. "She's trying to destroy the protection spell around the castle. I can feel it weakening as we speak. Get the wizards. Only they can reinforce it."

"She's lying, baby!" Faux yelled. "I told you she was weird."

Despite the creature's appearance, he had the uncanny feeling she was Alamir. Why else would she be inside Laugharne? He sidestepped the spider and offered a hand to Faux. "She is pretty freaky. Why don't we get out of here?"

"We can't leave *her* in here."

Freeblood gave the creature a good once over. "How do you know it's female?"

"I told Spirit I would straighten up. This thing might undo all my hard work. As soon as I'm done, I'll find you. Take *it* with you."

Spirit? He hadn't seen the woman since they'd arrived. He noticed the candle in the bowl of water and thought it odd. He licked his lips and turned to Faux.

"You were supposed to take a nap." Something in her mannerisms didn't ring true. He had to admit, the girl had been different since they left L.A. "Come on. If you don't want to rest, we can make fun of the Ambassadors in their silly robes."

The creature huffed but he ignored what he thought was an accusing glare.

There. He sensed a fog around Faux's mind.

"You're wasting time." The spider launched into the air, intent on the demon girl.

"No!" He screamed.

Faux lit in a golden shimmer. As the spider-scorpion neared her, its stinger bumped the table. When the bowl hit the floor, water splashed across the floorboards and the candle, extinguishing the flame.

Faux disappeared before the spider reached her. With nothing to slow its advance, the creature banged into the wall and slumped to the floor. The spider-scorpion façade faded.

Freeblood pulled up short to avoid sliding into the unconscious woman. He kneeled next to her and checked if she was breathing.

"I don't know who you are, but I believe you," he said. "I'll be right back." He raced downstairs. Whether Faux was successful or not, he hoped the wizards would be able to strengthen whatever remained of the spell to keep the *Bok* from entering the compound.

Linq was the first person he ran into, and he reasoned, was probably his best bet. "Linq, you have to get the War Wizards. They need to strengthen the protection spell around the castle."

The Elf raised a blond brow. "Has something happened?"

"No! No." *Calm down, man.* "Just a precaution." Freeblood tried to act nonchalant. *How do I do this without incriminating Faux?* "Uh, I've noticed a few weak spots."

Linq crossed his arms. "I did not know you were magically inclined."

Freeblood shrugged. "Funny thing about this Alamir stuff. You never know what's gonna come along."

"Spirit is a strong mage. Her spell will hold. The wizards have enough to do. If you will excuse me, I have things to do myself."

"No, Linq. It has to be the wizards." He sounded more desperate than he'd intended.

The Elf turned. "Why?"

He sighed. "The spell may not be as strong as it once was." He had his full attention now.

"Did you tamper with it?"

"Does it matter? Just get them to fix it."

Linq crossed his arms again and leaned against the wall. "Not until you tell me why you think it has been weakened."

"Shit, man." He pushed his hands through his hair. "It was Faux. Okay? She was reversing the spell. The spider woman thing stopped her."

Whether it was his words or his delivery, Freeblood had no idea, but the Elf grabbed him by the arm and marched him to the front doors. "Where is Faux now?"

"I don't know, but I'll find her."

"Take her to her room and make sure she stays there." Linq squeezed his arm to emphasize the importance of his advice. "If you cannot control her, the wizards will."

"I'll take care of her." Freeblood rushed off in one direction, while Linq headed in the other.

Blood of Kaos

"**S**o kind of you to join us, Lady Etain and Master Taurnil." Rana's clipped words carried across the hall.

Etain spoke before her partner could answer. "It's my fault, sir. He was helping me with personal business."

"The training hall is the only 'personal business' you need be concerned with during the day. Save the rest for the evenings when it does not interfere with the Black Blades. Now, shall we get to work? Present your blades."

She wanted to give him a piece of her mind but a slight shake of Taurnil's head warned her to remain silent. She pivoted and walked away, drawing her sword. Taurnil followed her to the center of the room.

"Lady Etain!" Rana yelled. "Where is your black blade?"

She glared at the man. "*Nim* is my blade."

He paced across the floor. "We go into battle with black blades. Nothing less will be tolerated."

"My *Nim'Na'Sharr* was handcrafted especially for my hand by the High Lord himself."

"You will submit to the rules as *set* by the High Lord himself when he established this organization so many turns ago." His words were spoken with the greatest distinction. "They are in place for a reason."

"With all due respect to the High Lord, the Black Blades, and the rules, none of those blades in that closet..." She pointed her *Nim* toward the armory, "fit my hand. Should you wish me to continue to train, I suggest you let me use a sword I am accustomed to."

"I am the *Megiltura* of the Black Blades and will not be questioned or spoken to in this way. You will submit."

"I will not—"

"Did you not agree within these very walls to be a Black Blade? To teach and be taught? If I have mistaken your intent, leave this place." Rana sounded resolute. "Now."

Etain impaled the *Megiltura* with her gaze. Other than the flare of her nostrils, she did not move. Rana remained cool and confident. The novice Blades lowered their weapons.

In time, murmurs passed amongst the students, their eyes on the sword at Etain's side. The once clear crystal had turned black. Without breaking eye contact with the *Megiltura*, she presented the blade and cocked a brow.

"Is this how you intend to enter battle? With your mind and matter split? Is it the best way to make use of your energies?" Rana stepped into her face. "How dare you show such disregard not only to your partner but to the hundreds, no..." He lifted a finger to emphasize the importance of his words, "*thousands* of men and women who have proudly given their lives as Black Blades for more turns than you could possibly comprehend. A blade is either black or it is not. If you do not wish to train with a black blade, your time in this hall has come to an end."

Her left eye twitched. She clenched her teeth, wishing she had the power to cast a hex on the infuriating Elf. No matter how angry she felt, though, she had to accept the truth in his words. She shoved *Nim* into her scabbard, straightened her shoulders, and strode across the immense hall toward the armory at the other end.

Metal clashed, weapons crashed, and strange mutterings carried from the armory as she searched for a blade. Within a short time, Etain emerged through the opening, a shamshir in her right hand and a nasty-looking dragon-headed dagger in her left, both with black blades. She walked straight to Taurnil and resumed her position.

The young Elf's Adam's apple bobbed up and down, as he stared at the weapons. When his gaze met hers, she raised a brow. A bead of sweat trickled down the side of his face. He drew in a breath and presented his blade. The *Megiltura* clapped his hands and practice began.

After an intense training session, Etain returned her weapons to the armory and stormed out of the training hall, despite Rana's bellowed orders to wait until being dismissed.

"Shall I go after her, *Megiltura*?" Taurnil asked.

A simple lift of a finger approved the request.

An anxious Taurnil rushed down the hallway and found her leaning against a bank of windows. "E?" She turned and collapsed into his arms. "E!" With no one else in sight, he carried her to her room and laid her on the bed.

She woke just as he sat down to bathe her face with a cool cloth. "Taurnil?"

"At least, it's not fatal." He dabbed her temples and forehead.

"What're you talking about?" She swatted at his hand and tried to sit up.

"You fainted in the hallway." He set the cloth aside. "Luckily, I was there to catch you."

"Fainted?"

"Aye, fainted, and you will stay right here." He pushed her back into the pillows. "No need to rush into anything."

She offered no resistance and closed her eyes. "Maybe I'm more stressed than I thought. The cloth does feel nice."

"Good." He placed it on her forehead. "When was the last time you ate?"

"This morning, I think. I grabbed a bite on my way to the training hall."

"Must not have been much." He sat back, happy to see the color returning to her face. "You have to take care of yourself around here, E. We practice hard. You must feed the machine to keep your energy at a high level."

"I'll try to be more diligent. I'm feeling better. Can I get up now?"

"Are you sure?" At her nod, he offered his arm. "Take it slow."

"Really, I'm good. Thank you."

"Please tell me we are not going back to the training hall."

She chuckled. "Perhaps I should get something to eat."

"Good idea, but I will go. You stay here and rest."

"No, I need to move." She squeezed his arm. "I need to keep busy or I'll drive myself crazy, thinking of things I shouldn't think about."

His resolve melted under the ice-blue assault and sensuous red lips. *I imagine you taste like fresh summer berries.*

"Taurnil?"

He cleared his throat. "Aye, I understand."

In the hallway, she offered him one last opportunity to bow out gracefully. "You don't have to come with me. I'm sure you have more important things to do."

"At this point, you are the most important thing on my list. You are my partner. How can I train without you?" He intertwined his arm with hers as they strolled down the hall. "There is plenty of time for me to kick your butt in the arena."

"Aren't we the confident one?" She laughed. "You know, I'm not a total novice. I *have* trained with the High Lord."

He laughed with her. "Which means your defeat will be all the sweeter."

"The challenge is on, Lord Taurnil. I shall make you eat those words."

He grinned. "Lord Taurnil. I like it. Say it again."

"You're incorrigible." She glanced at him from the corner of her eye. "Lord T."

Although he enjoyed the company of the High Lady during lunch, he escorted her back to her room with strict instructions to rest for a while. She was reluctant, but his offer to sit with her until she dozed off changed her mind.

Etain sound asleep, the prince of Nunnehi tiptoed from the room to find his mother for a chat on the recent happenings. He told of Etain's introduction to the Blades and ended with the intense workout of the morning, but purposely omitted the episode in the hall. In return, Alatariel advised her son of the events as they had unfolded at Laugharne.

"What do you think of our High Lady, son?"

"I like her, *Móðir* (Mother). She is intelligent, quick-witted and a tad spoiled." He maintained a cool façade, but his gaze repeatedly roamed toward the door.

"Just a tad?" she teased.

"Perhaps spoiled is a bad choice of words." He contemplated for a moment. "She is a woman who knows what she wants and expects to get it."

"At any cost?"

"No. She *is* determined, but she understands what is at stake, *móðir*."

"She may understand, *son minn* (my son), but she is impulsive. It sometimes eclipses her better judgment."

His grin lifted the mood. "I can deal with impulsive. Her heart is in the right place."

"Tread carefully, *son minn*."

He came to his feet and kissed her cheek. "Always, Your Grace."

"Get out of here." She laughed. "I will see you and our Lady Etain at dinner."

Taurnil walked through the hallways, doing his best to appear calm and in control, when what he truly wanted to do was sing and dance his way to Etain's room. She was so different, so unattainable, and too irresistible.

At her door, he knocked several times. "Etain? E?" With no response, he chanced a peek inside. "E, are you awake?" The bed was neat and tidy. He checked the adjoining bath. "Perhaps she has gone to supper?"

Taurnil passed the training hall where Dalos, Valin, and several other novice Blades loitered. "Have you seen Lady Etain?"

"We haven't seen her since this morning. What's up?" Dalos asked.

"She was not feeling well." Taurnil glanced up and down the corridor. "Are you sure you have not seen her?"

"Sorry, Taurnil," said another of the Blades. "Shall we assist you?"

"No thanks. I will see you at supper."

"Sure. See you there."

Dalos waited until the others were gone before he spoke. "Maybe she is visiting with the queen."

Taurnil startled at the invasion of his thoughts. "I have been with my mother most of the afternoon. I left E in her room to rest and promised to escort her to supper, but she was not there."

"She has friends here. Maybe we should check with them."

His frown turned into a smile. "Oh, aye! I forgot about them." He slapped Dalos on the back. "You do not mind going with me?"

"Not at all. Supper is not for another half-hour, plenty of time to find the missing Lady."

They sped off to the other end of the palace to speak with Chelri. With a light tap on the door, they were bid entry and were met by a smiling Swee. "Hello. Can I help you?"

"Hello, milady." Taurnil bowed. "Please excuse the interruption. You must be Swee, the healer. I am Taurnil and this is my best friend, Dalos. Welcome to Nunnehi."

"Thank you. It's nice to meet you both."

"Hallo, young Blades. What brings you to my part of the *Modertræ*?" Chelri's voice was close to a growl.

"Have you seen the Lady Etain?" Dalos asked, an interested eye on the Alamir.

"I had hoped she came here to visit with Ms. Swee." Taurnil nudged Dalos in the ribs. The wood Elf pried his gaze away but continued to peer out of the corner of his eye at the unusual woman.

Swee turned to Taurnil. "I haven't seen her since we arrived yesterday. Is everything all right?"

"I am sure she is exploring the palace. Sorry to interrupt." Taurnil pulled Dalos by the sleeve.

Chelri took Dalos by the other arm and escorted them to the door. "Our day is done here, gentlemen, and we were about to leave for the dining hall ourselves. If we see the Lady Etain, we will be sure to let her know."

"Thank you, *Frábær Heilari*." Taurnil tilted his head in a show of respect and shuffled his friend out of the room. As he closed the door, he gave Dalos a push, making him stumble.

"Hey, what was that for?"

"What have you been told about staring at others? I know you have not met many Alamir, but that was about the rudest I have ever seen, even for you, Dalos."

He frowned. "I was not rude."

"You were. Did you not see how uncomfortable she was by your staring?"

"I could not help myself. She is very pretty." His eyes brightened with an idea. "Should I go apologize?"

Taurnil caught him by the arm and whirled him around. "Not a wise move. We have a High Lady to find. Perhaps our *Nai Turamin* has seen her." He dragged the Wood Elf with him.

They hurried to the other side of the palace to the doors with the Tree of Life. Before either could knock, the doors opened.

"Come in, my young friends," Sylvan called. "Have you met Spirit?" Without waiting for a response, the *Nai Turamin* made the introductions, listened to their story, and assured the young Elves they had not seen the Lady Etain.

They bowed out of the room and faced one another in the hallway. Dalos' brows rose, but just as quickly fell into a scowl as the Elf bit his bottom lip.

"What?" Taurnil snapped, his patience worn thin.

"Do you think she went back to find Zysha? She was not too happy to hear about what happened at the Gathering, you know."

Taurnil's silent stare made him step back. "I doubt she would bother." He rubbed a hand over his eyes. "Go on to supper."

"But, Taurnil—"

"No." He took the Elf by the shoulders and pushed him in the direction of the dining hall. "Go on. I will be along shortly. I think I know where she has gone. No reason for you to be late too."

Taurnil closed his eyes to focus on the eerie feeling niggling at him since his discovery of Etain's absence. A hunch urged him to go toward the main gates and toward the portal. Everything in his being assured him he was doing the right thing.

I cannot let her go.

With Elven speed, he bridged the distance she would have already traveled and found her on her knees at the base of the mountain. She looked at him with a tear-stained face.

"Taurnil, go back. You can't come with me. It's too dangerous."

"You should have waited for me." He kneeled beside her.

"I have to get to Dar." She choked on her words and coughed.

"E, he can handle a skirmish. He has fought more than I can count."

"Not this one."

What he thought was fear in her eyes he realized was in fact pain. "E."

"He's in trouble." She glanced in the direction of the portal.

"What do you mean?"

"His emotions were so strong, they woke me." Her gaze came back to him. "I don't know what's happened, but to reach me here it has to be bad. When I left, I told him nothing would keep me away if I knew he was in trouble." She stood up and ran a hand through her hair. "I was headed up the path when another bolt ripped through me. All I know is he's in serious trouble. He needs me."

Taurnil stood with her. A novice Blade he may be, but he was experienced enough to recognize a determined soul when he saw one. "Then I will not try to change your mind." He moved past her toward the portal. "But you are not going alone. The *Bok'Na'Ra* will be en masse."

"This is not your fight."

He stopped and faced her with all the authority of the Prince of Nunnehi. "I will not allow my High Lady to walk into a trap. If you and I must come to blows to prove my point, so be it." He touched the hilt of his black blade.

Etain glared at him, her hand on *Nim*. Taurnil refused to be the first to break the link. To back down now would be suicide.

"If it would keep you here, I would love nothing better." Her eyes darkened to violet. "However, the love of my life is in mortal danger, and I haven't the time to argue." The violet light disappeared. "Let's get going." She rushed past the Elf.

Taurnil followed her toward the location of the portal. Once the shimmering gateway opened, she took his hand and stepped through into rain-drenched chaos.

Dar woke at the soft tap on the door. "Be right there."

As he turned the door handle, Inferno pushed into the room. "It's not a good day to do battle."

Dar scrubbed a hand over his face. "There is never a good day, Inferno."

The Alamir chieftain paced back and forth. "Bloody clouds rolled in whilst you were asleep. It'll be rain soon, and it won't make our job any easier." He stopped, fisted hands on his hips. "Do we have a chance against these bastards?"

"We do if I call in a few favors." Dar retrieved his boots from the shower where he had left them after a thorough wash. "There are many who owe me and would be more than willing to answer my call to remove their debts. However, no one here is going to like it."

"What do ya have in mind?"

"Demons."

"For fuck's sake, have ya lost yer mind?" Inferno set off in a new blaze of pacing, eyes glaring, hands jabbing this way and that. "I will not have goddamned demons anywhere near me home. Bad enough we have the soddin' *Bok* on their way, but now ya want to bring in a bleedin' lot of fucking demons?"

Dar stood, stamped his feet in a final adjustment of his boots, and proceeded to strap on his blades. "They will honor a blood pact."

"The bastards got no blood to bargain with!"

"I will use everything at my disposal to keep everyone safe. You have to trust me on this, Inferno. My demons are more trustworthy than the *Bok* who plan to ride over that hill." Dar opened the door and waited for Inferno to join him.

Even if it costs me my life, they will not have her.

"There has to be a better way, man."

Dar glared into his stubborn gaze. "I am not asking for permission. You warn the others about what I have planned. I have demons to command."

Before Inferno could protest further, Dar vanished.

An abysmal land stretched before him. Protocol demanded he present his petition in the guise of Lord Darknight, the High Lord of Kaos. Anything less could result in his immediate demise – blood pact or not.

Dar called for his black armor. The second skin encircled his throat and spanned across his shoulders to cover his chest, and out to his fingertips, the VonNeshta family crest, a flame surrounded by a crown of swords, emblazoned on his breastplate. It circled round his waist, continued over his hips, extending down each leg, and ended in dagger-pointed tips over each boot. The headpiece was the last bit to slide up his neck, leaving only his eyes visible.

He made his way to where the Council of Eight awaited his arrival. A heated debate raged between several of the demon lords.

"It is good to see a demon is true to his word." As an exhibition of his power, the High Lord of Kaos chose not to sit with them. "The time has come to honor the pacts made between myself and each of you."

One demon lord stood, attired in an elegant suit that changed in color as he moved. When he spoke, his deep voice bubbled as though he were underwater. "It has yet to be decided, Lord Darknight." Dar knew him as Leviathan, a rather innocuous-looking demon, the lord of flesh-wearing demons. Tall and graceful with a perfect coif of yellow seaweed that set off his pale blue skin. Human flesh was the most highly prized fabric, worn only by the elite. "Tell us what you want so we can be on our way."

"I am calling in the oaths sworn to me."

"We owe you nothing," growled another demon lord farther down the table. "We made no pledges to you."

Dar recognized the voice. There was no way to disguise the gravel rattling in the demon's throat. He turned on *Aslan başı*, a Buer demon with the head of a lion and a round body with five goat legs.

"Each and every one of you swore a blood pact to me." Dar slammed his fist on the table. "If you do not honor it, I promise I will lay waste to your homes and your kingdoms. Nothing and no one will be spared." His eyes transformed into golden slits. "Many of you know from personal experience the meaning of a promise from me." He placed both hands on the wooden surface and leaned toward them, glaring at each lord as he spoke. "As an added incentive, I will consider your debts paid in full with no further obligations to me or my bloodline."

They discussed his offer, each shaking his head as they engaged in private discussions. In time, Granach stood. Distinctive by his contrasting features, one side of his body appeared almost human, save for its exaggerated size, while the other side of his face and body was a metal skeleton beneath a horn-like substance. He spoke in heavily accented Latin. "*Non petis nobis res simplex. Hinc etiam, si opus sit ad potentiae sapiens devitare. Praeterea, appellat, et inclinaveris cor tuum, nisi quod debetur nobis in animo de pactis* (It's not so simple a thing you ask of us. There are powers at work here you would be wise to avoid. Furthermore, your request only invokes and resolves one of the pacts owed by us)."

"Do this and I will release you from *all* oaths. You will be free of me and any bonds we have." He was ready to draw his swords if his methods of persuasion needed a boost. "Or does it require a blood oath as well?"

The suggestion intrigued the demon lords and a fresh barrage of private discussions raced up and down the table. They took their time, forcing Dar to wait.

Eventually, Leviathan raised his head and spoke on everyone's behalf. "To see the High Lord's blood spilled in any capacity is an enticing offer. However, we have come to an agreement that does not require such a commitment on your part. To know we owe you nothing is sufficient. If you ever return to any demon realm, you will be torn limb from limb and your remains distributed throughout every realm as a reminder of our power."

Granach added one more assurance. "*Familia tua patietur eodem fato* (Your family will suffer the same fate)."

All heads nodded in agreement. Leviathan's slit of a mouth turned up at the corners. "In what manner shall we enter this Alamir realm?"

The terms were no less than what Dar expected. "When the time comes, I will open a portal for each of your worlds. How soon will your armies be ready to march?"

"We *are* ready." The perplexed expression on Dar's face led him to explain. "We have known of their intent for a while. It was only a matter of time before either you or the *Bok* came to request our services. How fortunate for you and your Alamir subjects you were the first to arrive."

With their business concluded, the demon lords bid farewell and passed through their respective portals, back to the hells from which they originated. Dar watched the mass exodus without saying a word, but his mind raced with colorful curses directed at each demon upon their exit.

She clung to his arm, pouting like a small child. "You can't leave me here alone. What am I supposed to do?"

Freeblood placed a hand over hers. "You're supposed to stay in your room and behave. No fighting, no conjuring, nothing, nada. Just stay put until I come back."

"Where're you going?" Her nails dug into his skin.

He winced and tried to loosen her hold. "I'm going to help."

"No! You can't go out there!" Her mannerisms became frenzied, and her tail snaked up, encircling his hips. "You have to stay here with me. There's no telling what kind of trouble I'll get into without you to watch me."

He spoke each word distinctly as he disentangled himself from her clutches. "*You* are not going to get into anything."

"I will." She stomped a foot. "I can't stay cooped up in here." She dashed to the window, but her only view was of the sea. "You can't go out there."

He drew a deep breath through his nose and sighed. "You're going to stay here, out of harm's way, and I'm going to go out there and fight. When I get back, we're going to sit down and discuss what the hell you were doing upstairs." He went to her, but she stepped away. "I can hold my own, Faux, and you will do as I say. If not for me, then for the sake of your baby."

"I don't care about the stupid baby!" she screamed. "If you stay here with me, you won't get hurt. He promised—" She bit her tongue.

"He?" Anger burned away any concern he had for his safety or hers. He snatched her wrist before she could escape. "Who the hell is *he*? Are you talking about Dar?" She twisted her arm trying to get away and made a stab with her tail. Freeblood's fury boiled to the surface. He pushed her against the windows, pinning the malevolent tail between her and the glass, making her yelp.

"It doesn't matter right now," he said between gritted teeth. "I'm in this fight whether he likes it or not. The next time you make a deal with the devil, you'd better make sure I'm on board." He let her go and stalked to the door. "If you don't stay put, I'll tell Dar what I saw upstairs, and I won't do a damn thing to help you." He slammed the door and went to face whatever future Lady Fate had in store for him.

TAKEN

A mist fell over the Laugharne warriors. Inferno, the Black Blades, and other Alamir volunteers sat in wait outside the shield Spirit placed around the castle. The Ambassadors stood with the War Wizards along the ramparts. Inferno noticed a black-armored warrior come from the compound. He placed a hand on the hilt of his blade and watched the stranger stop to speak with a Black Blade who immediately ran toward the stables. Inferno thought it odd and was taken aback when the black knight approached him as though it were nothing unusual. His grip tightened on his sword.

"The time is almost upon us, Inferno. Does everyone understand their part?"

He blew out a relieved breath. "Dar! Ya bloody wanker. Me damn heart nearly stopped."

"Ah. Sorry, Inferno. A necessary evil." Dar retracted the headpiece.

"Aye. There was plenty argument about those blasted demons."

"No need to worry. I will deal with them once the battle is underway." The Black Blade returned, leading a feisty, black stallion. "A demon for a demon. Thank you, Blade." Dar vaulted into the saddle. "I am not waiting for the *Bok* to attack. My demons and I will do all we can to keep the fight away from Laugharne." The stallion stomped and snorted. "Stay close to the barrier."

"Aye. Don't get yerself killed."

"By the way, I do not know if they will get this far, but should you encounter anything resembling a goblin, do not engage. You will only get killed." The protective headpiece spanned over his head again. Dar whirled the horse with a pull on the reins and was gone.

Once a safe distance out, Dar murmured a spell to form his own protective barrier between his friends and the demon hoards he went to call. Those within the invisible barrier watched as dozens of portals opened. Although safe from any intended attack by the hundreds of demons passing through, the barrier could not protect them from the smell of hellfire and pure putrescence exuding from the portals. The demon army gathered in front of him.

"I am the High Lord of Kaos." Great white wings extended from his back, a glow of power surrounding him. "Most days, you and I stand in opposition. We battle. Some days, I win; other days, you take the trophy." A concerted chuckle of agreement pulsed through the throng. "The one thing we have in common is our freedom. Freedom to live. Freedom to fight. Freedom to do as we damn well please. This *Bok* would make slaves of us all - Alamir, Krymerian, Elf, and demon. Today, we take the fight to the enemy to protect our worlds from their dark rule. Today, we fight to secure freedom for us all."

The demon army responded with raised weapons and cheers of death to all *Bok*. Dar and his horde rode out. Cresting the first rise, he was surprised to find the enemy had moved so close to Laugharne.

He called out as the *Bok* scrambled to pick up their weapons and grab their mounts. "Turn back now and we may let you live." Dar's muscular thighs held him fast in the saddle as his mount reared from the energy raging through him. "Pursue this fight, and you shall come to the same end as your murderous brothers. No quarter will be given. You will *all* die."

Their answer came in the form of fire blasts that devastated most of the front line. Dar's demon lords honored their oaths and filled the gaps with more demons. The High Lord retracted his wings and spurred his mount into the oncoming mass of *Bok*.

For this auspicious occasion, Dathmet wore armor the color of his morbid castle, deep, dark red, his helm shaped into the head of a snarling lion. Astride his fiery stallion, he overlooked the battlefield from a nearby hilltop and listened to Dar's inspiring speech to his hack of an army. His words impressed the blood-skinned demon, but it was the fact the man led the charge into the expanse of *Bok* that won his respect. His fall would be the hardest and the most gratifying.

One of the many lessons Dathmet learned from his father was nothing ever went according to plan and to always have an alternate course of action. Thankfully, he had several avenues to pursue this time. Some were necessary; some were for pleasure. The destruction of this Krymerian and his Alamir addressed the pleasure aspect. With them eliminated, *she* would naturally turn to him.

The growing list of failures set his teeth on edge. The botched plan to destroy the protection spell around the castle brought a flame to his eyes. When the second magical barrier appeared, it sharpened his irritation into a burning rage. He was ready to ride down the fucking Krymerian and kill him right then and there. Were it not for Thamuz and his wise words, all may have been lost.

Once done here, he would sponsor a hunt for the spider bitch and let the champion who caught her choose her end. As for his promise to Faux, she would be disappointed over the fate of her meddling prick. Perhaps his men would keep her too busy to be of much concern.

His flaming steed shifted its weight and rolled the bit in its mouth. The only end with any meaning for Dathmet was possession of the woman. The capture of the stones was well in hand, but she would be the crowning glory, the key to open the door to his future. Her show of power at Deudraeth had saved him the trouble of disciplining Cromorth for his blunder. Kromok's severed head atop the western turret of his blood-red castle served as an example of failure.

Straddled atop his chestnut mare, Inferno watched the dark swarm converge upon the Krymerian and his horde. He turned slightly and with the wave of a hand, signaled the wizards who stood on the castle ramparts. A chorus of chanting voices rose to the heavens. Grey clouds billowed and churned as black lightning slashed through the dark skies in a heavenly dance of death and tore into the battlefield, ripping into the *Bok* as well as Dar's demons. Scorched earth sizzled as the falling rain swirled blood and ash into a miasma of muck.

Inferno pondered if this was Dar's plan from the beginning, or had the wizards chosen to ensure no demons remained alive once the battle was done? His mount shifted bringing him back to the scene before him.

"Doesn't matter much. The only good demon be a bloody dead one."

Those *Bok* who were able to avoid both the wizards' fire and Dar's demons slammed into the Black Blades shield wall. Metal rang against metal, horses screamed, and men cursed as the day erupted in a spray of blood, bone, and flesh, the rain soaked ground red with blood. The wizards turned from Dar's battlefield to the skirmish threatening the gates of Laugharne. Aided by the wizards' magic, Inferno's clansmen joined by the Black Blades halted the advance and began to push the enemy back.

At the northeastern corner, Linq circled his squadron of Blades to the rear of the *Bok*, placing the enemy in between the allied lines, and strategically complicated the avenue of escape. Aramis followed his instincts and turned his Dragon clan to the west to secure their lines from that direction.

Amid the fighting, a deafening war cry echoed from the north. A band of unknown Alamir charged down the hill. The fact they carried no banner showed they were independents. Inferno felt a surge of pride prickle over his skin at the sight of the swarm.

His pride soon turned to horror when another wave of evil surged into the conflict, the front line led by a string of the biggest and ugliest goblins he'd ever seen. They also came from the north and proceeded to mow down the unknown Alamir.

Fuck me.

Although sight of the goblins was a shock, the allies were prepared for such a move thanks to the tip from Sion. Inferno turned his horse from the fight and signaled six Blades who were designated for a special task. Their horses snorted and pulled at their reins when the Blades came to a standstill before the Alamir chieftain.

Inferno lit a fireball in his hand so intense, it defied the falling rain. Each rider grabbed a torch strapped to their saddles and dipped it into the flame. The torches blazed as bright as the fire in Inferno's palm.

When the northern enemy line veered toward the castle, Inferno cocked his head. The six Blades lowered their torches to their sides, three to their left and the other three to their right. They raced like the wind toward the goblins and the *Bok,* then split, three riding northeast, and three riding northwest. One from each group pulled up at a strategic spot, while their brothers raced on. Several paces later, another two broke off, until all arrived at their assigned posts. The final two reached their mark just as the *Bok* cleared the line.

A signal from one Blade to his partner had the final two lowering their torches to the pitch camouflaged by the green grass. Fire swept through the shallow ditches in the blink of an eye. The Elves threw the torches into the flames and steered their horses away. Although an initial surprise to the *Bok*, they laughed at the primitive attempt of the Elves to hinder the advance and hurried on to join their comrades.

With the end fire ablaze, another signal passed between the first set of Blades. Again, torches touched to the ground sent another line of fire across the field, dividing the frontline of goblins and *Bok* from the Alamir. Pressed by the rear, those in the lead were unable to escape the wall of flames. Goblins sneered, howled, and lashed out. Horses screamed and collided as they fought to avoid the fangs of the panicking goblins and the bite of the flames. A few were able to turn their mounts from the fray, but others were not as lucky and either succumbed to the wrath of the goblins or crashed into the burning wall.

Between the rear and front lines, the two central Blades waited for those who remained seated on their mounts to circle back. Just as the enemy moved toward the break between the flame walls, the Blades set the final piece of the trap. Two fresh lines of fire completed the circle. The center Blades now joined by their brother torchbearers drew their blades to cut down any who might escape the flaming circle.

Once the flames united, several Black Blades stationed near Laugharne lifted their bows and sent a curtain of flaming arrows into the mass of *Bok*. Four trails of flames quartered the circle. Trapped in the fiery furnace, the enemy squadron was too busy fighting to stay alive to be of any use to their cohorts. The certain demise of the northern force freed the six Blades to rejoin the Laugharne ranks.

Dathmet clenched his fanged teeth at the annihilation of the *Bok*'s attack. With the wave of his hand, a single archer stepped forward, bow in one hand, arrow in the other.

"Make it count."

The bowman turned his longbow to the ground and rested the arrow against his hand. With the arrow nocked, he brought the weapon up and took aim. Two fingers drew the string in line with his ear. He breathed in.

Dathmet smiled at the sound of the sweet release, watching the arrow sail through the air.

East of the writhing throng, the black stallion circled round, guided only by the pressure of his master's powerful thighs. Dar tapped into his demon bloodlust as he tore into the enemy, his only objective to protect his family and friends at any cost. The pair opened a bloodied path of destruction as they worked their way through another squadron of *Bok*.

In time, he found himself positioned above the conflict. He tucked away his blades and took advantage of the moment to assess the scene. His canteen in hand, he released his black armor down to his waist, exposing his upper body to the cool mist, and observed as the hoard of demons fought as heroically as any Krymerian.

The stallion stomped and shook his massive head, eager to be off again. Dar looked beyond the smoke toward Laugharne to see how Inferno and the others were faring. The grey day amplified the blackness of the infection spreading ever closer to the great castle.

We cannot keep this up. A sudden empathy wriggled in as the memory of what caused this travesty manifested in his mind. *I understand, a chuisle. My solar ultimà may be the only way.*

Ready to rejoin the battle, he slipped the canteen away when a hot flash seared into his left shoulder. Dar grunted and grabbed the horn of his saddle to keep his seat but his mount screamed and reared with a heated snort. Dar scrambled to hold on, but with the arrow jutting from his shoulder, he was unable to do much more than leap away from the frightened animal in the hopes neither ended up injured or dead. He hit the mud with a jolt that ripped a sharp pain through his shoulder. The horse kept his balance, but shied away, nostrils flared and eyes wild.

"Whoa, easy boy. I'm the one on his ass." He staggered to his feet and grimaced. "*Réiteach, mo chara* (Settle, my friend)." Dar carefully approached. "*Tá tú ceart go breá* (You are fine). Shh."

"I ain't sure what you said, but he looks okay to me. Afraid I can't say the same for you."

Dar smirked as he stroked the horse's nose and turned to a ragtag bunch of what appeared to be fresh Alamir. Their dirty faces reminded him of the clan Etain belonged to when she first came to this world. "You boys should not be here. It is not safe."

The shaggy-haired mouthpiece of the gang showed off his shiny new pistol. "I got a CZ here says different."

Dar eyed the rest of the gang, who also seemed compelled to show off their toys. Not an expert in the use of a gun due to their ineffectiveness outside of the human realm, he recognized a few – Ruger .22, XP100, AK-47, even a shotgun or two. He chuckled at their naïveté.

"Serious toys you have there. I guess it is safe to say this gift…" He indicated the arrow in his shoulder, "is not from you."

"We ain't lame ass Robin Hoods." Shaggy's response elicited snickers from his buddies. "What we got gets the job done a lot faster than sticks 'n stones."

The rain tapered off and the wind shifted. Dar caught the slightest hint of *Bok* taint. *Fresh recruits.* Were they seasoned *Bok,* the smell would have been much stronger, and they would know the weapons they so proudly displayed were worthless in this realm.

"You will soon learn it is an entirely different game here."

The boy snorted, glanced at his crew, and cocked his head. "Only difference is I'm in charge and got the muscle to back it up."

"Do you know why you fight?"

"I know a big reward's been offered to bring in the big man, and I ain't seen no one bigger 'n you." Chuckles passed through the boys. "That's all we need to know."

The stallion stomped his hooves. The show of impatience reminded Dar of the passing time. "I guarantee it will not be what you expect."

"Not your problem, old man." Shaggy stepped toward him. "You coming? Or do we need to add a few more holes?"

Dar did his best not to smile. These boys posed no threat whatsoever, but he believed it imperative they be taught a lesson. "What about my horse?"

One of the other boys came forward in a show of bravado. "Forget the horse."

"Then you will not mind if I do this." Dar slapped the stallion's rear flank. He jumped back when the enraged creature kicked out and tried to bite him. Dar hissed at the movement of the arrow but kept his eye on the stallion to make sure the animal headed in the right direction – straight to Laugharne. The sight of thick smoke told him the firepit had been activated. It was a good sign. Several clicks from behind made him turn.

"Let's go, asshole," the boy with the CZ commanded.

"Oh, one more thing, boys."

"No, old man. Let's go."

Dar called to his demon blood. His lips pressed together was his only reaction to the explosion of pain in his shoulder as his height stretched to eight feet. An inner fire set the golden eyes alight. Gasps of surprise passed amongst the boys. Dar reached up and broke off the point of the protruding arrow and engaged his black armor just as shaggy boy squeezed his trigger.

Click.

He tried again.

Click.

"What the fuck?"

Another boy squeezed the trigger of his Ruger.

Click.

"I loaded it before we left." He dropped the magazine. "See? It's full."

"This is bullshit," said one, a shotgun aimed at Dar. The boy squeezed the trigger and the barrel exploded, spraying blood over the others as the boy careened back to the ground. His screams joined those from the valley below.

"What the fuck did you do?" the shaggy boy yelled.

All barrels aimed and fired. This time, bullets emerged in a direct line toward their target but came to a halt when they hit the dense atmosphere. The useless bullets fell to the ground.

"It is called magic. Your toys have no power here." All eyes turned to Dar, who now stood with his great white wings outstretched to their full span and talons extended from his knuckles. "Time for sticks and stones."

The boys slipped on the wet earth and stumbled over each other to make their escape. Two stopped long enough to grab their injured cohort and dragged him away screaming.

Dar raised his taloned hands into the air and called upon his Krymerian ancestors. "*A Thiarna an ama a chuaigh thart, líon mé le do neart, cuir isteach mé le do chumhachtaí* (Lords of the past, fill me with your strength, infuse me with your powers)."

His core grew warm as he envisioned the white light speeding through his veins, filling him with its intensity.

"You can run, but you cannot hide." A bright beam of light blasted from his eyes. It ripped into the earth, upending rocks, boulders, and trees, turning them into projectiles that brought the hasty retreat to a deadly halt. Amidst the drifting smoke, lightning strikes lit the sky and swallowed their screams with its thunder.

Dar extinguished the light. "That should be a lesson learned."

"Can the same be said for you?" asked a voice from behind.

Dar turned. He recognized the red-skinned monster from his visions. His blood told him this was the one responsible for the attack and much more. "She is beyond your reach." He grasped the hilts of his blades, gritting his teeth against the pain from the broken arrow in his shoulder.

Mocking lips spread over a row of pointed fangs. "But I have the perfect bait."

"You have a death wish." He planted his feet and spun the blades.

Dathmet laughed. "Only for yours." He tipped his head and his parasites moved in.

Dar slammed the hilts of Day Star and Burning Heart together with such force, the two swords became one. The fire in his shoulder further fueled his determination to end this demon fool's existence. He set the blades to work, weaving from side to side. They spun in such a rapid and precise dance, they sliced several of the minions to shreds before they could raise their weapons.

The one who threatened Etain would be the next to fall. He knew the abomination was close behind him. Dar ripped the two blades apart and rotated with Day Star in the lead followed by Burning Heart. He felt a momentary surge of gratification at the ease with which his blades sliced into the flesh and bone, separating the torso into pieces. As the blades passed, Dar caught eyes of ice blue in a fixed stare.

He stumbled.

His beloved Etain lay broken and bleeding at his feet. She had not screamed. Her blood had not sent a warning. Nothing of her spoke to him. Yet there she lay, dead by his own hand. Had his passionate need to slay the devil deafened him to her cries?

"Etain." The blades slipped from his hands and his wings disappeared. The mighty Krymerian collapsed to his knees. "Etain!" He reached out to her mutilated body and stroked her rain-drenched hair.

Dathmet loomed over the grief-stricken warrior, his gaze on the bloodied sections of her body. "The bigger the man, the harder the fall. What a waste. Had she stayed with Midir..." He clutched the shaft of the arrow protruding from the fallen hero's shoulder and turned it with a savage twist. "She would still be alive."

Dar groaned and his body jerked. Blood oozed from the wound and trickled to the ground, mixing with that of his beloved. This would be the last mingling of their precious blood. His heart constricted at her empty stare and her cheeks hollowing before his eyes. He reached for the dagger in his boot as his armor retracted into itself. If he could not be with her in life, he would be with her in death.

ODD TURNS

T he remnants of the *Bok* army fell back. Inferno nudged his mount toward Linq. "What the bloody hell? I've never seen 'em turn and run. Should we go after 'em?"

Linq watched the shadows turn, row by row. "They are not running. They are taking their time to leave the field. It could be a trap, but I think it is over. Best we regroup and wait."

"Sounds good to me." Inferno turned his horse to confer with Commander Crom. After some discussion, they decided it best to fall back themselves to safeguard against not only any lingering *Bok* but also the remaining demons from Dar's initial offensive.

The demons kept a watchful eye in the same way the Alamir and Black Blades watched them. Leviathan, the most powerful lord of the demon realm, gathered his fellow chiefs for a discussion. "What game do you think is played?"

Aslan başı, the lion-headed demon, narrowed his amber eyes as he spoke in his gravelly voice. "I've not seen the *Bok* do such a thing in all me years. They fight to the death."

"*Spero neminem eorum. In pointy AURITUS pythones occidi sicut plures ex nostris, sicut Bok,*" said Granach.

Leviathan nodded in agreement. "I noticed, Granach. The wizards did not discriminate between *Bok* and free-thinking demon. Do we view the act as a betrayal by the Krymerian dog and answer it in kind?" Grumblings of war passed amongst the lords. "Or do we accept it as unavoidable, go home, and consider our debt paid?"

"He runs off and leaves us here to rot," grumbled Raddick, Lord of the Necromancers.

"*Proditione dico, sed quia non Krymerian bello omnes parati.*"

"You're right, Granach," responded another chief, Zalil. "The *Bok* are up to something, but war with the Krymerian would be a waste of our power. I say we leave these Alamir to whatever the *Bok* have planned for them and return to our realms. We can deal with the Krymerian's betrayal another time."

"What say the rest of you?" Leviathan asked.

Aslan başı grunted. "Wouldn't take long to rip these puny Alamir apart. They'd get the message not to toy with the demon world." He wheeled around the group. "But Zalil is right. We should wait until the Elves and their wizards are gone."

The demons argued for several more minutes. In the end, all agreed to return to their respective realms. They knew where the High Lord slept.

After the departure of the demon army, a relaxed sigh passed through the Alamir and their allies. The men took a quick inventory of those warriors in the vicinity and decided it would be prudent to scout the area. Elfin, Wolfe, and BadMan split the clansmen between them and rode in different directions.

"Be on yer guard, laddies," said Inferno. "The bleedin' *Bok* could be lurking about."

Commander Crom sent a portion of the Black Blades after each group to assist in the reclamation of the injured and the dead. He ordered the other Black Blades to the castle.

Linq turned to follow those Blades returning to Laugharne, but Inferno did not move. The Elf cocked a brow. "Inferno?"

"Have ya seen Dar lately?" He eyed the eastern horizon, hoping to see a sign of the Krymerian, but the darkness of the day and the smoke from the still burning fires made it impossible.

"He was at the head of his demons last I saw." Linq brought his mount next to Inferno's.

"He had to have seen the same thing we did."

Linq slapped him on the back. "Do not worry, Inferno. Dar is always the last off the battlefield. If I know him, he is making a final sweep of the area."

"Reckon ya know better than me." The Alamir chieftain shrugged and nudged his horse toward the trees, away from Laugharne.

The horse on which the Elf sat swished its tail and snorted, its breath billowing in a cloud of steam. Linq watched his friend guide his horse in a slow walk through the mud and muck. "Where you going?"

"Something don't feel right," he said over his shoulder.

The rain turned to mist again, the kind that saturated down to the bone. Linq reached into a small pack behind his saddle and pulled out his cloak. Pulling the hood over his head, he clicked his tongue and went after Inferno.

The farther east they went, the more bodies they found. There were demons and *Bok,* Alamir and Blades. Linq and Inferno made a wide pass around the bodies, knowing the Blades would collect them for proper burial.

The two moved into the trees. Fortunately, no Alamir appeared to have ventured this far. All they found were demon corpses already in decomposition. Eventually, they came to a clearing. The horses shied away, twisting and turning. Unable to make any headway, they left their mounts to inspect the area on foot. Inferno lit a fireball in his hand for illumination and entered with no hesitation. Linq stood at the edge.

"Holy shite!" Inferno stopped. The air was heavy and hard to breathe. Even the fireball reacted in spits and sputters. "Ya feel it, don't ya?"

"A great wrong has been inflicted here."

They both spotted two black scimitars in a pool of blood.

"It can't be." Inferno moved toward them and flared the flame in his hand. "Are they his?"

Linq crouched and touched one of the blades. "Aye, I am afraid so. I can only assume this is his blood."

Inferno pointed to a grey mass near the great swords. "Ashes are everywhere. He must've fought long and hard." They searched the area further and soon came across a set of distinct tracks. "Here. Something was dragged off."

"Or some*one*." They followed the trail of blood to the edge of the clearing and silently stared toward the horizon.

Inferno's mind raced as fast as the hooves of his horse. He wanted to be on the *Bok's* trail as soon as possible. It was easier to ambush on the road than wait until they were safe in their own hellhole. Names ticked through his head on who would be best to include in a search party. He thought about anything to avoid the contemplation of what occurred in the clearing and why.

Elfin and Wolfe can fetch Spirit and Swee. Spirit can scry with the blood. Swee can help with the healing. Then he remembered Étain. *For fuck's sake...* And the kids. *Bugger it all.*

He spurred his horse faster. Thoric and several UWS clan members ran out to meet the chieftain as he careened into the courtyard.

"Did you find Dar?" Thoric asked, catching the reins as Inferno jumped off his mount.

"How the hell did ya know?" Inferno barked.

"His horse came in alone."

"Bloody hell." He kicked at the ground and blew out a heated breath. "The *Bok* have Dar." Thoric shoved the reins at a stableboy and rushed toward the house with Inferno. "We can't afford to lose any more time. I want to be ready to leave within the hour." The chieftain charged through the front doors and met Cappy, Arachnia, and a bloodied Freeblood on their way out. "Where's Aramis?" he asked, breezing past the surprised group and into the lounge.

"They haven't come back yet, Inferno," Freeblood said. "The Dragon clan split off to the west to make sure we weren't blindsided."

"I want him with us. They better show up soon. Cappy, can you and Thoric stay here and run things whilst we're gone? I'm sending Elfin and Wolfe to get the girls."

"Uh, Inferno?" Freeblood interrupted. "I can move as fast as Elfin. Let me go with him instead of Wolfe. We'll have them back here in a flash."

"Wait." Arachnia quickly interceded. "What about the demon girl? Who's gonna watch her while you're gone?"

"She's not a threat." Freeblood glanced at Inferno. "What should I tell Etain?"

Inferno's gaze shifted back and forth between the two before he answered. "I doubt ya have to say anything, lad. She'll be gone the second she knows yer there. Get cleaned up. I don't want ya scaring me wife or the kiddies. And be ready. I expect Linq will be coming in soon accompanied by me clanmates."

Everyone turned when Linq entered the room accompanied by Wolfe and Elfin. "Inferno." He held a fisted hand over his heart, stretched out his arm and opened his hand. "We found this."

Inferno snatched the purple-stoned ring from his hand. "Where the hell did that come from?"

"A Blade found it in the ashes near Dar's blades. Is it significant?"

"It belongs to Etain. A gift from Dar." Inferno whirled away and stormed to the fireplace, the ring clenched tightly in his fist. "She's as hard-headed as the demon she's married to." The pounding of his heart filled his ears.

Wolfe approached the fireplace. "It doesn't necessarily mean she—"

"How else would it get there?" Inferno snapped. "She didn't take it off. Ever."

Linq came up behind him. "It does not make sense. The *Bok* are not strong enough to overtake the two of them. Look at the devastation on the battlefield just from Dar."

"She knew he was in trouble." Inferno pushed past the Elf. "The *Bok* will pay for messing with me family. They can't be far." He pulled up short at the sight of a dirty, blood-covered warrior in the doorway. "Aramis."

The Dragon chieftain made a poor attempt at a smile and leaned against the jamb, holding his side. "There was a small patrol to the west." He drew in a careful breath. "We took them by surprise, which gave us a slight advantage." Thoric and Elfin helped him to the sofa. "We lost Unknown and Ciara."

"Bloody shame. Unknown had a knack with the horses and Ciara..." Inferno thought his heart would explode. "She was comin' along nicely with the blade."

"You need a medic." Linq headed to the door. "We will put the bodies with the others and tend to the rest of you."

Aramis accepted a glass of whiskey and downed it in one gulp. "Funny thing, though. Right in the middle of it, they quit. They snapped to attention, turned, and rode away."

Inferno refilled the empty glass and sat on the opposite sofa. "Aye, same here. Bastards cleared out completely."

Aramis nodded his thanks. "It was a good thing for us. Otherwise, me and mine would all be dead. How bad is it?"

"Don't have a final count yet. We lost some independents who came in from the north, and a few Blades, now my two clansmen. Thanks to Dar and his demons—" Inferno choked on his words.

Aramis lowered his glass. "You okay, man?"

Cappy placed a hand on Inferno's shoulder and gave it a supportive squeeze. "We've lost Etain and Dar."

Two swords stand in a pool of blood. A ring lies in a pile of ashes. Has the promised legacy come to a gruesome end?

Scan the QR code for **FLESH AND BONE** and find out.

Journey behind the scenes of the Blood of Kaos series - a world of warriors, magic, intrigue, and love. A monthly email will provide you with insights into the series that you won't find anywhere else.

In exchange for sharing your email, I have a special gift for you. It's a quick read that will give you the lowdown of when Dar met Etain.

Scan the QR code and register to access your copy of

Once Upon A Darknight.

NOTE FROM NESA

If you loved the story or even if it wasn't your cup of tea

It doesn't have to be fancy or a 5-star rating

Scan the QR code for **DREAMREAPER**

and share your journey into Kaos.

ABOUT THE AUTHOR

After marrying her special someone, Nesa decided life was too short to spend it all in one place. Instead of him moving to Texas (her home), she moved to England (his home). Since then, life has been an adventure!

Nesa is a 'learn as you go' kind of gal, which can be challenging, especially when it comes to writing. Although it took a backseat to raising her three children and work, the desire to write never died. Now that her kids are grown, she can indulge in her fantastical stories.

You can find Nesa Miller here:

* 9 7 8 1 9 1 6 0 6 3 7 1 6 *